In
GOLDEN
SPLENDOR

An Heirs of Ireland novel

To dd,

May your roads
ahead be paved with
gold.

1/16/14

In
GOLDEN
SPLENDOR

An Heirs of Ireland novel

MICHAEL K. REYNOLDS

PUBLISHING GROUP

Nashville, Tennessee

978-1-4336-7820-2

Published by B&H Publishing Group,
Nashville, Tennessee

Dewey Decimal Classification: F
Subject Heading: ADVENTURE FICTION \ HISTORICAL
FICTION \ ROMANTIC SUSPENSE NOVELS

Scripture quotations are taken from the New International Version
(NIV), Copyright © 1973, 1978, 1984 by the International Bible
Society. Used by permission of Zondervan. All rights reserved.
Also used is the Holy Bible, King James Version.

1 2 3 4 5 6 7 8 • 17 16 15 14 13

For my wife, Debbie,
whose encouragement shines through every chapter
of the book we share.

For my daughters: Kaleigh, Mackenzie, and Adeline,
who dance so preciously through the pages of our lives.

Prologue

THE WHITE DEER

ROSCOMMON, COUNTY ROSCOMMON, IRELAND
Summer 1843

 "Tell me again. About the white deer." Davin Hanley, his nest of brown curls riffling in the wind, peered up at his teenage brother and raised a tiny hand to shield against a sun briefly escaping the clutches of dark Irish clouds.

Seamus sighed, his tweed hat tipped down, arms crossed, and he leaned back against the white wooden post, as behind him the red walls of the tavern hummed with muted frivolity. "Oh, little brudder. Must I tell again of the white deer of Mallow?"

"Yes." A smile punctuated by dimples lit up Davin's lightly freckled face.

"All right, then. Here goes." Seamus paused dramatically and bent his tall, slender frame. "With me own eyes, I saw them, the white deer wandering the green, green grasses of Mallow Castle."

"A castle?"

"How can you be surprised? You've heard this story about four score times."

"I like the story."

Seamus dusted off a few specks of field dust from the front of his white tunic. No sense making it any more obvious to the town's young ladies that he was a bogtrotter. Although with his clothes being a tad small and patched at the knee and elbow, the fact he was a country lad would be plain enough to see. "What about the story? What do you want to know?"

"Were they really white? The deer. Were they, Seamus?"

"White as your bum."

Davin chuckled and covered his mouth, which was shy of several baby teeth.

"And with antlers like these." Seamus held fingers splayed out from either side of his head.

"When? When did you see them?"

"The same as the last time I told you. And the fifty times before that." Seamus lifted his hat and brushed back his wavy hair before returning it on his head, adjusting the cap until it was plumb. "It was when I ran away from home. Made it all the way to Cork, I did. The big city of Cork. It was on the way there, just off the road some. That was when I saw the castle in Mallow."

"Would you take me? Would you, Seamus?"

"What's this?" Seamus spotted a couple of local girls carrying on with each other. They were approaching along the muddy road lined with buildings, each springing out of the mossy, gray-stoned background with unique and brilliant colors. "Hush, hush. Time to be serious now, Davin. Here comes sunshine."

Seamus leaned back again and shifted a few times until he was confident in his feigned nonchalance. He looked down to see his brother was trying to mirror his efforts.

From the corner of his view, Seamus was pleased to see the young ladies appeared to be close to his age of nineteen. One of them was lanky, wearing a yellow dress and a large white ribbon in her hair, and toting two loaves of bread under her arm. The second girl's dress was faded blue, her shoes appeared worn, but her long hair and tight features made her the prize of his affection. She tucked behind her friend and Seamus soon realized it was an effort to disguise a heavy limp.

They drifted to his side of the road, leaning into each other and giggling, and this didn't surprise him. His father, Liam, who held even a tighter grip on compliments than he did on his beloved mugs of stout, told Seamus if it wasn't for his sporting looks, he would have no stick to lean on, and Seamus took this as gospel.

"She's walking crooked," whispered Davin.

"We all limp a little." Seamus turned to face the arriving girls, warmed a grin, and gave a curt nod. "Why, little brudder, we must visit this town more often, what with the likes of these two charmers."

The two girls conspired with a glance, pursing lips to withhold expressions of amusement, and the tall one moved forward. "The little fellow is quite handsome, wouldn't you say, Hannah?"

"He is that," Hannah said gamely, but her attention wandered toward Seamus.

Seamus met her gaze, which was both interested and demure. "And what about the big fellow?"

"Ah . . . he's all right, I s'pose." Hannah shifted uncomfortably and stumbled a bit, and Seamus pretended not to notice. There was a gentle sweetness to her countenance he found beguiling, her eyes shimmering pools of kindness he yearned to explore.

The tall girl alternated disbelieving glances between Hannah and Seamus, apparently more accustomed to being the draw. She tilted her head. "He's all right for a farm laddie. If you don't mind the stench of muck on his boots."

The grin melted from Seamus's face, but only for a moment as he saw he still had Hannah's endearment. He sensed Davin tensing up with anger, and Seamus gave him a wink. "Even the rose rises from the soil." His courage replenished, laughter returned to heart. "And if I had in me hands a couple of roses, I would surely offer them to you."

They heard a noise from behind and Seamus stiffened. What timing! Their father had left them to loiter in front of the pub for two hours, and just as they were being properly entertained, he came stumbling out of the doors.

Liam stopped and steadied himself, measuring the girls with a glazed glare. He was not an old man, but he was labor hardened and his skin was coarse and blotched from years in the sun and wind. Unlike his son, he made no efforts to conceal the soil and wear of his clothing and appeared rolled in the ground itself. "Be about your way, ladies. You can do much better, I can promise you this."

The two girls nodded uncomfortably and Hannah's face softened with empathy before they continued on their way.

"Did you mind the wagon, boy, as you were told?" Liam lumbered over to the sagging cart, which was yoked to a tired mare, flies circling its sad eyes. "Those are prize tubers I bought there for seeding." He reached in and patted the canvas sacks. "It's a fine thing that, as I'd cane you good if any of them were took."

"They are all there, Da." Seamus slid his sweaty hands in the back of his pant pockets and his pulse climbed, as it always did around his father.

It took Liam a few missteps, but he finally climbed his way up to the front seat of the cart, and he grabbed the reins and let out a large belch.

Seamus lifted Davin up over the side rails and lowered the boy atop muddied straw in the back of the wagon and patted him on the head. Then he circled around to sit alongside his da, and the wood creaked as he settled in the passenger's side. All the while, he was gathering the strength to speak what he needed to say, and then it came out with a bit of a stammer. "Should we . . . uh . . . not forget about the barley flour and honey?"

Liam dismissed this with a wave of his hand.

"But Da. We were s'posing to get those while here in town. Clare told us as much." Seamus knew his older sister would hold him accountable.

"Don't have enough to pay for it."

His flesh toiled with apprehension, as if walking bare through a thorny patch, but Seamus somehow let the forbidden sounds pass his lips. "Did you have enough before saddling in the pub?"

He wished he could grab the words from the air, desperate to pull them back, because his father's eyes narrowed and his old man turned toward him with deliberation, the corner of his mouth quivering. His da curled his finger, beckoning him closer, and Seamus leaned in and closed his eyes for he knew what was next.

The leather knots of the reins cracked against the side of his face, and it was all Seamus could do to keep from giving his da the pleasure of his tears. Still, he could not keep from rubbing his cheek that rippled with pain.

"Get back with you," his da said with a nod.

Seamus's nostrils flared and he clenched his fists. For just a moment. Then he stepped down, retreating to the back of the wagon, and lifted himself over the flimsy wood walls. Just as he barely had one leg in, his father whistled and the horse lunged forward causing Seamus to tumble into the bed. Davin reached helplessly to cushion the fall.

Seamus unraveled his limbs, dusted off the straw, and soon he and Davin sat side by side, the rumbling of wooden wheels on the gravel road and rusted squeaks of the wagon filling the numbing silence.

As their cart moved down the street, they passed by the two girls, who both waved, and Seamus feared it was in pity and he turned away.

After a while, Davin spoke. "Why do you fancy girls so much?"

Seamus's stomach burned, but when he looked at his brother, his stony glare melted. He put his arm around Davin's shoulder. "Sometimes, it's just about being liked, you know."

Davin pushed out his lips, wrinkled his brow, and nodded unconvincingly. Then his expression lit up as they bounced in the back of the wagon. "Seamus?"

"Yes?"

"Tell me about the white deer. And the castle."

"Again?" Seamus wanted to decline but, as always, was disarmed by those brown eyes looking up to him with unmerited awe.

Someday, when Davin was older, Seamus would tell the boy the truth. He would one day explain how the stories of the white deer of Mallow only renewed bitter memories of dire guilt and pain.

And rekindled the dark reasons that once caused him to run away from home.

Chapter 1

MAN OF THE MOUNTAIN

WILDERNESS OF THE SOUTHERN ROCKY
MOUNTAIN RANGE
September 1849

 His sunken face windburned and forested by an icicle-encrusted mustache and beard, Seamus Hanley exhaled a steamy billow through his cracked lips into the frosty mountain air. Then the Irishman held his breath and lowered his rusted Brown Bess musket, his hands numbed by the frigidness breaching his torn and frayed bearskin gauntlets.

The pain of hunger in his stomach had long subsided, and now only the trembling of his grip and weariness of his soul impressed upon him the urgency of this unpleasant task.

He closed one of his lake-blue eyes, the last remnant of the promise of his youth, and sighted the muzzle of the weapon at the unsuspecting, rummaging elk.

Even at a distance, the ribs of the great beast showed through its patchy and scarred chestnut fur. Through the barrel's eye, Seamus tracked the young bull as it limped its way over to an aspen tree. The elk raised its head, crowned in mockery by horns uneven and fractured.

Did it catch his scent?

Then the animal relaxed, bared its teeth, and tugged on a low-lying branch, releasing a powdery mist of fresh snowfall and uncovering autumnal leaves of maroon, amber, and burnt orange. Brilliant watercolor splashes on a white canvas.

In the deadly stillness of a finger poised on a trigger, Seamus shared a kinship of loneliness and futility with his prey, whose ear flapped and jaw bulged as it chewed.

This wasn't the way it should be. For both were trailing the herd at this time of season.

This was when both mountain men and wildlife should be well fattened by summer's gracious hands. For the fall offered only last provisions, the final stones in the fortress. Because, like shadows in the distant horizon, the bitter enemies of winter were approaching.

Seamus tried to steady his focus as the wind shrilled. "It's me or you, my friend."

The frizzen was closed, the powder set, and his very last musket ball was loaded. This would be his only shot.

For it had been another disappointing trade season amidst the dwindling market of beaver, otter, and marmot pelts. The fashion shifts in faraway places like New York and Europe were flushing out trappers like Seamus throughout the Western outlands of this sprouting nation.

But he expected as much. Seamus's past was rife with disappointing harvests.

With a pang of regret, his numb finger squeezed ever so gently and spark and flame breached the touchhole, igniting the gunpowder and sending a lead ball, laced with hope and desperation, through the icy air. Sounds, though dampened by the snow, ricocheted through the woods.

The creature leapt into the air, thighs and legs flailing in a moment of frenzy. Then it gathered itself, turned, and bobbed its white tail up through the embankment into the sheltering embrace of the frozen forest.

A flash here. A speck of brown again. Then it was gone.

And Seamus was alone. Completely alone.

Seamus lumbered over to a tree stump mushroomed by snow, and with the back of his glove he gave it a firm sweep to dust it clean before sitting down on the iced, jagged surface.

"Arrgh!" He flung his musket in the air, watching it spiral before being enveloped into a bank of snow. Then he lowered his face into his moist, fur-covered hands and sobbed.

No one would see him cry. No one ever did. Here, in the high country, emotions were shielded by solitude.

Though just two years had passed, it seemed forever ago when he chose self-exile. When he tried to hide from the memories.

Seamus could barely recall the laughter of his youth and his passion for whimsy. Growing up in the green-rich fields of Ireland, he would feast off the sparkle of cheer that echoed through the farmlands of his people back home.

But that was many tragedies ago. Now that all looked like someone else's life.

He dwelled in the blackness of despair for a while, but eventually the chilling lashes of the winds pried him from the depths of his misery. Survival still lorded over the emptiness.

Seamus retrieved his musket from its snowy grave. It was useless without ammunition, but he couldn't part with one of his only friends.

With slumping shoulders, he headed home. Home. His misshapen cabin in the hollow of the woods. Despite his best efforts to acclimate to the wilderness, he was still merely trespassing. And where was home when your spirit wandered?

Yet there was a more pressing question. Would he even make it back to the cabin? The moment the hobbled elk escaped, it became Seamus who was hunted. He had risked the chase and strayed far. Now his hunger grew fangs and eyed its prey.

The weariness. The throbbing of his temples.

Every step mattered.

Seamus popped the top of his canteen, lifted it, and poured water down his dry, aching throat. Then he surveyed this unfamiliar terrain.

He rarely traversed this patch of backcountry and for good reason. Civilization had encroached following the opening of a United States Army outpost not far away. It intersected with the Oregon Trail, the main pathway for travelers to the West, who of late were drawn in droves to the resonating whispers of gold in California.

The army fort was tasked to free the flow of commerce from the growing hindrance of the Indian population. Seamus had no quarrels with the brown-skinned natives of this territory. In fact, he coveted their ability to thrive in this cruel environment, which had buckled him to his knees.

But he was terrified of the American soldiers.

At the thought, he reached up to the scar on his left cheek, hidden beneath his scraggly facial hair. The image haunted of that branding iron growing in size as it was pressed down on him, the burning flesh both his punishment and permanent mark as an Irish defector in Polk's war, the battle against the Mexicans.

He bristled at the word *defector*. People confused it too easily with *deserter*. Seamus had fought bravely in the war and never wavered amidst firestorms, death screams, and the lead-filled chaos. Even when, like many of his countrymen, he chose to change allegiances and fight for the other side.

Suddenly, the whinnying of horses pulled him out of his trance. Seamus bent down behind a bush and strained his eyes high above in the direction of the repeating and frantic neighing sounds.

Of course. Fools Pass.

It was daunting enough for wagons to climb this section of the main trail during the warm and dry months. But trying to scale it during wintertime only validated its name.

The horses sounded again, this time blending with the curses of a man and the cracking of a whip. From Seamus's vantage point far below, he could see a wagon drawn by two steeds straining to make it up the crest of the hill. Its driver beseeched the creatures with a mad flailing of his arm whilst they slid and grappled for traction.

The two great horses managed to find a steadiness in their hoofing and the wagon straightened and lunged forward with the wooden wheels digging into the deep snow. The vehicle moved closer to the crest of the peak.

Then there was a hideous splintering of wood. One of the horses reared and broke free from its bindings causing the other to stumble. In the matter of a moment, the still-yoked horse, the carriage, and its horrified teamster started to slide back down the slope, angling toward the trail's edge that dropped hundreds of feet below.

Slowly. Excruciating to watch.

First one wheel cleared the edge. Then another. And all was lost.

The driver leapt from his bench, but much too late. The full momentum of the wagon and its cargo ripped violently against the futile efforts of the horse to regain its footing. The helpless creature was yanked through the air as if it were weightless. Its neck flexed unnaturally backward.

Then launching downward, in one flight of wagon, wooden shards, scattering luggage, and flapping limbs of man and beast, the behemoth plunged in fury to depths below amidst hideous songs of anguish rising above the wind's mournful cries.

Seamus shielded his eyes from the horrific imagery. But his ears weren't spared the tortuous screeching. He loathed to hear the conclusion of violence, the anticipated clash of rock and timber, metal and flesh.

Instead, there was a muffled thud.

Was it possible they survived?

Energy surged through his flesh and he dropped his musket and ran with abandon, boots sinking through fresh powder and legs tripping over fallen pine boughs and sunken boulders.

After bloodying his face and arms through dashes between patches of trees, he arrived with his lungs ablaze at the scene of the carriage accident.

The collision with the ground had been softened by a deep snowdrift, and as a result, the wreckage was relatively intact. But the driver hadn't survived the fall. His body was bent grotesquely in a rose-colored embankment.

There too lay the horse, still trained to the wagon. Amazingly, the poor creature still showed signs of life, though it was reduced to a dim wheezing, and tiny flumes rose in the coolness from the flutter of its bleeding nostrils.

Seamus curled up beside the fallen beast and stroked its

head. "Shhh . . . dear fellow." He sat beside it in an honoring silence until the last flicker extinguished in its eyes.

He then pushed to his feet and walked over to the mangled body of the driver dressed in a soldier's uniform and young enough to still be in the daily prayers of a heartbroken mother.

As he looked upon the dead boy, he was struck by the emptiness of the wide-open orbs gazing into the murky skies. Seamus's thoughts jarred to crimson-drenched fields, haunting memories of explosions, the flashing lights, the whirring of cannon shot hurled through the air against crumbling stone walls, battle equipment, flesh and bones.

How could he had ever fired at another human being? Back then they were faceless uniforms, just flags flapping in the winds of war. Yet this soldier lying below him could have been his brother. Maybe even the brother he lost.

Oh! Why bring back those haunting visions of his youth? Would they ever go away? Would he torment himself in even crueler ways than did his father?

Seamus looked around for anything that could serve as a shovel, and the best he could find was a wooden panel he ripped off of the carriage. He used it to drag snow over the body. It was a crude burial at best, but it would at least keep the corpse from being dragged away by scavenging predators for a day or so before the weather warmed again.

Perhaps he just couldn't bear to see the boy's face any longer.

He then explored the wagon, which had landed on its side and was twisted and embedded deep in the snowbank. Seamus reached down and pulled on the door, which tore from its broken hinges, and he tossed it out of his way. He climbed down inside, discovered several canvas sacks, and threw them up and out of the carriage's womb.

Getting out was a much more difficult proposition. Whatever parts of the cabin he tried to pull himself up with shattered to the touch, and the walls of snow around him threatened to collapse. He feared being crushed and suffocating.

After much exertion he managed to claw his way out, and when he was back on his feet, his muscles writhed and his breathing wheezed. Dizziness swept over him and he had to close his eyes to regain his balance.

There would be little time now. His stomach clenched. He must return home.

Could there be food?

He propped up the first of the bags and hesitated for a moment before unfastening the slender rope binding it shut.

Was this right to do? Wouldn't this make him a robber of graves?

Ridiculous! He was starving.

He removed his leather gauntlets and worked the knot with determination. Then it was freed and when he opened the mouth of the bag his spirit sank.

Mail.

Then the next bag. It was the same.

Another. Uniforms. He flung the sack down, and the clothing scattered, blue against the white.

The heavy bag? *Please. If there is a God above, then have mercy on me.*

Cans! But there would be no way to open them out here.

He untied the last bag, which proved to be the most stubborn. Finally it was freed and, once again, it was mail. But this one also had parcel boxes. He reached in to pull one out and several letters scattered in the wind.

Seamus stared at the box and shook it. Looking up, he saw the sun dipping below the crowns of the trees. He couldn't squander any more daylight.

He returned the package in the sack and gathered the letters from the ground. As he did, one letter caught his eye.

In addition to an address on it was written *PLEASE OPEN IMMEDIATELY.* He stared at it for a moment and went to fling it but paused and examined it again.

Not understanding why he was compelled to do so, he tucked the envelope in an inner pocket of his doeskin jacket. Then he lifted the bag of canned goods and slung it over his shoulder. Too heavy. He would have to do something.

Yet he couldn't fully embrace the thought of throwing away some of its contents. How much would he regret leaving any of these cans behind? The indecision was amplified by the pounding of his head and a surge of nausea.

Something drew him out of this. A movement in the trees behind him, a rustling of leaves.

He spun, now alert, and gazed through foliage beginning to be shrouded by dusk.

Silence. Even the wind had stilled. Only his breathing remained.

Then. It happened again. The snapping of branches.

Something or someone was approaching.

Chapter 2

THE WIND SPEAKS

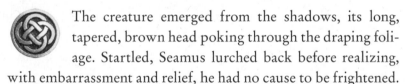 The creature emerged from the shadows, its long, tapered, brown head poking through the draping foliage. Startled, Seamus lurched back before realizing, with embarrassment and relief, he had no cause to be frightened.

The horse approached timidly, its hoofs making soft indentations in the white pillowed ground cover, large black eyes darting around with apprehension.

This was the lucky one. The one that broke free.

Seamus looked up toward the peak of the embankment for some explanation as to how it had traced its way down the hill, managing to end up here at the crash site.

Dragging on the ground behind the frightened animal and attached by leather straps was part of the carriage shaft tangled with twisted branches. Seamus pulled his buck knife out of its worn sheaf hanging from his belt and cut the cords connected to the harness and bridle. The mare nickered in a way that sounded like relief and gratitude.

Then he examined the muscular, sweat-sheened body, sliding his hands along its hide until it came to the branding mark of the U.S. Army on its hindquarters. The animal appeared to have been spared injury.

"What's your name, lass?" He stroked the wiry braided hair at her nape and she withdrew her head and snorted.

"It is all right, pretty one. You're gonna be just fine." Seamus followed the gaze of the creature. She was staring at her deceased yoking partner.

He eased her head away. "It's better you don't look hard, I would think."

Would she be willing to take a mount? He rounded to the side, but she snapped up her head and pounded a hoof in the ground.

"All right then, lass. It will be as you wish." He patted her on her shoulder. "But there's a fine chilling coming, and night as well. So if it wouldn't be too imposing, I'm hoping you would agree to sharing a wee bit of the load."

He labored to lift the sack filled with cans onto her back, and she bore it with little protest. Then using ropes he salvaged from the debris, he tied the cargo down firmly and then attached a leather strap to her harness to use as a crude lead.

Seamus began to walk her away, but the mare hesitated and then looked back at what once was her carriage to pull.

"Ah, there's grizzly, mean ones, and packs of wolves and coyotes out here. You won't be wanting to stay here by yourself, you should know."

This time he gave her a firm tug and the two headed out, making tracks in the hardening snow, through the chilling winds and closing darkness. It would be several miles before they would be back at the cabin, but Seamus found himself comforted by the notion that he wouldn't be journeying alone.

Seamus named the horse Clarisse, after his older sister, Clare, who emigrated to Manhattan with him from the potato farming village of Branlow three years earlier.

Together they endured a harrowing sea journey, the threat of starvation, and survived getting embroiled in the dark under-world of Five Points, New York. Seamus last saw his sister when he enlisted in the American army in haste, more in an effort to flee his troubles than any pursuit of some noble cause.

He missed Clare more than anyone because she was one of the few people in his life who believed in him, more than he ever could himself.

Seamus considered bringing Clarisse into his cabin for safety and warmth, but there wasn't enough room, and his handmade dwelling was in such poor condition he feared she would knock a beam and bring the roof down upon them.

Instead he tied the mare to a splintered post and kept open his wood-slatted front door, which would allow her to peer inside and feel a bit of the warmth from the vibrant fire he had built in the crude chimney.

The horse stepped forward to the length of the rope and poked in her head with curiosity.

"What? Are you here to criticize my wee home? Never was much handy with a hammer and what of it?" He smiled at her and opened a bag of oats. After a sniff, she reached down and nuzzled until her mouth was full and then her jaw muscles began to ripple. "I wasn't expecting a guest or I would have surely tidied up some."

He looked back inside his cabin. It was dusty and bare other than a pine-log bed frame with a straw mattress and wool blanket, a crudely made table and chair, and some empty shelves against the wall. The only effort at decor were a couple of drawings he nailed to the wall. They were ink-sketched portraits of him made by the eleven-year-old granddaughter of Jeremiah, his only neighbor for miles.

"Now look what you've done. You've eaten my finest oats. And the last of them as well. Ah, 'tis all right. The Yanks don't know how to grow oats for nothing."

Seamus tried not to think of Ireland, with its lush green fields, centuries of traditions, and hearty food that warmed his soul. It only made him homesick and yearning for the song and dance of his persecuted people, reveling in their unshakable merriment.

"Well, Clarisse, now that you ate it all, I s'pose I should see what we've got in those cans, eh? Wait. Where's the manners? You must be a might thirsty."

Seamus walked inside and lifted the tin pail he had been using to collect the heavy dripping from his roof. It was nearly full of water. With two hands, he tipped the pail and drank some, pausing to pull a leaf from his lips. Then he carried it over and set it beside Clarisse.

"There you are, lass. A pint to share with my new friend." He rubbed his hands together. "Now I should tend to those cans, if you don't mind. And who knows? Maybe there's an apple in one of these here for you."

He grabbed the chair from the table and placed it in front of fire that shone brightly, thrusting heat outward from the blackened stone hearth.

"Can you feel that, Clarisse? Let 'er snow outside now. Won't be a bother to us none."

He drew the duffel bag toward him and read the bold letters,

Property of the United States Army written outside of the coarse material.

"That would be you, would it not? Says so right on your rear. I'll just tell 'em you gave it your full authorization, isn't that so?"

After unfastening the rope tie, he widened the mouth and pulled out cans one at a time and stacked them beside him in neat piles. Before long, the sack lay empty, and all of the cans rose like a castle.

"I don't suppose you brought an opener with you, Clarisse?"

Seamus held up one of the cans to the glow of the fire and scratched his bearded chin. What a way to starve. He took out his knife and poked at the top with the tip, but it merely made a shallow dent.

Then he reached up and pulled his rusted ax down from its hook on the wall, carried the can outside, and after clearing away the snow, he placed it on the stump he used for splitting wood. He thought about it for a moment and then raised the ax head in the air and brought it back down with his full weight.

The blade sliced through the can, splitting it in two and a splattering of stewed tomatoes and red juices flew through the air. Seamus embedded the blade back in the wood, picked the red chunks from the snow until his hand was full, and then he shoved the food in his mouth.

He closed his eyes and savored each of the bites. He could feel life returning to his ailing body. When he was almost finished, he put his hand out to Clarisse, who lapped it clean with her long tongue.

"Quite a chef, am I?" He scratched the horse behind her ears.

After going through the process with six more cans, he had enough to fill two tin plates with baked beans, corn, carrots, and beef stew.

He added logs to the fire and nestled himself in his chair with a fork in his hand and the plateful of food in the other.

"I'm just goin' to nibble on this slow and easy. It's been far and long since I've eaten this richly, I'll tell you that." He measured the remaining pile of cans with a glance. "If we find a better way of opening these lids, I s'pose we have ourselves a good ten days' worth, maybe twelve."

It didn't take long for his hunger-shrunken stomach to be filled, and he took a deep sip of water and enjoyed the warmth of the fire.

Then he remembered the letter in his coat pocket.

He set his plate down on the floor, ran his fingers through his beard and mustache, and wiped his hands on his pants.

With a degree of reverence, he pulled out the envelope. Why did he take this? Why didn't he just leave it with the others?

Guilt surged as he read that it was addressed to a Captain Percy Barlow of Fort Bradley. Was this what it had come down to? He had to open someone else's letters because no one would write to him?

But that wasn't true. No one knew where he was. It was his choice to hide.

The letter was from an A. Whittington of San Francisco, California. He flipped it over. It was sealed in wax with a W signet. Seamus ran his dirty and cracked fingers over it as if it would somehow reveal secrets of what was inside.

California. Even a man of the mountains had heard about the great world out West.

Then he turned it again and read the words that had drawn his focus: *PLEASE OPEN IMMEDIATELY.* Could it be that this note was intended for him?

"What do you say, my new friend? Do you think I should open her up and give it a right look?"

He patted the letter against his palm and gazed into the fire. *Am I really going to do this?*

Then he pulled his knife out, slid the tip of the blade under a corner of the envelope, and sheared it with ease.

After sheathing his makeshift letter opener, he removed the parchment inside and opened the letter. Something fluttered through the air and landed on the dirt floor. Seamus plucked it from the ground and blew off the dust.

A photograph of a young lady. Not just any woman, but to him at this moment, one of the most beautiful and alluring he had ever seen. Was this true? Or had it just been so long?

Dressed with poise and elegance, with draping auburn curls, a face sculpted from ivory, deep brown eyes—she was vibrant yet with a touch of melancholy.

He tried to put the photograph down but there it remained in his hand. Seamus dragged his chair closer to the fire. Just to have more light. To see her face clearer.

There was a piercing sensation on his forehead, and he slapped his hand and pulled it back to see the shriveled corpse of mosquito in a splash of red. A few more cold spells like this and they would be gone for the year. He stood and put the letter and the photo on his chair and then moved to the door.

"I'm afraid the critters are getting inside." He untied Clarisse from the post and guided her a short distance over to a grove of pines. Then he dragged his boot to clear some snow, revealing a small patch of wild grass.

"Not much more to feast on, I'm afraid." He glanced out into shadowy terrain of darkness and worried about what might be lurking in the night hills. "You be careful out here, will you?" He patted her on the side. "I'll keep you untied so you can run if you need to."

A blast of cold wind stirred up and Seamus stepped lively to the front door. He turned and peered back. Would Clarisse be there in the morning?

Then he closed the door behind him. Hurrying to sit down, he opened the letter and placed the picture up against it, so as to imagine the woman speaking the words. The letter was short, but the precise handwriting showed it was authored with some care:

Dearest Percy,

As you'll discover from the tone of this correspondence, I write you with a great sense of urgency. To date I have yet to receive a response from you to any of my prior letters, which leaves me in a most difficult place of uncertainty.

The worst of all concerns, and one that makes sleep difficult for me, is fearing you have been harmed while in the proud and noble service of our country. It's unbearable to imagine this for even the briefest of thoughts.

I must confess, in my weaker moments, to be disquieted by another possibility. That the distance between us has somehow faded your affections toward me. I comfort myself in these times of vulnerability by remembering those sweet words you shared with me before you left me back home in Virginia. I so long for those precious days of our youth and pray that what you said that night was indeed true in your heart!

But I will not burden you further with my frailties. What I share with you is of great import. As you know, my father brought us to California in the pursuit of his fanciful dreams of gold. His way of reliving his glorious past, I suppose.

Father has left me to the safety of this seaport city while he has plied his trades in the hills of gold. If any of the rumors around here are true, I am quite certain he has made a great discovery!

Yet I cannot confirm this because I have not seen him for months. And as is his practice of caution, he has left no details of his whereabouts. Father is so terrified that someone would jump his claim. Oh, Percy, you know how foolish and stubborn he can be.

I find myself in a dilemma without easy resolution. Father would be just furious if I were to use strangers to help seek him out. It would be betrayal. But he would think much differently if you were to find him. He has always thought favorably of you.

I am ashamed to burden you with this request. I know how committed you are to your service in the army. But I beg you. If you have any love left for me and my father, please come and assist us without delay.

Yours with love and admiration,
Ashlyn

After reading the letter several times, Seamus found himself in a conflicting swirl of emotion. How could he intercept something of such intimacy that was never meant for him?

Or was it? What if this Captain Percy Barlow had been ignoring her letters and was scorning her requests? Who would be there to help her?

Perhaps this was just him being disingenuous. Trying to condone his behavior as some far-fetched attempt at chivalry. Besides, what good could he possibly bring into this poor woman's life? He was broken in spirit and worth. He could imagine his father's face, scoffing at him, laughing at the mere idea of Seamus believing he could come to this lady's rescue.

But when again he peered into the sad eyes of this woman from San Francisco, his heart persuaded him further. Was this

his fortuitous moment, the one that had evaded him all of his life?

Finally, after an hour of going back and forth with indecision, he found the will to tuck the letter and the photograph back in the envelope.

This was exactly what he was missing in his life. A cause. A purpose. Something to mute the pain of disconnection. Of loneliness.

Was there someone who could need him? Could he find restitution from his personal failings through the salvation of another?

Yet, such madness!

There was someone he could ask for advice. Someone who would know what to do.

Tomorrow he would head out to see Jeremiah.

Chapter 3

WORDS OF JEREMIAH

"Now son, I'm wanting to see things your way, understand, but what these ears are hearin', ain't lining up with the way I see it." As he leaned back on his chair on the porch, the old man stroked narrow, wrinkled fingers through a long white beard, which would lift up and wave on the occasion of a feral breeze. "'Cause what I see here is a horse you done took with a brand on her fanny saying, 'Hang me high.'"

Jeremiah was head to toe in hides, and the slight hump on his back made him appear to be bent over, and he peered through his one good eye while the other was wandering and glazed. "All this about a letter and gold and some lady you got your mind set to chasing, well now, that there's a whole other jar of foolery."

Seamus twisted his lip and tilted his head and sat up uneasily in his chair. In any city, by appearance, Jeremiah Travor would be one of those you would pass by on the street and pity.

You might even be tempted to throw a coin if he held up a tin cup. But in these parts of the high country, this wisp of a man was legend, and Seamus was trying to take in all he was saying.

"Well, I suppose if you're looking about it that way, I could be seen as a bit daft."

"And that's with only one good eye, which means you're surely twice that." Jeremiah cackled and rocked in his chair, kicking his boots.

He could back up his bravado. The old man's porch was overrun with trophies of success, dozens of pelts hanging from the eaves, there to dry in the wind before being taken to market. Mostly coon, plenty of beaver, otter, a few deer, and a bearskin as well.

Jeremiah's mountain cabin was a testament to his craftsmanship as well, with the logs interlocking with perfection and glistening with resin.

"Daddy, you be nice to Shay." Jeremiah's eleven-year-old granddaughter Becca leaned out of the window. She handed Seamus a piece of paper with a hand-drawn portrait.

He paused for a moment to take in the high cheeks, even brows, wavy black hair, and eyes of sparkling blue that almost always drew the poorly shielded gazes of women. "Me again? Why it's beautiful. But you forgot the beard again."

"You look much more handsome without it."

"You're too young for the word *handsome*, dear lady." Seamus examined it closely. He was amazed at how well she was able to draw him, especially since it had been two years since he was clean shaven. The face looking back at him seemed like a man in his far-distant past.

"I'll treasure this like the rest." Seamus clasped it against his chest.

The girl looked back at him with deep brown eyes that matched her dark skin and long, straight hair. She was orphaned at age eight when both her Cheyenne mother and Jeremiah's son had succumbed to a smallpox outbreak.

"This is grown-up conversin', Becca." Jeremiah winked at Seamus.

"I'm not listening all that closely." She smiled at Seamus and rested her chin on her arms, which were crossed on the ledge of the windowsill. "But can I see her face? The lady you love."

Seamus smirked at her grandfather and pulled out the photograph tucked in his shirt pocket. "I could use a more ably reasoned opinion, that's for certain." He handed it to the girl. "Perhaps a young woman's advice would be more suited to such things."

"Ah . . . she's beautiful."

"Let me see that." Jeremiah held out his hand.

Becca pulled back from the window frame, and in a moment she came out the front door and held the picture out to her grandfather with one hand while she put her other arm around him. "Isn't she pretty?"

Jeremiah took the picture from her soft hand and placed it just a few inches before his eye.

"Well, Grandpa. What do you say?" She glanced over to Seamus and nodded with glee. "She is beautiful, isn't she? What's her name, Shay?"

"Ashlyn."

"Ashlyn? I like that. Don't you like that name, Grandpa? It's pretty, just like her."

Jeremiah handed the photograph back to Seamus. Then he clasped his hands, closed his eyes, and rocked in his chair.

"He's thinking on it, Shay. He knows she's beautiful. I've seen it on Grandpa's face. He likes her too."

They both watched as the old man swayed back and forth, cogitating at his own pace. Then suddenly he opened his eyes and slapped his palms on the arms of his chair. "Yup."

Seamus held his hands up. "Yup what?"

"You should tail it out of here, that's what." He stroked his beard.

Becca clapped her hands. "He loves her too, Shay." The girl's expression changed and she pushed out her lips. "But that means you'll be leaving."

"So that's it, one glance at her face and I'm no longer a fool?"

"Oh, she's pretty enough, all right, but you're plenty still a fool. Which is just why you need to clear out of here."

Seamus glanced over at Becca who shrugged. "I don't . . . understand."

"If that there picture is what it takes for you to head west, then I say it's a good thing. Anything to get you out of this place."

"Grandpa. Don't be so mean."

"Believe me, girl, it's the kindest thing I can say. Why your friend Seamus has got to be the sorriest excuse for a mountain man as I've ever seen. This place has spit you out, boy."

"And that's you being kindly, eh?" Seamus put the photograph back in his pocket and buttoned it closed. His smile belied the pain in the truth of the words he was hearing. Would he spend his entire life proving his father's low opinion of him?

"Listen, son. You never were here but to hide from shadows. Ain't a single man gonna make a life of it doing what isn't right here." He patted his hand against his heart. "Especially in these parts. Out here, you'll end up buzzard pickin's."

Seamus rubbed his hands together. "That's the way you see it?"

"I do."

"Well, have you heard as well about my people? Out there in California?"

"The Irish folk? Hee . . . hee . . . hee. Where there's gold, eh?"

"Aye . . . I heard they're thick there, indeed, chasing it good.

I must say, I miss hearing a tin whistle, a song of paddy's tears, and a taste or two of home cookery." Seamus's thoughts drifted to years before, simpler and sweeter.

"And then again . . . there's the other mess of it." Jeremiah nodded over to the horse grazing where tall grass rose above the melting snow.

"Oh her. Ah, she won't cause me any troubles. She's promised not to mention a word of it."

Becca giggled and put her hand over her mouth. "She doesn't talk."

"She does indeed. Why Clarisse told me as plain as day you were just about the loveliest little girl she's ever set eyes on."

"And I'm supposin' your friends in the army will enjoy your fine wit while they are busy tying up a rope for you." Jeremiah shook his head. "This is serious, son." He turned and placed his age-spotted hands on Becca's shoulders. "Now you go in and set a couple weeks' provisions for our friend here, and get yourself ready for good-byes. Oh . . . and fetch me the box."

The girl's moist eyes looked over to Seamus. "Yes . . . grandfather." She turned and disappeared into the cabin.

"Ah, now Jeremiah you didn't have to unsettle her so."

The old man looked up from his drooped posture at Seamus and squinted. "Now listen, young man, and you listen well. You just leave that mare here and I'll set her free. Then you need to find the closest road and make good use of it."

Seamus scoffed. "Really . . . Jeremiah."

He waved his hand. "I know a few things I haven't told you. They know about you. I've heard things. They talk about the Irish traitor who lives in the hills. Word's got out. They see you with that horse or find you with some captain's letter or his girlfriend's photo in your pocket and that's all they'll need to draw and quarter you. Who knows? With their friend dead from the crash, that might be on your head as well."

Seamus was reminded of the cargo bags that were sprawled on his cabin floors, and the warning he was hearing from the old man was sinking in. But he wasn't ready to go. He still wanted to make something out of this life. Or was it that he wasn't prepared to face his shadows?

"I don't know, Jeremiah. It would be days before they make their way to the accident site. I've got time to clean things up a bit." Seamus lifted his hat from his head and scratched his scalp.

The door opened and Becca came out with a wooden box, which was meticulously engraved with the image of a mountain lion perched on boulder. "Thank you, child." Jeremiah opened it and pulled out some bills.

Seamus raised his hand in protest. "I am not too keen on charity."

"Here's fifty dollars. That will get you a ways. You can consider this purchase of your cabin."

"Why, it's not worth ten."

"If you were trying to hock it to me, I'd only give you five and that would be four too much." Jeremiah jabbed the bills at Seamus who took them with some reluctance.

The old man patted him on the arm. "That's good, son. And what about her?"

Seamus looked over to Clarisse and realized he had grown fond of the mare. "I need to go to my cabin first anyway. I'll let her loose close to the crash scene so they'll find her easy."

Jeremiah put his hands on his hips. "Well . . . I've got an old saddle here somewhere that you can put to use."

Becca returned again, this time with a bulging sack over her shoulder, leaning over from the weight.

In a matter of minutes and with some urgency, they had Clarisse saddled and bridled and with the packs neatly tied down. Seamus climbed up and prepared himself to leave the only two friends he had. "I wish I could have made you prouder, Jeremiah. I thought I could make it out here, I did."

Jeremiah patted the horse and Becca nestled close to her grandfather. The old man was struggling with his emotions. "You be careful now, son. The road's gotta way of takin' people where they shouldn't go. Keep those eyes on the horizon and your reins tight."

Seamus tipped his hat and turned Clarisse away, and in an unhurried pace, the two ventured on, mournfully, with a touch of uncertainty, but also with a hope in the unknown.

With the sun setting behind him, Seamus peered down from the path's ledge, where far below was his cabin by the creek. He rubbed the side of Clarisse's neck as he watched the soldiers teeming around the place he had called home. There would be no going back now. It was done.

"What do say, girl? Should I leave you here? You'd find your way down, wouldn't you?"

Seamus climbed down and untied all of the packs. Now more than ever he was grateful for Jeremiah's provisioning. Not only did he have food for a few weeks, but a bedroll, some warm clothes, and a canteen for water.

He slapped Clarisse hard on her hindquarters, turned, and set off down the path alone, swallowed up by the sprawling wilderness that lay ahead.

It reminded him of that day when he and Clare clung on to the railing of their ship as it pushed off the shores of the harbor in Cork and watched as the Emerald Isle slipped down the horizon. He always experienced such a sense of loss in good-byes.

After a good twenty minutes or so, he craned his neck to see what he left behind, and there only about forty yards behind, Clarisse was trailing his steps.

"You're going to get me in the thick of it all, aren't you?" But, in truth, Seamus was relieved to have a companion.

He pulled out the picture of Ashlyn from his pocket while he waited for the mare to catch him. Was it the woman's eyes? The innocent pleading of her letter? What was the source of his madness?

Playfully and with a surge of joy, Seamus kissed Clarisse on her jowl when she arrived. "C'mon, lass. Let's go find a lady."

Chapter 4

NOT FORGOTTEN

 "Do you believe any of that?" Clare raised the delicate bone china cup of tea from its gold-trimmed saucer as she peered out the bay window at the flower-speckled garden in their backyard, where a few hummingbirds dodged and sipped at the dwindling dewdrops of fall.

Andrew held up today's issue of the *New York Daily.* The headline across the top stated, "Chase for Gold on in California." He dropped the paper on the end table and looked at her through his round, wire-rimmed spectacles, which provided a gentleness to his high cheeks, square chin, and tightly groomed blond hair. "Of course it's true." His voice tinged with sarcasm. "We wouldn't print it in our newspaper if it wasn't so."

Clare put her free hand behind the curve of her back and arched, pushing her belly out further. She had been with child for seven months now and every part of her body ached. "But really, Andrew, that much gold?"

He came from behind, stooped down, and embraced her, and she smiled and leaned her head back against his face, close enough to know he hadn't yet shaved. Clare saw their reflection in the window, and it always struck her how well they fit together, even with her long, flowing, dark hair, fair complexion, and the Hanley blue eyes.

Andrew rocked her gently and kissed her on the cheek. "So you're going to leave me to become a prospector?"

She rolled her eyes. "But California seems so far away." Then she asked the question that was on her heart. "Do you think he's there?"

"Seamus? Well, the records do say he was spared the gallows. That much we know. Most of the men came home after the war. Even the Saint Patrick's Battalion. Could have gone back to Ireland, of course. But yes, many of the soldiers when out West."

It made Clare ill to imagine her younger brother receiving the prescribed fifty lashes and then having the letter *D* for defector branded on the side of his face. Was this better than being spared the noose? She wasn't sure. And how could he have ever been so foolish to shift allegiance from the Americans to the Mexicans? It was just like Seamus to be on the losing side. He never seemed to get a fair shake in life.

"Come." Andrew spun her gently, led her to the polished mahogany dining table, and sat her down in one of the purple upholstered chairs. "You need to eat something."

Clare knew better than to protest his caretaking, which gave him more solace than her. "All I do is eat."

"I wish that were true." He reached for a crystal pitcher of orange juice and filled a glass in front of her. "Despite all entreaties and skillful persuasions, I can't keep you away from your desk at the newspaper. And you, young lady, with the obstinacy and arrogance to believe we'll need to close our doors without your journalistic forays, poking the eyes of the bourgeois and raising a triumphant chalice for your downtrodden Irish."

She laughed. "And who will defend my people, with you and your English brethren pressing their aristocratic boots to our foreheads?"

"Who would have thought such words to be uttered in this house?" It was Andrew's mother, dressed in a floral shirtwaist with a laced stand-up collar and a sage-colored back-pleated walking skirt. "Why, Andrew, your poor father will never rest in his grave knowing how his beloved newspaper has become such a shamble, the vulgar voice of peasantry."

Clare smiled at Andrew, who pulled the head chair out to seat his mother. "Now, Mrs. Royce, your son has done a marvelous job as publisher."

"And remember, dear Mother, it was not I who sought the role." Andrew slid her chair in and snapped one of the cloth napkins and lay it in her lap. "It was only upon your most strenuous urging."

"Had I known! Had I known! And don't remind me so callously of my failures." She raised her wrinkled forehead toward the ceiling, fluttering her hand in disgust. "My precious husband, however will you find the grace to forgive me?"

Caitlin entered the room with a jump in her step, her pearly hair draped down her blue cotton dress. She circled around Clare and placed her hand on her stomach. "How is my niece or nephew?"

"They are both fine." Clare removed her younger's sister hand and felt the blush come to her face. "Will you be so kind as to beckon the man of the house?"

"I'm right here." Her eleven-year-old brother's voice came from the adjoining sitting room.

"Davin Hanley," Clare said with huff. "Have you been in earshot all this while? What have I told you about your eavesdropping?"

He appeared in the doorway and leaned against the frame, his brown curly hair astray. "If you're weren't gossiping, you wouldn't be minding so."

Andrew walked over to Davin and dug his fingers into his sides, which provoked a spasm of shrill laughter. "Perhaps I'll just tickle you until you find your manners."

Mrs. Royce shook her head. "Such insolence in the boy."

Cassie burst in through the shuttered doors leading from the kitchen with a plate full of scrambled eggs and bacon in her plump hands. "Must I be fetchin' the po-liceman? Mercy! Master Davin and Mister Andrew." She put the platter down and patted her glistening black forehead. "Peace and quiet done left this house years ago. Ain't that so, Mrs. Royce?"

"Isn't that so?" Mrs. Royce tapped her napkin against her pursed lips. "You say it this way, 'Isn't . . . that . . . so?'"

Cassie, whose cheeks exuded joy, tightened the strings of her apron. "Ain't. Isn't. I'll get better, ma'am." She paused and then spoke slowly with a delicate English accent. "Isn't that right?"

Andrew clapped and the table laughed. "Imperially stated."

"Well!" Mrs. Royce lifted her eyes to the ceiling. "And now even the servants are mocking me. Oh, my dear husband, I pray that I'll be home with you soon."

"Cassie is going to join me at the meeting again." Caitlin, who had just turned nineteen, glowed with youthful jubilance. "Ain't that right, Cassie?"

Cassie raised her arms and retreated back into the kitchen.

"Do you think that wise?" Clare never relinquished her role of matriarch. "There are people who are not as fond of the abolitionist movement and would see to do you both harm."

"I see." Caitlin sat upright. "You can write stories about the Underground and the evils of the slave trade, yet your sister can't even attend the meetings?"

Andrew sat in his chair beside Clare and raised his brows above the rims of his glasses. "She's your blood, that's for certain."

"So . . ." Davin, who always sat at the end of the table, spoke loud enough to break into the conversation. He poked his silver fork in the air, with a strand of bacon dangling on it. "What's this about Seamus?"

Clare leaned in. "You, young man, should be ashamed of asking any questions about what you overheard."

"Have you heard from Seamus?" Caitlin looked from face to face at the table.

"We have not." Clare shook salt out of a silver shaker on her eggs.

Cassie entered again, this time with a tray full of sliced fruit and berries. Several of them reached in and helped clear space in the center of the table.

"Thank you, Cassie," Clare said. "No. Andrew and I were just speaking about this discovery of gold in California."

"Do you believe he's there?" Davin's expression was full of hope.

"Perhaps." Andrew took the fruit tray and placed some on Clare's plate. "Just about every Irishman is shipping to San Francisco with a shovel in their hands and a dream in their hearts."

"That's certainly a fine thing." Mrs. Royce pointed to her plate and Andrew scooped some berries onto it. "It's a good place for all of them to go, present company excluded, of course."

"We should go get him." Davin's brow furrowed.

"Yes we should," echoed Caitlin. "I do miss him so."

"Nobody will be getting anybody," Clare said. "Seamus is a man of his own, and when he wants us to know where he is, he will correspond with us." The words didn't sit right with her, though. Her brother never seemed capable of taking care of himself, and it pained her to imagine him out there somewhere fending for himself alone.

That was if he was alive.

The thought caused her to shudder. She thrust out her hands. "Now. Let's say our grace."

As they shared their thoughts of gratitude and began to enjoy their meal, Clare's mind drifted and she tried to disguise her concern while the breakfast conversation continued around her.

Please, Lord, help him find his way.

Chapter 5
THE NUGGET OF WONDER

The distinctive blue hat was always a comforting sight.

As Davin approached the bustling harbor docks of the East River, which framed the southern flank of Manhattan, his eyes sought out the green painted bench where his friend Nelson almost always nested from sunrise to sunset. From behind, Davin could see the back of the navy felt admiral's hat, which was an easily recognizable silhouette against the morning sky, even from a distance.

He jogged up, passing by street vendors with brightly colored and carefully stacked fruits, vegetables, and nuts. There were well-built cart pushers, mostly blacks and Irish, taking cargo from the docks and bringing them up to the streets where horse-drawn carriages and mule-led wagons awaited. Davin darted in and out of the humanity, apologizing and lifting his cap as he bumped and pushed against the grain of traffic. Mostly he was invisible to the world around him, bent on the frenzy of commerce and trade.

Approaching larger in the horizon, were what must have been a thousand mastheads, dipping, bobbing, and bending with the sway of the winds and tides, encircled by screaming gulls and terns, picking at whatever might spill from crates and luggage streaming on and off the ships. The great steamers billowed angry fumes in the sky, as their mighty hulls sliced through the sea waves, their cargo a thousand empty faces leaning over rails.

"What news today, Nelson?" Davin swung himself over the side of the bench and landed beside the young man whittling away at an orange with a pocketknife.

Davin watched intently as Nelson, who was in his late teens, with long black sideburns and furry whiskers, concentrated on his task. "Hey, Nelson? What are you doing? Why don't you just peel it with your hands?"

The boy turned to Davin and grimaced, as if he had heard the strangest of questions. "It will make my hands orangey."

"Oh." Davin had learned to always take the first answer he got from Nelson. There was no use arguing with the boy as you would always circle around to the same place the discussion began. Davin didn't even know his friend's real name. Nelson was a nickname he received on account of the hat that never left his head. It was the same style once worn by Admiral Horatio Nelson, the famed naval hero. Some claimed Nelson's hat actually was a gift from the admiral himself, but Davin didn't really believe that one.

"Which one is leaving next, you think?" Davin usually didn't hang around on the green bench for very long, unlike his friend who could be found here all day. But still, he enjoyed watching the movement of people, great ships, and cargo coming and going as well.

He had the spirit of adventure, and though he dearly loved

his sisters Clare and Caitlin, he longed for the lofty fellowship of pirates and knights and rope-swinging heroes, which he believed only boys could share. Having lost his brother Ronan, who was close to his age, to the potato famine and his younger brother Kevan to a drowning accident, his only hope for fraternal bonding remained with Seamus.

Davin worshipped Seamus most of all. Perhaps because he was much older. Or maybe it was that he protected him from their father, rest his soul, when the old man was cruel, which was almost always.

He just had to find Seamus!

Nelson freed the last of the peel, all in one long piece, and laid it carefully on the bench beside him. Then he went about separating the slices of the orange one at a time and placing them in the shape of a sundial on the green wood.

Davin leaned back and stretched his arms out along the top of the bench. Shadowing the bright sun, he saw one of the longshoremen pushing a cart from the dock in their direction. It was a jovial chap they only knew as Jimmy.

"Hey, lads," the short man greeted them when he arrived, bright red staining his cheeks. He pulled up his cart and pulled his gloves off his hands. "A right, fine morning, wouldn't you say?"

"Seems fine enough." Davin thought of something. "Hey, Jimmy?"

Jimmy nodded.

"Which of these ships go to Fran-chesco?"

The man ran his stubby fingers through his thinning black hair. "I think you mean San Francisco."

"Is that the place with the gold?"

"You intendin' to strike it big?"

Davin shrugged. "Maybe." He had heard men were getting rich by living in the wild mountains and digging for gold. Why couldn't he as well?

"Well, in that case, just about every other ship is heading out that way. You can see them Micks lining up over there with their pickaxes, shovels, and fancy ideas spinning in their foolish Irish heads. Good thing you don't have a touch of the fever."

"I'm not sick." Davin looked over to Nelson and saw him straightening out his orange slices. "Nelson looks fine as well."

"They are looking for help on the *Tarentino* over there. A couple of strong lads like yourselves ought to be able to land a job."

"Do you think?" Davin tilted his head. It was hard to tell when Jimmy was being serious, and he didn't like when adults didn't take him seriously.

"There's no harm in seeing for yourself." He turned and pointed. "It's the black beauty over there. She's a fine one. I guess their captain lost most of his crew on landing, and they are trying to push out." He started putting on his gloves again. "Hey, Nelson. What about a slice for your sea partner Jimmy here?"

"Ah, you know better . . ." Davin started to say until Jimmy winked at him.

The man pulled up on the handles of the cart and started to turn it. "All right boys, don't forget about ol' Jimmy when your pockets are full of yellow stones."

Davin squinted from the sunlight and watched as Jimmy weaved through the crowd. "What do you say, Nelson? Should we see for ourselves."

They probably had stood for two hours on the wooden dock, just watching the dockworkers loading and unloading the massive *Tarentino*. Davin was determined to ask one of the ship's crew if Jimmy was telling the truth about there being jobs aboard, but each time he mustered enough confidence, he would get a disparaging look or grunt that would put him back in his shell.

He'd show all of them someday what he was capable of doing. Then they wouldn't look at him as a child.

But for now, both he and Nelson just observed over the side rail of the pier, as frazzled seamen, sunburned and full of anxiety, came on and off bearing the luggage of passengers who sauntered on throughout the day: ladies holding parasols, dressed in European finery, and men with expensive jackets, stovepipe hats, many of whom were smoking fragrant pipes and cigars.

"How far away is San Francisco anyway, Nelson? A few days, you think?" Davin twirled a seagull feather in his fingers. "Hey. See those fellows coming this way? They can hardly walk straight. Looks like they are coming to the *Tarentino*."

He viewed their arrival with some amusement, as there must have been nearly a dozen of them: tall, short, wide, and all of them full of drink, vulgarity, and laughter. They were being guided like the Pied Piper by one of the ship's officers who waved to the boatswain as they lumbered up the dock.

"Nelson. Look. They're going to get a tour or something. This is our chance." He grabbed his friend by the elbow, and as the merry fellowship stumbled past them, they both melted in with them, trying their best to remain unnoticed.

"Just ahead, boys, as I promised ya," the officer said. "Keep 'er steady."

They moved onto the ship platform and noisily made their way aboard, as some of the passengers cleared out of the path and exchanged disconcerted glances.

"Can you believe it, Nelson?" Davin whispered in his friend's ear. Right before them a large man stumbled, only saved from a tumble by two men who steadied him on either side.

As they lumbered through the ship to the forecastle, Davin gazed with his mouth agape as he spun about, taking in the black masts that reached high in the air, ducking under great ropes, and passing the steady work of the crew as they skillfully began to unfold the sails.

Up front, they came to some stairs leading down, and the group staggered forward and descended into the darkness. Davin was grateful for every step, expecting at any moment for large hands to reach down and clasp them by the napes of their necks to escort them off the ship. Until then, he would savor each and every glorious moment.

They reached the lower deck, the voices of merriment now growing louder as they reverberated through the oak-paneled hallways. Then they walked through a doorway and pressed body to body until they were all squeezed in a short-ceilinged room as tight as fish in a pail.

"Where is it?" shouted one of the guests with a heavy Southern twang.

"Yes. Show it to us, you ol' cudgel."

"I'll show it to you soon enough, but how about we share one last drink together first?"

Cheers ascended, and Davin peered through arms and bodies to see there was another officer now in the room and he was passing out tin cups. The other officer had a large uncorked jug in his hand and he was pouring from it to greedy, jabbing hands.

Two glasses made their way back to Nelson and he handed one to Davin, his mouth grinning to full capacity. Hoots and hollering erupted and the two boys stuck their glasses out through the tangle of hands. Once poured, they pulled it back and covered their mouths with glee.

"Now . . . now boys." The officer in the blue jacket with gold buttons, a balding pate, and crooked nose hollered above the fray and pounded on the side walls for good effect. "Those of you who have wagered against me, are about to see her in all of her glory." He reached out and the accompanying officer, whose young face looked intimidated by the gathering, handed him a small wooden chest.

"In here is the source of our pride. The true prize of the Pacific, dragged from the fertile fields of California, which serves these up like coconuts from palms." He gave the other officer a nod, and the man lifted the jug from the floor and proceeded to provide second helpings of the brown liquid he was pouring.

Davin held out his cup toward Nelson, who offered his up as well. Then in unison they leaned their heads back, emptied the contents to the back of their mouths, and snapped their heads backward.

Immediately, Davin started to choke and gasp and he grabbed his throat. If this was what whiskey tasted like, he would never drink a drop again for the rest of his life. And to think his da drank this all of the time.

"Drink up, lads. Have your fill. And then lift your dollars in your fists. If what you're about to see is not the largest nugget of gold you've ever witnessed. If it's not greater than the size of this clenched fist . . . then I'll . . ."

His words trailed as the room began to spin, and Davin reached out to clasp the arm of the man in front of him. But this man, just as many beside him, began to wobble, and the last thing Davin remembered was bodies collapsing and crumbling to the wood floor.

The cold, dusty, floor.

Then came the darkness.

The words pierced through the rippling of a distant dream.

"Son. Son. Son."

Then the cool splash of water on his face, and the echoes of cruel laughter.

"Should have thrown this one back in the water. Looks like we've got ourselves a couple baby dolphins snagged in the nets."

The receding tides of Davin's vision began to sift with clarity and as he put his hand to his throbbing head. He began to make out faces: grizzled, scarred, and jeering, looking down at him.

"Wah? He's just a wee scallop." The man's face was coal black, and his lips were cracked and swollen.

"Did you bring yer mammy?" said another.

"I hope he brought his mammy," a deep voice echoed, followed by laughter.

Davin's eyes widened and he reeled back. What danger was upon him?

"That's enough, boys." A tall man with a sharp, angled face but with brows of kindness bent down and lifted Davin up in his arms. "I'll be takin' this one."

As he was swept up into the man's arms, Davin was too terrified to squirm.

"Why's that, Dusty? Yer spoilin' our pleasure, poking at the lad."

"You'll have to find amusement elsewhere," the tall man replied. He bent down to lower his head in the doorway and carried Davin out of the room, into a hallway lit by lanterns as the voices trailed behind.

"What's happening?" Davin managed to squeeze out of his blurred consciousness.

"You've been recruited, son. Shanghaied as it's known here."

"I need to go home." The nausea crawled up his throat.

"Well, boy, as she's already a couple hundred miles out to sea, you won't be hugging your mother for a while. I've won you a right fine job, I have. You'll be with me in the galley and be thanking me later."

"No." Davin felt himself drifting again. "Clare's going to be so angry."

"Clare? Would that be your mother, boy?"

Davin felt his lips moving, but there were no words, and he succumbed to the blackness once again.

Chapter 6

STRANGERS OF THE ROAD

 "What say you try that by me again, mister? You're saying a soldier sold that horse to you, straight up, for a few bottles of Irish rye?"

"That is the most of it. Just as I said, although I am uncertain as to why it'll be any of your concern." Seamus's resolve dissipated rapidly as the stupidity of his actions was sinking in. What was he thinking? A shaggy-bearded, non-uniformed mountain man riding a U.S. Army issue horse down one of the busiest roadways of the West?

"Umm . . . right." The man twisted his rotund body, reached up from his seat at the front of the wagon, grabbed his rifle, and laid it across his lap.

He glared at Seamus with beady eyes, peering through a plump, red-cheeked face. "How about sayin' we look at this differently? Let's say, I'm a deputy from a neighboring county." He reached into the inside of his coat jacket and pulled out a star, then held it toward Seamus and rested it on his leg.

"Now, if a man in my position was to clip this on, why I'd been a sworn officer of the law. And I could shoot you right here. No one would question a word of what I'd say. But then I'd have to get out of this wagon here and spend a half of day in the sun digging a hole.

"Then again. Perhaps I could get that horse there from you. I could tie it to the back of this wagon and ride her back to the fort up ahead, where I'm guessing she's been missing from. Then when I got there, I could let them know about a man of your description just missing the flight of one of these slugs." He tapped on his rifle.

"Sounds to me, either way I lose," Seamus said.

"Not the way I see it. Not at all." He lifted the rifle up and pulled back the bolt and eyed the barrel. "One way, you're dead right away. The other way, you get a little time to ask God for forgiveness and repent of your thievin' ways until they catch up and hang you."

Seamus climbed down slowly from Clarisse.

"Easy boy." The man aimed the rifle at him.

"Mind that trigger, sir. I am onto your reasoning well enough."

The man lowered the rifle. "Now, of course, there's the part about my fee . . . what do we say, twenty dollars or so?"

Now who was getting robbed? Would he regret giving up so easy?

Seamus slid his hand into his pocket and pulled out a small pouch with the fifty dollars Jeremiah had given him. He pulled out two ten dollar bills and handed it to the man. "And how much more would it cost for your story to be you found this horse a wandering on its own?"

The driver shook his head. "I'm a lawman, sir. I'd be willing to sell a little time your way, but that's my best offer."

Seamus smiled with derision. "It is a fine thing to know there be still a few men of honor left out here." He handed the two bills over and put the pouch back in his inner pocket. Then he turned toward Clarisse and began to unstrap his bags.

He could imagine the heat of the weapon pointed at his back. Seamus moved deliberately, to make sure there weren't any motions that would be misconstrued. Then he took the mare to the back of the wagon and attached her lead.

"Well, lass, we only shared a wee time, the two of us. But your luck will surely prosper without the likes of me bringing you down."

The man waddled his way around the back of the wagon with the rifle tucked under his arm. "Now how about you start heading your way, and when I see you round the bend, I'll be on my way."

Seamus leaned into his bag and slung it over his shoulder. It was heavier than he thought, but this would be no time to dawdle. He nodded at the man, strangely grateful he was as corrupt as he was, and then headed down the trail. After a few minutes, he managed the courage to look back. Through the faraway dust, Clarisse was rounding the corner and then she was gone.

Now he truly was alone.

"Ahhh!" Seamus nicked himself on the cheek. He put his hand to his soapy cheek and there was a wet pink smudge on his hand. What did he expect? It had been a couple of years since he had last shaved to the skin.

He dipped the knife into the stream and the soap spun in trails along the current. It took him a few dozen more strokes with the blade until he could no longer feel whiskers. Seamus found a still pool of water to serve as a crude mirror and bent down low and examined his handiwork.

Yet he wasn't finished. Keeping a close eye on his reflection, he started to work the area around the scar on his cheek. Slowly he dragged the edge of the blade through the uneven edges of the damaged skin. He had long since scraped away the letter *D* from the side of his face, but the scar would always remain. All things considered, it didn't look that bad.

He gathered his belongings scattered around his makeshift camp in a clearing in the woods. He had set up far enough off of the Oregon Trail to be beyond the sights and sounds of passing travelers. Having lived almost entirely alone for the past couple of years, he was still adjusting to blending back into civilization, and he enjoyed last night's solitude, save for the stars and the choruses of crickets.

Seamus slung his pack on his back and ducked under branches and vines, while he took in the sweet smells of pine, mountain brush, and the moist soil. Sounds filled the air of quarreling squirrels, blue jays, and mockingbirds. Although it was indeed time for him to come down from the mountains, there would be much to miss of forest living.

As he came out from the sanctuary of the trees, this well-trodden branch of the Oregon Trail now sprawled open to him far to his left and right. He drew a deep sigh.

He pulled Ashlyn's photograph from his pocket and brushed off a piece of dust covering her lips. How terribly horrified she would be if she discovered this was in the hand of some stranger.

Yet Seamus was drawn to her with a soul of innocence. It wasn't that she needed him . . . it was that she needed *someone*. It wasn't just in her picture, but in her words. She yearned for a friend, a person to share in the burdens and joys of her life. And now Seamus knew he did as well. If nothing else, they were kindred spirits in their shared desires.

But there was more. And it was deeper. More profound. They shared a sadness, a hole in their lives. After so many years of trying to fill it with loose women, drink, riches, and affirmation and failing, Seamus knew he could not do this on his own.

There was an inexplicable sense that he had some role he was to fill, some unfulfilled purpose that lay ahead. What exactly it was? He had no idea.

Or was this all merely about proving his father wrong? How disappointing that would be!

Yet something told him the answer lay somewhere along this trail. Somewhere out West. That's where Ashlyn would be. And his fellow Irishmen.

One thing was certain. It was time to leave everything behind him. Time to start anew.

He began walking on a path deeply rutted with the tracks of wooden wheels and heavy livestock.

Seamus hadn't gotten too far along before he heard noises. He turned and saw a cloud of dust behind him. Were they on to him already?

He found a place off the side of the trail where he would be out of sight, but that would allow him a vantage to see what and who would be passing by him. As he waited, he pulled out his canteen, swatted a horsefly, and then moistened his mouth with the cool stream water.

In a matter of moments there were a few men approaching on horses, sentries, and behind them came a covered wagon, pulled by six grunting oxen and driven by a man conversing with a woman. The vehicle rattled with tools and pots tied to its sides, and the springs of the chassis creaked as it bounced on the road. As it passed, a boy with one leg dangling out over the rear hatch leaned back in boredom.

Then there was another, and many more. Faces peered out mostly with disinterest, some laughter; women cradling crying babies; children taunting and shouting in play; men in serious dialogue. The long train of wagons was interspersed as well with those who walked briskly alongside, stray yapping dogs, riders on neighing horses, snorting pigs, and several head of lowing cattle. The clanking of chains, whistles of cowboys, creaking of the canvas-covered ribs of the wagons, the pounding of hooves—these all added to the clamoring of what was a moving village. It stretched for what Seamus guessed was more than a hundred yards.

Seeing all of the humanity pass before him reminded him of the chattering vibrancy of his youth growing up in his small town. The community festivals, the weddings, the wakes, the dances, and even the interaction with family and friends on the farm. He seemed so removed from that life. Distant. Like a dream outside of his reach. After all he had been through, would there be a place for him? Or would he always be looking from the outside, a nose pressed against the window?

That all seemed to have been ripped away from him, leaving him abandoned on some lonely shore, as the lashes of his war punishment striated his back.

When they were far enough ahead, Seamus stepped into the road and watched the figures in the distance get smaller until all that remained of the train was dust in the air.

"Are you intending on just standing in the middle of this here road?"

Seamus spun around.

There was another wagon that had creaked its way upon him. But not just any wagon. It was a panoply of circus colors, painted brightly with purples, greens, and vibrant reds. And in giant gold lettering on the side was proudly proclaimed:

"Granny Portner's Miracle Cure." There as well was the meticulously crafted portrait of an elderly woman holding up a bottle as if it was the salvation of all that ailed.

Glaring down at him from his perch on the wagon sat a man who must have been a preacher, dressed in a black suit with a white collar and his head was crowned with a tall, tapered, black otter-skin hat.

Sitting next to him, its ears perked out of a motley array of bluish fur and tongue dangling from a smiling muzzle, was a small dog.

"Father?" The word stumbled from Seamus's mouth.

"Father? Hah! Sure, I can be that if you'd like. Father. Pastor. Preacher." The man had the eyes of a raven. "Hey. Don't supposin' you're in the market for a Bible?"

"Pardon me?"

"A Bible. Got 'em for sale right here with me." The man scratched his crooked nose.

"A Bible?"

The man pulled up the brake, swung his legs around, and stepped down gingerly. Then he stretched his scrawny body to its full short stature. In a moment, his canine partner made his way down and joined them with a hopping gait, his front paw curled. "Yes. A Bible. You know . . . something about in the beginning . . . let my people go . . ." The man made a sling motion. "David and Goliath . . . Matthew in the oven." Then he spread his arms wide and lowered his head, and then opened an eye. "C'mon. Baby Jesus, grows up a man, dies on the cross to save us all. A Bible!"

Seamus was getting his feet back under him. "I know what a Bible is. And I don't recall Matthew being in any oven."

"Well . . . then. What's keeping you, then? Genuine cowhide bound, soft, durable papers. Made with reverence and fine craftsmanship, to accompany you all the way to the high holy."

"Who are you?"

"Yes. Why, of course. How unfriendly of me." He lifted his hat, which revealed blond curls, though compressed and sweaty, and he gave a short bow. "Friends of mine, and more than few enemies, call me mostly Winn. Though it's short for the one my mama gave me, that being properly, Phineas Blake."

"Winn? Did you mean Phin?"

The man laughed and spoke to his dog. "He's a smart one, ain't he?" He turned to Seamus. "Yes. They called me Phin. But I changed it a bit to something more . . . promising."

Seamus glanced up to the side of the wagon.

"Hmm?" Winn turned back. "Oh yes. Grandma. No relation. She came with the wagon I done bought from a fellow in N'Orleans, along with the twelve wooden crates of the King James along with some preacher garments. Those are fine quality too. I've even got me some left of the Miracle Cure. He ran his fingers through his moist locks. I used to be balder than a duck's egg."

He paused for a moment, winked, then laughed heartily. "Just pokin' at you, boy. Was gonna have her painted fresh." He flashed his hands as if he was framing a picture on the sidewall of the wagon. "Imagine this. The gates of heaven opening, with a scroll pouring down, cherubs with wings playing harps and—you're with me, right?—at the bottom the Ark of the good Covenant opened wide with my smiling face looking at you holding out one of them there Bibles."

Doing his best to avoid laughing, Seamus kneaded his lips tight.

"There's a sad truth, though." Winn lowered his shoulders for effect. "The new painting was going to drain all of the profits before I even set out. So, for now at least, Granny Portner goes everywheres I go." He jabbed a finger at Seamus's chest. "But you wait, boy. As soon as we get through the starting inventory here, she'll be as pretty as that just described." Winn peered back at the side of the wagon for a long moment as if he was imagining it already there.

The dog barked.

Winn reached down and scratched behind its ears. "Yes. How impolite of me! This is Trip."

"Trip?"

"On account of his three working paws, and because . . . well, poor fella trips a lot." Then Winn turned around. "I best be getting moving. I'm gonna lose me that train."

"Oh, are you with those folks ahead?"

Winn lifted Trip and worked his way back up to the driver's seat. "Not precisely as such. I mean, I was for a while at least, sittin' with them and sharin' stories and all that. Guess they tired of my efforts to move a little product. Too many heathens, I suppose. Didn't manage to sell one of these Bibles to the whole mess of 'em. Can you believe that? But they don't seem to mind much if I keep my distance, far enough so I ain't eating no dust neither. But still close enough for safety and to pick up the pro-visions they scatter behind. Come on up. Why don't ya join me? I've got room here."

Seamus looked in both directions and pondered his choices for a moment. It wouldn't be difficult to get off later if the stranger seemed too bent. He tossed his bag up and Winn placed it in a cavity behind the bench. Then he offered his hand and gave Seamus a pull.

Trip tilted his head and eyed the newcomer briefly with sus-picion. When his mouth opened and his tongue wagged, Seamus reached out a hand cautiously, but pulled it back following a flash of teeth and a growl.

Winn adjusted his tall hat. Then he reached down and opened the top of a thatched basket, which was lying between them. "Ol' Trip will warm to you. See here. Fresh biscuits."

He pulled one out. It was fluffy, browned on the edges, and he brought it to his nose. "They left all of these behind, wicker and all. Why a train that large, with all of those children, we'll find all kinds of good things in their wake." He tossed the biscuit to Seamus. "What about you?"

"Me?" Seamus bit into the biscuit.

"Your name, your name. You've gotta have one, I'm sure."

"Seamus." The biscuit made his mouth dry already. "Seamus Hanley."

"Well then, Seamus. We've got food for days, time for conversing, and the wind at our backs. What say we journey forward, wherever that may be?"

Winn pulled on the handle beside him, lowered the brake, and whistled and snapped on the reins, and the two large, black horses lurched forward as the man howled with delight.

He glanced over to Seamus, his brows raised and a grin twice the size of his mouth.

Seamus turned away, took another bite from the biscuit, and was grateful to see the terrain around him passing by while he sat in comfort.

Ahead of them, the cloud of dust rolled forward. What were the real reasons for this strange man's exile? Although Seamus already had a few clues.

Chapter 7

THE THUNDERING PLAINS

Seamus settled into one of the most peaceful sleeps he had in years, in the warm air under a blanket of stars and with his stomach full of food. But just as first light glowed warmly above, a rumbling of the ground beneath him broke him out his slumbers.

"What's that now? Lightning?" Winn was sitting up and rubbing his eyes.

"You mean thunder?" Seamus said.

"Lightning, thunder. Both of 'em." Winn leapt to his feet, his eyes filled with panic. "It's God. He's done come for the Bibles."

"What are you saying? Did you steal them?"

"Now's no time for a confession."

Trip whimpered and hobbled in a circle. The pounding grew in intensity and off in the wake of the sunrise, a low-flying cloud of locusts was speeding toward them.

"My, my. We better hope these eyes are lying." Winn started hopping into his pant legs.

"Just what are you seeing?" Seamus stared in awe at the sight before him.

"Buffalo. They are trampling mad—and coming right at us!"

Defenseless in the open range, they sprinted for the wagon, with Winn only halfway in his trousers and one leg flapping at the side. Seamus bent over and scooped up Trip.

After fumbling in a panic to get the door open, they dove inside, spilling wooden boxes stacked inside, just as the great horned heads were upon them. There was a loud splintering of wood as the wagon's door was ripped away into an ocean of rising and falling waves of brown.

Winn and Seamus gripped each other tightly as Seamus felt the awesome power of the rampaging beasts surging by on either side of the wagon, occasionally clipping it, causing it to lurch, groan, and bend.

Seamus struggled against frightening foreshadows of horns bursting through the back wall and his heart and lungs trembled in wild palpitations.

The terror, which struck every ounce of his being, lasted only minutes, but it passed slow like eternity. And he wasn't certain, but he thought he was screaming throughout. Once it became evident they would not perish, he experienced gratitude. Not only for surviving it, but for being able to witness such an impressive spectacle of nature.

After the brunt of the incursion had ceased and the noise lowered, the two of them crawled to the doorway, where the trailing members of the herd were all that remained: the aged, the lame, and the calves galloping alongside their mothers.

Trip had worked his way out of the wagon and started to bark high-pitched protests at the interlopers.

Winn collapsed and sat against the doorway, holding his hand to his heaving chest. "Whoooh."

Seamus just nodded, as he could fathom no better descriptor of relief.

"Whoooh," Winn said again, this time much louder. He rose and stepped down to the ground outside.

Hoping to catch a glimpse of the herd before it disappeared, Seamus got up as well and tripped over several of the Bibles that had spilled out of the crates. He picked up one of the books from the ground. When he emerged from the doorway he took in the panorama of the earth transformed, as the once-smooth ground cover was now pockmarked with hundreds of deep divots from the fury of hooves.

"What now? Where did those horses go?" Winn stepped on a rock and looked in all directions.

"Were they not tied up proper?" Seamus was thumbing through the book.

"No. Which is a darn fine thing, or they would have been hoofed good. They'll be coming back soon enough."

"Hey . . . uh . . . Winn?"

"Yeah. What?"

Seamus handed the leather-bound book to Winn. "What kind of Bibles are you trying to peddle around here anyway?"

Winn snatched the book from his hand. "What? You've never done seen the Good Book before?" When he glanced at the cover, his expression fell. Then he opened it, slowly and painfully, and as he fanned through the pages, his brows burrowed further with each turn. "Weeell . . . I'll be."

"'Tis strange writing, no?"

"This one here's in French." He hustled into the wagon and from outside, Seamus could hear the thumping noises of frustration. In a few minutes, Winn lugged his body back out and slumped back against the giant face of Granny Portner.

Seamus paused before speaking, but the obvious question burned. "Did you not . . . a . . . you know . . . give them a good look over before buying 'em?"

Winn shook his fist at the sky.

Seamus regretted asking. "You didn't actually—"

"Yes, we done already figured on how they were acquired." Winn put his hand over his forehead. "Curse of Napoleon, all in French. I never put to thinking about opening them there crates. Just took to figurin' they were all the same." He looked over to Seamus and he wrinkled his forehead. "Why are you looking at me all cross like?"

"Well . . . now I should be the last of any to be questioning how a man makes his decisions. But, you know, stealing Bibles and all?"

Winn let out a deep sigh and looked at his feet. "It ain't exactly stealin' when you're pinchin' a thief. At least that's the way I see it. That dodger conned me well enough into buying this wagon along with a couple hundred miserable bottles of miracle cure. It didn't take me much time to be learned on the fact that he and his granny had already worn out townsfolk to the point of wanting to stone me at the mere mention of miracle cure. Turns out, his grandmama's recipe for healing was nothing more than swamp water.

"I finally caught up with him as he was skipping town, and I demanded all of my hard-earned back. Every last dollar of it. He refused to give me a thin nickel, insisting that 'Curing takes time.' When I threatened to put a hole in him, why that's when he revealed his next venture. One he said would make me both 'rich and righteous.' Seeing as I was short on both accounts, the hook sunk in."

Winn crossed his arms and kicked the ground. "I'm shamed to say, in a short while this wagon was twelve crates of Bibles heavier, but I didn't have any money to pay him. So that night when he liquored up a bit, I made off with it all, figurin' fair is fair."

Seamus had poked in far enough to something that wasn't his business. "What are you going to do with all of these Bibles now?"

Winn shook his head and then rubbed his chin. Suddenly, his disposition changed and his eyes widened. "Look at me with my cheeks full of lemons. Mama would have strapped me good. Why, we could have been resting below soil. But here. Look at me breathe. And these legs? Not even touched once by buffalo." He slapped at his chest and stomach. "Alive! Whooh."

He put his arm around Seamus's tense shoulder. "All we need to do is find ourselves some Frenchies out here in the West. Why, they are probably hanging from the trees on these roads ahead. Up from Louisiana, down from Canada." Winn held up the Bible in triumph. "And thirstin' plenty for a good word on these dusty plains. Why, ain't no stretch to think we can probably charge two, maybe three times as much for the same product. Hah! Fortune is smiling on us now, boy.

"No, Seamus, my new Irish friend. We ain't bearin' a single gripe out here. Whooh. You just needs to look on things proper." He dug a finger into Seamus's chest. "Manna from heaven. Remember this day. Remember it well."

Seamus couldn't help but smile. There was something both pathetic and likeable about his strange new friend. At the least, he provided amusement to break up the travels. He kneeled down and Trip allowed him to scratch behind his scruffy ears.

"Now," Winn said, "let's go get at them horses."

Chapter 8

THE UNDERGROUND

Clare snugged her knit shawl around her and looked back to the dark, gusty street that was undoubtedly brewing with lurking dangers. It was reassuring to see her coach and driver parked in front of the church, but even he was uneasy in this part of the neighborhood. She turned to the giant oaken door and swung hard three times on the knocker.

It echoed through the moonless night, and she was certain she had alerted the area's entire nest of thieves.

Steps could be heard and then there was a slide of the door vent and a lantern from inside revealed a man with a large rounded nose peering out, his eyes darting left to right. "What is the meaning of this clatter at this time at night?"

"You know precisely why I am here." Clare shuddered in the cold.

"The church will be open in the morning, ma'am. Surely this can wait."

"I know about the meeting."

"The meeting?"

"Is it in your nature to lie? In the halls of the church?"

There was a long pause.

Clare pressed. "My sister is in there. I intend to stand here continuing to clatter, as you say, until you allow me to pass, and I will scream if I must."

"You can holler all you wish, miss. This is the Five Points. None will know the better."

"Truly, sir. Will you keep a pregnant woman standing in the cold?"

He squinted at her. "Mrs. Royce?"

"You know my name?"

"Of course, Mrs. Royce. But I must ask you something."

"Hastily. Before I freeze myself."

"Are you coming as a sister or a reporter for the *New York Daily*?"

"Whichever you choose. Now please, open this door."

The man disappeared from the window, and then there was a large clack and the great door opened. The man who was dressed in brown robes stepped out briefly, and his hawkish eyes surveyed the darkness. "The coach?"

"He's mine."

"Have him wait down the street."

Clare lifted the hem of her dress and walked out to the driver. "James. Why don't you go down the street a ways. We'll come to you."

James leaned down from his seat, his top hat perched high on his head. "Are you certain about this, Mrs. Royce? Is it safe?"

"No. It most certainly is not. And if you mention any of this to Andrew. I mean, if he knew I was out here at this time of night . . ."

"Yes. Mrs. Royce. Then for just this reason and in consideration for both your safety and my continued employment, please be careful."

"I will, James."

Clare returned to the church door, pulling her jacket in to fend from the cold. When she arrived, the man was waiting for her and he was quick to close the door behind them and then latched it shut tightly.

"Follow me, ma'am."

They winded their way down the church pews, and then he continued to the back of the church, where they arrived at a creaking wooden stairway leading down to a basement. As they descended, the voices of argument lofted toward them.

When they reached the bottom of the stairs, Clare saw that she was in the back of a large room, with perhaps seventy or eighty chairs, all of them full with a crowd blended with whites and blacks, rich and poor, with others standing off to the side. Up at the podium, a diminutive man spoke with an authoritative bellow. He was bald atop his head, but for what he lacked in hair above, he more than made up with what protruded from his sides.

"If we remain silent, if we are to hold our tongues, then we will be bullied and shamed . . ."

His voice trailed out for Clare because she had only one thing on her mind. Her eyes scanned through every row of chairs until she got to the back, and there in the farthest seats off to the right, she saw the back of Caitlin's head, and sitting next to her was Cassie.

Clare lifted her nose and stormed toward her sister, having to restrain herself from giving her sister's hair a firm yank in salutation. But as she got closer, she noticed Cait was sitting next to a young man in his early twenties, and the two were holding hands. Clare's temper rose even further.

"Never shall we let this so-called King of Cotton . . ." the voice drawled.

She tapped Catlin firmly on her shoulder, and the girl looked back startled. Abruptly Caitlin stood, and Cassie looked over, her brown eyes widened in horror. The young man released Caitlin's hand and he rose as well, and put his hands in his pockets.

He was strikingly handsome with brown hair and matching eyes, a scruffy beard, and a sense of rebellion in his air and his posture.

Clare pointed a finger at him. "You." Then she motioned for him to sit and he did, but only after receiving a nod from Caitlin.

"This enterprise they are now embarking on is the grandest insult of them all to the Free Soilers . . ."

Caitlin and Cassie walked sheepishly around their chairs, and as two scolded children came their eyes shifted downward. The three went over to the staircase.

"We thought—" Caitlin began.

"I was asleep?"

"That's right."

"How could you do this to me, Cait? And you, Cassie, for that matter. It's been only three weeks since we've lost your brother Davin, and I've been crying my eyes dry on account of all of this, and you promised me you would take a break from your . . . your . . ."

"Underground. It's called the Underground Railroad."

"Of course it is," Clare said. "What do you think I do at the newspaper?"

Caitlin's eyes grew stern. "Well, you haven't written for a while about this."

Clare let out a deep breath. "Listen, Cait. I know you have grown to be a caring woman." She caught a glance of the young man who was looking back and she shot an arrow at him with her eyes. "And who . . . who is that . . . boy?"

"His name is Aidan. And he's a freedom fighter."

"To the point, young lady."

"The point is, I'm not a young lady. I'm sorry you are sad about Davin, and know well that I am too, but this . . ." Caitlin pointed to the filled room. "This is important to me."

"But . . . it's just so dangerous. And for Cassie as well."

"I's be fine myself, Missus Royce, really I is."

Clare looked at the brown eyes staring at her, and for the first time she could see an underlying passion in the woman.

"Listen," Caitlin said. "You have your work. This is mine. I mean, do you know who that is?"

Clare glanced to the podium and didn't recognize the man, but he did seem important.

"That is a senator from Washington. He says the South is upset about the possible statehoods of California and New Mexico and he's warning us of talks and deals. The rumor is they will be strengthening the Fugitive Slave Act."

Clare was caught off guard. She didn't know if she should be impressed with her little sister or still angry. Cait had indeed become a woman. "And what will that mean?"

"It means the slave catchers will be getting bolder and bolder. They are taking runaway slaves right off the streets of Manhattan. Do you know what this means? Do you?"

"Of course, I've heard about this at the *Daily*."

"Then why don't you write about it more often?"

"We can't. We're getting ourselves in enough of a bother there with defending the Irish in the Five Points. We can't take on every cause. We can't take on the battle of every household."

Caitlin lowered her eyes. "Even if the fight is in your own home?"

Clare didn't understand what she was saying. She shook her head, but when she looked at Cassie, tears were forming in the woman's eyes. "You Cassie?"

Cassie looked over toward Caitlin and she received a nod.

"That's true, Missus Royce. I's run away when I's a girl. My mamma brung me."

"Does Andrew know?"

"No." Her eyes filled with fear. "If Andrew's mother knows, she's sure to throw me out."

"I told her it would be safe to tell you," Cait said. "But she's so frightened."

Clare pulled Cassie to her and embraced her. "You told me your mother died."

The woman sobbed, and there was a pause before she spoke. "Mamma got took years ago. Just the same as she die."

Clare pressed the woman back and then pulled out her handkerchief and gave it to her. Then she turned to Cait. "Well . . . in this case, I believe we should go back in and see what the man has to say."

Chapter 9

THE MEN OF CLOTH

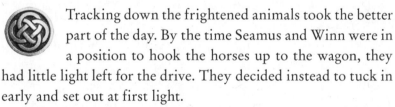Tracking down the frightened animals took the better part of the day. By the time Seamus and Winn were in a position to hook the horses up to the wagon, they had little light left for the drive. They decided instead to tuck in early and set out at first light.

When morning had broken, Seamus discovered Winn's mood had shifted to anxiousness as they warmed up hot water over a fire.

"What is it that's troubling you, friend?" Seamus tossed more dry kindling into the flames, which caused embers to rise like flaming moths.

Winn glanced up and tried to disguise his worry with a half smile. "Oh, there's not much in it. I'm just grieving a bit about us losing the wagon train." He handed Seamus a cup about a third full with dry oats topped by what appeared to be a crawling speck or two.

"Who needs them anyways?" Seamus asked. "You said they didn't want you around."

"They didn't mind me too much." Winn face flushed. "Just said I scared their children some, that's all." He glared into the fire. "But not only were they good about keeping us fed with their leavings behind, but now we're alone here in probably the worst of all Indian territory." He glanced up as if he heard something. "Why those natives are surrounding us surely, and these ain't the sort that would be fixing to trade beads for Manhattan."

"The caravan surely is just a ways ahead." Seamus picked through the oats with dirty fingers. "Maybe we just need to hurry ourselves along."

"'Fraid not. They are a good day, day and a half in front of us now."

"Couldn't we just wait up on the trail for another train to catch up to us?"

"That's not a fair wager." Using a cloth to protect his hands, Winn lifted the steaming canister from the flat rock in the middle of the fire. He nodded at Seamus who held out his cup and soon it was filled with boiling water and floating oats. "The one we lost might nearly been the last of them coming this way. At least of that size. We're at the end of pioneering season now. Those there mountains ahead of us will be sheep white with snow soon and the passes will be shut like a frosted iron gate. As it is, we may be waiting it out 'til spring melt."

The thought of being delayed that many months to reach Ashlyn seemed unbearable to Seamus. If it would take that long, he might as well not bother. "Then we'll just have to lively it up, I s'pose."

Trip came to Seamus and sat, his moist eyes now tracing every movement in his cup of oats. He gave the dog a wry look but then spooned a portion in his hand and allowed Trip to lap it up.

Winn slurped water from his canteen and then wiped his face with the back of his hand. "First we need to get you suited up proper."

Seamus didn't know what he meant and just shrugged.

"This preacher's gear I've been wearin'," Winn said. "It's not much in the way of comfort for travelin', but it serves its purpose rightly."

"And what would that be?"

"It'll buy us safe passage through tribal lands."

"How so?" Seamus scraped his metal spoon along the inside of his cup to get the last bite. He lifted his spoon and opened his mouth but then couldn't avoid Trip's hungry gaze. He lowered the spoon to the grateful dog.

"I've heard in these parts, the Indians they kinda see preachers as some kind of magical spirit man. Like their own healers. I don't know if it's about respectin' or fearin' them, but either's just fine by me, if it means keeping the hair on our heads."

Seamus was surprised that his friend's logic actually made some sense. There was another benefit to the preacher's outfit as well and probably even more important. It would provide both a disguise and perhaps draw some grace when they passed soldiers along the way.

"You've got one that will fit me proper?"

Winn's face curled with a grin. "Tailored with the finest-bred wool, with a full range of sizes to suit you well."

It felt good to be back on the trail again, heading into the western skies. The terrain alternated through patches of forested areas and wide-open, tall-grassed plains.

Seamus felt tormented by his new clothes, unable to get used to the tight collar that made him feel as if he was choking.

"It's convincing, if you ask me." Winn chirped at the horses and snapped the reins.

"Was that me you heard asking?" Seamus glared at his companion.

"No truly. It fits you well. Have you put much thinkin' to being a pastor?"

"I'm only wearing this because of you telling me it will keep me from getting scalped." Seamus swatted at a wasp, venting some of his frustration.

"The ways I see it, it's a crafty way to earn, if you're looking at it fairly."

They hit a divot in the road and they both lurched, but it didn't deter Winn. "People just hand you money like it's poison in their pockets. Invite you for supper at their homes. Tripping over each other to get you meeting their pretty daughters. Hands stay soft and your back don't get crookedy. Lot of good to it if you ponder it some."

For a few cherished moments, Winn took a break from conversation giving Seamus time to consider his new clothing. Would he be incurring God's wrath to be so falsely adorned? He had to admit to be dressed in this way brought him some comfort, bringing him back to a simpler time in his life when he believed God would protect him from all harm. He didn't know why, but he saw Grandma Ella's face shining at him from back in the old country. Now there was a woman who had faith! It brought him a smile.

Then he saw something strange in the skies.

Seamus pointed ahead to where there were a circle of dots in the air. "Over there."

Winn's gaze followed and he nodded. "Buzzards. Fixin' for a good meal by the looks of it."

"They've got themselves something, that's for certain." Seamus's imagination strayed to figuring out what it could be.

"We'll know soon enough." Winn fumbled with the reins.

They bounced on for some time in uncomfortable silence. After a while, Seamus sensed that Winn had a question surfacing, one which had loitered with him since he first picked Seamus up at the side of the road. "Why don't you just get out with it?"

"With what?" The man was a poor actor.

"With what's been niggling at you. It's been bothering you for a few days now."

Winn appeared curious but conflicted. "Maybe I've figured some things are best kept in a bottle."

"All right then. If you lack the courage, I'll uncork it for you. You want to know why I was wandering on the road, poorly dressed for travel and without more than a few day's provisions."

Winn glanced over to him, then returned his eyes to the road ahead. "There's two types of people on this trail. Those who are running away *from* something and those who are running *to* something. If I was guessing, I'd say you've got both pullin' at you . . . and hard like. I've got the running away part figured out fine."

"Oh, you do?"

Winn looked over again and raised a brow, as if probing to make sure it was safe to answer openly. "Them army boys. When we pass them you tighten up and kinda hide your eyes."

Seamus thought about denying it. Was it foolish to be sharing his story with this man he still hardly knew? "Have I been that obvious?"

"Still, I haven't figured out the 'running to' part yet. 'Course, it wouldn't much be gambling to see it doing with all that gold out there they've been talking up."

"Every man's digging up some type of gold, so that's a fair enough guess. My weakness has always been of the sort of gold that smiles back at you." Seamus unbuttoned his pocket, pulled out the photo of Ashlyn, gave it a glance, and then handed it to Winn.

"Hello there, daisy! Whooh. The mystery done solved itself."

Seamus laughed and reached out to get his photograph back. "Well if that be the case, then I'll have you explain it proper to me." His attention shifted abruptly to the sight up ahead in the distance. More birds of prey were amassing and hovering above what seemed to be dozens of lumps of brown scattered across the grassy landscape. "Say. What do you s'pose it could be?"

"It'll be plain enough soon. That's right where the trail leads."

They watched in discontented silence as it soon became evident the brown patches were actually the carcasses of many dozen fallen buffalo, lying across the yellowed plains.

"Woah." Winn pulled back on the reins and the wagon rolled to a stop with a rusted groan. He engaged the brake and the two men stepped down from the wagon, their shoulders lowered in disbelief.

"What could have happened here?" Seamus asked mournfully. They approached the lumbering bodies, which were motionless, save for the dark curls of their manes that danced with melancholy to the dirge of the whistling, brooding winds. Large flies feasted upon the surrendered, their green hues and translucent wings buzzing loudly with greed. Several of the corpses were steeped with crouching vultures that pecked hungrily at the moist, red wounds.

Trip alternated between sniffing at the fallen and yapping at the birds.

Winn bent down on one knee beside one of the larger bulls. "Bullets . . . not arrows."

"No. This couldn't be blamed on Indians." Seamus waved away a group of birds on one of the crumbled beasts.

"They wouldn't gone and been this disrespectin'. They'd treat the buffalo more kindly than they would you and me. No, this here has been done for sport."

"Sport?"

"This ain't me forgiving it none, but the trail can be long and boring. A herd of buffalo is gonna be too tempting not to shoot at for some. A good chance of it being the folks from our wagon train." Winn pulled out a buck knife from his leather scabbard and began cutting through the buffalo's thick hide, deep into the flesh.

Seamus could not believe what he was seeing. "What are you doing there?"

"They may have wasted these buffs, but it don't mean that we have to do as well." The blood began to seep from the wound.

"Ah, Winn. You're making a real fine mess of it, and we won't be able to use a bit of it anyway. Surely it's good and spoiled now."

Winn put the back of his hand to the side of the buffalo and rested it there briefly. "No. He's still warm and ain't been rigored yet. Trust me, boy. Never will you taste sweeter meat than buff. On the whole of the trail, we won't eat none better than tonight. Now won't you leave me to cutting us up a couple of steaks here." He looked up to the descending sun. "We'll get in another trail hour or so before finding a good spot for camp. Then we'll get on to puttin' these beauties to flame."

They considered gathering up more meat to fix up some jerky, but in the end decided they had neither the time nor the proper ingredients to handle it properly. The two left the scene of brutality behind them, Seamus laboring under no shortage of disgust. They only managed to travel a few miles before pulling off to the side of the trail. Soon, under the lantern of a full moon, the two settled around a fire as two large steaks sizzled in an iron pan.

When Winn pulled the meat off of the fire and put them on the blue tin plates, the seared cuts hung over the edges. Seamus gaped at the meal before him, which was heavy to hold and seared to perfection. With the crackling of the fire and cool sounds of the evening in the background, Seamus held his knife and fork, his mouth watering.

Winn sliced a large piece and stuffed it in his mouth, and a thin stream of juice slid down the corner of his lips. "Whooh." He looked over to Seamus. "Now, come on. Don't be staring or you'll make her nervous."

Seamus sliced a large piece, blackened on the outside but tender, red, and juicy on the inside. He lifted the piece up to his nose and grimaced.

"What? Are you still worrying yourself?"

"Smells a bit odd, don't you think?"

"Of course it does. It's *buff-a-lo*. It ain't heifer and don't be expecting it to moo neither." He took another bite, closed his eyes, and moaned.

Seamus put the meat in his mouth, and with one taste he was over the cliff and down the falls. The flavor was pure succulence. "That's . . . that's . . . oh my . . ." He shoveled in a large piece that he wolfed down.

He held out a strip to Trip, but the dog merely eyed it with curiosity.

"Mama didn't raise no liar, boy. I told you as much. This should learn you good about looking at me cross again." Winn took another bite and lifted his head to the stars and made a loud howl. "Gotta love the travelin' life. I hope this road never ends. And mark these two words, my friend: trust Winn."

"I will do my best to remember them well," Seamus said, his mouth filled so wide it was hard to chew.

"It'll be a right shame when we finally end up getting where we're going." Winn let out a loud belch. "By the way, Seamus. Where exactly is that?"

"Where's what?"

"Where are we going?"

"You're asking me? I'm just along for the ride."

"I'm a businessman. As well as there are customers to be had, makes little difference to me."

"Don't you have family?"

The question seemed to jar Winn. "Of course I do." He took another bite of his food and shook his head with a smile. "It's just . . . I'm not all that certain where they are."

"How's that?"

"My wife done walked out on me and left me to our farm in Carolina."

Seamus tossed a piece of gristle into the fire, and the flames responded with a flash. "Sorry to hear that. Didn't mean to meddle."

"Oh, no apologizing to me, friend. It was for the best. I mean, look at this life I live now. Free. Wild." His eyes glazed as he stared into the fire.

"Did she give you any reason for her leaving?"

"Yes. His name was Ethan Turner."

"That's a hard one. You didn't find them . . . you know, catch them in some point of compromise?"

Winn gave him a confused look. "Oh no. It wasn't a'tall like that. Ethan Turner? He was the man who sold me tulip seed. A convincing fellow he was. Told me I'd get twenty times the yield if I planted tulip. Said I had better soil than the Dutch and it would grow as simple as mushrooms after a good rain."

He took out a handkerchief and wiped his face. "So I . . . uh . . . tore out the tobacky plants from my wife's family farm and seeded it up with tulips. I worked that field from the sun rising to the sun setting. Hardly slept a wink, nursing them even by the light of the moon, babes on milk. Of course, it didn't take all that long to learn about the little problem."

Seamus set his plate down and leaned back and rubbed his bloated belly. "Problem?"

"Dandelion."

"Dandelion?"

"Yes. Old Ethan done sold me dandelion kernels. That turned to be all poor Beverly could take. I set out to track Ethan, aiming to get my money back, but no blue ribbon hound dog would have hunted that filcher down. He had slipped good. When I got home, there was nothing but shutters flapping in the wind. And a note from Bev."

Winn took a knife out and worked on his teeth. "It said: 'You can find us when you're good and done chasing the wind.'"

Seamus stared at him. "Why didn't you find her?"

"Oh . . . I know where she was well enough. She has relations up north. By my thinking, I didn't want to be coming back to her with my head down. There's a fortune out there somewhere for Phineas Blake. That you can count on, my friend. And for you just the same, Seamus." He wiped the knife on his pants and sheathed it. "Bet you never knew how many uses there are for dandelions."

They stared at the dancing sparks in the fire for a few minutes and then Seamus pulled out the picture of Ashlyn from his pocket. "San Francisco."

"What's that?"

"San Francisco. That is where this young lady lives. You already knew I wanted to cross the Sierra. This is where the trail ends for me. I'll go as far as you're heading and then make the rest of the way on my own."

"Yeah? Who says I ain't fixin' to go to San Francisco? What's her name anyway, this here lady?"

"Ashlyn."

"She your bride?"

Seamus laughed. "No. She doesn't even know me from a rock in the road."

Winn leaned forward and cocked his head. "Let's see if I'm hearin' you plainly, boy. You intendin' to walk more than a thousand miles or so, all for a woman who don't even know your name?"

"Well, when you go about it that way, it doesn't fair me too well." Seamus crossed his arms to fight the sudden chill. "I s'pose I'm hoping it's not just chasing the wind."

"Granted she's a might fine purty little gal, but I thought I was the desperate one between us." Winn cackled and mixed in a couple of howls.

"If it all wasn't so true what you're saying," Seamus returned the picture to his pocket, "then I'd be obligated to defend myself with these." He held up his fists and then laughed as well.

Seamus wondered what he liked about his new companion. Perhaps there was comfort in finally meeting up with someone with poorer luck than his.

"They got French people in San Francisco, you know," Winn said. "The Barbary Coast."

"What?"

"That's what they call it. Frisco. They call her the Barbary Coast. I think I should try my hand at diggin' me up some gold.

Why, I can sell these Bibles off or just trade them straight up for mining tools."

"So . . . you're thinking you might go all the way through to San Francisco?"

Winn leapt up. "Well, can't find any good reason to say no." He wiped his hands on his trousers and then outstretched a hand toward Seamus. "Barbary Coast?"

Seamus hesitated for a moment and then shook on it.

"That's it you see. The two of us. We're gonna be good for each other. You can trust ol' Winn on that one, my friend."

Seamus lay on the ground beside the wildly blazing fire when he suddenly felt the ground tremble beneath him and it began to crescendo. Buffalo!

He wanted to get up and run, but he found himself completely paralyzed and unable to move. When he tried to scream, no sounds came out. The pounding of the hooves came closer and closer and despite his greatest struggles, he was unable to budge. He closed his eyes as the great beasts approached, and though he couldn't see them, his entire body clenched at the impending pain of being trampled by a thousand feet. He covered his head and curled himself up tightly.

The pounding tremors lasted for an unbearably long time and then as quickly as it came, it was gone.

He got the odd sensation of warm breath on his face and eased open his eyes to see a bull only inches away from his face, ogling him as if he was some sort of threat. Then anger appeared in the creature's eyes and the great beast reared back, preparing to gore him with its horns. But instead, it relaxed, turned, and strolled away.

Seamus jerked upright, drenched in sweat. It was only a dream. He drew in a deep breath and let it out slowly. What was that disturbing sound? He turned to see Winn on his knees retching. Just then, a deep pain knifed Seamus's gut.

The fire had long since faded to dimly glowing embers and he struggled to his feet, grasping his stomach. And before he could stand and take a few steps, he vomited as he had never done before.

Chapter 10

TALES OF GOLD

It took two days before Seamus and Winn had recovered enough from the bad meat to be able to travel again, and by this time there remained little hope they would be able to catch up with the wagon train that had left them behind.

Over the next few days, they did manage to pass a few other travelers on their journey coming and going in both directions. There were trappers, hunters, and those who resided nearby; as well as a fair number of prospectors returning from California, both in victory and defeat from the fields of golden glory. Few spared much time to offer a report or suggestion.

But a man named Zeke agreed to share lunch with them. He was fresh from Coloma, which he proudly proclaimed was where gold was first discovered more than a year prior.

"Is it true what they are all saying?" Winn asked, not allowing the old man to take his first bite of the beef jerky they shared with him.

Zeke sat cross-legged on a tree stump and scratched his beard. "Sure as I'm standing here, it is. We were picking up nuggets the size of acorns in the riverbeds, and just as easy as pulling cherries from a tree. It's true what you hear and much more."

Seamus eyed the man closely. "But there were many who passed us who said they didn't find enough to cover passage back home."

The man bit into the piece of jerky, which was tough enough he had to tug his jaw sideways to cut it loose. "There's cunning to it, that be true. And plumb luck won't hurt nobody neither. But the way I seen it, you don't need much of either."

"What say you show some of what you dug up?" Winn's voice squeaked and he rubbed his hands together. "I've never seen it raw myself."

The gold miner narrowed his eyes at them. "Supposin' I do and I shows you, and the next thing you're strippin' me clean." He reached into his vest and pulled out a Colt revolver. "Then I'd have to introduce you to the missus."

"Hold it, old man." Seamus's service as a soldier made him cool to the sight of a gun. But he still spoke with caution. "We aren't aiming to pinch you of anything but a bit of news and maybe a wee drop of wisdom."

Zeke closed one eye and gave them both a good look over and finally unclenched. "Well, I don't mean to be unfriendly-like, but out there miners have their own code. You just mind your own and you hope to live long enough to leave with what you find—and that's if you find any. There's no thieves or murderers in gold country. Surviving is what makes right or wrong. My advice for you two fellers would be to mind your questionin'. I've seen men hung from trees for blinkin' their eyes in the wrong way."

Winn handed the man another large piece of jerky. "But you're sayin' there's gold?"

"Oh, it's there all right." The miner reached for the jerky and chomped away at it with the few good teeth remaining in his jaw. "Not that you'll be seein' any soon."

The very sight of the meat made Seamus's stomach lurch at the reminder of the buffalo meal. "What are you saying to us, old man?"

Zeke pointed the finger of a gnarled hand toward the sun. "The days are shortening. Too little left for you to make it to the passes before winter strikes. Sure. You can try headin' all the way south and looping up. That's a long, hard ride, and you'll surely have to do most of it without water in that desert. And the passes? Those mountains are pretty enough, and pregnant with gold. But try crossin' her during winter, and you'll be bones for someone to step over when the spring comes around. Nah. Those ranges will treat you right well, but you needs be showing them proper respect, or they'll gut you in a heartbeat."

"We've got time aplenty before winter." Seamus looked at Winn to see if he was concerned.

"Suit yourself." Zeke shrugged. "Won't tell another man his business. But the right decision would be to settle in to Salt Lake for the winter and head out when the melts come around again. There'll be gold when you get there, and it spends better if'n you're still breathin'."

The thought of delaying his trip to San Francisco for a season disturbed Seamus, and he chided himself for his foolishness. What kind of spell was he under? Was it this woman, or was it the gold after all?

"The leaves are still in color." Winn's face was turning a shade of red through his unshaven blond whiskers. "I'm told winter won't be bearin' down until December, and maybe not even then."

"Not here to argue with you fellers. Just right advice is worth more than the gold itself. Here's to hopin' you find yourselves both." The miner stood and grabbed the small of his back before what seemed to be a painful mounting of his horse. "The Green River is just two, three hours ahead. Ask the ferry-man about what he's been hearin'. They tend to have a ripe ear. There's soldiers camped out at the bank as well. I'll wager you'll hear just what I'm sayin' from all of them." He gave a curt nod and winked. "Good day to you fellers."

They watched him trot away, his frail body bouncing on top of the young mule.

"Did you hear that old curmudgeon?" Winn climbed up to the seat of the wagon and unclamped the brake. "You can't be believin' a word from those gold diggers. They grab theirs and don't want no one else to get their share, just in the chance they someday may want to come back. Hope the greed doesn't grip us. We ought to promise each other that."

Seamus stood beside the wagon, having hardly heard what Winn was saying. His mind was stuck on the news about the soldiers ahead.

"What's the matter with you, boy? We got time enough, but not so much to be wastin'. Green River crossin' is just ahead."

"Yes. That's where the trouble is." Seamus lifted his hat off his head and wiped away the sweat. It wasn't right for him to drag Winn into his difficulties, even though the thought of los-ing both transportation and companionship was unpleasant. "I can't go to the ferry."

"What do you mean? Are you 'fraid of water?"

Seamus paused. How much should he share? "You were right about me not wanting to run into any soldiers."

Winn's face scrunched up. "You're a deserter?"

Seamus rolled his eyes. "Well . . . not a deserter, more of being on the wrong side of things. But there's something about a horse as well."

"I don't see a horse anywhere. And they can't hang you but

once. As long as you know I don't much tolerate pain and will be turning on you quick-like if them soldiers get around to torturing me. But we ain't gotta go to no crossin'. There's a narrowing of the river to the south, just a few miles. It's got a few more whitecaps in it, but should be safe enough for traversin'." He glanced up to the sun. "We ought to get there by midday still, that is if we don't take to tarryin'."

"You are not understanding me, my friend," Seamus said. "There is no good reason for you to be bound to my troubles. Go on. You'll be much better suited on your own."

Winn put his hand on Seamus's shoulder. "I've got plenty of my own share of worries. C'mon, Seamus. No more talkin' like that. We two, we're good for each other."

The thin log he was using as leverage snapped, and Winn fell into the water and cursed to the elements and anyone who would listen.

They had tried just about everything they could to free up the rear wheel of the wagon deeply entrenched in the mud, while the shore waters of the Green River flowed over it just a foot shy of flooding into the cabin where the Bibles and their provisions lay.

"Any other way about this?" As twilight approached, Seamus sighed and leaned his back against the wagon, the chilly waters up to the knees of his black preacher's pants.

Winn stepped out of the river and swatted at the swarm of mosquitoes that fluttered by his sun-reddened and sweat-soaked face. "We could wait until the river works its way on these wheels. Eventually it might break itself free. We ought to empty the cargo, for sure."

It seemed like a poor option to Seamus, but seeing as he was the reason they had taken this alternate route, he didn't feel he was in a proper position to complain. With them now being miles away from anyone who could assist them, there weren't many choices left to them.

"I'll be about getting the fire lit while you try to find some dry clothes," Seamus said. "Then maybe we'll cook something up."

"Until we find another host wagon train, there won't be much cooking to do." Winn waded out to the wagon's doorway, leaned in, and drew out a stack of garments for them to sort through. "Yessum, just about plain out of food."

He joined Seamus who was working with some matches on kindling.

"But there is a feast all around us," Winn said cheerfully. "We just need to start hunting, 'tis all."

Seamus didn't want to be the one to dampen Winn's spirits any further. "I've got a musket, but not a single ball for the chamber. What about you?"

"I've got a revolver, but it doesn't shoot all that straight. Mostly to scare away animals, not hunt them down." After fumbling through the pile to find the right size, he held out some new clothing. "Hey. We're at a river. It's gotta have some fish, right?"

Seamus perked up. He wasn't much of a fisherman himself, but the thought of putting a trout or two in a pan sounded appealing. "If you find me some line and a hook, I'll get going with it."

Winn's brow lowered. "You didn't bring any?"

"You're the one with the wagon, Winn. You don't have any fishing line, poles, or hooks?"

He raised his hands, palms upward. "If you paid any heed to

my story, you'd darn well already know I was having to be . . . hasty . . . in sayin' my parting with N'Orleans."

"Wonderful indeed. We're a well-suited pair, the two of us." Seamus rose and surveyed the wooded area surrounding them. "You finish up with this fire. I'll go about seeing if there is enough mountain in this man to scratch us a meal."

Chapter 11

WHERE THE RIVER LEADS US

 The sun woke Seamus to a choir of angry blue jays fighting over the morsels of squirrel left over from last night's dinner.

"How about some coffee, boy?" Winn asked with a brightness of spirit unwelcome at this early in the morning. "We don't have but a few scraps of food, but we've got coffee beans enough to last us for much of the whole trail. You get yourself rised good and I'll give 'er a look to see if the wagon's loosed up on us."

Seamus struggled to his feet, and glanced toward the wagon. Something was amiss. His pulse rose and he shouted out to Winn, "Where are they?"

"What?" Winn turned around.

"The horses. They're gone."

Winn trotted back toward him. "Didn't you tie them up last night?"

"Yes." Panic crept into Seamus's thoughts. "I tied them to that tree over there. Sure as I'm standing here in these boots."

The two walked over to the tree and saw the ropes had been sheared with a knife.

Winn held the frayed end of the rope. "Well, I'll be. We didn't hear nothin'."

Seamus bent down. "See these footprints? Moccasins. You've been talking up your friends the Indians the whole trip. Looks like they made a visit." He stood and his gaze panned the area.

"Should we track them down?" Winn's lips were trembling and Seamus didn't know if it was in anger or fear.

"Yes . . . that's a fine notion there. We'll track them right to their camp. And we'll have you go up to them and say, 'Mr. Sioux, I was wondering if you happened upon a few of our horses, and if so, we were wondering if it would trouble you too much to give them back. You know, seeing as we've got this musket here without ammunition and this pistol that won't shoot straight. And while you're at it, Chief, if we could get about a half-dozen of your finest lads to assist in prying free our wagon, we'll surely appreciate it.'" He turned to Winn and raised an eyebrow. "What do you say about this plan?"

Winn crushed a pinecone under his foot. "No need to be so wise about it. You were last with them horses anyways." With his shoulders slumped, he waddled over to the wagon, where Granny Portner still smiled broadly, and gave it a shove. Then again. And another, with curses.

He slouched against the wagon, put his hands over his face, and sobbed. "What are we gonna do? How am I gonna go about selling these Bibles?" Then he suddenly snapped up, kicked at the stuck wheel, screamed, and then hopped in the water with his foot in his hand.

Seamus had seen enough and he headed over to console him.

"We just lost our two horses, I believe you're going to be needing that leg."

"That's it!" Winn shouted.

"What about it?"

The pain and tears on Winn's face were replaced with a beaming smile. "Yes, that's it! I shoulda been thinking that way all along." He brushed away the moisture from his eyes. "This is a turn of great fortune."

"No. No." Seamus shook his head. "I can't take another one of your *turns of fortune*."

"C'mon, Seamus. Raise your chin, boy. I just had to remember. That's all."

"Remember what?" Seamus didn't want to ask.

"The fella I got this here wagon from."

Seamus nodded toward Granny Portner's face.

Winn looked in that direction. "Yes. That's his mama. Right. He told me this wagon could float if need be." He splashed his hands on the water. "Ha, ha! What do you say to that?"

"You mean the man who sold you the miracle water?"

"Yeah. That's the one."

"The same one who sold you the Bibles?"

"Yeah, yeah. I see where you're aimin' at good and all. But look." He reached behind the driver's seat and pulled out a map, then he unfolded it as the wind tried to press it down. "We don't need to get that wheel out. We just need to detach it. And the other three as well." He struggled to flatten the map against the wagon and pointed. "Right here. See it?"

Seamus wanted to rip the map out of the man's hand and watch it float down the river. But he sighed and leaned in. He was the reason they got in this predicament in the first place.

Winn's boots stumbled on the river rocks below, but he regained his balance and jabbed his finger at the outstretched paper. "Here. This is the Green River, where we're standing. You see where it goes?"

"Not to San Francisco," Seamus answered dryly.

"Stay with me, boy. Down there, say forty, fifty miles, is Fort Bridger. There we'll keep you clear of sight of any army boys while I get this wagon fixed up right and provision us up with a couple new fillies and food to keep us fed the rest of the way. Why, if all goes well, we can go farther south."

Seamus was looking at a madman. "You're telling me we're going to take the wheels off, and this big square coffin will ride us down the river, like a raft?"

Winn nodded. "You've got it now." They stared at each other for a while until Winn broke out a smile, peeled away, and climbed into the wagon. Soon he hopped down with a large hammer in his hand. "Now are you fixin' to be useful, or are you just intendin' to pout about the horses you lost us?"

"I lost?" He snatched the hammer from Winn's hand, now eager to smash something.

As he grudgingly followed his friend's directions, Seamus tried to think through whatever alternatives they might have. The best he could muster was to abandon both the wagon and Winn and hoof it on his own on foot. He was beginning to question the wisdom of not traveling alone. Then he decided to lose himself in the task before him.

Surprisingly, it progressed much more smoothly than Seamus imagined it would. It turned out that Winn had a smattering of carpentry skills, and after only a few hours, they had managed to remove the wheels, prop the logs under the wagons, and secure it all together tightly. They also removed the front and sidewalls of the wagon, which would allow them to navigate the crude vessel with two long pine poles.

When it was all done and their creation stood before them ready and loaded, Winn broke out in a jig and laughed. "See again. Look at you doubtin' Winn." He slapped the side of the vessel. "Why she could probably handle the Atlantic, this one here. You'll see, my friend. This is the best that could happen."

Winn splashed some water on his face and then lifted his tall hat to his head, adjusted it, and then saluted Seamus. "Shall we set sail, Captain?"

Seamus started to loosen the ropes tying the wagon to the trees along the stream but froze. In the corner of his view, he noticed movement in the trees across the water. "Shhh."

"What?"

Seamus whispered, "Some shadows are moving over there."

"Horses?"

"Not unless they're learned how to walk on two feet. We best be pushing out."

Winn shuddered. "Have you ever felt an arrow pierce your flesh?"

Seamus shook his head. "Have you?"

"No. Just wonderin' what it felt like."

"If we don't get moving, you might get your answer."

Seamus motioned to Trip and the dog hobbled over to where he got a lift on board the crude vessel.

The two men got on either side of the raft, with Seamus deep in the water and they ran over the wet rocks until the raft had enough momentum to drift into the current. Winn managed to stumble and ended up clinging awkwardly on the side of the cabin before steadying himself.

Quickly, they both climbed up and took their positions on either side of the makeshift raft, jabbing at the water with their pine poles to keep it upright and going in the right direction.

The currents of the river immediately turned them into a spin and it wobbled horribly. But after a few panicky moments, it spat them out into the center of a wider, flatter and quieter section of the river and they managed to get their bearings.

When things stabilized, Winn let out a hoot. "Yee . . . waah! Isn't this something your mama never told you?" He splashed his pole in the water.

"You fool." Seamus's gaze darted behind. "Have you forgot already?"

"Ahh . . . we're past them now, if you wasn't just seeing a ghost anyways. It's all down river now, my friend. Yee . . . waah!"

Seamus fiddled with the pole in his hand. The water wasn't so deep he couldn't reach the bottom, but they would have been much better off with oars. He decided to fashion a seat out of one of the Bible crates, but when he started to walk toward the carriage door, the whole raft surged and swayed like a broken cradle.

"Woah." Winn tried to counter it from the other side, but this just made it worse, leaving the two of them desperate again with their poles in the water to regain the wagon's balance.

All of the sudden, hoots echoed from the opposite side of the river, and three Indians moved out of the cover of the trees, laughing and pointing fingers, presumably at the spectacle of the two of them floundering in their wobbly barge.

"Are they laughing at us?" Seamus shouted.

Winn smiled and waved to the natives and he nodded at Seamus to do the same. "Don't turn an eye from 'em or they'll be raising our scalps to the skies."

"I don't know," Seamus said as they drifted away from the three bronzed and painted men on the shore. "They don't appear to be all that unfriendly."

"Just mind your pole."

They winded around a gentle bend in the river opening up to an even wider and flatter stretch of river. Seamus was stunned to see across the way in the meadows several dozen members of the Sioux tribe at work gathering food and bearing babies on their backs. At the sight of the raft, several of the women and children moved behind the men who came to the river's edge.

Winn's face twisted with worry. "Steady . . . steady."

Seamus tried to focus on the task of keeping the shimmying raft from buckling, but now he was equally concerned with what was staring back at him from the shoreline. He feared at any moment he would hear the whir of an arrow's feather. But when he looked over, he saw the men of the tribe were waving at them frantically. "Do you see what they're doing now?"

"I ain't blind, boy," Winn blurted out, agitation growing in his voice. "Eyes on the water. She's turning on us."

"But it looks like they're trying to warn us of something," Seamus said amidst the growing and indiscernible shouts.

Winn scoffed. "Yes. They're surely invitin' us for dinner. Now press, Seamus."

They came around the next turn, but this time rather than opening up on either side, the river narrowed and up ahead were whitecaps of churning water.

"That's what they were trying to telling us," Seamus shouted.

But at this point, there would be no more discussion, just shouts of panic. The wagon spun slowly and Seamus and Winn poked desperately at the growing number of boulders and rocks they were passing as the currents grew angrier and the pace started to build to a torrent.

Seamus tried to plant his pole deep below a large boulder to brake their momentum, but it snapped up and smacked him across the side of his head before plunging over the side and disappearing behind them.

Finally, when it seemed certain the raft would keel fully to its side, Seamus spotted the rising terror in front of them as the river was leading to a solid thirty-foot drop.

Both of them dove off either side of their raft, and as soon as Seamus hit the frigid water, he grasped desperately for a boulder,

gripping tightly to the moss-covered behemoth. Just in time to
see Granny Portner proudly displaying her miracle cure to the
end before dropping down out of sight to a chorus of shattering
wood above the roar of the waters.

But then Seamus's hold was compromised and he spun backward and the pull of the massive torrents beckoned him until he
surged over and down the wall of water himself. Then there was
light and then water and suffocating and bashing against the
rocks, all of his limbs worked independently flailing and flapping for a chance to live.

A protruding log flashed into view. He reached for it and the
ragged edges cut through his skin, and then the limb broke off
and he was tumbling. Then pain pierced his head and he surrendered to the currents before renewing the struggle once again.

And then it stopped, as the whale spat him out to a still
pool on the far side of the river. He choked on the water, then
stumbled in the sandy bottom and staggered up and crawled to
banks of the river, pulling himself up by an exposed tree root.

Then he was out of the water, facedown. He lay there for a
while, paralyzed with exhaustion and grateful to be alive.

After several minutes, he took inventory of the damage to
his body. Nothing seemed to be broken, but everything was in
pain and he was bleeding all over.

Where's Winn?

His eyes strained through the sunlight filtering through the ·
trees, and all he could see drifting by was the flotsam of their
shattered raft and its contents.

He climbed up to a standing position and limped over to a
boulder to get a better view. But there was nothing. His heart
sunk. As big of a blubbering fool Winn had proved to be,
Seamus had grown fond of the man.

Please, Lord. Bring back that idiot to me.

He pressed farther down the bank in the chance that his

friend may have rolled past him. After a few hundred feet, he feared the worst. There was no sign of him anywhere.

He hobbled his way back up the embankment to retrace his steps and still there was no sign of Winn. Remembering the Sioux upstream, Seamus continued as far as it was safe, then decided it would be wiser to head down current again, where he would most likely discover his unfortunate companion. Or at least recover his body. This thought grieved him.

Seamus decided to look for salvageable items that might be critical for surviving the rest of the journey. After nearly an hour of passing through the gnarls of limbs and bushes, staying as close to the river's edge as possible, Seamus accepted the obvious.

The rest of the trail he would be traveling by himself.

So he pressed on. Recalling from Winn's map that there was a town southbound, forty miles or so, Seamus shifted from his mission of rescue to a traveler once again, although he wasn't ready to stray far from the water.

A sense of loneliness swept over him, and suddenly he panicked. Reaching into his pocket, he opened the button and cheered inside when his fingers touched the moist paper.

He still had Ashlyn.

He tugged on it ever so gently, fearful that now in its water-logged state it would tear easily. *Please, Lord. Don't let it be ruined.*

He discovered it had been tucked in his shirt in a way that somehow it wasn't completely soaked, and there staring back with her alluring eyes was the woman who had such a stranglehold on his heart. He kissed the image.

A little time on a flat rock in the hot sun and it would be good once again. Worried it would be crushed if he returned it to his pocket, he held it flat and upright in his palm, unable to take his eyes off of it, even as he moved forward again.

What was it about this picture? Perhaps it had merely become the rope that was pulling him out of his darkness.

The trees thinned out and then the river went to a great clearing that seemed to stretch out for miles.

Then he heard barking.

"Hey, Seamus!"

Seamus spun around and saw Winn standing in a canoe with two Indians, one in the front and the other in the rear, each stoically dipping paddles into the water. Trip was barking and looking anxious to plunge in toward him. Winn's face was filled with joy and he nearly rocked the vessel over as they headed toward shore.

"You were right all along, Seamus. These are friendly Indians."

The canoe slid to the sandy bank and Winn was already leaping out and embraced Seamus with the full strength of his arms while the Indians stood motionless and expressionless in the canoe.

"Seamus. Can't say their names, but they are Sioux as we were guessing. They were just taking me—and now you, surely—" Winn shook his head. "I thought you were dead." He hugged Seamus again. "They are going to take us a little farther down, shy of Bridger, because they don't take kindly to soldiers much neither. Of course, they'll be keeping the horses. But loo-kee, Seamus!"

He pulled out a roll of dollar bills from a sack hanging around the white collar of his neck. "I've still got forty-seven of these babies, a bit soggy, but it will buy fine. Ain't that a sight? See, my friend? I told you. Just got to keep a proper perspective and trust ol' Winn."

God had answered two of Seamus's prayers today. Ashlyn's picture had survived and the idiot was indeed still alive.

Chapter 12

THE DANCE

SAN FRANCISCO, THE TERRITORY OF CALIFORNIA

 Ashlyn Whittington had to fight all urges to adjust each and every one of the four layers of her miserable dress for the ball. She wanted nothing more than to be back home in much more practical and comfortable clothing.

For a precocious, emerging global city such as San Francisco, this was as high society as it would get in what used to be a mostly forgotten little village on the bay. But in the past year people came from all corners of the world in a swarm of ships and by endless wagons overflowing with wide-eyed prospectors. Even Ashlyn herself, along with her father, came with the first waves of those pursuing golden dreams.

She had no problems portraying the part of a well-bred Southern woman since her dear mother, Hazel, had infused those customs into her since she could barely walk. Ashlyn enjoyed uttering in the slow, musical qualities of her refined drawl, which she knew found favor with those who heard it, but she never understood why wealthy women would choose to suffer through these intolerable fashions. Let the haughty Parisians and Londoners keep those for themselves.

For Ashlyn, the dress was also a difficult reminder of how short she was in the shadow of her mother's grace. Mama was the perfection of Southern virtues: God fearing, an encouraging wife, beloved by her community, and overflowing with hospitality and dignity.

When Mama died a few years ago, Ashlyn lost her champion and gentle mentor. It would be cowardice to blame her shortcomings and personal tragedy on her mother's death. Mama did all she could to raise a better woman and deserved a daughter of higher standing.

Ashlyn's particular dress, trimmed in violet and flourished with taffeta, lace, and intricately crafted glass beads, was a gift from Henry Parnell earlier this week. He was not only her father's closest friend and partner, but her patron as well. At least as long as her father was away in the mines. As cloying as Mr. Parnell could be, without his caretaking, Ashlyn's little orphanage of babies and toddlers would have been shut down many months ago.

"Come now, Ashlyn." Mr. Parnell held a brandy snifter and leaned his portly body toward her. "You should try to disguise your distaste of all of this."

"Am I to remind you, Mr. Parnell, that this was entirely your idea and not in the least way mine?" If he only knew the turmoil of her inner thoughts.

"Now, dear. Calling me Henry will do and please, chin up."

It had been a difficult year for Henry as well, and his hair had silvered as a result.

"Miss Ashlyn." A tall, brown-skinned man with a distinctive white mustache, matched in color with his tailcoat jacket, came up and reached out for her hand, which she gave him and in return he kissed. "You have brightened up my little celebration." He turned to Mr. Parnell. "Henry, it was so kind of you to bring this lovely young lady. I only wish we had more than just *viejos* to greet you. My young sons are out in the hills." He waved his hand dismissively. "Seeking out fortunes of their own. I suppose their father's is not good enough for them."

"We are most charmed by the invitation, Señor Santiago. It's a splendid affair." Ashlyn admired the Mexican land baron, who remained one of the most respected *Californios*, despite the humbling loss in the war with the Americans.

His wife, Esmeralda, whose olive skin made her look youthful despite her long, gray-streaked hair, put her arm in his, almost possessively. "*Sí. Es verdad.* So many languages I hear this night, Felipe. So far they have all come for your little fiesta."

Señor Santiago was handsome and dignified, even as he looked at his wife with amusement. "It is all about the gold, my dear. Nobody cares about a *ranchero* and his cows."

"So much fuss over a shiny rock, no?" Esmeralda sipped from her glass of red wine.

"*Esposa mía,* you seem to love the shiny rock enough to have me buy it for you so many times." Señor Santiago kissed the woman on her cheek, which she delighted in, as a cat when petted.

"San Francisco should be grateful for this shiny rock," Mr. Parnell said. "It's done so much for the city."

"Call us . . . how do you say . . . nostalgic, yes, but some of us preferred Yerba Buena as she was. A woman is most beautiful when clothed in humility, like our dear Miss Ashlyn, *sí*?"

Ashlyn was embarrassed and wanted to change the discussion. "Is that gentleman over there from the French consulate?"

"You most certainly aren't saying that the discovery of gold was a detriment to San Francisco or Yerba Buena, however you choose to call it." Mr. Parnell's voice was tainted with drink.

"*Sí*, Mr. Parnell. This was a wonderful discovery by that Swedish gentleman, what was his name? Which, most coincidentally, happened shortly after your brave American soldiers conquered this territory and claimed this land as your own."

"Yes," Esmeralda said, rolling her eyes. "Ashlyn, dear, that is Gerard Clois, the Frenchman. I know he is probably now saying bad things about this wine from Felipe's . . . ¿*como se dice?* . . . oh yes, vineyards. And Klaus over there is a royal German, at least he say so."

Señor Santiago gently squeezed his wife's arm. "Esmeralda hates it so when we speak of such matters."

"So boring, no?" Esmeralda exchanged her glass of wine with a full one from a tray held by one of the servants. "Tell us about the *bebés*. The little babies."

Mr. Parnell cleared his throat. "That's precisely why Ashlyn is here tonight. To thank those who have supported her."

"Yes, Señor Santiago. You cannot begin to fathom just how much your generosity is appreciated." Ashlyn felt her breath leaping and choking her words. She hated talking about money.

"All thanks go to you, Miss Ashlyn, for your devotion to the lost children of Yerba Buena." He held his glass up to her. "To the orphanage. *Salud*."

"Well . . . I would have to confess it is hardly an orphanage," Ashlyn said. "Why we have just a few babies and infants."

Mr. Parnell glared her down.

Ashlyn tried not to notice and gave Señor Santiago a warm smile. "But we are oh so terribly grateful for the new house." She looked to Mr. Parnell and he nodded. "Which is why we wanted you to hear for yourself this evening we are intending to name it *La Cuna* in your honor."

Señor Santiago's face blanched with anger. "No *Casa de Santiago*?"

Esmeralda giggled and covered her hand to her face and he broke a smile. "Oh, Felipe. You make me laugh. La Cuna. The Cradle. So beautiful this name."

"*Sí*, Miss Ashlyn. This is a great honor for me, for it to be named in the words of my people. But others gave as well, no?"

"None as graciously as you, Señor Santiago." Mr. Parnell emptied his brandy snifter. "And I'm . . ."—he turned to Ashlyn—". . . the young lady is hoping she can continue to rely on your altruistic spirit."

There was a slight break in the land baron's expression as he looked at Mr. Parnell, but then he recovered and turned to Ashlyn. "The rumors about me, my dear, are true, I am sorry to say. My investments have not done well, as of late." Then he bowed. "But you can expect me to do all I can for the *niños*."

Ashlyn wanted to shrink away as heat rushed to her face. But it's all for the children. Anything for the children.

Esmeralda looked at her husband and then turned to Ashlyn. "What about your *padre*, dear? Your father?"

"Yes," Mr. Parnell said. "Ryland Whittington is, of course, known for his high standing and his benevolence, not just here, but back in the proud state of Virginia where we came from. But we are sorry to say, poor Ashlyn has not heard from her father for several months now. It's left La Cuna's finances quite fragile."

The Mexican woman's expression flushed with compassion. "I am so sorry, dear." She turned to her husband. "Is there nothing we can do, Felipe?"

"That's just it," Mr. Parnell said. "We don't know exactly where Ryland is or we would send out a recovery team ourselves.

You know how these gold prospectors are. They don't want anyone to know their whereabouts, what with claim jumping being
such a serious concern."

"I assure you all, there is nothing to worry about regarding
my father." The words seemed so foreign to her emotions as they
came from her mouth. Should she drop the pretension and beg
for help?

Ashlyn shifted to try to shake the numbness in her legs. Her
corset had been fastened much too tight. "My father learned
the craft of gold mining in the Appalachians. He is quite experienced, and it certainly is not unusual at all for us not to hear
from him for long periods of time. In fact, this usually simply
means he has found what he had intended to find."

She tried to take comfort in her own words, which she knew
to be the truth, intellectually at least.

Señor Santiago smiled curtly, and his eyes wandered. "Well,
we shall all hope so. Both for you, dear, and for the ongoing
provision of La Cuna. Now. My wife and I must apologize, but
we must not be impolite to our other guests, even if they are not
as delightful."

He nodded and they turned away, with Esmeralda glancing
back over her shoulder and waving gracefully before leaning her
head into her husband's shoulder.

In the front of the room, a flamenco guitarist began to play
and the crowd drifted toward him, leaving Ashlyn and Mr.
Parnell somewhat abandoned.

"That did not go as we had planned," he said.

"And what exactly did we expect? After all those people
have done for the children, and here we're already back again
with our palms outstretched. Really, Mr. Parnell." Ashlyn
glanced over to the door. Would anyone notice if she slipped
out?

"About your father . . ." Mr. Parnell seemed uncomfortable.

"Oh not that again. Perhaps this is not the best time."

"We need to talk about this." He raised a hand to signal for another drink, and one of the servers nodded.

"My father always treated you kindly. Like a brother."

"I know, Ashlyn. And I've done my best. But he is perceived by all as the financial backer of this bank. If word spreads further that he is lost . . . or worse, failed in his endeavors, my investment—our investment—will collapse. It's all Ryland worked for, you do know this?"

"We will certainly see my father soon again." She must see her father soon.

He reached out for the newly filled snifter glass that arrived. "Ashlyn, dear. I know I've asked you this more than once. Many times. But if you have any knowledge, any understanding of his whereabouts whatsoever, I can't emphasize enough how important it is that you share this information with me."

"Do you really believe for a—" She caught herself speaking with anger and lowered her voice. "If for a moment I knew where he was mining, I would most assuredly be seeking him out myself. Truly, Mr. Parnell, do you think so little of me?"

He watched her over the glass as he sipped the amber liquid. "All right, then. I won't ask again. But if you hear of any news, you will let me know?"

"Yes. Of course. And you have heard of nothing yourself?"

Mr. Parnell looked over to the gathering on the other side of the room, where a flock of guests were now dancing to the intricate melodies of the guitarist. "It's as I have told you before. There have been rumors of Ryland landing himself a most profitable location. But he has covered his tracks well. There is no claim registered in his name. And those who I have sent after him have not been able to catch his scent."

She glanced around to see if anyone was watching. "I'm going to leave now."

"Ashlyn. There's one other issue, as you know."

"We are not extravagant with our needs, Mr. Parnell. What we get is just enough to feed the babies."

"Everything has a price, my dear. Even those things meant for good. I simply can't extend any more credit to your accounts."

"But are you not the president of the bank? And you have not forgotten it is my father's investment as well."

"That well has run dry, Ashlyn. You need some other benefactors. I can no longer continue to support both you and . . . those children. As it is, I have grave concerns for the bank. If we don't locate your father soon . . . well, let's not think that way."

Ashlyn was fuming inside, but she did not want to draw attention and was desperate to get out of the room and this throttling dress. But the poverty of her situation also knotted her stomach. How could she and the children survive without some turning of their desperate fortunes? So much depended on her success this evening and she had failed them. How much longer could they continue?

"Yes, please forgive me. You have been so kind to us at the house. We will just keep praying for Daddy to come home. And he will. I am quite certain of this."

Now if she could only convince herself. This was indeed a long time for her father to be out of contact. And would Percy ever respond to her letters? What would it take for him to come and rescue her from this situation? Not only for her fragile finances and for the safety of her father, but to revive what few scraps were left of her dignity.

Mr. Parnell smiled weakly. "Yes. Keep praying, dear. But look to your ledger as well."

She nodded. The musician, dressed in the clothes of a Spaniard, flailed his hand at the guitar and the dance floor

cleared as Esmeralda, with a rose clenched in her mouth, began to dance with vigor and grace in front of the distinguished gathering. The music pulsated louder, the guitarist and dancer playing off each other's intensity, and the alluring performance enraptured all of the guests, that was, except for one.

Ashlyn slipped out the back door, removed her shoes, lifted up the hem of her dress, and scampered barefoot through the lantern-lit streets. She was finally on her way back home.

"Ma'am."

The woman's voice broke into Ashlyn's distracted thoughts.

Ashlyn was at the door of her home, freshly painted in white, with the shadows of newly planted hedges and flowers surrounding it. Into the light from the glow of the moon emerged a woman cradling a cooing baby in her arms.

"Sarah Mae?"

"Yes, ma'am. How did you know it was me?"

"We heard you might be coming."

"You must think I'm a miserable person, don't you?" Sarah Mae had long, wavy blonde hair, which was marketable in her line of trade.

"Of course I don't." Ashlyn could see the woman was on the edge of crying. "Are you sure you want to do this?"

"No. I mean. I'm not sure. But it's the only choice I have now. They won't let me keep her at the house, and I need to start earning now that the pain's gone."

"What's the baby's name?"

Sarah Mae looked at her baby and tears from her heavily painted eyes streaked down her cheeks. "Isabella. I named her Isabella."

Sarah Mae kissed the child on her cheek and Isabella seemed to stare back at her with longing and confusion. Then the woman gathered her courage and handed the baby to Ashlyn, and the baby began to cry.

Ashlyn nodded. "That is a lovely name. She will be well cared for."

Sarah Mae put her hand to her mouth, wrapped her shawl around her dress, and then spun around and shuffled away into the night.

Chapter 13

FROM BACK HOME

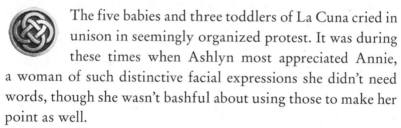 The five babies and three toddlers of La Cuna cried in unison in seemingly organized protest. It was during these times when Ashlyn most appreciated Annie, a woman of such distinctive facial expressions she didn't need words, though she wasn't bashful about using those to make her point as well.

Annie was calmly distributing the bottles of milk in the cradles evenly spread around the second floor of the house, which still smelled of wood and fresh paint. She held up one of the bottles in her slender ebony hand for Ashlyn to see it was nearly empty.

Ashlyn sighed. "Yes. I know. I'm going to market soon. Are we that low?"

Annie held the bottle up again and raised her eyebrows as if it was obvious to see it was less than a quarter filled.

Priscilla, a redheaded girl of fifteen, who volunteered her time whenever she was able, peered down through the staircase with a toddler on her hip. "Miss Ashlyn. Gracie is asking for you."

"Thank you, dear." Ashlyn reached out and took the one-and-a-half-year-old girl with the head full of tight cinnamon curls from Priscilla and pressed her close to her body. "The others?"

"Both James and Zachary aren't sharing well again, but they're fine." There was a loud noise and Priscilla's eyes widened. "But I shouldn't leave them alone." She thumped back down the stairway.

"No she shouldn't," Ashlyn said to Gracie, who was reaching out to tug on her long braided hair. Ashlyn gently removed the tiny hand and touched her fingertip to the child's nose. "Gracie, have you had the pleasure of meeting our newest young lady?"

She walked over to the cradle where Isabella lay, with the pink face and feathery black hair of a newborn. "Her name is Isabella. Isn't she a tiny one?" Gracie leaned forward to reach her hand toward the baby.

"Isabella is not yet old enough to play."

Annie came over with outstretched skinny arms toward Ashlyn.

Ashlyn gave Gracie a kiss on her cheek and grudgingly handed the child to Annie. "I know. I am leaving shortly."

"We don't get us some more milk, we's going to have a riot with these here little 'uns." Annie's brown eyes widened. The woman had a tough life, yet there was a strength and gentleness still exuding from her bent and worn body.

"I am leaving. But you are certainly going to have to pray for me. That horrid man gets grumpier and greedier by the day."

"On account of him not gettin' paid? I'd be grumped too." Annie nodded for Ashlyn to leave.

"All right. I am gone." She scurried down the squeaking stairs and waved to Priscilla who was crouched on the floor with the two toddler boys. Then Ashlyn left out the front door. As soon as she was in the open air, the knot of worry returned to her stomach.

"Now, Ashlyn, we've already had this discussion." Mr. Jensen wiped his hands on his white apron and tucked his pencil behind one of the ears of his squat, balding head.

"But this is an entirely new day. You know good and well my father will be home to us soon, and he will most definitely reward you handsomely for being so faithful and patient." She grabbed a sack of flour from the shelf and laid it on the counter. "Eggs?"

Mr. Jensen started to point but stopped himself. "No. No more credit, Ashlyn. Credit is for people who pay us back."

Ashlyn tilted her head and pursed her lips. "Mercy, Mr. Jensen. After all, it is for the children. It would heartbreak us all to just let them starve."

"Don't you play on my emotions, young lady. You know it's not just about the food. Ryland has quite a tab going on with equipment and supplies, and word is patience is on short supply with all of them."

"Thurston?"

Ashlyn recognized the deep baritone voice of Reverend Charles Sanders, or Brother Chuck as he preferred to be called. She turned to see the tall man, dressed in his black jacket and white collar, arms folded behind his back, leaning forward, with his deep furrowed brows glaring down at the proprietor.

"Reverend Sanders." Mr. Jensen's face flushed with an expression of guilt.

"Are you taking good care of our dear Ashlyn?"

Mr. Jensen began to puff up and prop his shoulders as if to make a stand, but his resolve quickly melted. He whispered, "There's some concern with her account, Reverend."

"Really? You have concerns?" Brother Chuck bounced forward and back on his heels. "That's hard to imagine that would be possible." He picked up a shovel. "How much is this?"

"Those are imported from the East. Steeled in the coal fires of Pennsylvania. Those are fourteen dollars."

"And how much were they just last week?"

"Those?" Mr. Jensen's voice weakened.

Brother Chuck shook the shovel, testing the weight. "Yes. These."

"About ten."

"And they are now selling at fourteen?"

"They are quite in demand. Quite." Mr. Jensen eyes were pointed at the floor.

"Sounds to me as if you are a blessed man, Mr. Jensen." His voice was starting to boom and a few of the patrons turned to watch.

"Could we discuss this . . . outside?"

"A blessed man with few concerns, as I would see it."

The proprietor shrugged. "I suppose it's true."

"And all blessings come from where, Mr. Jensen?"

A tiny woman with an infectious wrinkled smile said with breathy adoration, "The blessings come from the Almighty, Reverend Sanders."

Brother Chuck leaned down and put his hand on the woman's shoulder. "Yes, they do, Mrs. Granger. And would you say a man like Mr. Jensen, showered with God's favors, should be abounding with joy and far, far removed from any concerns?"

"I ain't seen joy on Thurston's face unless you're handing him a wad of dollar bills," a man said, and laughter rolled through the store.

Mr. Jensen leaned over to Ashlyn and whispered in her ear, "Last time, young lady. The very last time."

Ashlyn hugged Mr. Jensen and winked at Brother Chuck as the crowd continued to gather around him and the sermon continued.

As she went to the front of the shop, she gathered whatever supplies she could as she believed Mr. Jensen would be good to his word. She loved the reverend, but would he continue to be so kind to her if he discovered who she really was? How far she had fallen?

At the counter, Mr. Jensen's son, Carl, wrote down everything she was taking and then helped her bag them up and load them on a handcart he said she could borrow. Fortunately, the boy made up in kindness what his father lacked.

From outside, thunder echoed through the streets and Ashlyn gave a startled glance through the paned-glass windows to see the sky had become almost black.

"You best be heading out, Miss Ashlyn. Those clouds look to be splitting soon and those wheels don't roll much in the mud."

"Thank you, Carl, truly. That is so sweet of you to be concerned for me. However, the house is not too far from here as you know."

"Would you like some candy?" Carl asked, before checking to see if his father would notice. "For the children."

"Why yes, Carl. That would be delightful and they would appreciate that most kindly."

The sandy-haired boy filled a white bag with candy, twisted the top shut, and then placed it carefully on top of the other groceries. Then he pushed the cart out to the front of the store and onto the street.

"I best be getting back, Miss Ashlyn. Pa doesn't allow me to leave the counter. He don't much trust all these foreigners."

Ashlyn smiled and nodded with gratitude. He turned and went back inside just as the dark skies broke loose with instantly pounding rain. A gusty wind blew through as well, causing her to shudder. She buttoned her jacket and gripped the wooden handles of the cart and began to push. Then she paused and looked around.

She had the strangest sensation she was being watched.

She expected it to be Mr. Jensen, no doubt chasing after her because she had added more items to her list. But when she turned, she didn't recognize anyone in the crowd, all of whom were scurrying for cover.

She started to push forward but heard a shout from an angry driver as a horse-drawn buggy brushed by and splattered her legs with mud.

Ashlyn let out a deep breath and scanned around her again. Just like that, the streets had emptied of all beasts and persons, and walls of water were coming down so heavily, she could barely see ten yards ahead. She suddenly felt alone. Carl was right. She needed to make it home quickly.

The roads of old Yerba Buena were widely despised because of their wretched conditions and when wet were nearly impassible. But just as it was with the buildings of this burgeoning metropolis, everyone was too busy getting rich off of the gold rush to take the time to construct anything properly. Everything would be done in the future, and the future would have to wait until the gold in the hills was thoroughly harvested.

After one difficult block, Ashlyn's situation became grave as the wheels grew more and more entrenched in the thickening sludge of mud, animal droppings, and the dumped contents of chamber pots. She looked down to see her boots sinking to her ankles. The rain intensified and so did Ashlyn's sense that someone was following her.

She looked back quickly. Nothing.

Ashlyn leaned into the cart, but rather than moving forward, the front wheels dug into the ground. She pulled back on it, but her hands slipped on the handles. She lurched it forward again and all it did was dig in deeper. She was thoroughly stuck.

God. Is this my punishment for taking too many supplies?

"Looks like you made a right mess of it, Ash."

At the sound of the voice and the uttering of her childhood nickname, Ashlyn froze. *Impossible. How did he find them?*

She made a slow turn as the cold rain drenched her clothes, hair, and face, masking her tears of frustration and now shock. There before her was Cade Gatwood, thousands of miles removed from his birthplace deep in the Appalachian Mountains, but he was dressed as if he had never left home. He grew up to be a strong, wiry young man, unshaven but becoming, dressed in soaking denim overalls, a white shirt underneath, and wearing his familiar black bowler. Rivulets of water streamed down the rim of his hat.

"Why, Ash, don't look so surprised to see me. You knew I would be back some day. And imagine how I felt after coming to our pretty home to see you and your pa had just up and left. No note or nothing. It was almost as if you were all intending on leaving me behind."

"Yes. Cade. I am surprised. You left with such cruel words and told us yourself you were never coming back."

"That's right, I s'pose. Just had some learning to do. Found some things out too about your pa. All on my own. See there was a man I met who goes by the name Cotton. And he had much to say."

Ashlyn turned and tried to yank on the cart again.

Cade stepped forward and pushed her away gently. He wiggled the cart and then gave it a firm pull backward and freed it up. Then he wheeled it over to the side of the road and under a wooden overhang.

She looked down the road and wished she could just run, but the truth was, those supplies meant too much for her to abandon them.

"What is it you want, Cade? If it's more money, then you will be sorely disappointed to know you have traveled so far in vain."

He laughed and turned away, then spoke as if he couldn't look in her eyes. "Now, Ash, that little back-home-girl charm may work with these here city folk, but we both know your father is highly skilled at what he does. This all don't concern you any. It's just between me and your pa."

"It does not concern you either, Cade Gatwood. Not anymore. My father long ago paid you his pound of flesh. And for what, may I ask? Now if you don't mind—"

"Oh I mind. I mind all right." Cade reached into her cart and pulled out a small basket of cherries and ate one and spit out the pit. "You s'posin' I ain't got nothing coming my way? That how you see it?"

Ashlyn's teeth clenched. "What is it you are asking of me?"

"That's plain simple, Ash. Just tell me where he is and I'll fast be on my way."

She turned and watched as the water continued to pool in the road. "What are you planning on doing?"

"Now that's the right question. I am aiming just to talk to the man. That's all. I've got some things need saying."

Could he be trusted? There was a time when Cade was as sweet as butter. It was later when he became bitter and angry. What was worse? Not knowing where her father was or not knowing which Cade she was dealing with?

She gazed deep into his eyes, seeking to see through the heart of the boy she had grown up with. *God, please give me an answer.* Finally, as the drumbeat of rain grew eerily around her, she lowered her head and uttered the words.

"There is a map."

Chapter 14

LIVING WATERS

 "Just as I have been sayin' all along." Winn jabbed his finger at the tattered map that fluttered in the desert winds and then flashed it toward the horizon. "Can't be but a half day up ahead, my friend."

Seamus had long lost the will to rebuke the man's futile optimism. What fools they must have appeared to the turkey vultures circling in the skies. Two drifters, pastors without a flock. Their hats had survived, their clerical collars were still intact, but their black garments were faded and stained with sweat and the alkaline dust thrown in their faces across the windy desert basin. Even Trip was showing ribs, although he continued to keep up gamely.

Their last encounter with civilization was more than sixty miles ago, when they parted ways with a Mennonite family who were traveling out West by covered wagon from Pennsylvania.

They had met on the trail and invited Seamus and Winn to enjoy a last supper, a mercy killing of their last ox that had taken lame.

The father, a long-bearded man with a stutter, decided to return back to Salt Lake to camp out there for the winter before moving forward again in the spring. He pleaded for the two men to join them as they both were obviously short on supplies and strength. But emboldened by the meal and stubbornly clinging to their visions of what lay ahead, the woebegone travelers left on their own into the treacherous arms of the most lethal leg of what was now the California Trail.

It didn't take long for Seamus to seriously reconsider the madness of the pursuit. But soon they had crossed a point in the desert where it would be as difficult to retreat as it was to press forward. There would be no turning back.

"It's right there yonder. Can't you see it?" Winn's cheeks were gaunt and his arms and fingers were lanky. "That glimmer way out there. Squint your eyes just so. Those are the water holes on this here map. We'll be drinking until we drown."

Seamus sat on a hill of sand and sunk. He pulled out his canteen, unscrewed the top, flipped it, and then willed whatever last drops would fall on his dry, cracked tongue. Would he ever rise again? He was so dizzy and his vision was blurring.

Winn bent over and put his hands on his knees. "If we stop, we might as well bury us here."

"Why don't you just ask our friend over there to take you the rest of the way?"

They both glanced back, and just as was the case for the past three days of their journey, the shadowy figure of their unknown pursuer remained.

Yesterday, in anger and in absence of wisdom, they had tried to go back and confront their mysterious tracker. But whoever it was kept their distance, and with agility and ease.

"C'mon, Seamus. We've got to git to those holes." Winn's

face was red with burn and exhaustion, and he reached his hand down and helped lift Seamus grudgingly to his feet before stumbling himself.

It was less than a hundred yards later when Winn collapsed in the sand, and it was Seamus's turn to pull him up. He put his arm around his friend's shoulders to guide him the rest of the way.

Up ahead, the shimmering reflections drew tantalizingly closer, but at such a slow pace Seamus wondered if they would make it there alive. But finally, and gloriously, he spotted the clear evidence of water: the fronds of desert trees and vegetation.

Now also coming to clarity was the gruesome evidence of the trail's savagery. Lining either side of the pathway were the tragic debris of failed crossings. Sun-blanched rib cages and scattered bones of oxen, horses, mules, as well as broken wagon frames and wheels with missing spokes. Even more haunting were the discarded dolls and toys and even cribs, a reminder of how death dealt no better hands to the young.

Winn's knees buckled and he began to drift in and out of consciousness. Seamus lifted his friend up in his arms and cradled him for the last few hundred yards, tapping into the last of what little endurance he had.

He was left alone to the whistling of the desert winds and a wearying Trip, and he looked back to see their pursuer had closed the gap, although with the fading of his vision and the spinning of his head, he still couldn't ascertain more than a muted shape.

Mercifully, Seamus climbed one final peak of sand, bearing Winn's limp body, and he saw a large hole that had been dug into the ground of this slender oasis. It was framed by more bone fragments and rubbish flew by, whirling in the currents of the wind. There were short trees and low bushes, but they were browned and shriveled by the encroaching winter.

Seamus gently lowered Winn's body, laying him on the ground and shoveling some sand with his hand to cushion his friend's head. And then with all the energy that remained, Seamus crawled to his feet and staggered toward the first hole and collapsed beside it, gusts of wind now growing in intensity and throwing sand in the air and in his eyes.

A rankness rose to his nostrils, and when he looked down in the well of water, he could see the decaying body of an ox, which apparently had drowned in its last desperate effort to ward off thirst. Flies covered the flesh of the beast, which was peppered with holes, presumably from the beaks of scavengers.

He reached down, scooped up the water, and held it before his nose. It smelled so rancid he threw it aside and put his head to the ground, tears streaming from his eyes. The putridness was so intense he could hardly breathe, but he no longer had the will to rise. As his head gyrated with throbbing and nausea assaulted his stomach, he closed his eyes and drifted further and further down into despair.

Then it all became quiet.

The smells of roasted nuts and seared meat floated into Seamus's dream and it filled him with a sense of rejuvenation and hope. He feared returning to his precipice of despair but opened his eyes nonetheless and was cheered by the crisp air and the peppered lights of the evening sky.

There was laughing, a familiar voice echoing through the emptiness of the desert, to the accompaniment of a crackling fire. Seamus found himself tucked in a weaved blanket, and he sat up slowly to see Winn sitting on an abandoned piece of worn luggage. Across from him was a dark-skinned boy in his late teens with long, straight black hair tucked under a two-feathered headdress.

The young man's face was painted with two red stripes, horizontal across his cheeks and he wore leather leggings and a beaded breechcloth. What stood out most, however, was the large woolly buckskin coat he must have acquired by either trade or chicanery, as it was something you would only see worn by a high-country frontiersman.

"Hey . . . I see moving. There's life in you yet, Seamus. Wait 'til you hear this, old friend." Winn seemed quite animated for a man who so recently heard the drumbeats of death.

"How long?" Seamus rubbed his head and crawled to his feet, keeping the blanket wrapped around his shoulders. He lumbered over to the fire and was greeted by a healthier-looking dog.

"It was a long sleep. Meet our new friend, Seamus. He calls himself Shila. How do you say?"

The boy smiled and his cheeks dimpled. "Shi-la."

"Is he the one?" Seamus asked.

"Yes. He's been trailing us alright. Good thing it is. He nursed us like a bird to its chicks. Water. Food. Wait 'til you taste this." He scraped some of the food cooking on a flat rock into a cup and handed it to Seamus.

Seamus gave it a sniff. He reached in and put some to his mouth, and the mixture of nuts and meat at this moment tasted as good an any other meal he had on the trail. He closed his eyes and moaned.

"That's a mighty fine taste, ain't it?" Winn shook an appreciative finger at the boy who beamed white teeth in return. "He ain't speak more than a word here or there, but we've been talking with drawings. That's snake and pine nuts, if the dirt there don't lie."

At this point, Seamus didn't care what it was, as long as he could keep eating it. "So could you tell by any of this lad's pictures why he was tracking us?"

"That's just it." Winn slapped his knee. "This will tickle you some. What do you call us, Shila?"

At first he appeared confused, but then Winn pointed to his stained white collar and the boy's expression turned to understanding. "God . . . man," Shila said with deliberation.

Winn laughed heartily and then howled to the sky, and then started to cough and drank some water from his cup. He held out the cup to Seamus, who hesitated.

"Nah, the water's good. The boy dug a hole a ways there, tapped a fresh spring."

Seamus sipped the water and it was cool and refreshing.

"So hear this," Winn said. "The boy thinks we're preachers, on account of these here outfits, and ain't no good sense in correcting him as I see it. And all this time you were giving me fits of doubt."

"What about his tribe? And the rest of his people? Where are they hiding?" The boy might be setting them up for ambush.

"As far as I can tell from his sketches and all, he's done strayed on his own. Or his tribe set him on his way. All he keeps saying is God-man. I've been thinking maybe one of them Indian-evangelizing types got to him, poisoned his thinking so his people ain't want him around no more."

Seamus ate the rest of the food in his cup. "Maybe the same man who gave him that coat."

Winn whistled. "Yeah, she's a beauty. Strange wearing for the desert."

The boy tried to follow the conversation, shifting his head from one to the other, but there was no change to his perpetual smile.

"How are you so certain he can't understand each and every word we've been saying?" Seamus smiled back at the boy.

"Already done tested that," Winn said. "Told him I was to

skin him alive and boil his guts through, and he just glowed back at me like I was only telling him his moccasins were purty."

"You best be right about that, Winn. And what keeps you from knowing there aren't friends of his ready to give us a jump?"

"He had fine chances for that, on account of you and me being out like rocks. And in the desert, we can see plainly for miles. I ain't seen nothin' but these bones, and none of them got up and danced neither."

Seamus raised his cup to the Indian boy. "Thank you kindly, son. For the food and water and everything."

Shila rubbed his stomach and said, "A-men," which drew laughter from the two men.

"Amen is right." Seamus helped himself to some more of the meal.

Winn poked Seamus in the arm with a stick. "You ain't even given me a chance to tell the best of it all. All of your suspicions of our new friend been distracting me off the main point, but here 'tis: Our boy Shila knows the way."

"What do you mean he knows the way?" Seamus bit into something that cracked between his teeth, and he pulled it out to see it was pine-nut shell.

"A short trail. One that will get you your girl yet."

"All right. You have me listening."

Winn unfolded a map that was lying beside him and moved it close to the fire. "Go ahead, Shila. Show us."

The boy came over rather sheepishly, still unsure of Seamus. Then he leaned over, flattened out the map, and tucked his long hair behind his ears. After examining it for a moment, he pointed a finger on the map.

"That's us right here," Winn said.

"We're there? Aren't we s'posed to be much higher up toward the trail?" Seamus couldn't hold back his disappointment.

"A right shame, I know. My reckoning was off. Different water holes, it would seem."

"Then all is lost." Seamus shook his head, disgust burning in his gut. "Your reckoning has been off this entire forsaken journey. We'll never make those passes now."

"Now don't get in a snip. Listen here. You ain't seen the boy's way yet. Go ahead, Shila."

Shila appeared disturbed by Seamus's frustration and gave him a hopeful glance as if to pierce through his malaise. The boy pointed back at the map and then slid his finger across in a western direction. "Way."

Seamus looked to Winn and grimaced. "Those are mountains."

Winn nodded weakly and the boy mirrored this as well.

Seamus covered his eyes with his hands and pulled on the taut flesh of his face. This was all he could bear. He was done with Phineas Blake and his miracle cures, French Bibles, his buffalo steaks, river rafting, floating wagons, and ox-stinking water holes. Seamus had fallen prey to the last hoax at the hands of this pathetic man. He was certain if he heard even the most whispered utterance of the words "trust Winn" one more time, he would throttle the man with his bare hands.

Then the enmity transposed to twisted humor. Seamus just laughed. For the first time in many years, full, hearty, and with so much vigor it began to hurt his stomach, and he spat out some chewed up pieces of pine nuts and rattlesnake.

Winn's shoulders sagged and the young Indian appeared uneasy. "Seamus, you're scaring the boy. You ain't need be mean about it. I've gotten you this far, or have you forgot?"

"You've gotten . . . ?" Seamus nearly choked. "You've gotten me far? Far into the deepest, hottest, steaming pile of misfortune I've ever put my boots in, yes. Before I met you, sir, I was entirely capable of messing up my life. But you . . . you friend, are an artist. A most talented man."

"I'm not denying there's risks with this here plan."

"Risks? Every man, woman, and child, donkey and pig has told us we're too late. Missed the season. And that is using the trail passes. You are actually suggesting we go straight up mountain peaks through unchartered wilderness? The madness ends here, my dear Winn. You should deal with yourself kindly and go back to New Orleans and try to sell Bibles."

"Bi . . . bles." Shila's face brightened. "Bi . . . bles."

"Wonderful. Simply wonderful." Seamus didn't want to be hard-hearted, but all of his patience was drifting in the wind. "There it is. You just found yourself another salesman, Winn. You and your Indian preacher friend, you two go into the mountains and may your path be true. This Mick here? He's going the other direction. You going north? I'm going south."

When he finished, he was breathing hard and his heart was hammering against his chest. Before him, two astonished faces stared back in the flickering light.

They all sat there silently for several minutes as Seamus rocked slower and slower as his fury subsided. He begged the night skies that Winn would just let it be, but he knew better than that.

"What . . . about—?"

"What . . . about what?"

"Your lady," Winn whispered.

"My lady? My lady?' Seamus reached into his pocket and pulled out the photograph, surprised to see it was still preserved fairly well. "It's been a lie. One big lie. There is no lady. It is only some poor woman whose mail was opened by some desperate, lost soul." He curled his wrist back to flick it in the fire, and tried once, and then twice. Then he looked at it again, and he hated that his resolve was melting. What a plague this woman was upon him! Who was this Ashlyn? Was it about a girl? The gold? A chance for redemption? To prove his father wrong? It all blurred and blended back into this portrait of a woman he had never met.

Defeated, he returned the picture back in his pocket and buttoned it shut once again.

In the uneasy silence, the evening sounds around them rose. Trip lapped at a bowl of water Shila had set down for him.

Finally Seamus sighed deeply. "Just . . . if—"

"I just knew you'd be seeing things proper. I just knew it, Seamus." Winn held up his hand. "Now listen here. The boy showed us that way 'cause he knows it well. That's what I figure. And aren't you a mountain man anyway?"

"A very . . . very . . . poor mountain man."

Winn shook that away with his hands. "Listen, I reckon luck ain't been too familiar with us lately. But I feel this one, Seamus." He clasped his chest. "This is the right way." His eyes traced Seamus's every movement. "And I won't go without you. We are yoked for this . . . this time of our lives. If you say no, then that's it. Good and sure."

Seamus took his tweed hat off and ran his fingers through his knotted hair. "All right. Let's . . . just . . . sleep. In the morning. The morning . . . I'll decide."

Winn patted him on the shoulder and Shila broke out into a smile. "God . . . man."

The exhaustion sunk in soon, and it didn't take long for the three of them to set up their sleeping blankets around the fire, which they livened up by throwing in a wagon wheel.

Before he laid his head down, Seamus glanced out west. In the light of the almost full moon, he could see the hulking shapes of the mountain ranges in the horizon, looming, daring them to enter.

Seamus felt several firm tugs on his shirt and rose quickly from his slumbers. Shila stood before him with excitement on his face. He was waving for him to rise. "God . . . man."

He tugged on Winn with equal fervor, who seemed even more disheartened by the interruption of sleep. It was still only in the first light of morning.

Seamus's gaze panned their setting quickly to see if any man or beast approached. Relieved to see no imminent danger, irritation began to set in.

When the two of them had risen to their feet and after rubbing their eyes, they traced to where the boy was pointing.

He had a glow about him, both a peace and a sense of fulfilled purpose. "Sun."

"Yes, Shila. That's the sun." Winn turned and shrugged at Seamus, but the boy tugged again.

The boy pointed to west. "Sun . . . die. Sun . . . die."

Then he pivoted and pointed directly to the east, where a brilliant sun peered above the tips of the far ranges. "Sun . . . rise. Sun . . . rise."

"Yes, boy." For the first time, even Winn seemed annoyed with the Indian. "We're going to where the sun dies."

Seamus watched the young man with a whole different level of respect, and even with the barriers of language, he could sense the depth of Shila's character and he found himself profoundly drawn to it. "No, Winn. There's more to it than that."

He held his hand out to the boy, who was slow to reach out his, still measuring Seamus's motives. But then his familiar smile breached and he put his slender brown hand in Seamus's and shook it with all firmness.

"Let us get on with our journey, Winn. Wherever it may lead us." Seamus shot a stern glare at the great towering mountains that reared up in the distance. "I have a feeling the trail is about to give us its best."

Chapter 15

NO GREATER LOVE

In all of his life, Seamus had never pushed his body as hard.

Shila forced a pace that varied from a steady jaunt to almost a full sprint at times when they were sweeping downhill.

The Indian moved along the rising terrain of the Sierra Nevada range with a fluidness and oneness with his surroundings that reminded Seamus of the wild prey he had so often sighted with his musket in the Rocky Mountains.

While watching the boy was one thing, trying to keep up with their guide was quite another.

Fortunately Shila treated them with kindness and patience. Whenever he realized he was losing them, he would pause, sitting on a boulder or leaning against a tree, or taking in the scenery of an overview.

But most of the time he would use this time busying himself with the task of making sure they were all well fed and watered.

Though none of them had anything in their packs that could be considered rations, Shila treated the wilderness as an open market. He would often be found scavenging for edible roots, nuts, beetles, snakes, and lizards, and constantly tracking down early winter streams. They never tasted hunger during their passage through this magnificent landscape of granite peaks, crystalline lakes, evergreen foliage, low-lying manzanita bushes, and forests of pine, fir, and thousand-year-old sequoia groves.

On one level, Winn was right. As they left the desert plains and entered into the sinewy trails of the pine forests, Seamus began to feel alive and at home again. He was perhaps not designed for a life of solitude and survival in the wilderness, but his time in the mountains had indeed honed his skills and sensibilities for high-altitude subsistence. And in many ways, he was inspired to follow in the lead of their indefatigable guide. He even accepted the task of assisting Trip by carrying the grateful dog under his arm for most of the journey.

Yet as they went deeper into remote territory and ascended the boulder-strewn bluffs and peaks of the Sierra, Seamus noticed a subtle but clearly growing unease in Shila. He would pause and listen for something beyond the bleating of mountain goats, the quarrels of gray squirrels, and the chirping tapestry of kingbirds, tanagers, and blue jays. More and more he would stop to carefully inspect markings and scrapings of bark and prints in the soil, and even he encouraged them to duck for cover when something out of the ordinary would alarm his attuned senses.

When they would ask for explanation, he would shake his head and then wave them forward, leaving them with the mere choice of following or being abandoned in the middle of this glorious, yet imposing alpine backcountry.

Shila also began to shorten their break times, barely allowing them more than a few minutes before he was anxiously waving them to rise, and once again they would be huffing their way forward, desperate not to lose sight of the heels of his moccasins. During one of these rare moments of respite, Seamus put his hands on his hips, and Winn bent over trying to recover his wind while they conferred regarding their scout's increasingly odd behavior.

"What do you think about our lad here?" Seamus sipped from the cool mountain stream he had scooped into his canteen.

"Can't tell you much." They watched as the boy cracked open pinecones between rocks. "Hope he's not fancying an ambush with some of his friends." Winn, who had long since abandoned his tall hat, put his hands behind the back of his head to catch his breath.

"No. I don't believe so." Seamus looked up from the spectacular rise of the mountains up ahead. "He has caught the scent of winter. I know I do."

Winn jeered. "Really? You can smell it?"

Seamus nodded in the direction of a grove of pines, which were bending with surging gusts. "Those trees speak of a storm coming our way. We get ourselves caught in a snow flurry up here in the mountains, and we'll end up buried in a drift."

Winn gazed at the skies with concern.

"But that is not the full of it," Seamus said. "I wish it was, I do. The boy has an enemy out here, that is for certain. I don't know what it is, but I am guessing it will be an enemy of ours, just the same. Even Trip here has been growling at something at times."

Shila was waving them to proceed, but Winn was still breathing heavily. "Oh, that boy is gonna rip my lungs out and feed it to the crows."

Seamus elbowed him. "It is just the mountain air. Believe me. It is not the air we have to fear."

For the first time in their passage, there was a trace of anger in Shila's face. "God . . . man. Come."

Reluctantly, painfully, but with submission to the young boy's urgency and leading, the two followed and were soon again dancing through the trees, lifting above brush, leaping over streams, and rising, rising to greater and more painful heights.

There lay a terrible beauty before them.

The whipping breezes of the exposed mountain crests would have been unbearable if not for the strenuousness of their assault on the terrain, which warmed their bodies and distracted them from the added challenge that Shila's unspoken concerns now took them off of established trails through rockier and more ankle-twisting footing.

There was no explanation, but at this point none was needed. Through the growing seriousness of the boy's gaze and with his ears and senses raised like a doe in the morning, they trusted and submitted to his will.

It was getting more and more difficult to find soil untouched by early winter snowfall. Although it appeared there hadn't been any heavy snows for a while, they were now at a high enough elevation where it was cold enough to keep it crusted and free from melting.

At times they would hit a frozen sinkhole or tree well, and a leg would become buried to the knee. And as temperatures sank, the sweat in their clothing began to freeze and stiffen.

After a couple of days and as they headed deep through the heart of their journey, Seamus sensed Winn was also reaching the limit of his physical capabilities. He was still a young man, and the ardors of his cross-country travels had provided him with fortitude and endurance. But the mountains provided the blade of separation between most men, and Winn was faltering on these testing grounds.

Seamus, too, was wearying at the pace and the tyranny of the altitude, but his experience with the unfeeling grips of this terrain was proving the difference. For the first time as well, even their forerunner was starting to show the wear of their relentless assault, and there were times when he would be seen up ahead with his hands on his slender waist, struggling to find his air. It was a sight welcomed by his two pursuers, who reveled in his mortality.

Hardly sufficing to overcome the pains of their ascent, they were at least rewarded by some of God's most spectacular brushstrokes across the landscape. Even Seamus was amazed by this scenery, and he had lived daily amongst wilderness grandeur.

It was at one particular turn in the path, close to the highest point in their journey, when the three sojourners were so awestruck by what gloriously unfurled before them that they suddenly halted. And for the moment they became immune to the daggers of the merciless cold and the blazing of their lungs.

There spinning beneath them, breathlessly and seemingly miles below, was a valley finely tailored in a stunning cloak of white and generously covered with snow-flocked forestry. It lay at the base of a symphony of granite that reached like grateful hands up to the heavens. Tears of adoration poured freely from great waterfalls that descended with fullness, despite the lateness of the season. Behind this all, the sun lowered its head beneath the distant edge of the crucible, pouring into the sky cottony plumes of pink, rose, and rusted orange.

"If this ain't the finest sight I've ever seen," Winn said in between staggered breaths and with mist rising from his lips.

In Ireland, Seamus had been raised amongst the unparalleled rain-drenched greenery of Irish farmland, peered over the edges of the Cliffs of Moher, and had witnessed much of America's outdoor brilliance. But would he ever see something so striking in his lifetime? He stumbled over to a boulder, sat down, and then put a handful of snow in his mouth, which tasted as pure and refreshing as the air he was breathing.

He looked over to Shila whose eyes devoured the great valley below as if seeing it for the first time. He turned his brown-skinned, sharply carved face to them and pointed. "God . . . make."

"That, He did," Seamus said, and it sunk to belief in his heart. There could be no other clearer understanding of majesty than from this precipice.

"This . . . would be a wonderful place to die," Winn said.

There was a darkness in the statement considering their predicament, but Seamus understood his friend's sentiment.

Shila handed them each a handful of nuts and dried fruits, portions he handed out with meticulous care.

"You know," Winn started in a way usually followed with some absurd notion, "lately I've been doing some figuring."

"And what would that be, Winn, or shall I ask?"

He appeared disappointed with Seamus's tone but continued. "I've been wondering hard about my family coming out. Out West." He sighed. "I'd fancy my girls seeing all this."

Seamus was surprised. Besides his initial explanation of his family trials, he had never heard Winn mention his daughters.

"Soon as I get my gold that's coming to me," Winn said. "Then I will. After I fill these here pockets, I'm going home. I'll say, 'Look what your ol' pappy did for you. He ain't all that bad.' They'll sure be proud of me then."

Seamus took another sweeping view of the scenery and exulted as if it was nourishment to his soul. When his gaze drifted back to his friends, he saw Shila staring with disquiet at the trail behind them. Seamus followed the boy's gaze to what were deep indentations in the snow. In that moment, he knew immediately what had been Shila's concern all along.

No animals would use footprints to do their tracking.

Trip started to growl and pace furiously.

Seamus nodded to Shila and there was an understanding between them.

"Indians?"

The boy nodded. "Ah-wah-nee-chee."

Winn, who had been oblivious to what had been going on, raised his arms and howled. "What greater day than this—?"

Before he could finish, there was a strange whistling noise, a whirring of feathers in the cool air, and suddenly an arrow's tip dug into Winn's forehead. A circle of red grew around it, his eyelids closed, and his body crumpled back and folded over the edge of the cliff.

This all transpired so quickly, there was scarce time for horror or remorse. Instead the surge of survival burned through Seamus's veins. He was back on the bloody battlefields of Mexico, and he was a soldier again, letting out a scream blending fear and fury. In one leaping motion both he and Shila hurtled through trees and bushes as two rabbits scurrying from the foaming jowls of a pack of wolves.

Behind them native shouts and yelps of their attackers echoed with wicked pleasures, and Seamus looked back ever so briefly. Emerging from behind the trees were nearly a dozen Indians brandishing knives and spears with some pulling back on the strings of their bows.

Seamus made a jagged turn and heard the whistling of arrows flying behind him. He shifted back toward Shila and chose to place his life in the decisions and pathway of the one who had guided him thus far. His vision flashed back and forth from the branches and shrubbery ahead and the rugged terrain beneath his feet. For all it would take was one trip, one stumble, and his pursuers would claim deadly victory. With dusk shedding its final glow, this task grew more and more onerous.

"Come!" Shila pivoted and started to race up a wide-open slope.

Without giving it thought Seamus darted behind his friend. But he questioned the wisdom of this direction once they started flailing at the sharp embankment with arms and feet in desperation. The ascent was barren of trees, exposing them as clear targets, and with each step forward, the snow grew deeper, grinding down their momentum further.

More whirring sounds and then a howl of surprise from Shila, as an arrow bounced off his thick fur-lined coat. "Come!"

Seamus thought each step would be his last, certain an arrowhead would seek its way through his flesh. He risked another fleeting look back, and in the dim light he could see several were on one knee and aiming with lethal intent.

He turned forward and stumbled just as he realized they were at the top of a peak. Shila leapt with all force into a wall of snow and Seamus followed in blindly as well. They slammed through the hard crust and emerged through the other side of the massive cornice and shot out into the air, landing hard on the icy sheening of a dramatic slope. Seamus immediately experienced the joys of freedom and escape.

But now, something else was happening.

They were sliding down the other side of mountain, bouncing and rolling and their momentum increased with ferocity. Seamus struggled to roll on his back, but he couldn't manage to plant hand or foot, and as he plummeted helplessly, he felt his body being bumped and bruised.

He had lost all control, and as he spun, he panicked at the thought he would be lanced by a tree branch or his head or bones would be suddenly shattered against a protruding boulder.

Suddenly he hit a bump and was launched again through the

air, this time slamming with the full length of his body into a hill of snow. He felt his legs embedding several feet deep as if he had landed into the caring hands of a giant.

Then the world stopped moving.

His eyes strained to see in the darkness, and about twenty yards away, reflecting from the remaining light, he was able to make out two legs kicking.

It had to be Shila and he must have landed head first into the snowbank. There were only seconds, maybe a minute, before the boy's life would end.

Seamus started to press himself up from the snow, but he was buried from the waist down and it seemed every effort he made only sank him deeper. Yet, unrelenting in his frantic efforts, Seamus managed to press himself up and then he crawled his way out of the hole. Then he ran, awkwardly, because something was wrong with his left leg.

Seamus dove to the spot where Shila's legs were still protruding but now were no longer moving. He was too late.

Please, Lord. No.

With one tremendous motion that drew a strength well beyond his own, Seamus yanked hard on the thighs of the boy and sprung him upward in one firm stroke.

He laid Shila on his back and crawled to his face, then cleared the snow off of his face. The boy loudly gulped in air and coughed.

Seamus hugged Shila, gripping him tightly, and sobbed.

The Indian's eyes were open, but he was in shock. "God . . . man."

"Yes . . . yes." Seamus laughed. He pointed at the boy. "You . . . God . . . man."

The boy smiled back sweetly while Seamus groomed away the dirt and specks of branches around his eyes. Then there was more snow on the boy's face and he brushed that away as well.

Seamus's gaze turned slowly upward and coming down, as with a fluttering of wings, were large drifting and swooping white flakes.

Shila struggled to his feet and Seamus lifted him. They both knew there would be no safety here so they were fleeing again, despite their pain and exhaustion. The tribe of the Yosemite might not have abandoned the chase and could be upon them shortly.

But now there was another, even more frightening enemy. If a full winter storm was upon them, they would stand little chance of surviving, and their deaths would be much more excruciating than the piercing of an arrow.

They hobbled forward, leaning on each other for stamina. Seamus quickly was reminded of the pain in his leg and he looked down to see that a branch had impaled his calf. Even in the dim light of the moon glowing through the clouds, he could see he was trailing red in the snow.

He reached down and tugged on the limb and it slid out without breaking. Fortunately the branch was thin and it had not made it all of the way through. The frigidity of the air had already numbed his flesh, and though the slicing winds tore at his nose, ears, and face, he was grateful he couldn't sense much pain in his leg.

The two moved as brothers in the night, one collective will to survive and to encourage each other to rise above the misery of their situation. Yet with each step, the storm's anger rose and the soft ballet of the initial snowfall now howled with side-shifting winds, blinding them for all but a hand's length before them.

They had hoped to find a cave or some barrier from the night's tempestuous assault, but their eyes burned with the sleet and their feet sank deeper and slower into their drifting futility.

Finally, once they decided they could journey not one step farther, they crawled over to a nestled grove of pines, which would need to serve as their last stand of defense. They tried to gather some branches to build a windbreak, but they were at the cliff's edge of their consciousness.

Instead, they sat together at the trunk of a large tree and gripped each other tightly, giving and taking whatever heat they could draw from one another.

Seamus fought to keep his eyelids open, knowing that if he shut them, he would probably never rise again. His body shook with convulsions, and his head began to ache while a drifting dizziness swept over him.

He couldn't . . . fight . . . any more. And his will was seeping into the whistling dreariness of the storm raging around them.

Seamus glanced deep into the brown eyes of the young Indian, and he saw a well of strength and joy that he yearned for. And he heard the whisper of "Come" in the air, and he smiled and reached out his hand.

* * *

He wasn't certain if it was the bright rays of the sun or the cheerful morning song of the jays that made him stir, but Seamus woke.

Or was he dead? It seemed like such a different day than the night before. The sun was bright, the temperature was already warm, and the wind that had been so fierce the night before was restful and silent.

Not only was Seamus no longer cold, but he was sweating. As his gauze of slumber faded, he looked down to see he was wrapped up in Shila's frontiersman coat, which was fur lined inside and out. Still lying beside him was his Indian friend, wearing only a leather tunic, and Seamus gave him a nudge.

But rather than waking, the boy's body dropped softly to the snow. Shila must be really snared in a heavy sleep. Seamus stretched, then nudged the boy again. No response. The beauty and warmth in this day was sucked from his soul and his heart thundered with denial. *Nooo!*

He flung himself beside Shila's snow-crusted and stiffened body and carried him to a flat area in full sunlight. The boy's lips were content with peacefulness and innocence but tinged in blue, and his brown face was now pallid.

Seamus took off the coat and draped it over his friend, embracing him, and then he tried to warm the life back into the boy, rubbing his arms and then his legs.

But Shila was gone, and the Irishman was terribly alone.

He sobbed at first with modesty and restraint, but then opened up into tears and shouts of anguish.

Yet strangely, this anger didn't last and was replaced with profound sadness. Not for the boy. But for the emptiness he left behind.

The young Indian had made the ultimate sacrifice. He had laid his life down for Seamus.

"Greater love hath no man than this . . ."

The words came to Seamus as if in a dream, a whisper in his heart, some memory of his childhood or a glance into his future.

For the very first time in his life, Seamus experienced true love in the death of his friend.

He wrapped the fur coat around Shila's corpse and limped forward with the boy's body cradled in his arms for miles and miles until he descended to a clearing where the snow had melted.

He labored for hours to dig a hole in the ground to bury him, but it was too frozen and the best tool he had was a pine bough. So finally, he laid the boy's body down and then covered it with a pile of small boulders, stacking them high.

Seamus stared for quite some time at what lay beneath him before he heard a noise. What's this? Barking? Tears flowed from Seamus's eyes as Trip emerged from the trees and limped toward him, and the two embraced like old friends.

Still, the pain of loss burrowed deeply in his soul.

There in the lonely high mountain air of the Sierra, with the sun shining on his shoulders, Seamus planted a wooden cross.

Chapter 16

THE SHORES OF PANAMA

 Davin felt miserable for his sister Clare. What with her not knowing what happened to him, she must be terrified.

But if it wasn't for this occasional suffering of guilt, he couldn't have been more thrilled with his new adventurous life. Because as it turned out, being shanghaied wasn't necessarily a bad thing. Especially considering the *Tarentino* was one of the fastest ships in the sea.

Initially, it was quite a shock for Davin to learn that San Francisco was farther than a couple day's journey. And it took a good week for Captain MacDonald to warm up to him enough to consider him a somewhat useful addition to the crew.

Of course, the other men who got shanghaied seemed less grateful about their service aboard the ship. Apparently one or two of them went on a long swim and never came back. Davin wasn't certain how they could have swam that far, as there were rarely any other ships on the water or land to be spotted.

Although he befriended most of the crew, he had a hard time thinking too fondly of the passengers who he found to be unreasonably demanding and lazy to boot. Why they never helped out with any of the chores and expected to be served as if they were the Prince of Wales.

Fortunately for Davin, his assignment as the cook's assistant allowed him to mostly keep his distance from the ungrateful masses and allowed him a position of some honor. Because no man second to the captain himself was more honored and more valued by the crew than Dusty, the ship's cook.

Davin finished peeling his eighty-second potato. He knew this because he always practiced his math when he was in the kitchen. It was his plan to appease Clare when he got back home. He was sorry about leaving home for a while, but at least he kept up with his lessons. His sister would be pleased with this.

Dusty wiped his hands on his apron, which bore evidence of the last few meals he had served. He was a lanky man, with a wild tuft of sandy-brown hair. "How many lost?"

"Just six blackies. I threw them away already."

"Rotten through the heart, laddie?"

Davin looked up to the man and squinted.

The cook held up his hands in surrender. "All right, but you doesn't have to be bitin' me with those eyes, there. I guess I'm s'posing to know no Irishman would allow a good tater to be wasted."

Dusty must not know what emotions were stirred up by potatoes. His father hadn't died on a potato field. His mother and brother hadn't died of starvation because of the potato famine. But Dusty was a nice enough man so Davin never burdened him with his difficult thoughts.

"Where's Nelson?" Davin scratched his ear and ended up getting a peel stuck on his cheek before brushing it off.

"Now, laddie, you a fine worker, but that boy's a lubber, not much worth the grub he's eating."

"You just don't know him, that's all. None of you. He knows all about ships. Sails. Rigging. The knots. Why he could captain this ship if they only gave him a try."

"It's all I could do to keep them from feeding him to the sharks already." The cook heaved a bag of onions onto the table. "We're good for taters, boy. Slice the ones there and then give these a peel and cut. But save your cryin' for your ma."

"Ah, I never cry about them onions." Davin sliced into the potatoes with the large knife. "It's just my eyes leak sometimes." One important thing he learned from his father was that boys never were supposed to cry.

The cook opened the door to the large iron stoves and put in more wood to the flames.

Davin continued to rattle on the cutting board. "Dusty?" It wasn't his real name. The crew called him that because they claimed he never stopped talking about his dreams of discovering a pail's worth of gold dust.

"What is it, boy?"

"So tell me about us getting rich."

"Again?" The cook slammed the doors and cranked the handles closed. "Haven't you enough of me tales?"

"Does the gold really grow like mushrooms in California?"

"Aye. They do and more." Dusty turned a chair backward and straddled it. "In fact, if you rise before sun break, you'll see nuggets hopping like frogs. You catch 'em with a net."

Davin laughed.

Dusty's expression turned serious. "And I s'pose you'll be sleeping while I'm out there grabbing 'em. You won't get a taste of my share."

"I'm not aiming to get rich. Just need to find my brother." Davin's eyes watered at the thought of Seamus, so he grabbed an onion and started cutting.

The cook put his arm on his shoulder. "We'll find 'em all right. The two of us."

Davin knotted his brows. "The three of us."

Dusty rose. "Sure enough, laddie. Nelson too. Why we'll have such good diggings, we'll buy him a new hat, one made of gold."

The door to the galley swung open and Captain MacDonald entered. He was an angry-looking man with a head disproportionately larger than the rest of his body, which was short and stocky.

"Why, Captain, what brings you?" Dusty stood nearly at attention and swept his apron with his hands.

The captain ignored Dusty and glared at Davin. "I've been hearin' some disturbin' rumors from somes of the crew." His voice rattled with a Scottish bent.

Davin shrugged. But his heart pulsed as it was just as if his father's anger was rising before him.

The captain removed his hat and brushed the thinning strands of his hair across his balding pate. He poked a stubby finger in Davin's chest, who was now standing stiffly as well. "Is there truth in it that your fadder is one Mr. Andrew Royce?"

"No. None at all."

"He's not your fadder?"

"No. He is just my sister's husband."

"Are you twistin' me, boy?" He placed his hat back on his head.

"Sir." Dusty inched forward. "You must be givin' the lad some grace. He speaks plainly but means none by it."

"Plain enough to earn the back of me hand. Were you aware of this, cookie?"

He winced. "I was, sir. The boy confides in me."

"And you thought it too much trubble to learn me of this?"

Dusty looked sheepishly at Davin. "Now, when you says it that way, it surely was deservin' of mention."

The captain bent over and Davin could smell whiskey on his breath, something he had learned accompanied anger. "You'll get me hanged, you know that, boy? We only take orphans and drunks. They'll take me ship. Are you happy with that news?"

"No, sir." Davin bent his head downward. "I will just tell them I tricked you. That I snuck on board and you begged me to leave. I love this ship, Captain. And when I get to San Francisco—"

"San Francisco?" The captain shot a vile glance toward Dusty.

"As soon as this ship unloads in Panama, we'll be taking you full sail back to New York so I can kiss your sister's hand and tell her husband he married a bonnie lass."

"But sir . . . I've got to get to my brother."

"Your brudder better live in New York, 'cause that's all you'll be seeing."

Davin's eyes moistened. "You see, sir, Dusty and I are going to find gold."

As soon as the words came out, Davin could see his betrayal across Dusty's deflated face.

The captain's huge head snapped to Dusty. "That's the other rumor we'll end here. Cookie has a dash of the goldie, does he?"

"Well . . . sir, I—"

"I'll remind you well, you'll finish the full tour, you will." He glared back at Davin. "Sure as I'm standin' before you, if one fungus-filled toe steps off this ship when we port her, you'll both be filled with holes. Clear enough?"

Dusty started to protest but caught himself. "Yes, sir. Quite clear, it 'tis."

The captain stepped out the door but only halfway, and then he turned back with a smirk. "And anudder thing. You might wanna see about your idiot."

"Sir?" Davin asked.

But there was no answer and the door slammed behind the captain, and it was as if it brought a close to their dreams as well. They stood in numbed silence for a few moments.

Davin knew he had let Dusty down, but there was something else to be concerned about now. He risked interrupting his friend's mourning. "Was he talking about Nelson?"

The name brought Dusty out of his funk, and he stood and untied his apron with sudden urgency. "We better be off. It's a good chance we're too late."

The salty winds raged across the wave-splattered deck, which meant the passengers of the ship would be away sheltering in their rooms. This left the crew alone to their own sordid imaginations, which oftentimes during this trip meant making a plaything out of Nelson.

There, clasping one hand on the masthead pole and the other clamping his navy bicorn hat to his head to keep it from fluttering to the depths of the sea below, was Nelson, who looked both on the point of exhaustion and exposure from the cold.

"Nelson! Hold still." Davin panicked as they elbowed their way through the drunken and mocking crew of onlookers.

"Hang tight, boy." Dusty climbed up over the rail and tried to get himself into a position to grasp Nelson, but the ship's lurching made it almost impossible for him to brace himself properly.

"Just standing there?" Davin scowled at the dozen or so who

pointed and laughed from the deck. He curled a fist at them, which drew more laughter.

"Old Nelson looks prettier than a mermaid," one hollered.

"Aye. Careful yourself, Dusty. We don't care none for the moron, but a cook's hard to replace."

Dusty continued to try to scale the ropes but turned and snarled. "You think you'll be eatin' anything soon?"

"Ah, c'mon, Dusty. We're just funning the boy."

"Let go of the hat, Nelson, and grab 'er with both hands." Dusty's voice hinted with anger.

Davin knew well enough that wasn't going to happen.

The cook shimmied his way out to the masthead pole, but when he reached for the draw wire, the ship surged and he spun around, then latched his arms and legs around the pole.

One of the men turned to the others. "That's enough, lads. We'll starve without cookie, and the captain will have our heads."

A few of them grumbled and moved their way forward, cursing and moving awkwardly due to heavy drink and the undulations of the sea.

After a few struggles they assisted Dusty back to deck and then, as promised, pulled Nelson back down as well, the boy refusing to weaken his grip on his hat. But as soon as he reached the deck, as if his mission was complete, his knees buckled and he tumbled to the ground, his body trembling.

The men laughed lustily and returned to sharing the jug in their hands and shifted away down the deck into the darkness.

"Let's get him by the galley's fires." Dusty lifted Nelson over his shoulders, which was no easy task, and Nelson's beloved hat fell to the deck and bounced.

Davin pounced on it and returned it to his friend's head. He wanted to be a protector of Nelson just as Seamus had always been to him. Because he knew all too well the pain of being bullied. He may not have had the courage to stand up to his father when he was young, but now that he was nearly a man, he would take nothing from no one.

"Don't you worry none, Nelson. Dusty's getting you a hat of gold."

Chapter 17

TEA TIME

"What flavor of tea is this, laddie?"

The question startled Davin, and for a moment he glanced worriedly around the table of officers gathered for their morning breakfast. But determining it was asked with innocence, he answered coolly. "They brought it up from the docks, sir. Seeing as we couldn't go off ship ourselves, by your orders we had them provision us. Said it was locally grown."

The captain leaned over to his cup, his hands shaking, as they always did, and he lifted it and sipped loudly. The others around the table glanced around and followed suit, as if not to offend the captain. "Lovely."

There were some nods and grunts from the others. Davin set the teapot down on the table, his hands sweating with nervousness. He pivoted on his feet and was relieved to be leaving after precisely following the directions the cook had shared with him.

"Davin." The captain's voice was stern.

Davin's face dropped and he made a slow turn to accept his fate. "Yes, sir?"

"Listen, son. I know you're a wee disappointed in me. When I return you to your sissie, how 'bout I seek her permission to bring you back? Then you can fetch your brudder."

The other officers seemed amazed to hear their captain speaking in such manner to the cook's helper.

The captain smiled. "Oh. Have you not met the laddie proper? Did you know his sissie is married to the publisher of the *New York Daily*?"

Their eyebrows raised with understanding and then they tipped their cups to him, some with ardor and others in derision, and they drank some more of the Panamanian tea.

The captain put his hand to his forehead and rubbed his temples. "I want the laddie to get proper treatment, like Irish royalty, be that as it may." He laughed, then his eyes started to close and he collapsed into his plate of scrambled eggs.

A few of the officers sprung to their feet, but almost as instantly they began to stagger, and in a few moments all were crumbled facedown on the table or curled up on the floor.

"Yes," Davin said. "Isn't the tea lovely?"

He watched his conquered foes with no little satisfaction. No longer. No one was going to push him and his friends around. Nothing would stop him from seeing his brother Seamus.

Then he scurried out of the room.

The *Tarentino* had only been a mile out to sea on its return voyage from the Panama coast before tea had been served. But

Dusty and Davin were anxious to keep the distance they needed to row the dinghy as short as possible.

At the cost of forgiving a large gambling debt to Dusty, one of the seamen assisted the two in lowering the boat to the water and even waved as they rowed away into the morning light.

They had a good part of the day before the slumbering officers would come off of their drug-induced nap, one caused by a root grown in the faraway land of India. It apparently was the same one used to get Davin and the other "volunteers" aboard the *Tarentino* at the beginning of the ship's journey.

Davin feared what would happen when the cruel Scottish captain and his crew arose to discover their getaway. But Dusty assured him there would be no anger that would cause them to turn a ship back to port just to get an old cook and his galley boy.

But this didn't keep them both from rowing as quickly as they could in what already was shaping up to be a day of sweltering heat. Davin was grateful to do his part in pulling the oars against the deep, clear waters, and that their effort in approaching the shoreline was accompanied with much jesting on account of their freedom. He was starting to believe the man with the dreams of golden adventures would be one of his best friends. Dusty didn't treat him like a child. And he never yelled at him or made him feel bad.

They were able to slip into the harbor relatively unnoticed as there were several large ships, but it was mostly blanketed with the small vessels of dozens of local fishermen. When they moored on one of the vacant docks and tied down, they were not surprised to see their friend Nelson sitting patiently on the shoreline, his silhouette easy to spot because of the curvature of his hat. The captain had not only allowed Nelson off of the boat, but had insisted he be escorted off at the dock.

After a few hugs and a brief few moments to stretch their arms, Dusty had the three of them off hastily to their next destination.

They passed by the lively markets in the streets, busy with carts and donkey-pulled wagons, as dark-skinned and strangely speaking merchants in mostly white clothing barked about their pineapples, dates, and coconuts. Skinned pigs hung upside down, and there were cackling chickens, goats being milked, and many children and elderly squatting with tin cups in their hands.

As Davin and Nelson watched this procession with wide eyes, Dusty pressed them forward, oftentimes grabbing them by their shoulders to keep them from getting lost in the crowds.

"Why the hurry?" Davin shouted.

Frustration displayed on Dusty's face and he wiped away the sweat beading on his brow. "Two rich *Tarentino* passengers 'tis all. Be lively mates or we'll be grousing through the jungle in our boots."

"There's a jungle in San Francisco?" Davin looked to Nelson and shrugged but then scurried to keep up with their leader.

It took nearly an hour for them to get to the river's edge, and they all were spent and their clothing was soaked and foul smelling.

"Wipe yourselves off, laddies. They won't hire us looking like this."

"Who's hiring us?" Davin bent down and scooped some water to his face, then sipped some as well. Someone was going to give them a job? He tried not to overplay his enthusiasm.

Nelson kneeled by the muddy edge leading up the water and removed his hat, dipped it into the river, then dumped it on his head.

Davin laughed. "What about me?"

His friend smiled and filled the hat again with water and

handed it to Davin, who joyfully emptied its contents over his overheated body.

"Are you blarnin' mad, the twos of you?" Dusty stood over them with his hands on his waist.

Chagrined, they crawled to their feet. "You told us to clean ourselves off." Davin drew his fingers through his wet hair to comb through the knots. He hoped Dusty wasn't going to end up being just another angry man after all.

Dusty nodded in the direction of some moored riverboats, which were long and slender and being tended to by what appeared to be Panamanians. "Those there richies won't want children along. Now look at yous, like wet monkeys."

Standing by the boats, an elderly man paced and glanced at his pocket watch while dressed in a blue jacket with a white vest underneath, which must have been intolerably warm in this heat. Beside him, fanning herself and hoisting a parasol, was a woman whose wide girth was only emphasized by the hoop beneath her pink dress.

Davin's heart sank. Of all of the difficult passengers on the *Tarentino*, these were the snootiest of all. What possible benefit could there be in being around these people?

Dutifully, they followed behind Dusty as he approached the couple, with his hat in his hand and fostering a fawning smile.

"Well!" The woman's puffy face scowled. "This? This is what we're waiting for Reginald?"

"My sorries to ya, Mister and Missus Matherson." Dusty bowed before them. "We're here now."

"Really, Reginald." She fluttered her fan.

The man didn't disguise his disappointment in Dusty's assistants. "It will have to do, Daphne, I'm afraid. If it gets later, we'll melt." He held out a limp, pale hand to Dusty. Leaning forward he whispered loud enough for the boys to hear, "Don't lose sight of these local boatmen. I'm told they'll pilfer every-thing they can touch. We didn't bring much, but what we have my wife and I would like to ensure it gets to our ship intact."

"And just that we'll do," Dusty said. "Now just for remind-ing. For our services, me and my men here, you'll get us passage from Panama City."

Mr. Matherson raised his brow. "Yes. As long as we and our luggage make it there intact. Passage for both you and your . . . umm . . . men."

Dusty grinned. "There's more to them than the eyes tell ya, Mr. Matherson."

"I should certainly hope so," Mrs. Matherson interjected.

"C'mon, laddies. Let's load 'er up for these fine folks."

Davin didn't see any fine folks before him, and when he turned his head to see the magnificent pile of leather cases, crates, and ornate boxes that needed to be packed into the two narrow boats, he scratched his head. Not a moment later, he felt the firm tug on his shirt from Dusty and the three of them set upon the impossible task of trying to find a way to pile it all up as neatly as possible while the Panamanian boat captain stood by in amusement.

"So this river goes to San Francisco, then?" Davin slapped his neck and pulled his hand back to see a half-dozen mosqui-toes squashed on it.

Dusty laughed as he organized the luggage for loading. "'Fraid not, son. We take these bungos up this Chagres River to Las Cruces. Then we mule it to Panama City. If we don't die of 'squitoes, gators, snakes, and fever, we hop another ship north ways to California."

The words were daggers to his heart. Davin's mouth dropped, but he closed it for fear the bugs would fly in. "We have been weeks into this already." He couldn't even imagine how angry his sister would be at him for leaving home. He might as well never return.

"Gold's the prize, son. Keep your sights on that."

"My brother," Davin mumbled. "Seamus."

"Can you believe the impertinence of these boys?" Mrs. Matherson's expression was twisted as if she had swallowed a sardine. "Keeping us, us of all people, thirty minutes in waiting, and now they move like pulled caramel."

Dusty tipped a hat to her. "We're on 'er, missus." He gave a piercing glance at the boys, and soon they were all scurrying to pack the two boats.

"That crate has our china, you indelicate moron. Those have my porcelain doll collection. Our paintings. My dresses. Oh, my dear Reginald! All these miles from France and England and China only to have our precious belongings sink in this malaria-and-cholera-infested cesspool. Why, it is all that we have in the world." She waved her fan and batted her eyelashes.

"They'll be fine, missus. These lads be gentle as lambs and lovers of the arts, they are."

It took another twenty minutes to squeeze everything in the two riverboats, or *cayucos* as the Panamanians called them. Much of the time was spent unpacking the lead vessel, so there would be ample room for Mrs. Matherson. This boat was larger than the other and featured a large overhang, which brought shelter to its passengers from the braising sunlight.

A kinship had already been forged between the Panamanian crew and Dusty, Davin, and Nelson, due to their common enemy. So when Mrs. Matherson insisted that Nelson be left behind, they all stood firm.

"That's the bargain. All or none of us."

The woman glared back at Dusty, who was perched in the back of the first boat. "Hummph! Aren't you going to say something, Reginald? The arrogance!"

All eyes shifted to Reginald who, much to his wife's dismay, merely signaled for them to untie the ropes and leave the shoreline to begin their forty-five-mile journey downriver.

Once they were afloat, a slight breeze brought with it some relief from the heat and the mosquitoes. Davin began to settle in on the pure pleasure of the sights all around him, and the relaxing motion of the boats. He had learned from the Panamanians there were *tigres* in the jungle, so he peered into the tropical forests of palm trees and mangroves and vines lining the river's shores with utter fascination, while brightly colored birds and chirruping monkeys filled the air with strange sounds.

It was only about a couple of miles into the trip when Davin looked back from his seat to see Nelson precariously perched on a stack of leather cases, gripping onto the sides of the boat with obvious discomfort.

Up ahead, he could see the backs of the Mathersons' pretentious heads as the lead cayuco bent its way around a curve of the La Chagres and disappeared briefly out of sight.

Davin sprung up to his feet and worked his way to the back of the boat.

"Get yourself up, Nelson. Now, be quick about it."

His friend appeared confused but did as requested. Once the teenager was up, Davin knocked over the crate of china and let it sink into the murky water, with bubbles rising. He took a quick look toward the approaching curve in the river, and then repeated this with two other crates as the boat captain laughed with approval.

He patted Nelson on the shoulder. "That should be a wee bit more comfy."

Chapter 18

THE BARBARY COAST

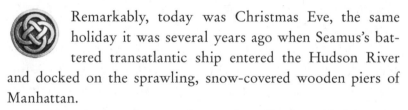 Remarkably, today was Christmas Eve, the same holiday it was several years ago when Seamus's battered transatlantic ship entered the Hudson River and docked on the sprawling, snow-covered wooden piers of Manhattan.

At that time, as he peered over the rails alongside his sister Clare and watched in awe as the Manhattan skyline grew before his eyes, America represented a new beginning, a chance to make his mark.

But now as he rode aboard the river steamship through the Golden Gate and into the bay, it was all so different. With the shores of San Francisco drifting toward him, his sense of victory was marred by plaguing guilt. At what price came his survival? His success in this venture?

As he glared into the waters shifting below, his thoughts drifted back to years ago, to that darkest of days. The one weaved through each of his deepest hurts.

There on the verdant banks of the creek near his family farm in Ireland sat his brother Kevan, the youngest of all of the Hanley children, looking up to Seamus with rosy cheeks, the soft blond curls of a toddler and a toothless smile of innocence, joy, and trust. Seamus loved the child as he did all of his brothers and sisters.

It was in the faintest of moments where Seamus turned and lost himself in playful banter with his childhood friend Pierce. Had it been a few seconds or minutes? He could remember neither the exact time nor the topic of conversation, but seared indelibly in his mind was the horror of glancing back to see the bank was empty, save for the green grass.

By the time he found Kevan, many yards down the current, the child was pale, moist, and lifeless.

The rest was a blur: the panic, the screams, the despair of his mother, the wake, the burial.

Clare bravely tried to intercede and fend off some of the blame for it, but his father had seen through it. One evening Seamus awoke in his bed to see Pa leaning into his ear and he whispered, "You took my last chance to have a son I could be proud of."

Seamus sought so many times to bury the memory forever. His first effort was to run away to Cork, but he returned hungry and ashamed. Then he thought by sailing from Ireland he could leave it all behind. When this didn't alleviate the hurt, he hoped the horrors of war might wash it away like waves lapping against a sandy shore. And when this failed, he sought life in the mountains, in the effort to elude the shadows that haunted.

He now realized there would be no burial of his suffering. All he was doing was covering it with rotted leaves, and it revealed itself with each new windstorm of his life.

Which was why Shila's sacrifice made no sense to him. Why wasn't Seamus the one God took? The one who was already suffering? The boy had his life ahead of him. And was gentle and deserving of mercy.

Was this what his pursuit of this woman in the photograph was all about? Just another hopeless effort to bandage the scars?

Trip's tongue licked his face and Seamus was surprised to see he was so lost in his thoughts he had nearly forgotten he had been holding the dog.

"I s'pose it's just you and me for now, eh Trip? Now which of us is more wanting of a bath?" He scratched behind the dog's ears and looked up to see the ship had reached its destination.

As the boat drifted to landing, it was impossible to miss the spectacle of hundreds of ships in the harbor, drooping, unkempt, and anchored so closely to each other they appeared shackled to the shore.

The masses aboard the crowded deck moved as one, and a voice hollered in his ear. "Have you n'ere seen such a sight?"

Seamus knew by the brogue the man was an Irishman, but he couldn't place the accent. "Where from?"

"County Derry. You?"

"Roscommon." They spilled down the ramp and were grateful for the space as the crowd scattered on the shore. "What is it?"

The Derry man shifted his pack from one shoulder to the other. "Those ships. All abandoned."

Seamus looked over but from this vantage point could just see the tips of the masts. "Why's that?"

"These ships come into harbor and before the ropes are tied, crew, cooks, the captain himself, can be seen rushin' to shore with shovels in their hands and hope in their hearts. They just leave those ships behind. And the Paddies? The city's green with them."

"Are they finding anything? You know. Is it true about the gold?"

The Derry man set his pack down and pulled out a small leather sack from under his tunic. Then he poured a dozen or more nuggets from it in his hand. "That's my passage home, it is. Less than I wanted, but more than I need. I have had me enough of blisters and bugs. I am ripe to be kissing Irish soil and me wife and kids."

"I miss back home myself." Seamus was surprised to be hearing himself say this, but for the first time in a long time, it was true.

"Well, if you want home, at least why you are here, go see McGilley's. The beer's stale and the ladies will pinch you clean, but there are plenty of Micks. There's Dublin Town too. Why we are all over here. I might just get back home and find Ireland emptied."

"Thank you, friend." Seamus patted the Derry man on the shoulder and headed for the center of the Barbary Coast, yet another name for San Francisco. Only after a request or two for directions and a short stroll, he found himself outside the doorway of McGilley's and the sounds of unrestrained revelry and Irish music brought warm memories to Seamus and he smiled. Yet as he opened the door and saw the many tables filled with mug-lifting miscreants, card cheats, arm-wrestling lads, off-melody drunks, and shady women leaning over their welcoming prey, it seemed so foreign to him.

Had he changed this much? Was this not the type of place he once considered his life's greatest joy? It reminded him of his friend Pierce, who had shared many a tavern with him before sharing the ship to America with both he and Clare. The last he saw of his redheaded friend was in a U.S. army encampment. Just shortly before Seamus changed sides.

Seamus bumped his way through, getting his share of threatening glances, until he made it to the front where he raised a hand to beckon the barkeep.

"You are not planning on ordering a drink, are you?" said the man behind the bar.

"And what if I was?"

"You one of the reverend's boys, are you not? He finds you in here with an ale in your hand, he will shove that book of his down my gullet."

Seamus had forgotten he was still wearing preacher's clothes and felt embarrassed. "This is just something I am wearing."

"You know the reverend?" the man sitting in the stool next to Seamus asked. He was a hefty man with large cheeks, thinning gray hair, a red face and nervous smile. Dressed in the clothes of a man of some means, he seemed oddly out of place in the room. His two hands gripped a mug of ale and lying beside him was a black bowler hat, which Seamus recognized as otter skin.

"Never heard of this reverend." Seamus addressed the bartender. "Could I trouble you for a glass of water?"

The portly man beside him leaned in and garbled his words as he spoke. "Water? Give this man a meal." He signaled the bartender with a motion that said he would put it on his tab.

"You heard Mr. Parnell." The bartender smiled. "And he doesn't open his purse too often."

"Henry," the man reached over stubby fingers.

Seamus looked at the bartender and then to Henry. "That's kindly of you sir, but—"

"No sir." Henry flatted his palm on the mahogany counter. "These lads from back home, Billy. Too much pride."

Billy uncorked a clay jug and poured water into a glass, stopping briefly to remove a spot with his forefinger. "Be back with your grub."

Seamus lifted his glass to his benefactor.

Henry lifted his glass to his lips and then wiped off the foam from his lips. "What brings you to the Barbary Coast? Hmm? Gonna stake your claim?"

"Perhaps." Seamus emptied the glass and was still thirsty.

"All over the world they come here to this place. Stepping up to the shores, dripping wet with their desires. Hunger. A strange hunger, is it not?"

Seamus looked down at his hands.

Henry wagged a plump finger at him. "So what's the story with that? Those clothes."

"Just came a long way, mister."

The man held up his hands. "Say no more. We all have our secrets."

Billy arrived with a steaming bowl of pottage, and Seamus couldn't help but lower his nose to it and smelled the sweet fragrance of potatoes, leaks, onions, and cream. "Thank you kindly," he said to Henry.

The man pointed a finger to his empty mug and Billy took it away with him.

"How 'bout a name?"

The spoonful of stew made him shut his eyes. "Seamus." He leaned over and shook hands with Henry.

"A good Paddy name it is. You staying at Dublin Town?"

"I have heard of it from a man from Derry. What is it?"

The freshly filled mug of ale slammed on the counter and Henry nodded his approval to Billy. He held it up to Seamus. "You want one?"

"No. But could I trouble you, barkeep, for another bowl?" Seamus buried a large spoonful in his mouth, and in a moment Billy plunked a tin cup on the counter.

Seamus took the cup, spooned several portions into it, and then lowered it to the ground for Trip, waiting patiently on the floor.

"You're getting more interesting all of the time." Henry tipped the mug. "There's no houses here in the Barbary Coast. All of the carpenters are in the hills digging gold. So the Irish boys set themselves a tent city. Must be a thousand or so, happily living in squalor."

"Sounds like the Five Points."

"New York, eh?"

"That's right." Seamus was grateful he had a piece of bread still, and he dragged it around the inside of his bowl.

"So what you really here for?"

Seamus paused for a moment and then decided this man was as good to ask as the bartender. He reached into his pocket and pulled out the now-frayed and faded photograph and slid it on the counter. Almost as soon as he did, he regretted it because the man's face drained.

"How do you know Ashlyn Whittington?" Henry sobered.

Seamus reached back and returned the photograph in his pocket, then pushed out his bowl and drank from his cup again.

"Who are you? Coming in here dressed like that and asking about Ashlyn?" Henry's face softened. "I don't mean to be harsh. I'm just a bit protective of the girl. She's . . . like a daughter to me."

"I understand." Seamus wiped his lips with his sleeve. "Can you tell me a wee bit about her? What is she like, would you say?"

Henry gave him a strained look. "You are an odd fellow. Seem harmless."

"I am that." Seamus spent enough time around taverns in his life to know that if the man wasn't willing to speak to him, the drink in him would.

Billy came by and wiped clear the counter with a rag.

"What would you say about Ashlyn?" Henry asked of the bartender.

"You know her as well as any. But if I am the one answering, I would say she's as fine a woman as this town has." He flung the rag over his shoulder. "Runs a little orphanage just down the street here. Pretty as can be but has her heart set on some soldier, in case you had any thoughts. You know her?"

"Not had the pleasure yet."

"But he's got her picture in his pocket." Henry gave a sloppy wink.

Seamus expected a rebuke from the bartender, but when he looked up, the man was looking toward the door.

"Well, here is good trouble for all of us now."

"Goodness no." Henry covered his face and shrunk in his stool.

Turning, Seamus saw a tall man in a black jacket and a collar walking toward him.

"I warned him, Reverend Sanders," Billy said. "And I didn't serve him a lick and I am happy to share with you he didn't ask for one neither."

"There will be no happiness in this establishment, Billy, until you aren't serving anyone a lick." There was a deep resonance in his voice that caused several bystanders to take notice.

Billy smiled. "Even the heathens need a place to be loved, Reverend."

"Speaking of heathens, why I believe it's our good friend the banker here drowning himself in your still." The reverend put his hand on Henry's shoulder. "Why if you're not idling your time with the root of all evil, you're sure to be here at the trough of indulgence. Didn't you just tell me last Sunday you'd be keeping clear of McGilley's?"

"Now, now, Reverend," Billy said, "it's better for the weaker brothers among us to share their vices among friends."

"I have all those intentions," Henry responded.

"And who are you, Pastor?" The minister looked Seamus up and down.

"Seamus Hanley." He extended a hand and pointed to his clothes. "But these don't suit me."

"Reverend Charles Sanders." He reached out a large hand, which engulfed Seamus's dirty grip. "The few who love me call me Brother Chuck. You can do the same. And why may I ask don't they suit you?"

"Forgive me, Reverend, but I am ashamed to say they were used to disguise us as men of the cloth to keep us from being harmed by Indians—" As soon as he said these words, Seamus was overwhelmed with the sudden image of Shila's death, blue-lipped, pale complexion, and with his eyelids sealed. Seamus fought back a sudden urge to sob.

The reverend's arm reached for his shoulder and his voice, still deep, was now soft and caring. "What is it, son?"

Seamus laughed awkwardly with embarrassment. "Nothing. Just went through a bitter journey."

"It always is. It always is." He patted Seamus on the back.

"He knows my Ashlyn." Henry struggled to keep the beer out of his tone.

"Is that so? Say, son. Do you have a place to rest your head? I can tell you're new to town." The man peered down at him with comforting bushy brows.

"I didn't know you were taking boarders." Billy acknowledged a customer's request with a wave of his hand.

"This one intrigues me. What do you say, son? A place to get yourself cleaned up?"

Seamus was embarrassed by his show of emotion. "That is certainly considerate of you, Reverend, but I would not feel comfortable to accept your kind offer."

Billy tapped a firm hand on the counter. "There is not much in the way of hospitality around here, and unless you want to sleep in the mud, you'd best tell the man, 'Thank you, sir' and be on your way."

Seamus looked from face to face and then raised his hands in surrender. "I suppose it would be foolish to turn down such an offer. Especially the cleaning up part." The truth was, he had an instant rapport with this Brother Chuck, and the idea of being out of the cold and sleeping on a mattress sounded as good as the stew he just enjoyed. Perhaps he was getting accustomed to accepting charity.

Within a matter of a few minutes, and following many waves and handshakes as the reverend parted from the patronage of McGilley's, Seamus, Trip, and their new hulking patriarch were walking down the lantern-lit streets of San Francisco, liberally decorated with the ribbons and wreaths of Christmas.

After a short distance into their sojourn, the man pulled up in front of a modest two-story house with the curtains drawn but candles burning brightly from within. "There it is."

"This is where you bed down?" Seamus had expected something that looked more like a church building.

"Oh? You didn't know. This is the orphanage," the reverend said with a smile. "This is where Ashlyn lives." He tilted his head. "But perhaps we should get you straightened up a bit before she sees you, huh?"

Seamus nodded blankly. They continued to walk with the reverend carrying the conversation, but Seamus couldn't help but glance back over his shoulder several times and the words echoed in his head.

This is where Ashlyn lives.

Chapter 19

CHRISTMAS EVE

 Seamus opened his eyes to an ominous golden glow emanating from the windows and shifting on the walls of the parsonage.

It couldn't have been long since he finally fell to sleep. Had he known that he would be sharing quarters with nearly a dozen of Brother Chuck's protégés, he would have preferred to sleep in the mud.

Not that he wasn't grateful for the hot shower, the comfortable bed, or the warm greeting he received from his roommates. It was just that he felt unworthy of being among so many of those who were fervent in studying their faith. He certainly was the least among them, from what he could tell.

But at this moment, all that mattered was determining why there were colors flashing in the room. There were the sounds of dismay, a shout, and then several followed louder and closer from outside, and suddenly it became clear to Seamus.

"Fire!" he shouted, and in an instant he was working to wrestle on his trousers and then tying on his boots. The other men were rising to their feet as well, but he didn't acknowledge any of their groggy inquiries.

His entire focus was on one thing, and without delay the door was open and he was hurtling down the streets, which were alive with terror and frenzy. Yet the screams of anguish, the rearing of horses, the people spilling into the roads and the passing of buckets of water—these faded in the background.

Am I too late?

Smoke rolled through the air and the brittle homes and buildings on either side of him burst to flame just as a match being struck. The smell assaulted his nostrils and walls of heat could be felt from either side of the road. He feared the entire city would burn in a matter of minutes.

Yet. There was only one building on his mind.

He was moving against the grain of the fleeing population. Mothers with children draped recklessly in their arms raced by bearing masks of horror. The aged, with canes and hobbling forward, were given no courtesy as they were shoved out of the way by those more able, and even horse-drawn carriages ripped through the pathway of tumbling pedestrians.

Up ahead, all that he feared was true, and his gut wrenched. The orphanage was fully swallowed in flames.

Out front a black woman, holding a baby in each arm, screamed for those passing by to help; yet even after trying to grab some by their arms, she was unsuccessful.

Without hesitation, Seamus ran by her and darted through the flaming door frame, and in a moment he never imagined, he came up to the very woman in his precious photograph, toting three infants in her arms.

He paused only for a second until he heard her holler, "Upstairs," and he lurched for the stairway.

Taking the steps two at a time, he probed his hands before him in a desperate attempt to fend off the hot, surging black smoke blasting down on him. Each breath now threatened to scald his throat, yet without adequate air, his head started to grow dizzy and his knees weakened.

The tragic sight of cradles on fire caused him to stumble with trepidation. Fearful of seeing tiny, shriveled black corpses, he was relieved to find the first two empty.

But tiny arms reached up from the next one and he pulled the little one up like a sack of flour, and again with the next, and he spun to see the blackened face of Ashlyn back up at the staircase and reaching toward him.

"There's one more," she shouted, taking the choking babies from his arms.

When he turned back, there was only a solid wall of flame, and the smoke had crippled him to the point of fainting. But without pause he was surging through the flames, his lungs emptied with his own shouts.

When Seamus landed, one of his feet broke through the boards and he was trapped, until he yanked his leg, feeling a shearing pain. He was blinded by the heavy black smoke and he reached out in the darkness until he felt the wood of the cradle. Frantically, his hands probed and then he felt the soft flesh of the baby and he gripped tightly.

And then they fell.

Seamus drew the tiny body into his chest as the floor collapsed beneath them and curled his body in a way where he would take the brunt of the fall . . . one he never felt.

In a haze, Seamus looked down to see his tattered and blackened shirt being removed, and when it was off, he heard gasps and the voices of men and women.

"He has been horribly burned."

Seamus felt hands on his back and fingers touching his scars, where soldiers had punished his treachery with fifty lashes.

"No. These are not from the flames."

"You are right. Those are old wounds. But he is bleeding here."

"Who is he?"

Seamus struggled to speak. "Is the baby . . . ?" The words did not seem to be his own.

Appearing before him, sliding into focus, were the beautiful, melancholy brown eyes of Ashlyn peering back at him with deep gratitude and concern. "She is safe. The little one is fine. You saved her life and the others as well."

She touched his face with tenderness, and he worried now that his wounds would be hideous to her. But if they were, Ashlyn had concealed any semblance of disgust or even pity.

"What's your name?" Her voice was as rich as her eyes.

"Seamus. Seamus Hanley."

Her gaze dove deep into his and she smiled and the sadness left her eyes. "My name is—"

"Yes. You are my Ashlyn."

She gave him an odd expression. "Pardon me?"

There were many arms that reached in, and he felt his body being lifted and carried away, pulled away from her and then a man spoke. "Let's tend to these wounds."

Chapter 20

WHAT NEWS

 "It would be wise of you to grant me a victory here and there, just to feed the delusion my opinions actually carry some influence."

Clare smiled in response at her tall, blond, bespectacled husband sitting at the other side of the small lacquered table, a candle providing the only splashes of light inside the building. Around them, the mighty presses of the *New York Daily* remained silent. Would she continue to love this man more every day?

"Truly, Clare. Of all your stubborn notions, and there have been plenty to spare, this undoubtedly is one of your worst. May I remind you, once again, you are no longer making decisions merely for yourself."

She needed no reminder of the late hour of her pregnancy and couldn't resist but to run her palm over the curvature of her midsection. The doctor had told her they were only weeks away, and with this being her first child, it could arrive at anytime.

"You are right to be concerned," Clare conceded. "But the stories were written with my own hand, and you certainly did not believe I would allow you to be here by yourself. This is your idea to be here, not mine."

"Yes. I suppose it is my own doing." He pulled a gold watch from his vest pocket. "The morning shift should be here in an hour. It won't be long now."

His expression belied his words. Clare held out her hand across the table and grabbed his. "Do you really believe they will do something?" She wondered who the faces were behind the threatening letters they had received at the newspaper.

"They will, I am afraid. The remaining question is when." Andrew pulled up the paper from the table and fanned through it before folding it back, laying it on the table before her, and pointing at a small notice. "Do you imagine it will attract a response?"

Just thinking of her brother Davin always gave her pangs of remorse and a knotting fear in her stomach. "We should have thought of this much earlier. It has been more than a month now." Where could he have gone? How could she have been so reckless with the guardianship of her little brother?

Andrew cocked his head tenderly and peered in her eyes with the soothing and reassuring look that always made her worries seem insignificant. He squeezed her hands. "He'll be fine. He will, Clare. That one is a hardheaded boy. Just like his sister."

"What does it say?" She pulled back and wiped away a tear welling in her eye with the tip of her finger.

He edged the paper closer to the light emanating from the candle's flame. "Let us see here." Andrew adjusted the glasses on his nose. "'Young boy missing. Eleven years old. Last seen at the harbor docks. Brown hair. Brown eyes. Fair complexion. Generous reward offered.' Yes. That would seem to express it well enough."

"Oh, I don't know, Andrew. I pray it will work. I do. I cannot imagine never twisting that boy's ear again." Clare glanced around the dark interior of the first floor of the newspaper building. The hulking presses, which wielded so much power, looked vulnerable as they rested in the night. Normally, they were almost always rolling. But Andrew insisted on giving his people a day off during the Sabbath on Sundays.

Just then, they heard some troublesome voices from outside. Clare met Andrew's gaze just before he blew out the candle. "Perhaps it's just the Monday crew," Clare whispered.

He reached down and pulled out his iron crowbar, which made a metallic sound as it dragged across the floor. "Please . . . Andrew. Be sensible."

He pointed his finger at her. "Now, you stay put. And I mean that, Clare."

What shadows were visible came only from the glow of the gaslights hanging from the black iron poles rising from the edges of the stone-paved streets. With the candle extinguished, they would be able to look outside the high, partially draped windows without being seen. Clare felt helpless as she watched Andrew move to the glass and strain to identify the source of the sounds.

She listened intently. No more voices. No sounds except the pounding of her heart. Clare rose from her chair slowly. Then she was relieved to see Andrew's shoulders relax, and he turned toward her and shrugged.

"They appear to be gone. Maybe they were only people passing by." He laid the crowbar on the table.

The shattering of glass exploded the evening silence, and Andrew spun around as Clare screamed so loudly it made her stomach muscles hurt. She saw in the limited light a brick sliding on the floor toward them.

Without hesitation Andrew grasped the crowbar, his face knotted in a vengeful grimace, and he moved toward the shattered window, his boots crunching on the shards scattered on the floor.

"Andrew!" She sought out anything that could serve as a weapon and grabbed the glass pitcher that had held their water.

Andrew gave the broken window a firm kick with his left boot, opening the hole wide and he lowered his head and stepped through it out of Clare's view, so she scurried behind him.

"Come out, you slithering cowards." He pounded the bar against his palm.

"Andrew . . . please."

He glared back at her. "Clare . . . for the love of heaven . . . stay where you're at."

Clare briefly considered ignoring his plea, but against her wishes and in reverence for him, she held back in the frame of the fragmented window. "Please be careful, Andrew."

"Come out from your hiding. Are you afraid of one man? Where are you?" Andrew's neck panned back and forth along the street.

"We're right here," said a voice, Irish and gruff and touched by drink. Five figures emerged from an alley and spread themselves across the other side of the road. They wore plug hats and dandified plaid jackets.

"Is that you, Braden?" There was surprise in Andrew's voice.

"It 'tis," The man stepped farther into the light, rubbing his hand across his whiskered chin.

"With all of what we have done for the Five Points, your people, and this is how you express your gratitude?"

The man almost looked chagrined as he lowered his head.

"That's all fine, Mr. Royce. But I fear the paper's taken a turn since your pappy passed, rest his soul."

"My father would be writing just as I am were he alive."

"Would he now?" Braden's voice was growing in confidence. "He would be favoring the darkies at the cost of we Irish? Your father knew how best to be selling papers in the Five Points."

"We are all exiles here, Braden. None of us are deserving better than the rest. The Africans need to earn for their families, just as the Irish and the English."

"Well, I fear we don't agree with those terms as jobs are scarce these days. Them Negroes need to be in line. And we've warned you plenty to keep the filth from your papers. There will be more than a brick coming to you."

"Then I will say to you and to any of your friends, that the ink on these presses will never be tarnished with fear. I will shut her down before allowing her to speak such lies."

"I don't believe he's hearing," said another man with a brick-bat in his hand. "Maybe his fat wife can be reasoned."

That was it for Clare. She had to respond before Andrew could lash out. She stepped through the glass so quickly, she nicked her arm. Feeling a bit foolish with the pitcher of water in her hands, she let it drop with a crash.

"That will be enough." Clare saw the violence in Andrew's eyes fading as he glanced back. "Your concerns are most duly noted." She clasped her husband's arm and could sense the rigor of his fury. "And . . . shall be properly ignored. We will write the stories as we see fit. And you, sirs, speak for no Irishmen."

"Hold there!"

A few men ran up the street toward them. She recognized them as members of their morning crew. *Thank You, Lord.* There were six of them and they stood alongside Clare and Andrew.

"What is all of this here?" said one of the newly arrived looking at the shattered glass.

Andrew stared at the five men across the street, who were now stepping back. "We were just concluding a conversation with some gentlemen who wanted to share some concerns they've had with our recent editorials."

"This hasn't ended." Braden spat to the ground. "You can listen or no. Be assured, next time we'll speak louder." With that he nodded to his men and they disappeared into the adjoining alley.

"Shall we go after them?" asked Winston, the lead pressman.

"No. There are too many who share their opinion. The presses will continue to serve as our cannons." Andrew's face cheered. "But we're certainly glad to see you arriving early for your shift." He patted them on the shoulders and shook their hands.

"Well, if that cheers you . . ." Winston looked to the others and they nodded with smiles. "We come bringing a report."

"What is it?" Andrew said. "What news?"

"It's Davin."

"What of Davin?" Clare stepped forward.

"We were having a wee sip on our way to work." Winston lowered his head, his cheeks turning rosy.

"I don't care about your drinking." Clare's voice wavered with joy and apprehension. "What about Davin?"

"We met a man," Winston said. "He wouldn't tell us himself. I'm thinking maybe he wants to be certain he'll be rewarded proper."

"Yes . . . yes. What is it?" Was it good news or bad? Clare's knees began to shake.

Winston nodded. "The man. He knows where Davin is."

Chapter 21

THE MAN WHO KNEW

As Clare entered through the hinged doors of the tavern, she shuddered at how comfortable she had grown in these surroundings. Although she had never enjoyed the pungent smell of spilled beer and cheap tobacco smoke, it was her job as a journalist to go wherever the story was, and too often the best material could be found in dingy places just like this one.

This didn't make it any easier on Andrew. He had been pleading with her to take leave of her job at the *New York Daily* for months now, despite the fact she had become a major voice in the community and one of the key drawing points of the newspaper.

"Do you think he left?" They stood at the entrance gathering their bearings in the crowded tavern. It always surprised Clare to see how full these establishments could be so late in the evening.

The crew had explained that the man they were seeking would be sitting at the end of the bar. Clare pointed. "Let us hope it's that gentleman over there."

She moved forward, Andrew's hand on her shoulder holding her back. "What's this?"

Clare looked down and saw her arm was blotched with red from where she had cut herself on the glass.

Andrew walked her to a tall table, all of the time she kept her gaze on the man in the corner, making certain he didn't slip away. "This will take just a moment," Andrew said. He lifted a glass of what appeared to be bourbon and put it on a handkerchief he pulled from his pocket, then dabbed the fluid on her arm. She jumped with the pain but then observed with affection as he lovingly cleared away all of the blood.

"It is not much of a cut after all, now that I've cleaned it out for you. Just bled out some. But it has ceased now."

"And now I smell like a drunk," Clare said.

"Are you ready for this?" He raised his eyebrows.

She wasn't. All they knew so far was this man claimed to know where Davin was. He made no indication of whether her brother was dead or alive. And even if he was alive, Manhattan was a cruel city to be swallowed by the streets. Clare had interviewed many dirty politicians, thieves, and dangerous people, but none on a subject so personal to her. She exhaled a deep breath and nodded to her husband.

The two of them winded their way through those engaged in evening pleasures and vices and came up to the back of the solo figure at the end of the bar. He was crouched over and nervously clinging to his glass, seemingly content to be in the darkest place in the room.

Something struck against Clare's sensibilities. This didn't seem like the type of character she would even want to know the whereabouts of her little brother.

Andrew tapped on the man's shoulder and he was startled, holding up an arm as if he feared he would be struck.

Then he turned, and Clare stumbled back in horror. There glaring at her was a face she recognized, with his unmistakable yellow-toothed grin, wrinkled forehead, and darting eyes.

Uncle Tomas. The man known as Patrick Feagles.

"What is the meaning of this?" Clare put her hand to her mouth.

"Shhh . . . shhh. Don't draw attention." Uncle Tomas threw a few coins on the counter and then nodded for them to follow out a side door of the brick building. When they hesitated he held up a torn-out section of the *New York Daily*, which had the notice seeking help in finding Davin. "Follow me."

"Let me go alone," Andrew said.

It frustrated Clare sometimes when her husband would even bother to say such things. No one despised her uncle more than Clare. The memories of his evils swept back: the betrayal of his sister, the theft of her family's money, and the events that caused her brother Seamus to flee the city and enlist in the army. These were all traced to the man leading them into the alleyway. And now he knew something of Davin? No. She most certainly would not be left out of this conversation.

"I thought he was supposed to be in prison," she whispered as they trailed behind.

"That was my understanding as well."

When they stepped down onto the dirt pathway between two tall buildings, the smell of vomit and urine pervaded. If not for a flickering gas lamp at the entranceway to the main road, they would have had no light at all.

"First, I know what the very sight of me does to the two of you. Believe me this, I have had enough time behind walls and in heavy irons to have long questioned the burden of my existence. Prison is a ghastly mirror to the soul and I faced such darkness."

"Enough of this." Andrew's voice came through clenched teeth. "Are you here to mock us, or do you indeed have knowledge about young Davin?"

Tomas lowered his shoulders and lifted tired and life-worn eyes. "I realize I am undeserving of any manners for what I put you through, but I must beg you lend me your ear and soon it will come clearly enough before you. For what I am to propose—"

"We are not welcoming any proposals from you," Clare said.

He sighed and lowered his brows. "I know this, dear. If there was a path to forgiveness, I would crawl—"

"There is not." Clare crossed her arms. She was growing weary of the conversation.

Uncle Tomas looked injured by her posture. His voice softened to a whisper. "Yes. Dear Clare. I suppose you're right. Then at least you might find the mercy to hear a few words from a dying man." He glanced up. "No. It doesn't matter to you." He coughed, and there was a deep rattling in his lungs.

Clare remained stern. "What news, if any, do you have of Davin?"

"Yes. About Davin. Yes." He held up the paper. "What joy for these old eyes to read this, I must say. Not that the boy was missing, of course, what horrible news. But that his uncle, after such a miserable life, might be granted in the last of his days to finally do some good."

"What are you saying?" Clare sensed he was speaking truthfully, but he had fooled her many times before.

"Yes. To the point, Tomas. To the point. Before being released, on account of mercy for my faltering health, I met a man who was in the cell beside me ever so briefly."

"Well? What did he say?" Andrew's patience was wearing, and Clare put her arm on his.

"Let him speak, Andrew."

Her uncle's eyes were alive with the story. "So he tells me of a night of hard drinking, one which he said he was no stranger to. But on this evening, he found himself waking to be out to sea. Shanghaied, he was. As were several others . . . and there was a boy."

"Was it Davin?" Clare asked.

Andrew gripped him by the collar. "What ship was it, old man?"

Her uncle's frightened eyes looked to Clare for rescue.

"Please, Andrew. Let him tell the story."

He let go of his grip and backed down. "I don't trust a single word coming from his lips and neither should you."

"Was it Davin?" Clare pressed.

Uncle Tomas straightened his collar and turned his neck back and forth. "That was the name of the boy, yes. He fits the description."

"Then Davin is here now and the ship has returned?"

"No." Tomas adjusted his hat. "That was it. My informant told me he had escaped two days into the trip when another ship came close enough for him to seek refuge."

"Where? Where was the ship heading?"

"That knowledge, I'm afraid would spoil penitence."

"You are not going to tell us?" Clare's voice tinged with anger.

"I will do much better. I will go myself and bring the boy back safely."

"We'll pay you," Clare said. "How much do you want? Just tell us."

"There are many people who would do me harm. It is no longer safe for me in the Five Points. I do want to be paid. By passage out of this town, for my life depends on it."

His story didn't make sense to Clare. "Then why would you come back?"

"I don't fear dying here," Tomas said. "I just want a little taste of redemption before I die. The boy will give that to me. I know you'll forgive me, Clare, when I have the boy at my side. I know you will."

"Shall I beat it out of this vile creature?" Andrew rolled up his sleeves.

Uncle Tomas gritted his teeth. "There is no pain for me now I can't tolerate. Not after what I've endured. Except for those screams in my heart. The guilt is real pain. This is my chance for it to go away. That's my offer to you. Enough for passage and I'll bring young Davin home to you. I am the only one who can help the boy now." He glared at Andrew. "And I'm no use to anyone dead."

Clare's emotions were in shambles. Hope flowed through her in the chance her brother was alive and that she might see him again. But Uncle Tomas? What a cruel twist to her fortune. Was there any other way?

"I'll buy you your passage." Andrew managed his tone.

Tomas grinned. "Clever man, you are. No. You won't know the ship I sail. I'll buy me own passage. I may be going north. I may head south. A hundred dollars will cover my ticket and provisions."

"It will cover much more than that." Andrew's anger returned.

"Why won't you just tell us?" Clare's voice cracked with tears. "Can you just do us that one act of kindness?"

Her uncle's eyes glistened as well. "It's God will for me, Clare. I know it 'tis." Tomas turned to Andrew. "I'll give you one hour. Return with the money and I'll get the boy. I'll even send a telegraph when I first find him. But if an hour passes and you haven't returned, you'll never hear from me again.

"One hour."

Clare heard the front door of the house open and then the sound of Andrew greeting their much-anticipated guest. She waited in the sitting room, biting on her fingernails.

Jack Turley came around the corner with her husband just behind. This was Andrew's best man when they had difficult assignments at the newspaper. As a longtime policeman he could dig up just about anything on anybody, and he was fearless in the pursuit.

But as he entered the room with his hat off and his coat slung over his arm, she could already see the disappointment in his eyes.

"How did you lose him?" Clare crossed her arms in anger.

"I don't know what to say, Mrs. Royce, other than he slipped me good. The way I figure it, he could be going through the Cape, to Cuba, China, England, or Canada. There's no way of knowing. I'm not even sure he got on a ship."

"Well, then what *do* you know, Jack?" She didn't care for the manner of her own voice, but she felt miserably uncomfortable with the pregnancy this morning, was short on patience and in no mood for ill tidings.

"I did check on his story. He definitely got released that day. But there were about twenty men who could have been the sailors in his story, and most of them are lost in the wind. Can't tell you he's telling the truth. But can't say he isn't neither."

"We appreciate your efforts, Jack." Andrew waved him to the table. "Can we offer you a cup of tea?"

"No. I'll be on my way."

Clare was disappointed with Andrew's hospitality and was grateful when their guest declined.

Jack put his hat on his head. "Oh yes. There is one more thing."

Clare's attention perked. "Yes. What is it?"

"We spoke to a preacher. One who visits every week."

"Go ahead," Andrew prompted.

"He was quite emphatic about it. The preacher says your uncle made peace with God."

Clare turned to the garden and spotted a butterfly fluttering from flower to flower. The thought of ever forgiving her uncle seemed such a foreign idea to her. She knew she was supposed to have a forgiving heart, but surely her uncle was an exception, after he had taken so much away from her and her family with his cunning and his lies.

There was one thing for which she could pray. *Lord. Take care of sweet Davin.*

Chapter 22

LA CUNA

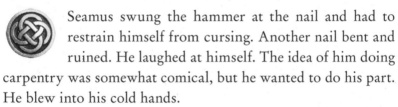Seamus swung the hammer at the nail and had to restrain himself from cursing. Another nail bent and ruined. He laughed at himself. The idea of him doing carpentry was somewhat comical, but he wanted to do his part. He blew into his cold hands.

Fortunately he wasn't alone in the task of rebuilding Ashlyn's little orphanage, La Cuna. The reverend had seen to it that all of the Brothers of the Parsonage took this as their mission, and Brother Chuck himself raised the funds for all of the materials necessary for the project.

Seamus spotted Ashlyn and Annie carrying a large basket between them, and after a few hoots the brothers were all climbing down from their ladders and greeting the ladies.

"What have you brought for us?" one asked.

"Hopefully some sunshine and heat," another said.

Annie reared with the basket with the glare of a mother looking to rap some knuckles, but Ashlyn merely giggled. "I hope you all find the sandwiches to your liking." The basket had hardly been set down before the hands of the men jousted for their meal. Then one of them reminded them all to first offer a prayer of thanks. No sooner had the "Amen" arrived, and they were playfully shoving one another again.

Seamus crossed his arms and waited patiently for his turn and was thrilled when Ashlyn approached him. She wore a long, green dress with a black wool petticoat and her brown curls had been carefully pulled up and tucked beneath her feathered hat. It appeared as if she had dressed up for this visit.

"Is it wise for you to be out here?" Her delicate brows were knit with concern.

"Where else would I be if not hammering my thumbs?"

She smirked. "It is not your thumbs we have been so worried about. May I see them?" Ashlyn asked in a way that was more demand than question.

Seamus shrugged and took off his jacket and then his shirt, which drew a few stray glances from the other brothers. It was a frigid day in January, and the sea-heavy winds made it even more biting. But what gave him shivers was when she traced the marks on his chest with her slender fingers. There was innocence in her touch, but it made him twinge nonetheless.

"The burns are healing well."

He nodded and put his shirt on again. Seamus knew she had been curious about the scars on his back for weeks, but he wouldn't make it easy for her to ask. He wasn't ready for that conversation. "Anyone watching my children?"

"Oh, they are yours now?" She smiled warmly. "They are with Priscilla and sleeping for the moment, although those moments like many sweet things in life never last. Annie and I should not tarry too long."

"How are your accommodations suiting you?"

Ashlyn grinned. "They are suiting us quite well, but I am certain the good reverend is using it as strategy to hasten the brothers in their work."

"Oh, 'tis a proper plan for you to use the parsonage for the orphanage until we get your home built up again."

She lifted the basket and opened it so he could pull out a sandwich for himself. "Yes, but the very thought of all of you living in tents in Dublin Town is making us feel terribly guilty."

Seamus took a large bite out of the sandwich.

"Nothing too fancy." She blushed. "Just boiled ham and some mustard."

"It tastes mighty fine." He rubbed the corner of his mouth with the back of his hand. "Dublin Town is not so bad, after all it reminds me of home."

"Ah. Is that where you were?" She lowered her head. "In Ireland before you came here to San Francisco?"

He knew she was looking for more than he was willing to offer. But he had many questions for her as well. "I was in the high country. Colorado. A trapper, although not a very handy one."

She looked up to him with her melting brown eyes. "Is that why you came out here, Seamus Hanley? Was it to find gold?"

He smiled. "You could say that in a way is true." Seamus took another bite and there was an awkward moment of silence between them.

Ashlyn glanced over to the house. "How long?"

"She should be ready for paint in about a week's passing, and I s'pose ready for your return in about two."

"Hmmm. That will be wonderful."

Seamus noticed a man leaning against a lamppost down the street, and he was looking right in their direction. "Is someone waiting for you over there?"

Ashlyn turned her head, and her eyes widened for a moment before she recovered. "Yes. He is . . . someone I was not expecting to see."

"Everything all right?"

"Yes. Yes, of course. He is a family friend." The sadness returned to her eyes, the same ones that enraptured him in the portrait he so cherished.

"Ashlyn." He wondered if it was improper to be so forthright, but when he saw the way she looked at him, he grew in courage. "If you need anything. *Anything*. Please ask it of me."

At first she seemed troubled by what he said, but then she smiled and looked down. Then she met his gaze. "Who are you, Seamus?"

The directness of her inquiry jarred him, but then he smiled back at her. "I'll let you know as soon as I discover a good answer to that question."

Ashlyn glanced nervously back to the man watching them and then back to Seamus. She lifted her basket. "I must go."

He watched as Ashlyn hurriedly went to the lamppost, and he did not turn away even when the stranger gave him a darting glance.

Seamus was intrigued by this woman. Ashlyn was a mystery he was determined to solve.

Chapter 23

THE PARSONAGE

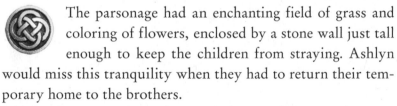 The parsonage had an enchanting field of grass and coloring of flowers, enclosed by a stone wall just tall enough to keep the children from straying. Ashlyn would miss this tranquility when they had to return their temporary home to the brothers.

She swung gently in the porch swing, alternating between the joy of seeing the toddlers at play on this sunny day and troubled by the reason she hadn't visited La Cuna to check on the progress. The front door opened and Annie came out with a tray of cookies she set on the glass table beside her.

"What time is it, Annie?"

"Oh's, I's say it's five minutes later than the last time you asked."

"Am I that nervous?"

"More. Missus Esmeralda's always behind."

"Yes. I suppose you are right. It's just—"

"I's know. 'Cause you says it five times just today alone."

"These cookies look lovely, Annie. Can we send some to the boys?"

Annie tied the back of her apron and looked down at Ashlyn. "'Course, you could bring them yourselves. It's been a week since."

Had it been a week already? This embarrassed Ashlyn. She would have to resolve her conflict soon. It was on the sharp point of rudeness that she hadn't visited there to encourage the brothers.

"That boy won't bite you."

There were never any secrets from Annie. "It is not *just* about Seamus."

"No harms in just walking by and sharing your graces. You know I ain't care none for your soldier neverways."

"Annie!" Ashlyn waved her fan, even though it wasn't hot enough to merit the effort. "Do you have no shame? Did we not just hear that he turned captain? Here he is at risk for the benefit of our country, not to mention—"

"Well. He could raise a pen and write you, dear. That Irish boy takes to you just fine, and no harm in that. And I say he isn't hard for looking at none."

He was handsome indeed, tall and strong. Even with the scar on his face and the strange markings on his back, Seamus was striking in appearance and his sapphire eyes were unlike any she had seen. More than this, there was something about his character, his courage and his humility, that was drawing her toward him. But how wrong this was! What would Mama think in light of all Ashlyn had been through?

Ashlyn's gaze drifted to where Gracie was digging with a shovel in the grass. She had grown so much it seemed in just the last few months. How she adored that child.

Ashlyn spotted a tall, flowered hat bobbing above the stone

wall and then the gate opened and in came Esmeralda, dressed in a white dress, delightful against her olive skin, and the woman's face brightened with a smile. In her hands she carried a large basket filled to the brim with fruits and breads.

Annie ran out to her and removed the basket from her hands. Ashlyn stepped up and straightened out her dress.

Esmeralda greeted Ashlyn with a kiss on each cheek, and then she motioned for both of them to sit on the swing. Then she gave the ground a push with her shoes and they were swaying softly. Esmeralda closed her eyes. "*Qué esta día bonita. ¿Sí?* What a pretty day."

Ashlyn felt her blood pumping in her body. What was she so nervous about? The worst that could happen was Esmeralda could say no.

"The priest. He nice man, yes?"

"Oh yes. We cannot thank him enough for his kindness in letting us stay here until La Cuna is back up again. And the brothers have been most helpful."

"*Sí.* And the new brother?" Esmeralda cast a curious eye toward Ashlyn.

Ashlyn bit her lips and tried to keep from revealing anything.

"So handsome, no?"

Ashlyn shot a suspicious glance at Annie. "Well, he does have that scar on his face."

Esmeralda braked with her feet on the ground, and she touched the side of her face. "That just makes the pretty boy a rugged man, no?"

"Yes." Ashlyn sighed. She handed the plate of cookies to Esmeralda, who took her time deliberating which to choose.

"The *niños*? They are good?"

"Yes. The children are fine. Well. Seemed to be fine, after the fire and all of this. However, now that you mention this—"

Esmeralda held up her slender brown hand. "I already ask Felipe about this."

"About?"

Annie's eyes opened wide. "I may have says something when I see the missus at the market. About us being short on food."

Esmeralda frowned. "Felipe, I am afraid. He is . . . how do you say? Concerned, yes?"

Ashlyn swallowed. "About?"

The Mexican woman looked up to Annie.

"Oh, I's go inside." The black woman scurried away, seeming happy to flee the scene.

When the door shut, Esmeralda grasped Ashlyn by the arm, and fear churned Ashlyn's stomach. "What is it, Mrs. Santiago? Speak plainly."

"Felipe say *hay problemas.* I mean, there are troubles with money he sent the last time."

"I don't . . . understand." The blood rushed from Ashlyn's head.

Compassion came over Esmeralda's face. "Is good, I am sure. He just say he wait to talk to your father. He come home soon, *sí*?"

"Yes." Ashlyn could hardly breathe. What problems?

The latch on the gate sounded and the door opened once again and it was . . . Seamus! And with him was his little dog, which immediately hobbled toward the children.

"Trip!" Seamus looked up with embarrassment and then ran after the dog, which made sport of making a retreat. The children laughed and joined in the mad chase.

Esmeralda laughed too and covered her mouth, then looked to Ashlyn, who tried to match her mirth but couldn't. She was too bothered by what the woman had said about the money they donated.

Yet even her worries were no match for the sight of the

Irishman chasing after the broken pooch being pursued by three giggling toddlers. Yes. He was handsome. And he had an extraordinary gift of serving as a distraction from her troubles.

It would be wrong if she was to pursue him. But if he was to pursue her? Would that change anything?

Esmeralda leaned in to Ashlyn and whispered in her ear, "I like the boy. I am happy for you."

Warmth rose on Ashlyn's cheeks. "Oh no. He is just a helper with the house."

"*Sí*, we all need a helper." The woman held both of Ashlyn's hands. "I must go. Do not worry. I bring some food. For the *niños*. When Felipe talk to your father, all will be fine. *Todos*."

Seamus seemed content that the dog had settled down and the children could pet him. He took off his hat and brushed his hair with his hand. "Ladies, would you do me the kindness of forgiving such a peculiar entrance. I only thought the children may have missed Trip. Well, at least Trip seemed to be missing them. You know how it is when somebody misses someone, do you not?"

Esmeralda held out her hand to Seamus and shook it. Then she looked toward Ashlyn. "*Sí*. The lady knows this well." Then she walked away, waved daintily to the children, and closed the gate behind her.

"Really, I am truly sorry," Seamus said. "It's just I thought . . ." He paused for a moment. "It's just you had not come by for a week. I was concerned about you. Am I interrupting your day?"

"As a matter of fact, I was in the middle of enjoying this most lovely porch swing. I have discovered it swings much truer when two are sitting upon it."

"That? Yes, it is a lovely swing." Seamus stood there awkwardly.

A voice came from inside. "Sit with her already."

Ashlyn spun around to see Annie's face pressed up against the window. She turned back to Seamus and the two of them laughed heartily.

Then he joined her on the bench, and they swung for a while until he put his arm around her, and she reveled at his gentle touch.

For at least this evening, Ashlyn forgot about all of her problems.

Chapter 24

DUBLIN TOWN

The rebuilding of La Cuna was nearing an end, but so too was the patience of the brothers.

It was a slow walk back to camp for the reverend's men because they needed to carry all of their tools. One thing about living in a vibrant port city where every material good was grossly overpriced was that thievery abounded. If they didn't bring their equipment back with them, it wouldn't be there in the morning when they returned.

When they arrived at Dublin Town, which was less a village and more a hastily constructed slum, Seamus could hear the murmuring of the brothers. Not all of them were as enthusiastic about trading their comfortable hostelry in the parsonage for what was essentially living in the outdoors.

For Seamus, he was grateful enough to have a tent for cover and blankets to keep him warm. After his arduous travels across the rugged western territory, this remained luxury to him.

He had not time to spoil himself with living in the parsonage because he had yet to enjoy a full night's sleep there.

Besides, he was comforted to hear the brogues of his fellow Irishmen of Dublin Town and to listen in on stories of back home, familiar tales of longing for family and life on the farm, lost fortunes and broken hearts.

What you didn't see in Dublin Town were women, at least those who weren't for hire, and even those shady ladies were reluctant to wander through the menagerie of tents, campfires, mud- and whiskey-drenched miners. For harsh was a community where most of its citizenry stayed only as long as it took to get off the ship, provision up, and head for the hills.

Which is why Seamus was so stunned when he arrived at the brothers' circle of tents to see Ashlyn standing there in conversation with Reverend Chambers.

"Well, will you look at all this good cheer as these boys return to their castles." The reverend laughed. "Have you ever seen a happier lot?"

His comments were met with a few begrudging smiles as most of the brothers lifted the flaps of their tents and retired inside with groans.

"Seamus," said the reverend, "our dear Ashlyn here was concerned with the living conditions of the boys while they are staying at the temporary parsonage."

"It's just dreadful." Ashlyn grimaced as she looked around. "How will we ever forgive ourselves for displacing all of you here?"

Seamus shrugged. "Actually, it's a wee bit like home. Back in Ireland."

Her face flushed. "Certainly I had no intentions of being insensitive. It's just—"

"I know what you meant, Ashlyn." He smiled, overjoyed in seeing her.

The reverend patted his broad hand on Seamus's shoulder. "Proof there for you, Ashlyn. It will be a sad day for these men when they're asked to tear down their tents." He turned to Seamus. "Son, would you be kind enough to escort the lady back to the parsonage? I was heading off in the other direction."

"That's not necessary—" she began to say, but her eyes betrayed that she didn't mean it.

"Of course, Reverend Chambers. It would bring me considerable pleasure."

"I thought as much." The reverend buttoned his jacket. "Well, off I go to see about a widow and her bedridden cat."

The reverend bade farewell and Seamus went to set his belongings in his tent. Brother Peter, who was sharing his tent, was reclining on some blankets and feeding Trip some type of beef strips.

Seamus dusted and patted his clothes and combed his hair as quickly as possible.

"You look so purty," Peter said, and he pursed his lips.

Dismissing the taunt with a tilt of his head, Seamus put on his cap, exhaled, and stepped outside. He had to skip to avoid landing in a muddy puddle and stumbled, but then carried through the motion into a deep bow as if he had intended it all along.

Ashlyn giggled, but then tried to appear serious. "Are you all right?"

"That, my dear, was an Irish salutation, passed down through many generations of Hanleys."

"I see." Ashlyn held out her arm, which Seamus accepted and then escorted her through the ragged maze of canvas hovels, twine-hung clothing, and curious, whiskered faces.

Seamus heard music playing and decided to see if Ashlyn was up for a short diversion.

"Could we give her a listen?"

Ashlyn bent her lip. "Oh, I suppose it will be fine. I can keep Annie waiting a little longer. After all this was her idea."

"Oh. The . . . camp inspection?" Seamus smiled broadly.

Ashlyn laughed and covered her mouth with her white glove. "Maybe."

They rounded the bend where a crowd gathered around three scraggly musicians sitting on oak barrels: a fiddler, a tin flautist, and a hand drummer. Near them was a large canister spewing flames.

The spunky tune had nearly all of the crowd tapping their feet or clapping their hands, and a few of the men danced in vibrant jigs to the delight of the onlookers. A line was formed as well leading up to a large kettle, where a bald man with the ash of his cigar threatening to fall in scooped out generous portions of some type of stew to any who extended a cup.

"Is this some type of celebration?" Ashlyn's eyes were wide open.

"Yes. We call it sunset."

"They do this. All of this every night?"

"They do." Seamus nodded to a muscular man across the way, one he had lost a close arm-wrestling contest to the night before. "The location changes, as do the musicians and who's willing to share grub, but yes, this is Dublin Town."

When the song ended, the bodhran player, who also did the singing, turned to Ashlyn.

"And what would the lady, the only lady I might add, wish for us to perform?"

"There's another lady here as well," an angry voice said, and this brought derisive laughter and cheers. It was one of a small group of working girls who had just made their way to the scene.

The hand drummer kept his gaze on Ashlyn. "Well, dear?"

"She's not from our parts, I'm afraid—" began Seamus.

Ashlyn held up her white glove. "I would be honored if the musicians would play for me 'The Green of My Tears.'"

Applause broke out as well as a few cheers and hoots. Then the music began, somber and slow. Seamus placed his arm behind his back, bent down, and extended his other out to Ashlyn who nodded and placed her delicate hand in his and they moved to an open space.

As they danced, slow and swaying, others joined as well, some with the painted ladies and other men with each other as they most likely imagined with sadness they were in the embrace of their loves back home.

Seamus rested his palm on the back of Ashlyn's shoulder and felt as if he was holding his dreams in his hand, and his pulse quickened. He leaned into her ear. "How did you know this Irish melody?"

"My grandmother on my mother's side is from Leitrim."

"Is that so?" What other surprises would this woman have for him?

"Grammy would rock in her chair on the porch, peering across fields lit up with fireflies, and she would hum these songs to the evening skies."

Then there was no more questions, no more conversation, just the silent enjoining of their hearts, and he reveled in the sensation of Ashlyn surrendering into his arms. Seamus closed his eyes and wished this moment could last forever.

But even though the band agreed to play the song twice at his urging, when the second version ended, Ashlyn whispered those painful words, "I need to go."

He walked with her as slowly as he could, with her hand in his, passing the evening clatter of carriages and hurried pedestrians on the muddy streets, but all too soon, they were at the front door of the parsonage.

Ashlyn turned to him with expectation. After an awkward moment, she spoke. "Thank you, kind sir, for your accompaniment. And the dances."

He stood before her, embarrassed at how paralyzed he was at this moment. So many times he had wooed girls back in Ireland, but now he was terrified. Perhaps it was because it was never with one who he had cared for so deeply.

Finally, he leaned into her, but then as she bent in toward him, he pivoted and kissed her on her cheek. When he looked at her, she was blushing. "Good night, Seamus Hanley." Then she opened the door and went inside.

As he moved down the stone paved walkway out to the iron gate out front, he struggled with himself. *Should have I kissed her on the lips? Should I have kissed her at all? What am I to do with a lady?*

He closed the gate behind and it rattled. When he turned, he was face-to-face with the strange man who had caused Ashlyn distress the other day. He was in his early twenties, unshaven, wearing overalls and a black bowler hat.

"Did I scare you some? I hope you don't mind much me follering you." The man pulled a pipe with a slender stem from his mouth and blew out smoke away from Seamus.

Seamus recognized the Southern drawl as one he had heard many times from other soldiers when he was in the war. "Who are you?" His voice was shakier than he would have wanted.

"Cade. Cade Gatwood." He held out his hand, which Seamus didn't shake, and the man withdrew it slowly and placed it back into his pocket and grinned. "Yours?"

Should he tell this man anything? "Seamus."

"Enjoy your evenin'?"

Seamus had gathered himself and now was on the offensive. "What were you discussing with Ashlyn the other day? It seemed to disturb her quite a bit just to see you."

"Same as I'm about to be discussin' with you." He pulled out his pipe and flicked out a few ashes from the bowl. "Ryland."

"Who?"

"Oh. You gonna tell me you don't know Ryland?"

Seamus shrugged.

"Ash is a strange one, that girl. Liking a boy as you, and not even telling you her daddy's name?"

"We haven't known each other all that much time."

"Long enough to be acting awfully familiar."

How long had he been following them? Had this man watched as they danced? And as they kissed? "I'll ask you again," Seamus said sternly, "what is your business with her?"

The Southerner's face grew serious and he leaned forward. "Ash is practically a sister to me. Her father done raised me. I knew her from this tall."

"She didn't appear too pleased to be seeing you. That is, if you're so much like kin."

Cade's eyes narrowed. "Listen. You and me. We gonna help each other." He reached into his coat pocket and pulled out a map, although it was too dark to see details. "Ash sent me off with this. This was her daddy's diggings, she says. Only, when I go all the way to see her old man, he done already pulled up and left."

"Sounds like Ashlyn isn't too concerned with having you find her father. Why would that be?"

"That's just it. I gotta little piece of news her daddy needs to hear. Needs to hear it something badly. And Ash. She's worried about her ol' man. And she needs her daddy's gold. So we both have mutual concerns. Problem is, I don't think she trusts me much."

"You think she knows where her father is? And she isn't telling you?"

Cade folded the map. "And I think my new friend Seamus knows more than he says he do."

"And if Ashlyn doesn't trust you, why should I?"

Cade grabbed his suspenders and watched as a lantern-lit carriage rode by them. "Ash's in a bad way. There are things about Ash that are hard to know. And worst is, there's things she ain't know, ones I can't tell her."

"This all sounds confusing to me." Seamus was struck by the sincerity in the man's voice.

"It's quite clear, Seamus. If you love the girl, and I see in your eyes you do. No denying that. You'll help me find her daddy."

"And if I agreed to that, how would I go about helping you?"

"Ash'll tell you where her daddy is. I know she will. And when she do, and Seamus, it needs be soon, for all concerned. You be sure and let me know."

"Saying I did decide to help Ashlyn find her father. Why wouldn't I just take care of it on my own?"

Cade smiled. "Now. That's proper thinking. Don't grudge you none for it. But let's say that would disappoint me some. And you'll need a man like me who knows about Ryland and where he would tuck himself away. A map gets you only so far in them mountains."

Seamus tried to discern the man's motives. There was a danger to him, no doubt. But could he have Ashlyn's best interests in mind? "I'll do some proper thinking on it."

"You do that, Seamus. You do that well and soon. There ain't much time for thinking much." With that, he tipped his hat and crossed the street, then disappeared around a dark corner.

Seamus drifted back to Dublin Town, his mind mired in worry. How deep was this trouble Ashlyn was facing? Would he even be able to help her?

One thing was certain. Seamus had a confession to make to Ashlyn. And she deserved to hear it right away.

But did he have the courage?

Chapter 25

SECRETS WE KEEP

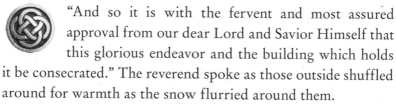"And so it is with the fervent and most assured approval from our dear Lord and Savior Himself that this glorious endeavor and the building which holds it be consecrated." The reverend spoke as those outside shuffled around for warmth as the snow flurried around them.

Annie leaned into Ashlyn and spoke loud enough for Seamus to overhear. "If the man don't stops his talkin' soon, we all gonna need funerals."

Ashlyn elbowed the woman gently.

"And without further ado . . ."—the reverend paused as this statement brought out a spate of hoots and cheers—"we present to you, the new La Cuna."

"Inside all, and quickly," Ashlyn said, and the remnant who hadn't already lost faith and gone home shuffled into the house.

The smell of fresh paint and potpourri filled the house, and set up against the walls of the small main room were a couple of tables crammed tight with hot apple cider, biscuits, fruit, and hot tea. The greatest draw was the fireplace, where most of the guests jockeyed for space to warm their hands.

There wasn't any room for people to sit, and they were not at all surprised when the guests grabbed some refreshments, shared a congratulatory comment with Ashlyn, and then were on their way. Before long, the only ones left beside Priscilla and the children were Ashlyn, Annie, Seamus, and the reverend. Soon even he was at the front door fastening his hat and preparing for the chilling walk home.

"Reverend Sanders, there are not any words to describe our indebtedness to you." Ashlyn helped the man put on his coat.

The reverend winked. "It is the people of this community who owe the debt to you, Ashlyn. Although I believe none may be more pleased than the brothers to be sleeping again in the parsonage."

"That was so kind as well for you to be sharing your home. Oh, I do hope we cleaned up after ourselves adequately."

"Well, I am certain the brothers have already undone any and all of your good efforts there." Reverend Sanders put his arm on Seamus's shoulder. "And on the subject of cleaning up, we are proud of this young man. We've had few who have progressed as fast in their studies of the Word as this one here. Why, I am sure we will have him in the pulpit before too long."

Heat rushed to Seamus's face, and he avoided Ashlyn's adoring eyes. "Ah, Reverend, you won't be getting me up on a box anytime soon. Surely, I'll be the last one you'd ever want to be telling people how to live rightly."

"There you are proving my point, son. A spirit of humility is the hardest lesson to learn and you have already mastered it well. Well, I will be on my way. You'll be joining us soon, Seamus?" His large brows bore down on him.

"Yes, sir, I will."

The door opened and the reverend departed as chilly gusts and a fluttering of snow invaded before they could close it.

Ashlyn rested her back against the door and sighed. "This may have been the longest of any of my days."

The cries of babies rang out from the back room, and she glanced over to Annie and pleaded with her eyes.

Annie waved her hands in the air. "No one seems carin' much about how longs my day be." She left the room and then poked her head back in. "This just so the twos of you have your lone time, right?"

Ashlyn pointed and Annie laughed at her own good humor and promptly disappeared.

Following Ashlyn, Seamus walked over to the white upholstered couch and they sat down. She prepared two cups of tea, pouring the water, adding milk and then sugar, stirring both with her spoon.

Silence settled between them as Seamus watched her go about her task. Then they both raised the cups of tea and sipped.

"Lovely day," Seamus said.

"Oh yes."

"Well attended."

Ashlyn nodded. "More than I thought would show."

They sipped again. Annie had been successful in quelling the babies' concerns and all that could be heard now was the crackling of the fire, the wind rattling the windows, and the ticking of the clock on the wall.

"Ashlyn?"

"Yes?"

He laughed at his own lack of courage. But then he felt his emotions rising. Was he going to cry in front of this woman?

Ashlyn must have sensed his unease because she placed her silky hand on top of his and it gave him strength.

"Ashlyn." His eyes began to water.

Her face shifted to concern and she seemed surprised but embracing of his emotion. "What is it, Seamus? You can tell me."

He squared to her and grasped both of her hands. "There is something I need to share with you. And I must warn you, it's something that brings me great shame."

Seamus thought she would pull back, but she looked steadily into his eyes. He squeezed her hands and then released them. He unbuttoned his shirt pocket, pulled out her weathered, tattered picture, and laid it on the table. He rested his chin on his clasped hands and waited.

Ashlyn's expression whitened, and she gave him a puzzled look. "Where did you . . . ?" Then she picked it up and her brows narrowed in anger.

She stood and stared into the fireplace. "Is he dead?"

"What? Oh no. I mean, I don't imagine he is. I found the letter. There was a stagecoach crash. The army courier died and I found all of the mail."

"You read my letter as well?"

He stared down at the tiny leaves floating on the top of his cup. "I did."

Ashlyn spun around. "But I don't understand."

He stood from the couch. "Nor do I, Ashlyn. Nor do I. I was alone in the mountains. Searching. Seeking. When I found your letter, I was a weak man."

"No. What I don't understand is, you came all of the way out here . . . for me?"

Seamus tried to read her. Was she furious at him? Or pleased? "You are the most beautiful woman I've ever seen. And your letter . . ."

"That wasn't the only letter," she said with sadness before her brown eyes widened. "Why are you telling me this? Why didn't you just keep it as your secret? This would seem to ruin it all."

"Yes, I know. But it wasn't settling with me to be hiding this from you. I felt it was in your rights to know. Besides . . ."

"Besides what?"

"I wanted you to know I was aware of your situation and your struggles. I was uncomfortable just standing by with all I knew, all I had learned." He stepped toward her. "Ashlyn, please. I don't want there to be any secrets between us. If there is an us, and I believe there is. I want to be there for you, to protect you. I don't want you to suffer." Tears pooled in her eyes, and he reached up to her cheek.

But Ashlyn stepped back and turned away. "This is all so sudden. I will need time to think through all of this, Seamus."

"Of course. I understand." Had he made a terrible mistake? Defeated, he picked his hat and coat off of the rack by the door and put them on. He turned one last time, but her back was still turned and her hands were on her face.

Seamus slipped away, into the gentle snowfall and the cool, cool night.

Chapter 26

THE RUN

"So Seamus, what have you to say about your time in the parsonage?" With gray clouds swirling above, Reverend Sanders ambled down the street with his arms clasped behind his back. He never seemed to be in a hurry but always had somewhere to go.

"I am indebted to you for my stay. And I cannot begin to thank you for your hospitality."

The reverend gave one of his knowing smiles to Seamus and tipped his wide-brimmed hat as two elderly ladies passed by, their parasols threatening to fly away in the wind. "Now, son, you know what I'm asking. We're not running a boardinghouse."

Seamus knew he would be asked this soon enough. "I am sorry to admit I don't share your confidence in me. I fear it is a wee bit misguided."

"So now I am misguided?" He raised a brow.

"That was phrased poorly, Reverend."

The preacher stopped at a fruit stand, picked up two apples, and handed a coin to the vendor. He tossed one of the shiny red fruits out to Seamus. "You are probably wondering what it is I see in you."

"It's been a thought of mine at times, 'tis true. Maybe all of the time."

He pulled up to a building where gold lettering spelled out *Assayer's Office* and they looked through the front glass into the building. There was a line of men carrying bags and sacks waiting for their turn on a large scale as a man with round spectacles studied each measurement with great seriousness.

"Did you know they come to this place from many nations, just for the chance to pour dust onto a scale? Two years ago you wouldn't have recognized this town. Fishing boats, some cattle, and a few lost mariners. Now there are tens of thousands and many, many more in the hills."

The reverend looked deeply into his eyes. "What about you? Do you have the fever?"

"There's a pull, certainly there is," Seamus said. "Even if some of the stories are fetched. A few months getting bit by mosquitoes does seem a fair shake for returning with your pockets full of nuggets. What about you, Reverend Sanders?"

"What would you say if I left all of this and staked a claim, maybe never to come back?"

It seemed a strange and impossible thought to Seamus. Brother Chuck abandoning his ministry and shoveling for pay dirt? "There would be an emptiness. You would be missed."

"Exactly." He bit into the apple. "I would be missed. And that, son, is the question for all of us. Would we be missed?"

"So, would I be missed?" Seamus asked with a wry smile.

"Not much. At least, not yet. And that is precisely the work we've set out with you at the parsonage."

The words rang hard. Seamus tried not to show they hurt,

but his face tightened. "'Fraid that is more work than can be had by the parsonage."

"This I would agree with, Seamus. But it's not too much work for God."

Seamus scoffed.

"You don't believe what I am saying?"

This discussion made Seamus uncomfortable. "With what I've done? Wouldn't think He'd want to lift a finger."

"Is this about the boy?"

Did he know about Kevan? The drowning? How could he?

"The Indian boy?" The reverend's brows showed kindness.

Seamus relaxed his shoulders. "That's what it is. It is some of what's troubling me. I'll never be able to repay that debt."

The reverend patted him on the shoulder with a heavy hand. "If you understand that, then you are further along than you may know."

They turned a corner in the street and up ahead a crowd was gathering, with many raising their fists and shouting.

"I believe that is Henry Parnell's bank." The reverend appeared alarmed.

They strode toward the building, with the clamoring increasing and the numbers of angry people growing. The reverend used his imposing frame to push through to the front door, and Seamus tucked in behind.

Inside, peering out through the blinds of the large shop window, from which hung a "Closed" sign, was a haggard Henry Parnell, whose spirit cheered when he saw them approaching.

The reverend reached the door and they backed down as he turned and faced the assemblage. "What's the meaning of all of this rancor?" he bellowed, cutting through chatter and summoning hushes.

"They've got our money in there and Parnell refuses to give it back," said a man waving a walking stick.

"Back off, you, I'll get in there, sure enough." A broad man wielding an ax moved forward as the crowd opened up for him.

The reverend held his ground and Seamus readied himself to take out the man.

"Now, Jonathan, you come to the church every week with your wife and children and are a man of peace and grace. But now I see you with vileness in your eyes and it's not at all flattering."

"But Reverend Sanders, everything that matters to us is in that building."

The reverend's brows raised with indignation and his voice boomed with authority. "Shame on you, Jonathan, if you believe a word of what you just said as it only proves you've brought deaf ears with you every Sunday. And not just Jonathan. All of you are behaving in such a disgraceful manner."

His gaze panned the entire group, seeking out one brave protester among them, but they all lowered their eyes and their shoulders sunk. "Now. Give me a chance to talk to Henry, who is a friend to all of us on any other day, and we will find a more orderly resolution."

The crowd backed up a few steps and the reverend turned and knocked. Henry responded by shaking his head.

The reverend turned to Jonathan and reached out his hand. "Give that to me."

Startled, the man handed over his ax.

"Henry Parnell, you will open this door or I will open it myself."

The door unlatched.

The reverend faced the crowd, then reached into his pocket and pulled out a ten dollar bill. "You all go see Billy down the street and have something to cool you down."

"Lemonade?" a woman asked.

"That would be preferable. Now go along, all of you, and I'll learn our news."

With murmuring and a slow dispersion, they made their way down the street toward McGilley's, and it was only when they were out of earshot did the reverend exhale. "Did you see my knees shaking?"

"No," Seamus said. "But I think I saw you buying the men drinks, which has my knees shaking."

"You don't think they'll drink lemonade?"

The bank door opened and a pale, sweaty Henry Parnell waved them in and then slammed the door closed. He locked down two bolts and then closed all of the blinds, leaving just the candelabra with five candles on his desk for light.

The portly man wiped his brow and sat behind his magnificent oak desk, then opened a drawer and pulled out a tin flask and a glass. "Apologies, Pastor." After pouring the amber liquid into the tumbler, he emptied it in one swoop and then motioned for the two of them to sit in the chairs facing him.

"It rippled from New York. One of the packet ships sunk and word made it here that it went down with banknotes. They are delaying our transfers by three weeks. I don't know how this became public, but once it did, they were on us, demanding their full deposits. After we gave the first few out, we had to close the bank until matters settled. And you can see what happened next."

The reverend picked up a bronze globe from the corner of the desk and balanced it in his hand. "What are you going to do, Henry?"

"But . . . I was hoping you would have an answer. We might need your . . . connections," Henry said looking upward.

"Prayer is certainly a good approach." The reverend leaned forward and placed the globe back on the desk. "How much time do you need?"

"Well . . . the ship should be here in a few weeks . . . but no one will give us that much time."

"And how much can you allow them to get? You know, enough for them to get by?"

Henry wiped the sweat off of his cheeks with his handkerchief. "There are a few of my loans I can call in. That would take a few days. For now, I suppose, if we can keep the withdrawals down to say . . . twenty dollars tops, we could make it out then."

Reverend Charles pressed his palms on the desk and rose to his feet. "I will see if I can sell it. The bank has helped build this town. It's time for the city to return the favor."

"That's all we need." Henry stood and shook the reverend's hands frenetically. "Three weeks and we'll be as solid as the treasury."

The reverend turned to replace his hat on his head. "Hopefully Billy took a little edge off of them. Seamus, would you mind keeping our friend here company, just in case somebody else pays a visit while I am . . . in negotiations?"

The bell of the door rang and Seamus locked the door, then turned to see Henry working his flask again. He held it up to Seamus.

"No thank you." Seamus walked over to the wall beside Henry's desk, where there was an older model pistol framed in a glass display box with a couple of rounds.

"That's a .44 caliber Colt Dragoon," Henry said with pride. "A gift from General Taylor. Never been fired, and never will."

Seamus gave a whistle.

"You know your pistols?" Henry leaned back in his red studded leather chair.

"This one I do. I served with a captain who had one just like it."

"Your name is Seamus, right?"

"Yes."

He waved to the chair before his desk and Seamus sat and put his hat in his lap and ran his fingers through his hair.

Henry held up his glass and peered through it. "You like her, don't you?"

"Pardon?"

"Ashlyn Whittington. She talks about you with fondness. Though you already know this?"

Seamus squirmed in his seat.

"I know. You're thinking it's none of my business. However, I am a friend of her pa's." He waved an arm around the inside of the bank. "In fact, he's been a partner of mine in this . . . and in many things. Including the mine work where he's at. Have you heard of the Appalachia Mining Company?"

"No, sir." Seamus kept his eye on the window outside. He didn't want to fall short on his scouting duties and allow them to be ambushed by any angry patrons.

"Ashlyn's father, Ryland. He and I have a long history together. We've done a lot of deals together. Some good. Others . . . not as much."

Was the bank another one of Ashlyn's concerns? "Are you saying he has something to do with . . . all of this?"

"Ryland has everything to do with this. He's our only hope, to be precise. Not only for me, but for Ashlyn as well."

Seamus's chin jutted out. "How does any of this have anything to do with Ashlyn?"

Henry rocked back in his chair and it squeaked with each move. "You, no doubt, are aware of the high regard she has in this community."

"She seems to be well thought of, yes."

"Oh, it's much more than that, Seamus. Ashlyn is revered around here. The saint of Yerba Buena. The rescuer of the downtrodden."

"I don't know if I like your tone, sir. She's that and more to me."

Henry waved a hand. "Forgive me. Yes. Of course she is, young man. To me as well." He glanced upward as if searching for the words. "It's just that reputation is such a fragile thing. It's here one day and it's gone the next."

"What are you saying, Mr. Parnell?"

"There is no ship coming in three weeks. The only ships that will save us now are those mules coming out of Ryland's claim with large sacks of pay dirt. Word is, he is doing quite well. He . . . just needs to bring us the gold."

"Why are you telling me this? The reverend is going to be back any moment now."

"I know, Seamus. I know. So listen closely." Henry sat forward in his chair. "You must convince Ashlyn to tell you where her father is."

"That seems to be a popular notion."

"This is very important. If the bank fails, why there will be many displeased customers. You've seen just a sliver of what it will look like. They'll drag me through the streets and they'll sift through the papers, and they'll know about Ryland and Ashlyn. Then I'm afraid her secret would be revealed."

Seamus leapt up. "What are you saying to me? What secret?"

Outside, the sound of approaching voices grew.

Panic returned to Mr. Parnell's eyes. "I shouldn't have said anything. Please forget I even mentioned it."

There was a knock on the front door.

"What is this secret? You will tell me."

"You can let us in. It's just me, Reverend Sanders."

Seamus clenched a fist and held it up. "I'll ask you only once again."

Henry sunk down in his chair. "Fine. But you'll be sorry you did."

The pounding grew louder.

"Go ahead."

"Sure, Ryland came out for the gold. But that wasn't the main reason."

"What was it?"

"I am going to get out that ax again." The reverend's voice was growing angry.

"Ryland needed to get Ashlyn away. From her hometown. From the shame. There was a reason why she started the orphanage. It was his idea. To disguise her indiscretion."

Seamus crossed his arms over his chest. "What are you saying? Speak plainly."

"When she boarded the ship to come out here, Ashlyn was already well with child."

Chapter 27

THE GHOST SHIPS

 Annie peered outside through the cracked door and her dark brown eyes widened. "Ashlyn. That young fellar, he comes to see you."

Seamus held a bunch of wild calla lilies and tapped his foot on the ground, glancing around to see if anyone thought he was as foolish looking as he felt. He hadn't spoken to Ashlyn since their last conversation and worried if she would ever want to see him again.

A muffled voice came from inside. "I am not in the least way presentable. And we still have baths to give. Can you thank whoever it is for the visit?"

Annie rolled her eyes and held up a finger to signal to Seamus, "just a moment." Then she spoke to Ashlyn in hushed tones, which were still easily heard. "Don't you think it'd be politer if you tells the man yourself? Specially with them flowers he brung?"

"Is it, Seamus?"

"Yes. The Irish boy."

"All right would you tell him I will join him in just a few minutes? And could you give him some sweet tea?"

The door opened wide and Annie's face appeared again. "She will—"

"Yes. Five minutes. And sweet tea would be most welcomed." Seamus sat himself down on the oak bench in the front yard and enjoyed the tailing sunshine of this unseasonably warm day as it was approaching dusk.

It was a good half hour and three glasses of sweet tea later before Ashlyn stepped out from the door, but when she did, he felt dressed like a peasant.

Ashlyn was wearing a comfortable yet exquisitely laced yellow dress, and her wondrous brown curls flowed freely and long down from her white Sunday bonnet.

He stood mute before her holding up his hand-gathered bouquet.

"Is there something wrong?" Ashlyn looked down at her dress.

"No . . . no." Seamus scrambled to reach deep in the well of his past, when he always was so confident around women. In fact, they would swoon over him. But that was many years and many hardships ago. And Ashlyn, to him, had always been different. "You . . . you look like spring has arrived early."

Ashlyn laughed and draped the hem of her dress playfully. "And I hope this is a good thing?"

"Yes. Quite so. Reminding me of fresh clovers in an Irish meadow."

She crinkled her brow. "There are bugs in the meadow."

"And butterflies."

Ashlyn held her hands up and smiled. "Would you mind terribly taking a lady to the harbor?"

"Of course. Not at all." He waved his hand for her to proceed. He noticed her shoes didn't match her dress and she must have caught him looking.

"A pretty mess, are they not?"

He was going to refute her but decided to be honest. "A strange pairing, perhaps."

She kicked up her back foot and smiled at them. "I know, but my dress shoes would only get me stuck in these muddy streets and they blister my feet."

"A practical and wise choice indeed."

They sifted through the busyness of the Barbary Coast roads, which were always bustling with the activities of street merchants and miners. As they continued forward, the smells of the bay, warm and musty, arose, as did the activity of seabirds. The traffic of carriages and pushcarts grew thicker and less patient as well.

"This is a treat for me," Ashlyn said. "Priscilla is away for a couple of days. It was kind of Annie to volunteer to watch the children alone." She grinned at Seamus. "If I am not mistaken, I might believe this is her way of lobbying on your behalf."

Seamus was surprised by her tone, because after their last conversation, he didn't know what to expect. But now he was enjoying their time together. "I was not aware I was in need of any lobbying efforts."

She chuckled. "You most certainly are."

"So, you have chosen to forgive me?"

"And what exactly was there to forgive?"

"I pinched your mail, Ashlyn. It was an awful and, I must say, a rather strange decision on my part. I carried your picture in my pocket. Look here, I still do, and it was never mine to have."

She looked over to him with a gaze of seriousness. "Did you really find my portrait that attractive?" Then she laughed and ran over to the piers, now just ahead of them.

Seamus followed, having to give way to a passing carriage before catching up with her. She had her shoes off and was walking precariously on a rail on the dock.

"You be careful up there." He offered his hand, which she received.

Behind her in the background, groaning and shifting and bending in the wind, were hundreds of marooned ships listing in the bay waters. The arguments of seagulls could be heard in the salty air as well as the boisterous braying of sea lions.

"My ship is out there, did you know that?" Ashlyn pointed far in the distance.

"Is that so?"

"The *Stella*. Yes. I believe that was the name. We left from Richmond and it took us around the cape in the wildest waters you would ever see. Thought on several occasions the ship would tilt and we would all be spilled into the seas. But nothing was as odd as watching the entire ship empty, all of them abandoning the ship and running to the mountains with the lust of gold in their eyes."

"And your father?"

Ashlyn hopped down from the rail and plopped down on an oak bench facing the waters, and he sat beside her as the skies to the west turned orange with sunset.

"Yes, my father was one of them. I believe he outran them all." The thought seemed to chase her from her whimsy and her eyes traced deep into the horizon.

"You are worried about him?"

"Who wouldn't be? Apparently he had moved his camp but did not see fit to tell his own daughter where his new site is."

"Is that unusual?"

"It is not, actually. But what is peculiar is that he has not sent any word home . . . or . . ."

"Support?"

"Yes. He is a man touched by the fever of gold. Why I remember being just a small girl when he first came back from the Appalachian Mountains with his eyes filled with madness, holding up his bag of dirt as if he were holding up the head of Goliath himself."

She laughed. "Now Mama. Mama didn't take so kindly to his . . . affliction. As a matter of fact, she tied him down good to farming for quite a few years. We grew up in the Shenandoah Valley, in beautiful country. And Daddy built himself up a large tobacco plantation. But that wasn't what was in his heart. He did all of that for Mama and me. Of course, when Mama passed a couple years ago, he was heartbroken and so lonesome. So when he heard about all of this great discovery and magical diggings in California, I wasn't going to be the one to fend him from his dreams."

It pained Seamus to think of the poor relationship he had with his own father. He never would have called his father "Daddy." It sounded so endearing and foreign to him. Could someone be friends with his own father? "You must love your pa."

"I do. Of course, he does have a pledge he made to me to keep."

"What would that be?"

"Daddy said he would take me back home after just one season in the mines. He would strike it rich enough to buy the *Stella* and hire a full crew. Oh. The promises of fools." She put her hand to her eyes, and Seamus touched her on the shoulder.

The light lingered faintly, and the masts of the abandoned ships appeared haunted, tangled silhouettes, a forest without leaves. The two of them stared silently into the emptiness.

"Do you know where he is?"

"My father?"

"Yes."

She seemed disappointed. "That is a question which seems to be on the mind of many people. Who exactly are you, Seamus?"

"Someone who cares."

"And why should I believe this? That there would be someone who would travel across the country to come into my life and solve all of my problems? Would you believe that story, Seamus Hanley?" Ashlyn stood abruptly. "I should be going home now. It is unfair of me to burden Annie much longer."

Seamus decided to take a risk. "Ashlyn. Do you believe God can place His hand in your life? And do things that would be difficult to explain?" He was surprised by these words coming out of his mouth. What was all of this time reading the Bible and discoursing with the brothers doing to him?

"Of course I do."

"Then why is it so hard for you to believe that this"—he pulled out the photograph from his pocket—"all of this, you and I, this was meant to be?"

She nodded for him to start the walk home, as she appeared to be weighing what he said. "So it sounds like the good reverend has you hooked well. Are you going to be a preacher, Seamus?"

"You can mock me all you want, but that won't change how I feel about you, how I know we were meant to be."

She skipped across the road, and Seamus picked up his pace to keep up with her. "Why won't you let me help you? Why can't you trust me? I want to be there for you. The one who lifts you up when you fall down."

Ashlyn stopped and turned. "I don't even know you, Seamus. What brought you here? And why are there scars on your back?"

"I will answer any question you have. Any. I'm not proud of where I came from and what I've gone through, but I am sure of all I'm saying to you now."

They arrived at her street corner and she paused again in

front of the gas lamp. She appeared as beautiful to him as she ever had, even with tears in her large brown eyes.

"Seamus. You don't even know about my scars."

He put his arms on her shoulders. "Ashlyn. I do. More than you know. And none of that matters to me."

"You have no idea what you are saying. How did you find out?"

"Will you let me help you?" He placed his hand on her cheek and her shoulders relaxed, then she sobbed. Seamus hugged her and rejoiced as her fears and anxiety melted into his arms.

She looked up to him as he moved her curls behind her ears. "No respectable man would ever want me. Not even my father."

"Your father hasn't left you, Ashlyn."

"How would you know?"

They held each other for quite some time. Finally, he pressed her away and held her hand. "Annie?"

Her expression flushed with guilt. "Oh, my poor Annie."

They walked the short distance to La Cuna, and as they did Seamus saw the sitting room was brightly illuminated.

"That woman. She is going to use up all of our few candles."

Together they went to the front door and Seamus wanted to give her a kiss but remembered something. "The flowers."

They had placed Ashlyn's calla lilies on the bench by the front window so they wouldn't have to carry them along. When he stepped over and reached down to retrieve them, he glanced through curtains and saw a man standing by the burning fire. He was not tall but stocky, with blond hair and was well trimmed in a United States Army officer's uniform.

Seamus froze for a moment, unsure of what to do. The soldier locked gazes with him. At first it was an odd look, one of surprise and perhaps even a bit of jealously or anger. But then it shifted to something else, one of recognition, and Seamus had to fight the temptation to flee.

When he turned back, he saw that Annie was leaning out the front door, her face stricken with dismay.

"What is it, Annie?" Ashlyn asked. "Are the children all right?"

"The babies, they's fine." She nodded over to Seamus. "There's the trouble. The captain. The captain he's here."

"What?" Ashlyn's expression was strained and conflicted. "Yes, I see. That is wonderful news." She turned to Seamus and looked sadly at the flowers.

"Captain Percy Barlow?"

"Yes," she breathed. "That would be the one."

"You don't need to say anything." Seamus felt his heart being torn from his chest. "This is good for you, Ashlyn. This is what is right." He fought with all of his strength to keep from screaming. Would God curse him again?

Shielding his disappointment as he walked away from Ashlyn and La Cuna, he pressed his shoulders up high. It was only a couple of blocks along the way when he realized he was still holding on to the flowers.

He tossed them into the street as a carriage approached and watched as the calla lilies were trampled in the mud by the hoofs of the horses.

Chapter 28

THE CAPTAIN

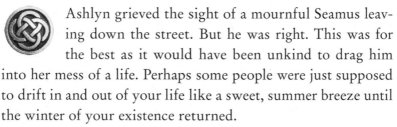 Ashlyn grieved the sight of a mournful Seamus leaving down the street. But he was right. This was for the best as it would have been unkind to drag him into her mess of a life. Perhaps some people were just supposed to drift in and out of your life like a sweet, summer breeze until the winter of your existence returned.

She straightened her dress and patted down her hair.

"Yous already look fine." Annie always knew what she was thinking. "Come in, Miss Ashlyn. Your soldier, he's gonna be s'picious of you."

Ashlyn took a deep breath and braved her entrance. She was relieved to see the sitting room empty of children and that Annie had cleaned up the usual smattering of wooden toys and toddler garments. Percy turned from the fireplace and his face warmed to a gentlemanly smile. He embraced her stiffly and gave her a firm kiss on the cheek.

Percy appeared more handsome than ever, strong and important in his dark blue double-breasted frock coat, with its two rows of seven buttons, gold-laced sleeves and shoulder boards. He stood erect with his blond tightly cropped hair and his head at a regal tilt upward.

"My dear Ashlyn, you look exquisite." He took her hands in his and stepped back to admire her. "What foolishness to leave such beauty in the window for others to admire."

She tried not to be affected by his charm, but he always seemed to disarm her.

He waved his arm for them to sit on the couch.

Ashlyn folded her dress behind her and sat down, and he nestled up closely beside her.

"Annie," he said bluntly. "Can we expect dinner soon? It was a terribly long trip."

"Oh my." Ashlyn went to stand, but Annie gave her a nod to sit back down.

"Yes sir, Mr. Barlow."

"That would be *Captain* Barlow, Annie." He glared at her.

Ashlyn sat back in the chair and gave Annie an apologetic glance, and her friend left the room. "Captain. We were certainly overjoyed to learn about your promotion. Although we had to discover this through our own channels. How precocious of you, Percy, to have moved up in rank with such haste."

He dusted off the sleeve of his coat. "I have much news to share with you. My expectations, as high as they were when I left back home, have proven to be dreadfully inadequate. I know you weren't fond of my enlistment, but I think you'll come around to the idea it was what was best for us."

"Yes. Yes, I am sure I will. Please do tell." She placed the back of her hand against the teapot, and determining it was sufficiently warm, she poured cups for the two of them.

"You know, Ashlyn." Percy lifted the cup and saucer. "Annie seemed very . . . odd when I arrived."

"Really?" She sipped from her cup. "How so?"

"She was quite . . . informal. Why I had to even ask for tea." He shook his head and lifted the cup to his lips.

"Things are different here in California, you know."

"Hmm. Yes. I suppose. In our territory as well. There is a distinctive lack of Southern sensibility in most of this savage country. Makes me long for Virginia." He set his cup and saucer on the table. "All this being true, Ashlyn, you must be more judicious with Annie. If you allow her to forget who she is, you will not be able to bring her back home. Gentility is quite fragile. Once it is broken, it can scarcely be healed."

She swallowed. "I'll keep that in mind." Ashlyn looked up from the rim of her cup to him. "I am so delighted to see you, Percy. What a wonderful surprise. Was it something you finally read in my letters that influenced this visit?"

"Now, Ashlyn. You must be aware of the responsibilities I bear when in service to my country. My reluctance to come out here was not any reflection of some fading of my affection toward you. Sometimes, dear, your imagination is much too restless."

"Yes. Perhaps." She offered to fill his cup, but he waved her off.

He reached into his shirt pocket and pulled out a small package. "Actually, there was a letter that made my visit here imperative. As it turns out, it wasn't yours, but it certainly concerns you. The both of us."

"A letter?" Ashlyn stirred sugar into her cup. "Who from?"

"Your father."

"My father?"

"Oh, believe me, dear girl, I was surprised as well. I was never entirely convinced Ryland considered me with fondness."

He put his hand on his stomach. "That was a grumble from a famished man." Percy looked toward the door to the kitchen. "I do hope that woman hurries herself."

"The pantry is a fair thin. Had we known you were coming, of course, we certainly would have made more proper arrangements."

The cry of a baby came through the door of the side room and she winced. "She might be calling for me."

"Goodness. Annie can certainly mind the children." He raised a questioning eyebrow. "By the way, what is all of this anyway? Really, Ashlyn, an orphanage?"

There was another cry from the room. She sighed. "I must see if I can help."

He shrugged. "Don't be long. There remains much to discuss."

Ashlyn wanted nothing more than to hear about her father, but without Priscilla to help out, she feared Annie might be at the end of her wick.

She entered the kitchen and discovered Annie flustered and pulling feathers from a chicken. "The bird ain't any happier than I is."

"This isn't one of our egg layers, is it?"

Annie looked up to Ashlyn with tired and frustrated eyes.

"Oh, don't mind me," Ashlyn said. "He unnerves me as well. Let me see about the children."

"No, you git with your captain. These babies ain't the trouble."

Ashlyn put her hands on her waist. "Now, Annie, you must warm up to Percy, no matter how much it pains you. Despite his unpleasantness at times, he is a man of some regard and improving standing."

"As good as he ain't standing in this here kitchen, bossin' about. Now shoo you." She flapped her hands.

"All right, then. Just . . . please Annie, hurry that dinner however you must." Ashlyn paused and then pushed the door open again. Percy had slid the teapot and cups to the edge of the table and now had a map spread out.

"What is that, Percy?" Ashlyn's mood shifted. "From my father?"

"It is." His expression glowed with pride. "This is what I wanted to show you."

"Why did he not send this to me?" Was her father that disappointed in her?

Percy handed the letter to Ashlyn, but when she reached for it, he snapped it back. "Uh, uh, uh. Let me read it to you." He seemed pleased with himself. "Some of Ryland's handwriting is most difficult to decipher, as I am sure you know, but here. Let's see. 'I hope this finds you in good health.' More pleasantries. Yes. Right here. 'These diggings are more plenteous than we ever could have imagined.' And a little later. 'I'm certain Ashlyn could use your immediate assistance in assuring that the shipment I had sent her is taken care of with great prudence. In times such as they are and with so much at stake, no one, absolutely no one, can be trusted.'"

She was taken aback. "I . . . do not understand." What shipment could this be?

"Now wait, Ashlyn. There is more here. Yes. 'I have enclosed this map and would insist you fully consider joining me without delay in this venture. The richer the claim, the more difficult it is to trust anyone, and with you being, by all practical measures, like family, I would want you to benefit from my good fortunes. Within the shortest of time, I'm certain we can all go on our way, and you will be very much rewarded for this brief diversion.'"

"This makes no sense at all." Ashlyn sat down and leaned against the back of the couch. "He says he sent us something, but we have received nothing. Are you sure this is what it says?"

Percy's countenance dropped. "Are you telling me what your father claims here is untrue?" He tossed the letter on the table. "This was a tremendous risk and sacrifice for me to come out here."

There was tingling throughout her and she tensed. Ashlyn picked up the letter and read it closely. "My father has many shortcomings, but he is no liar. If he says he sent something to us, then this is exactly what he did. Yes. This may explain things some. If he believed I had been cared for, he would not be as hasty to leave his claim. But what could have happened to this shipment he speaks of?" Her voice wavered.

"Or. Or." Percy's face began to flush with anger. "Perhaps this was more guile to bring me out here. Your father is capable of doing anything for you, Ashlyn. Anything."

"What are you saying?" Who was this man before her? Had she truly once loved him? Did she still?

He stood and grabbed the poker by the fireplace, pulled back the iron mesh, and jabbed at the glowing wood. "Nothing you would ever hear. Your ears are incapable of hearing anything contrary to your childish beliefs in that man. Well . . . here is the rub. I have an appointment with the general here in San Francisco, which is how I managed to get leave from my station. There is talk of a reassignment."

"Here?" She rose.

"Even with this being another of your father's hoaxes, there may still be some profit in this trip after all."

"I am so sorry you have traveled so far out here in vain." Ashlyn tried to rein in her emotions, which were conflicting and muddled. But there was clearly anger rising.

Percy spun around. "Oh, my dear Ashlyn. How brutish of me." He approached her and spread his arms. She entered and felt stiff in his strong embrace.

"You must forgive me." Percy slid his hand across her cheek

and beneath her curls, and she flinched. "To be able to spend even a few moments with you is worth every dreadful mile. Perhaps I am mistaken. Maybe your father meant everything he said."

Ashlyn allowed herself to settle against his chest, and he brushed her hair. His uniform was uncomfortable against her soft cheek. Would the young boy who once chased frogs in the pond with her ever return, or was this the man he would always be?

"There is one more thing to discuss." His officiousness returned. "This . . . man. The one I saw through the window."

Ashlyn worried she might be noticeably blushing. "Seamus?"

"Is he an Irishman?"

"Yes, I believe so. What is this about?" Was there something he knew about Seamus? Something she should not have missed?

"Did he have a scar on the side of his face?"

"Why are you asking?" Ashlyn lowered her gaze. Percy always was prone to jealously, but maybe he had a right to be. What kind of properly raised Southern girl would be plying the interests of two men?

"I would appreciate very much if you would just answer the questions."

"Well . . . yes, he does have a scar."

"Right here?" Percy pointed to the left side of his face.

Her anxiety elevated. "Yes. Percy, please tell me why. He is a friend of the reverend. They rebuilt this house when it burned down. You may not be aware of the fires as you have been so focused on your duties."

His gaze continued the interrogation and she could tell her every twitch, the flutter of her lids, the nervousness of her hands—they were all serving as clues.

"There is nothing to this," Ashlyn said. But there was. Was she betraying Seamus now?

Percy stepped back. "You dress as such all of the time? Annie said the two of you were enjoying a walk together. At such an hour?"

"I will not endure any more of this tone."

He gave her a contemptuous glare, but then this shifted to an amused smile. He placed his arm gently on her shoulders. "Ashlyn, my dear. It is only my concern for you that is surfacing."

"What concern?"

"Maybe I should be certain first."

"Certain about what?" Ashlyn stepped back. "What is it? You are frightening me, Percy."

He adjusted the pins on his sleeve. "I hope I am not correct in who I fear this man might be."

Ashlyn swallowed. "And what would that be?"

"It's quite possible the . . . person you came home with. He may well be a very dangerous man."

Chapter 29

SEA WINDS

 It had been a long time since Seamus had ordered a drink in any establishment, and on this evening he couldn't recall any good reasons why he ever stopped. In fact, he was desperate to see the reflection of his face in a shimmering glass of Irish whiskey.

Billy gave him a look of incredulity. "There aren't but two people I ever feared. My nana, who took pleasure in shredding my knuckles bare with a stick, and our good friend the reverend. Did you truly come here thinking I'd fix a slug of mash for you?"

"The reverend is not my father and any man is deserving of drinking what he rightly chooses."

Billy gave him a glance, which looked more than merely professional compassion. "What's bothering you, Seamus?"

"Nothing that can't be mended by a good taste of barley."

The bartender leaned forward. "Anything to do with those three over there asking questions about you?"

Seamus started to turn his head.

"Don't look," Billy chided. "What kind of trouble is it?"

"Are they soldiers?"

"Not unless Zach Taylor is enlisting boys."

"Boys?" Seamus spun around.

"Well, if you must look. Left. Far corner."

"Did you talk to them? What did they say?"

"Said everyone in Dublin Town told them to ask me. That I'd know where to find you."

Seamus raised an eyebrow at Billy.

The bartender held up his hands. "Hey, friend. I didn't betray a word about you. Forgetting is a necessary skill for my occupation."

"Well. There is no sense in letting the mystery linger." Seamus got up from the stool and headed in their direction.

"And make sure the reverend knows about me keeping your mouth dry," Billy called after him.

Wanting to make sure he wasn't wandering into more trouble, Seamus approached the three strangers with caution, glad their attention was on their meals. But as he got closer, the youngest one at their table looked strikingly familiar. Could it be? It must have been three years.

"Davin?"

The boy was drinking from his cup, and when he turned it nearly fell from his hand. He set it down brusquely, and water sloshed onto the table, but no one cared. Davin nearly leapt into his older brother's arms and began to whimper with joy.

Seamus squeezed him with all of the love he had left. Would there ever be a more perfect day to see one of his kin? "How is this possible?" With Davin's head buried in his chest, Seamus looked to the other two visitors. The tall, older gentleman was coming around to greet him as well. The other stranger with the navy hat kept busy with his food, as if he was oblivious to what was happening around him.

"Dusty's the name." The man shook hands with Seamus while Davin continued his embrace.

"How?" Seamus couldn't get over the shock of it all. "Is Clare here as well?" he said.

With the sound of his sister's name, Davin pushed back and lowered his head.

Seamus wondered what he said wrong. "What? Did you come straight from Ireland?"

Davin shook his head. "No. Clare came and brought us to New York. At least Caitlin and me."

"What about the others?"

"Ma. Pa. Ronin. They didn't make it."

The news seared through Seamus and he had to sit down. Had he failed them?

"I am sorry, Seamus. Should I have not mentioned this? I do not like you sad."

"No. It is all right. I will be fine. That is just hard news." He didn't want to spoil the moment for Davin. "But Clare? And Cait?"

"They're good. Clare got herself hitched. They live in Manhattan."

"And Clare let you come all of the way here by yourself?"

"Well." Davin put his hands in his pant pockets and looked down at his shuffling feet. "I left without permission. But on account of me finding you." He looked up and cocked his head. "She's forgiveful sometimes, isn't she, Shay?"

Seamus looked to Dusty for an explanation.

"Yeah. Crews bein' thin as they are, these boys got their gills hooked by the captain of our ship. But the boy had a mind to fetch you that couldn't be shook."

"He'll be shook all right, when his sister sees him soon." Seamus rubbed his hand over his brother's knotted and matted hair. "It's been a while all right, since she's run a brush through this."

"Clare don't brush me none now, Shay."

"Nor does anyone else it would seem."

"And what is this?" Davin pointed to the scar on Seamus's cheek.

"Oh this? Grizzly took a nip."

"Did you hear that Nelson?" Davin said to his friend, who having finished his food was standing and eyeing Seamus with apprehension.

"Or maybe it was a mountain lion." Seamus rubbed his scar, which was coarse with stubble. "Nah. How could I forget. A tomahawk."

Davin laughed and punched his brother in the arm. "See, Nelson? I told you. He's a right tease. You don't need to fear him at all."

Seamus held out his hand to Nelson and the boy returned with a limp grip.

"Dusty here has come for the gold. Told me once we found you, we'd be off to get him rich."

The man appeared embarrassed by Davin's words. "Aye, might see to havin' a dig or two, now that we're here close to them hills."

"It's mighty kind of you, sir, to see to my brother's safety. But I hope you understand I'll be needing to get him back to his sister as soon as we can."

"But Dusty says we can pick 'em like mushrooms." Davin's brows were knit in rebellion.

The man put his hand on Davin's shoulder, seemingly disappointed by hearing this as well. "Now, laddie, you best be respectin' what your brother is saying."

Seamus eyes were drawn to the front door, where there appeared to be some type of commotion. Was that Annie at the entrance?

"Boys. I will be back in a tad."

"What is it, Shay?" Davin seemed concerned his brother was leaving them already.

Seamus ignored this and moved through the tavern with growing intensity as he saw the black woman being muscled. He arrived there just as Billy was showing up with a brickbat in his hand.

"What's the scuffle?" Billy asked.

A crusty miner with an ear missing scowled. "We're just s'plaining she's got herself in the wrong place."

"Maybe I'll have some explaining of my own for you, sir." Seamus squared up to the man, whose friend, a bald man with a wild, bushy beard and more girth than brawn, stepped forward as well.

"That's enough, boys," Billy said, "or this door will be for all of you." He turned to Annie, who seemed more furious than distraught. "What can we do for you, miss?"

She looked at Seamus. "I just need words with the gentleman."

Billy glanced at Seamus and nodded to the door. "Would you do me the favor?"

Seamus felt his fists unclenching. He was already figuring on which of the two cretins he would strike first, but his temper quickly gave way to his immediate concern. What could be so strong on Annie's mind to have her risk such an entrance?

He escorted her to the front of the tavern, allowing the hinged doors to flap behind them. Then they found a shady spot under the overhang of the building, where they would be out of earshot of those passing by.

"Mr. Seamus. I's sorry to be a bother. The reverend tells me you is here."

Seamus laughed. "He's got fine instincts, don't he? What is it, Annie? What brings you?"

"'Tis good being hasty 'cause there's not much time." She reached into a bag she had strapped over her shoulder and pulled out a folded paper.

Seamus raised his brows. "What's this?" But he answered the question himself as he opened it up. "This is a map. Did the captain bring it?"

"Yes. But if Miss Ashlyn knows I gives it to you . . ." She glanced over her shoulder nervously.

"What is the map? Why are you so upset?"

"Just scared 'tis all. She's my friend. But the captain, he tries to tell the missus you is a horse thief. But I knows better."

The pains and truth of those accusations sank in, but this wasn't the time to correct her. "What does this map show Annie? Speak slowly."

"Is where Master Ryland is. Ashlyn's pappy. I draws this up from the one the captain brings. There ain't no horse thief in you, I tells her, but the captain's got her ear good."

Seamus held up the map. "What am I supposed to do with this?"

"Sees, I done a bad thing. A real bad thing, Master Seamus."

"Slow down, Annie. It will be fine. What is it you've done?"

"Miss Ashlyn. The captain. They say Ryland lies about the gold. She think her daddy just shamed to come back. But I knows. I knows, Master Seamus."

"What do you know?"

"See this man comes. A Mexican boy, I think. He drops this box to our house. Just before Christmas. Says is from Master Ryland to his Ashlyn. I want to keep a surprise for Miss Ashlyn on account of Christmas. So I hides it. Oh, I's done a bad thing."

"Christmas? Hmm. And then the fire, right?" Seamus scratched his chin. "What was in the box?"

Her eyes widened with surprise. "Hows you know I peeked?"

"Because I would have."

"Money. Dollars. And a note says something about a promise. And a star, made of wood. Master Ryland, he loves to whittle. Did it special for Christmas for Miss Ashlyn." She started to cry and put her face in her hands.

"Hey, hey, you." He reached into his pocket and pulled out a handkerchief and gave it to her. "How could you ever have known about the fire?"

"I looks hard and hard in those ashes. But . . . that was food for the babies. They all now gonna starve on account of my foolery." She looked up to him with desperation in her eyes. "You gotta find Master Ryland. He's gotta know we's broke as broke. Miss Ashlyn's too proud. And 'cause of me, she thinks he don't care for her none. Because of . . . well she thinks he's too shamed. But this is all my doing. I done messed it good."

"Didn't you say that Ashlyn's soldier brought the map? Why isn't he going after Ryland?"

"I's done told you that. He ain't trust Ryland none. Maybe he still go. But he ain't care none but for himself. Not like you, Master Seamus, the way you do for Miss Ashlyn. She is plumb thick on it, but Annie sees. Besides, you gotta leave anyways. The captain says he has pictures."

"Pictures of what?"

"I ain't seen 'em none. But he shows Ashlyn a piece of paper with your face on it, and now she says you is a horse thief."

The news was crushing to Seamus. He leaned back against the wooden walls of the building. It was certain now. Ashlyn would be lost to him forever. He opened the map and was amazed at how detailed it was, considering it was a copy.

"You did this?"

She nodded. "Miss Ashlyn, she says I is handy with the pen." Annie grabbed him firmly by the wrist. "Will you go, Master Seamus? Tell me you go."

He nodded while his mind wandered to thoughts of his love and dreams crashing. Just as the stagecoach did, the one that started this all. Perhaps having a mission would serve as the perfect distraction from such a disappointing life. Besides, he could do nothing else than think of Ashlyn. Even if she would never look upon him fondly again, he could at least ease his mind by serving her. He folded up the map and tucked it in his shirt. "Of course, Annie. You know I will."

A smile came across her entire visage and she raised a hand and closed her eyes. "Thank You, sweet Jesus."

Yes, thank You. He didn't understand it, but as strange and seemingly reckless as his life had been over the past few months, the only explanation he could find in all of the madness was that there was some purpose to it all. He would just have to let go of thinking he could orchestrate the outcome.

So he was now a horse thief on the run. A man probably despised by the woman he loved. But he drew peace in the knowledge that he now had a singular and noble purpose. He was to find Ryland Whittington. Was he indeed sitting on piles of riches? Would he be alive at all? Or had he left Ashlyn, disgusted with his daughter, as she had feared?

In an odd way, none of this mattered. The only thing that did was responding to the call.

And would the captain be in pursuit of Ryland as well? Who wouldn't want to hunt down the gold? Although Seamus didn't exactly understand why it was so important, one thing was certain. He would need to get there first.

"You should keep this conversation from Ashlyn," he said. "If she believes me to be a criminal, she won't be happy with the idea you gave me the map."

The words he just shared seemed to bring concern to Annie, and he hoped it wasn't regret he saw in her face. But she smiled and nodded. "Yous a good man, Master Seamus. Nobody gonna tell me different."

With this she crossed the road and winded her way down the street, glancing around to see if she was being noticed.

Seamus made his way back inside the tavern, and as he approached he saw his younger brother in intense conversation that cut short when they spotted him.

Davin cleared his throat. "We've been talking. The three of us. Well, maybe not Nelson so much, but we know good what's on his mind."

Dusty leaned in. "Aye, Seamus. We. The boys here. Having come so far and seeing as all the long ways I've been blabbin' me gums so much about mining—"

"Yes," Davin interjected, "you see, it wouldn't be fair to Dusty, after he's been so handy with helping us findin' you, to just leave him now—"

"I agree with you," Seamus said.

"Now listen, Seamus. Just because you're my big brother, I'm practically twelve now—" Davin cocked his head. "What did you just say?"

Seamus squeezed his brother's shoulder and looked at the boy's friends with a cheerful demeanor. "I say those Sierra Mountains are beckoning to us. There's a rich breeze in the air and she's singing to us now. What say you, boys? How about we get our fair share of gold?"

"You all wait on the street here." The gaslights shone brightly, allowing Seamus to see the two boys and Dusty nodding in agreement and happy to remove their packs from their backs.

Seamus wasn't familiar with this part of the neighborhood. This was one of the few places in the entire city where the houses were properly constructed with brick and mortar. Unsure he was at the correct house, he paused before drawing back the large iron door clapper. He rapped it three times and then backed up a step.

He admired the well-groomed landscape of the home on a hill. From here he could see the lights of the bay on the horizon. Seamus went to use the knocker again, but the door opened to a sleep-worn Henry Parnell who seemed none too pleased.

"Seamus?"

"I have news you'll want to hear. Would you let me in?"

"Yes. Please come in."

Seamus whistled to the others.

"Who are they?" Henry said, his voice laced with suspicion.

"My brudder and his two friends. They are with me."

Henry glanced around nervously. "Why don't you tell me your business here? At this late hour."

Seamus reached into his coat pocket and pulled out the map Annie had given him.

"Is that . . . ?" Henry's puffy cheeks rose.

"It 'tis. Now. Are you going to let us in? There is something I need from you."

Chapter 30

CHURNING WATERS

"We're going to ride on one of those?" Davin's mouth dropped open and his eyes widened.

"Not if we don't get aboard before she leaves." The great horn of the steamship blared in the cool March air of the busy gateway to the Sacramento River. Seamus handed the ship's mate four tickets. He tried to calculate how much of Henry's money remained in his pocket. He figured there were about eighty dollars left. As he had guessed, the banker had currency stashed away in some corner of his house.

He laughed at the thought of Henry's suffering as he reluctantly passed the dollars into Seamus's hands. Still, it wasn't difficult to get him to underwrite the trip to find Ryland. The challenge was explaining why he wasn't welcome to come along.

"What would your bank customers think if you suddenly disappeared for a few weeks? How many pieces would the bank be in when you came home?"

Seamus was surprised to see Henry still conflicted. "You do want the bank to survive, don't you?"

"Yes. Of course I do. That's nonsense. But if you don't get back to me in a couple of weeks with all that Ryland owes me, there won't be a bank anyway."

"And what exactly is it you believe he owes you?"

Henry drank down his brandy with a snap of his hand. "Something close to everything you find."

Seamus expected this to be followed by a smile or a laugh from the large man, but all he detected was desperation.

"It's serious, Seamus. Ashlyn's livelihood, her very place in this society, all depends on your great success. Then there is no room for delay." Henry set his tumbler on the marble counter top and noisily uncorked the lid to his bottle of brandy. "And how am I to be assured that you will return at all?"

It was a reasonable concern, but it still drove a stake of irritation through Seamus nonetheless. "You know as well as most."

The glugging of liquor pouring filled the air, and then Henry resealed the bottle and lifted his filled glass. "You're quite fond of her, aren't you?"

"Quite."

"Don't worry, Seamus. I will mind her for you while you're away." He raised an eyebrow and took a sip.

As Seamus now climbed aboard the deck of the steamship, these words continued to haunt him. *What did he mean by that?* There was always something about the man that unsettled him.

These worrisome thoughts were interrupted by a deep voice that could be emanating from the chest of only one man. Seamus lowered his head in defeat.

"Seamus? Have you forgotten something?"

He turned slowly, and there was the reverend with a small sack carried over his shoulder.

"Go ahead," Seamus said to the three of his companions. "I'll be on board in just a moment."

"You seem alarmed to see me." The reverend handed the canvas bag to Seamus.

"It would be foolish for me to be surprised about anything when it comes to you, Reverend Sanders. I'm beginning to believe God whispers in your ear."

"Oh, that He does." The reverend looked over to two seagulls jousting over a scrap of fish. "That and Brother Peter. He told me you are having him tend to Trip at the parsonage while you are away. He was uncertain if you were coming back."

Seamus struggled with the idea of parting with Trip, but with three working paws and failing health, it would be cruel to take the dog on the difficult trail. "If you're here to tell me I am making a mistake—"

"I am not."

"You could have sent any of the brothers with my bag, if that's all you wanted."

"No. I wanted that pleasure for myself." He crossed his arms and leaned back on the rail of the pier. "You'll find some food and fresh clothes and a few other things to comfort you." He paused for a moment. "Son, can you see how we might be concerned with you slipping out without even a good-bye? Without even gathering your belongings?"

The horn of the boat sounded again and the ship's crew were untying the mooring.

Seamus sighed. "You deserve much better, 'tis certain. I was just hoping to save you any more disappointment in me. You'll know about Seamus Hanley soon enough. Just ask Ashlyn. She'll tell you all you need to know. That doesn't take anything away from the kindness in your effort, Reverend Sanders. You're a good man. It's just some of us aren't worthy of other's hopes for them."

"Why would I ever be disappointed in you?" The reverend looked down at him with the compassion Seamus would have begged to see just once in his lifetime from his own father. How could he ever let this man down?

"Sir." The voice was abrupt. "If you're coming, it will need to be now."

"I'm sorry, Reverend. Truly I am." Seamus launched himself onto the ramp and holding the rails loosely, moved up as the boat lurched and black smoke and angry plumes of steam piled upward. He was terrified to look back as he couldn't bear to see sadness in his mentor's eyes.

He had learned all he could from the man. But as soon as the reverend, along with the rest of city, learned of his past, Seamus would never be able to return.

He couldn't bear to see the outrage in Ashlyn's eyes. Or the reverend's either.

No. Perhaps this was God's intention all along in sending him Davin and his friends. They would be able to return and deliver what was found. As for Seamus, he was better off in the wilderness. Alone. Not having to live up to anyone's expectations for him.

Seamus didn't want his brother to see him in this condition. He paused at the lacquered oak rail of the boat and braved a glance to the river's edge, which was pulling away rapidly. There he saw the tall figure of the reverend heading back toward the streets spilling into the city.

"Hello, friend."

Seamus gathered himself quickly. There standing beside him was Cade Gatwood, with his back to the guardrail and lighting up the pipe in his mouth. He appeared to revel in whatever unreserved expression of astonishment Seamus must have shown.

The man grinned mischievously and pulled the slender stem of his pipe from his mouth. "Now, Seamus, you didn't think you'd be leaving without Cade?"

Chapter 31

THE SACRAMENTO RIVER

"There won't be much sense in following us." Seamus leaned over the railing and peered out at the springtime trees on the banks of the Sacramento River, with hints of green sprouting from their branches. "We wouldn't be taking you where you're hoping to go."

"Now, Seamus, such an unkindly tone. Shouldn't we be mending things now we's partners and all?" Cade cupped his hand around a lit match and glowed up the bowl of his pipe.

"There aren't any partners from where I'm seeing things, and how I'm seeing things is all that matters." Seamus watched a couple of mallards landing, webbed feet first into the river below.

"That'd be a right shame, seeing as we're goin' about the same task." Cade tipped his hat to a couple of women who passed by, and they ignored him. "C'mon now. I done seen with these here eyes the black lady giving you the map. With mine own eyes."

Seamus thought about being coy but changed his approach. "Even if I had a map. Even if I was going to find Ryland. Why would I ever allow you to follow along?"

Cade shrugged and drew on his pipe. "Don't see really how allowing matters."

Seamus felt his blood rising. "Listen. I don't know what your business is, and it matters none to me, but you'll be wise to keep your distance."

"Why if I wasn't such a . . . gentle spirit, I might be thinking I just heard me a threat."

Seamus pointed a finger into Cade's chest. "Clear and plain, here is your threat, Cade Gatwood. I'll spare nothing to protect Ashlyn, don't you doubt that one bit."

The Southerner looked down and slowly moved Seamus's hand. "I told you, boy. That girl's like a sister to me. And her daddy? Ryland done raised me from a boy this high."

Seamus relaxed and tried to discern the truth in the man's distant gaze. "What is your business with her father?"

"I thought you had no interest in meddling? Ain't that what you just said?"

"That's your ticket," Seamus said. "You tell me all of your intentions, and if they are straight to me, I'll consider you coming along." Out of the corner of his vision, he spotted Davin alone at the end of the boat.

Cade's eyes narrowed and he stiffened. "I'll just trail ya. Ain't nothing you can say or do." He pointed to his forehead. "'Cept for to put a slug right here. And you don't strike me as having the courage." Then he grinned and nodded and turned his back on Seamus.

Seamus thought about lifting the man by his belt and tossing him overboard, but only for a moment. He retreated toward the back of the boat, his mind whirring with anger and wondering what he was going to do until he came alongside Davin and gave his brother a nudge.

"Shay!" Davin gave him a hug. Then he pointed to the massive wheel, which was thrusting loudly and creating a trail of white water far behind them. "Nelson and I've seen these boats in the Hudson. But I've never been this close."

"Where's your friends?"

"Dusty took Nelson to see if the captain would give him a tour."

"He doesn't seem to like me much. Your friend Nelson."

"Nah. That ain't it. He's just slow to warm up. You'll see."

"But I never hear him talk."

Davin gave him an odd look, as if determining whether Seamus was mocking his friend. "He says plenty to me. The way I see it, there's lots of people who use all their words and say nothing."

Seamus had always been amazed by his brother's innocent wisdom and pithiness. But it still always drew a smile. "From what I heard, they just shipped this boat all the way out from New York in pieces and parts." Even for Seamus, it was hard not to be impressed by the power generated by the spinning paddles. "Reminds me of Clare and me, coming all the way from Ireland."

The mention of their sister's name resulted in Davin displaying a pained face.

"That reminds us both, I suppose. We ought to get ourselves a letter out to Clare." He poked Davin in the arm. "We certainly don't want her angry at both of us."

Davin wrinkled his brow. "Nah, it would be all right. Clare's capable of doling it out good for the two of us."

"You are right on that one." Seamus chuckled, then a fish jumped out of the water. "Did you see that fellow hop?"

His little brother nodded, but obviously something else was brewing in his thoughts. "So, uh, Seamus. Why didn't you come home after the war? We waited and waited."

Seamus leaned over the edge and felt the mist of the water on his forehead and lifted his hat. "That's a hard question, Davin."

The boy kept his eyes on him. "Clare says you were a hero. She said you fought for the Irish."

"Hmmm. She's a good woman, your sister. I miss her so."

"So why didn't you come back to us, Shay?"

"'Cause your brudder isn't a hero of any kind." He looked to Davin and expected to see disappointment, but peering back at him was impenetrable admiration. "If I was, I would have done more for you back home."

"Clare was right." Davin squinted from the sunlight.

"What was she right about this time?"

"Clare says you had bad eyes. Because you never could see the good in yourself."

"That's what she said, huh?"

"But I see good enough for both of us."

Seamus smiled and put his arm around his brother's shoulder. "Never a truer thing has been said. From now on, you do the seeing."

They observed a pelican dip in the sky, angling up then plunging for the water.

"I'm afraid to say my nose works fine." Seamus laughed. "We got to get you a bath when we get to the city."

"Dusty says real miners don't take baths."

"Oh he does?" If on cue, Seamus saw Dusty and Nelson heading toward them. He pointed in their direction.

"Hey! Nelson. Dusty. Did you find yourselves the captain?"

"We surely did," Dusty said. "Nelson here done spun the cappy's wheel."

"Did you?" Davin's face was a celebration for his friend, who pursed his lips to hold back a smile. "Why wasn't I there?"

"That ain't the best of it, there." Dusty addressed Seamus. "What's tomorrow to you?"

Seamus shrugged and looked to Davin for help, who offered none.

"Fine Paddy you are. The both of you. Saint Patrick's Day it is."

"That's right." Seamus was embarrassed he had forgotten.

"Captain says Sacramento City teems with Paddies. Big day planned, food and dancing."

"It will be just as if we're back home," Davin said. "Nelson, can you believe it?"

Seamus hated to dampen the fervor. "I'm sorry to say, boys, but we will be just passing through."

Davin turned on him. "C'mon, Seamus."

Nelson tugged on Dusty's arm.

"We shouldn't mention it," Dusty replied.

"Mention what?" Davin glanced to Nelson. "What is it?"

Dusty gritted his teeth in apology to Seamus. "It's just the steamer races."

"They are going to have steamboat races?" Davin implored Seamus with all of his pleading charm.

Seamus gave Davin a blithe glare. "The undertaking we're on is one of earnest." But gazing from one face to the other, his resolve sank. "All right. Here is how it will be. I've got to find someone who can clear up our map. That'll give you the morning to provision up, and *if* there is time before we go, we can watch the race."

Davin hugged him and Seamus was surprised when Nelson followed suit, although not without some awkwardness.

"The boys and I'll hunt supplies. What it'll be? Shovels? Pickaxes? Burros?"

"No," Seamus said. "Just food, and maybe a few blankets."

Davin scowled. "What kind of mining is that? No shovels."

"Where we're heading, they'll already have their supplies. In fact, if all goes well, they'll already have the gold dug. We'll just be there to sack it up."

This was met with blank stares, including Dusty, who seemed the most disillusioned of all.

"That doesn't sound like we'll be real gold miners." Davin wrinkled his nose.

Seamus laughed. "Don't you worry yourselves, boys. We'll be sure to find each of you a hole of your own to dig." He happened to glance at the upper deck, and looking down on them was Cade, with his bowler hat and pipe in hand. He gave Seamus a curt nod.

A knot of concern festered in Seamus's stomach, but then an idea surfaced. Perhaps the steamboat races would provide just the distraction they would need.

Chapter 32

SAINT PATRICK

 Seamus thought he might be the only man left in Sacramento City since the only signs of life were the debris of celebration drifting across the main road like tumbleweed.

Last night they disembarked to find the whole town engulfed in unfettered revelry. It seemed everyone was anxious to get an early start on Saint Patrick's Day festivities, which rivaled those in vibrancy if not in scope of what Seamus experienced in the Five Points of Manhattan. It must have been true that every healthy lad from County Donegal to County Kerry had relocated from Ireland to dig for gold. And above this all, it appeared that the sense of isolation, the pains of loneliness, and of the ardors of the mining life would be forgotten with one licentious public exhibition.

In contrast, Seamus realized how decidedly prudish he had become. Only a few years prior, he would have been the leader of the parade and diving into the merriment with all of his being. But now, he found it all to be a bit boorish and he regretted telling the boys they could partake in any of this.

With most all at the river's shores for the steamboat race, Seamus delighted in this time of respite. The only sounds rising were the whistling of chimes, flapping of merchant signs dangling on chains, and the squeaking of weathered wood as the wind gusted through the street lined with mostly new stone structures.

Seamus sat in an oak chair at a small wrought-iron table on the porch leading out of the tacking station.

A few dogs were rummaging for food droppings left in the haste of it all. Even a few pigs grunted and snorted as they passed by Seamus.

What was taking so long?

They had chosen to spend the night in the Gold Hills Inn, which only by the good fortune of a drunken patron being thrown out for fighting with a prostitute was there a room available at all. Not only here, but in the entire city. Without tents or bedrolls yet, they needed the shelter. But this didn't keep him from fuming about the extortion-level rate they paid for the opportunity to cram the four of them in a room meant for one.

Although it set him back twenty dollars of Henry's money, it might have been worth it just for the tip he received from the hotel's proprietor. Seamus had asked him if he knew of anyone experienced and trustworthy enough to help to translate Annie's map.

"The honesty part thins the options out quite a bit." The proprietor tapped his pen. "I'd say old Ben Turney will be the best wager. Yes. Ben is your man. If he can't show you where you want to go around here, it probably doesn't exist."

"How would I go about meeting Ben?"

"Yes. That's the problem. I'll put out a word or two and see if Ben's willing."

And now, as Seamus sat at the table overlooking the abandoned streets, he worried if the plans had fallen through. After another twenty minutes, Seamus was just stepping up to leave when he saw a man with a heavy limp and tilting posture leading a burro toward him.

Please be him. The thought he had already squandered this much of the day's light was wearing on Seamus, and the arduous task of hunting his fellow travelers down yet remained. Something deep in his spirit pressed upon him that he was running short of time.

As the man came closer, he looked every bit the part of a hardened and claim battered gold miner. He was thin as a warped fence post, with a long, wiry beard.

"Are you Ben Turney?" Seamus put his hand over his brow to fend off the sun.

The man chortled out. "Depends on who's asking."

"The owner of the Gold Hill was telling me I would meet a Ben Turney here at noon."

"Then Ben I am." After getting tied to a rail, the burro's sad eyes pleaded relief from the load it was carrying, which seemed just short of tipping the poor creature over. "There's a map?"

"There is. 'Tis right here." Seamus unfolded it and ironed it out with his hands.

The man looked up to him with crooked and missing teeth. "See now. I already know you're a darn fool. Nobody knowing anything shows his hand to anybody around here. Specially a claim map."

Warmth rose to his face. "I was told you were a man to be trusted."

Ben moved his lips, like a cow chewing cud, and then spit a large wad of moist tobacco on the ground. "You know, you've got a kindly disposition to you, young feller, but out here, and especially in those mountains up there, they would just as soon slit your throat as shake your hand. Not a place for handshaking at all.

"Used to be you'd find a site, plant your stakes, and that would be respected. But there's no honor here. Those days been gone awhile. Swarming with thieves and villains. Villains and thieves. Why, if you ain't smokin' them from the hive, they'll be hiding in the bushes and skulking in the shadows, just waitin' to take what you got. Villains and thieves."

He held out a wrinkled, curled claw of fingers. "May I?" Then he took the map from Seamus's reluctant hand. "Hee . . . hee. Always git joy in the first look. Let's see. Well it's not marked too well. Not well at all." He scratched under his arm of his browned long johns. Tilting the map, he stroked his gray beard, which was stringy and hung down like icicles. "Yup. That there's Swallow Peak River. No mistaking that. Swallow Peak indeed." He dragged a cracked, soiled, and long-nailed finger along the contour of the map.

"What about that? Wouldn't think there'd be more than two specks in this part of the country. But who am I? Just someone who's dug into every piece of moist, worm-loving soil in these parts. Sure I'll get you there. For half the stake."

Seamus pulled the map back from him and folded it abruptly. "Thank you for warning me about thieves. Good day to you, sir."

"Hold it, hold it there, young man. You didn't offer up a counter. Ain't negotiating if only one's doing the talking."

Seamus looked into the eyes of the man and saw equal parts wisdom and a pleading for pity. Although Seamus hadn't dug a shovel into dirt himself, he was learning the get-rich dreams of most miners were shipwrecked on the crags of disillusion. It reminded him of what Reverend Sanders had shared outside of the assayer's office in San Francisco. They all were seeking redemption in something incapable of delivering it.

He softened his tone. "I am sorry, old man. It is not mine for bargaining. We're not here for the gold but to help someone concerned about kin."

The man scratched his cheek and squinted an eye. "Would that be a young lady?"

Seamus stammered.

"One goes by the name Ashlyn, perchance?"

"What? How did you . . . ?"

Ben chortled and swatted a mosquito on the back of his wrinkled hand. "Ryland's a bigger fool than you, that one. Yessiree, a big fool that one. But if he learns you've been flapping that map around like a piece of torn clothing hung to dry, he'd probably poke your eyes out. Yup. First eyeball and I knew it to be Ryland's site straightaway. There isn't a clip of rock or a pile of mountain cat poop I ain't stepped on 'round here. That oughta make some skittish, but it's flat true. Ryland? Fairly new round these parts, but he's real mining. One of us old timers. It's not about finding the shine, it's about the hunting. It's all we can think, breathe when it's deep in the dirt. No sooner we can hold it in our hand, and it's just dust again."

"Then you'll take us to him?" Seamus couldn't believe his turn of fortune.

"No, sir. Won't do that." He pulled out a pear from his pocket and rubbed it on his dirty shirt and then crunched a bite.

"You won't . . . I don't understand."

"I told you. Ryland's one of us."

"Then why won't you help us?"

"Oh, I'm going to help you, all righty. I only said I won't take you there." He leaned in to Seamus. "There's spies around us. Flies on a hot apple pie. Spies. Spies. Spies. That's why first I was testing you some. Figurin' your motives and all.

"Spies. That's why you ain't want me taking you. They spot Ben Turney leading you out, and it'll draw a bigger crowd than them two steamships. No. I wouldn't do that to my friend Ryland. Specially since he's on to something. On it good."

"He's done well?"

"Done well?" He slapped his leg and cackled. "He shipped out bags and bags of pay dirt by many a mule. I saw them myself. He's got some boys from South America working for him. Swears by them as well. Enough to care for the haul. But they parted in December."

"So Ryland didn't leave?"

Ben gave him a cocked eye. "You ain't been hearing well. Ryland is on it. And he's on it good. And once a digger is onto something, he ain't gonna depart until the dirt's done or they throw the dirt on him. Or snake poisons him or lion or bear tugs at his flesh."

"But is he of good health? Alive and well?"

The miner tossed the pear core to the ground. "Come to think of it, I ain't heard from Ryland for months. But they all kinda hunker down through snow season. Where he's at is hard to pass at winter. I s'pose you'll be findin' out soon enough."

Ben untied his burro. "So here it is, young man. I'm going to send one of my best with you. An Oriental fella. Trust him almost as much as this old, broken mule. He won't draw you any attention as there's a lot of Chinamen. Long ponytail. Face like it's been pecked by crows. He know these trails in the dark, which was good 'cause night is when you should go. You said you're at Gold Hills, right?"

"Yes. That's right."

"Have your people waitin' back in the alley. My boy will meet you in the lobby. I'll describe you well, and then you all can slip out back." He grabbed the burro's lead and wrapped it in his hand. "Give regards to Ryland. If he's still alive. Yup. If he's still upright. Regards to you as well, friend."

Seamus shook the man's hand and waited for him to waddle away with the burro. Then Seamus walked and then started to jog toward the river. Maybe there was still a chance he could catch the races.

Chapter 33

THE STEAMBOAT RACES

 "Have they raced already?"

A man leaning on a rifle looked back to Seamus with annoyance. "Just getting ready to."

Seamus was relieved. He had no intention this morning of even bothering to watch, but now that his plans were in place, he was able to relax some. And as Ben said, they couldn't really leave until it was dark anyway. Although the town was empty, it wouldn't keep them from bumping into travelers coming the other way down the trail.

Besides, even though he had seen many a steamship ferrying soldiers during his time in the war, he was always fascinated by the great power of the steam engines and they had changed dramatically in just the last few years. The idea of two of them racing intrigued him.

And apparently, many others as well.

His first glimpse of the riverbank was overwhelming. The entirety of the population was flocked against the shorelines, many dozen deep and for as long as he could see. It would be impossible to reconnect with the others in his party.

What he did find was the full spirit of Saint Patrick's Day. Though most had moved to elbow their way to a decent view of the race, dozens of kettles burned, skinned animals spun on open pits, kegs were flowing freely, musicians continued to pipe Irish tunes, and hundreds danced with drunken frivolity.

Intent on finding his brother and his friends, Seamus worked his way through the crowds. There were the palettes of many nations: Africans, Mexicans, South Americans, and Orientals. Although the predominant voices carried the familiar Irish brogue of his homeland, Seamus heard a variety of languages from all over the world.

Which was why in the blending of all of this mostly male humanity, the woman who approached appeared so extraordinary and so out of place. She was dark enough in skin color to be Mexican, but her facial features were European, with high cheeks and taut skin. Her hair flowed freely, brown and straight and nearly all the way to her glistening silver belt buckle. She glanced at Seamus with playful and alluring eyes.

Yet rather than being dressed in the bright, ornamental dresses of the painted ladies in town, she was dressed more as a man, with leather leggings, a red plaid shirt, spurred boots, and a black flat-brimmed hat. Most notably, she swayed with confidence and strength.

Seamus caught himself staring, then the steamship whistled, signaling the event was about to commence. He fully expected her to walk by him, as he was just another anonymous face in the thronging masses.

But she didn't. She came up to him as if she had known him for years. She warmed up a brilliant smile, white teeth against her browned skin. She nodded toward the activity in the muddy banks. "You're going to miss it all, you know. Come. Follow me."

Captivated by the moment and unable to protest, he didn't hesitate when she held out her hand to him and then proceeded to guide him toward one of the thinner patches of spectators. As she moved forward, just about every man gawked as she passed by them. They parted as the sea, and Seamus remained tucked in close behind her so they wouldn't be able to close in around her, shutting him out.

Her voice was a caricature of expectancy, so assured she was that each of her soft entreaties would be followed by the dull expressions of her mesmerized admirers, no doubt drought-stricken by the lack of a feminine presence in the mines. "Excuse me. Why thank you kindly. Pardon." In a only a few scant minutes, she had managed to navigate successfully to an unobstructed standing view at the bank of the great river.

A shot rang out and a cheer lofted from the crowd. Far away, like two small figures above the river's tide level, smoke rose from the two great boats.

She turned to him and shouted above the fray. "Well. Which is yours?"

"Mine?"

"Yes. Which of the boats? Aren't you wagered?"

The thought of gambling brought him back to his days in New York working for his uncle Tomas, handling fists full of dollars on the numbers games and fights with dogs, roosters, and men. That seemed a lifetime ago. "No. I've had my fill of gambling."

"Then root for mine, will you? The red one. The *Riviera*. Isn't that a pretty name?"

"What's your name?" Seamus felt a part of him, which he thought had died or at least gone to deep slumbers, coming back to life. He suddenly became conscious of his appearance, and when she wasn't looking, he spat on his hand and tried to wipe the dirt off of his face. He lifted his hat and brushed back his hair before removing it. But when he glanced down at his shirt and saw how filthy it was, he felt unworthy of her attention.

"You don't know?" She raised her brows. "That's probably a good thing." She held out a hand to shake and allowed their hands to linger before releasing his.

What am I doing?

"Dorrie. Dorrie Hayes."

"That's a fine name, Dorrie Hayes. It suits you well."

The shouts continued to rise all around them even though the ships were taking a while to gain their speed and hardly appeared to move.

"Thank you. My father thought so."

"They both seem as if they're painted with red. Which one is the *Riviera*?" Seamus got bumped into by a man behind him and he scowled back in return.

"The sleek one. With the smooth lines."

Seamus casually scanned the banks around him and on the other side to see if he could catch sight of his brother. Impossible. He decided to look for Nelson's captain's hat. But everything seemed blurred by the throb of the screaming, whistling, and arm-waving spectators.

Dorrie spoke, but at first he couldn't hear what she was saying and he shrugged. She leaned into his ear, her hair brushing his cheek. "Isn't this exciting?"

Seamus was startled by her touch and it enlivened his senses. *Yes. This is exciting. But isn't this wrong?* He pressed his hand against his shirt pocket and felt the shape of his photograph of Ashlyn.

Seamus turned his attention to the race now, as the maddening energy of the crowd drew him in. At first the two boats were tightly positioned, then one began to assert its preeminence, and as they got closer and closer, the one lagging appeared to be struggling.

"Looks like I'm going to lose a lot of money." Dorrie gave him a mock frown.

Seamus realized the boat in the lead was the one they had rode in last night, and he silently urged it on. It continued to stretch its gap, with its mammoth paddle churning up frothy white currents behind it. Aboard the boat were only a dozen or so passengers, raucously celebrating with drink and cheer, their hands cupping around their mouths to send taunting chants at their flailing pursuer.

Dorrie put her lips to Seamus's ear, close enough so they touched. "Would have loved to be on that boat."

"Who are they?" Seamus felt a pang of envy as outside of the crew on board the ship, all of the passengers were dressed in royal garb.

"You have to be a very important person to be on deck during the race."

"So why aren't you aboard? That disappoints me," Seamus whispered back and smelled the fragrance of her skin.

She gave him a sultry look, aware of his rusted efforts to charm.

When he took his eyes off of the smooth curvature of her face, he noticed many of the spectators were pointing toward the trailing boat. The *Riviera* now had billows of black smoke rising from its chimney, and its crew and passengers were shifting along the deck in a frenzy.

Right at that moment, a horrific sound reverberated, the grinding of metal and scattering of debris as a blinding flash of a violent explosion caused spontaneous screams and panic from the spectators, who pushed and pummeled their way from flying sparks and smoldering fragments.

Seamus's first reaction was to pull in Dorrie and protect her from the incoming shrapnel, and he winced as he felt a piercing of his back. The boat's passengers were frantically leaping from the rails of the floundering boat, now in full flame, and already several people were bobbing in the wide waters of the river with their arms reaching, desperate to cling to something floating by them.

Ahead, the lead boat was beginning to turn around to assist in the rescue, but Seamus feared it would be too late for those already struggling before him.

A shout pierced through the menagerie. "My son. My son. He's drowning."

Seamus sought to hear the source of the pleas, and a man in a drenched black suit was trying desperately to swim against the current to where a boy was losing the fight to stay above water.

For Seamus, there was never a stalled intention, and he launched himself into the water and stroked in a direct line for the boy. He didn't even pause to consider that he was not an accomplished swimmer by any means. His few experiences back in Ireland as a boy were in the chilly, pooled waters of the neighboring stream.

But there was a strength within him, one he had never experienced before, and it pulled him through the waters as he buried his head and pressed forward, believing at any moment his efforts would be in vain. During one mad stroke of his arm, he landed on flesh and he pulled up to see he had stunned the boy with a firm strike to his face.

Seamus grabbed the boy from behind right as the river picked up strength and carried them more swiftly. He reached out for a floating plank of wood, but it was wet and slipped through his grasp.

The boy was working against him, pushing him down, as Seamus tried to press him up. All the while he kicked furiously as the weight of the two of them was causing him to sink below water.

The pace of his rescue and his lack of swimming ability had conspired against him, and his strength was running dry. Seamus had a decision he must make.

It was either him or the boy.

His raw survival instincts screamed at him to toss the boy to the waters and use all he had to assault the shoreline. But something much more powerful and deeper within him prevailed. He pushed up his arms as high as he could to keep the now-unmoving body of the boy above water as Seamus continued to sink.

The water filled his lungs and he tried to cough, but it only drew in more water and his head grew dizzy and his mind drifted away.

Then. A stillness. A moment of peace. He saw Shila's painted face peering down at him through rays of sunshine shimmering through the water, the smile reassuring him in the expanding brilliance of the light.

What greater love than this?

It was then he knew it would be all right.

To lay your life down for another.

He sensed the laughter of pure joy and he was no longer holding the boy. His arms spread wide as he sank lower and lower into the depths of the murky waters.

Then Kevan's visage formed as a rippling apparition, glowing with the same joyful expression the toddler shared before succumbing to the creek.

Forgive me, little brudder. Please forgive me.

Then arms thrust down through the water and light, and Seamus loosely experienced himself being yanked to the surface by what seemed a hundred hands and dozens of worried faces.

Seamus was close to the river's bank. They must have drifted. As the shouts and screams continued, he was dragged through the sand. He spit out water as he kept both arms raised in triumph as the world spun around him.

Once it was settled, he was laid down gently, and above him many who were deeply concerned peered down. Then he remembered. "The boy?"

"The boy's fine," said a man who held his hand and looked down at him with kindness.

Thank You, Lord. Was that You, Lord?

"My son. Where is he?"

"He's right here. Over here."

Seamus struggled to a sitting position despite the protests of the strangers attending to him, but it was worth the effort to see the boy being embraced by his father.

The father's water-drenched suit clung to his body. He had a tightly groomed beard, unlike those of the miners. He was crying, running his fingers through his son's hair. He turned to Seamus with an expression of profound gratitude, one Seamus had never experienced before.

"Seamus!" Davin slid beside him, panting and with terror in his eyes.

"I am fine." Seamus took a deep breath and coughed, but his head was clearing.

Davin wrapped his arms around Seamus and pressed his cheek against him and sobbed. He continued this for a long time, until he pulled up and looked his older brother in the eyes.

"Clare was right about you, Seamus. Don't ever say you're not a hero. Ever again."

He had no energy to protest, and Seamus didn't want to anyway.

There was a peace abiding in him like nothing he had ever experienced before. It was an encouragement of who he was and an affirmation of where he was heading.

But this lasted for only a few moments before there was another message resonating, unvoiced but clearly present. It was urgent and pressing.

Time was scarce. They needed to find Ashlyn's father before it was too late.

Chapter 34

THE TRAILHEAD

"Shouldn't we sack it another night?" Dusty frowned. "Get you healed up?"

Seamus tightened the strap of his satchel with a full tug. "I'll be fine. Besides, tonight might be our only chance of getting where we need to go. We can't risk losing our guide."

Davin rubbed Seamus's back. "You ought to be listening to Dusty, you know."

"Trust me." Seamus looked over to Nelson who was sitting in the chair by the door appearing bored. "Now you've got it figured out rightly, Nelson. Hat's on and you're good to go. And no time squandered trying to mother me none."

The boy stood. "Ready."

Seamus froze. Did he just hear that? "Nelson, you just—"

Davin shot him down with his brows. "Of course he does. I told you. But not if you parade about it. It just means he likes you some. He saw what you did."

"Let's be along our way, lads." Seamus stood and felt a wave of nausea.

Dusty reached for Seamus's pack. "I'll tote this."

Seamus started to protest but decided against it. It would be better if it appeared he was just having a drink in the lobby and not getting ready to hunt down a claim. "Now remember the plans we made. You'll use the door at the bottom of the stairs and wait for me out back. When the guide shows, the two of us, we'll sneak out and join you. Remember, boys. No one sees us go."

He turned to Dusty. "Provisions?"

"Good with that," Dusty said. "A cook's supply of food. Bedrolls. Woolies. A canvas lean-to. All but the donkey to haul her all."

As his head started to ache, Seamus put the back of his hand to his forehead. But in response to the stares, he shooed them on their way. They filtered out, laboring to carry the supplies between them without Seamus's assistance. He was the last to leave and closed the door behind them, disappointed to hear them chattering loosely up ahead.

It will be a miracle if we aren't tracked by the entire city.

When he got to the staircase, he paused. He flushed with light-headedness. What stealth would there be if he passed out and tumbled down the stairs into the lobby? He took it step by step, regretting their room was on the third floor.

He heard the sounds of discussion and the clattering of glasses and silverware prior to reaching the lobby. He imagined today's tragedy would be the subject of discourse for everyone, and probably for several weeks at least. Seamus thought, somewhat morosely, this all might assist them in their efforts to leave town unnoticed.

The bottom floor of the hotel was more of a tavern, and tables and seats were mostly filled with guests, who apparently hadn't allowed the day's events to temper their enthusiasm for drink.

Seamus managed to find a small table, hoping to keep to himself. But the proprietor spotted him and approached.

"How did it go? With old Ben?" The man put his hands behind his back.

"Not too well," Seamus said, but he instantly regretted lying. "That's not actually the truth of it. He was quite a help to me as you said, but urged discretion."

"Understood. Drinking?"

"What do you have for a wee bite?"

He rolled his eyes. "It's a big crowd, but no one's much in the mind for eating. I was expecting on account of the good saint to be serving heavy, but now it seems we'll have coddle, mussels, and pigs feet until my last days."

Seamus laughed. "I'll help you with whatever you've got the most of, friend. And a cup of tea, if you don't mind."

It didn't take long for the man to return with his supper, and Seamus handed him three dollars. He kept his eyes on the room as he ate. Although it was fairly crowded, the atmosphere was noticeably subdued.

The food itself was surprisingly like what he would have gotten back in Ireland, and it was exactly what he needed to regain some of his strength and clarity. In fact, he enjoyed it so much, he lost himself in it.

"Some good grub served here, eh?"

Seamus thought he would never hear that voice again. Dorrie pointed to the empty chair across from him. "May I?"

Seamus wanted to say no but couldn't conceive of a tactful reason to do so. "I am expecting someone soon, I am afraid." He thought this would be enough to cause her to decline the seat, but the woman was unmoved.

He slid his cup of tea in front of her and poured it full.

She put her hand up.

"No really. Won't you have a cup of tea. How about some of this food?"

"Not hungry. But please do."

He didn't need much encouragement and scraped the last portions of his dinner from the edges of the bowl.

As he looked across the table now, however, he no longer felt at all attracted to this woman. In fact, he was sickened by a sense he had betrayed Ashlyn with the way he behaved this afternoon. Yet Ashlyn had her captain and Seamus was sure to be forgotten. Would he ever get over that woman?

Dorrie must have sensed his change of attitude toward her. She crossed her arms and rubbed her shoulders for warmth. "That was quite something today. Most impressive."

"How did you find me here?" Seamus pushed the empty bowl to the side and wiped his lips with the back of his sleeve.

She gave him a guilty smile and her eyes teased downward. It was a subtle move that was probably well practiced and surely irresistible to most. She was slick and stunningly attractive. But all Seamus could think of now was reaching into his pocket to see if his photo of Ashlyn was waterlogged and destroyed. He had dried his clothes before putting them on again, but until now had forgotten her picture.

He glanced toward the entranceway and spotted a power-fully built Asian man who had a ponytail and was eyeballing the crowd.

Dorrie clasped her hands, put her elbows on the table, rested her chin on her fists, and tilted her head slightly. "So, tell me about yourself, Seamus Hanley."

When did he tell her his name? Maybe his first name, but his surname as well?

The Asian man spotted them at the table and made his way over.

As Seamus watched him approach, Cade Gatwood, who must have slipped in unnoticed to the side of the crowded room, waved him over with urgency and Seamus's temper surged.

He stood from the table. "Would you spare me a moment, Dorrie? I'll be back shortly."

She started to object, but he was already sifting through the maze of bodies in the room.

"I thought I told you clear enough, Cade," Seamus said upon arriving.

Cade raised his hands in surrender. "Hush." He was focused in the direction of the back table.

Seamus looked back as well and saw that the behemoth Oriental had joined Dorrie and they were in discussion.

Turning his back to them, Cade pulled out a piece of paper and unfolded it. "You'll want to see this."

It was a ragged poster with a drawing of Seamus, much like the one Jeremiah's granddaughter had drawn. The soldiers must have retrieved it from his cabin. But most disturbing were the words printed above and below his portrait: "Wanted for Horse Thievery. $500 Dead or Alive."

"Get's much sweeter," Cade said with his drawl. "Your lady friend there? That be Miss Dorrie Hayes. The black widow."

"What are you saying?"

"Bounty hunter. And the big man, Wo Lin. He's her muscle. You need to get going."

Seamus stumbled on his disjointed thoughts. "But I am supposed—"

"I talked to Ben."

"What?"

"I'll sit out 'til the guide shows. We're hooking up at the Stanislaw Trailhead."

"How do you . . . ?" Seamus glanced back and saw the hulking Wo Lin elbowing his way through the crowd toward him.

Cade shouted, "Go" from behind, but Seamus was already well on his way toward the front door.

※※※※※※※※※※ ✦ ※※※※※※※※※※

They all hunkered down behind the sagebrush, a stone's toss from the trailhead's entranceway, which being a good mile from the town center was a challenge in itself to find.

"But it makes no sense," Davin whispered. "Why would they be after you? Didn't you just save the boy?"

"I'll explain everything to you when we're not being chased like a wild hare." The truth was, Seamus didn't know how to begin sharing the story. His little brother thought too highly of him, but it didn't seem kind to crush his heart either.

"If we be the hare, who is the coyote?" For the first time, a hint of agitation infused Dusty's voice.

"You have every right to understand this all plainly." If only it was plain to Seamus. It seemed surreal to be hiding in the wilderness and in pursuit of a man he had never met. All of this for the benefit of a woman who probably wanted nothing to do with him. If this was what love was, maybe he was better off alone in the mountains.

He shifted over closer to Dusty, managing to poke himself in face with a branch. "If I were you, I would head back to town and forget that you ever knew me." Then another moment of clarity came to Seamus. "For that matter, it would be a favor to me if you would take my brudder and Nelson along as well."

Davin clenched to Seamus's arm. "I will not leave nowhere without you."

"Fine then, Dusty. Do me the kindness of taking Nelson with you at least, and the two of you get out of here while there is yet a fair chance."

"No," Nelson blared.

"Shhh." Davin hushed him.

Seamus was beginning to think he preferred it when the boy didn't speak.

Dusty snickered. "The boys speak for themselves. Me? You know what breed of rapscallions end up on board a ship? Wouldn't have none to cook for otherwise. Just be good manners to know your wound 'tis all."

"Horse thief, if it's something you need to know."

"You aren't no horse thief." Davin let go of Seamus's arm. "My brother isn't no horse stealer."

"Please. Davin, calm yourself. That's not the full story, 'tis true, and there's another side to it. But now at least you know your brudder isn't aiming for sainthood."

There was a snapping of twigs and they silenced. Suddenly, Seamus had a fear they were being set up by Cade. How could he have known so much?

Through the trees and shrubbery, they saw the glow of a lantern flashing through evening. As the light approached, two figures became pronounced as did their voices and one of them was clearly Cade's.

Seamus motioned to the others to keep quiet. Should he let them just pass? Maybe they should just risk it on their own.

"This here's the trailhead you say?" Cade probed the lantern forward in several directions. "Seamus? You here?"

At this point, Seamus was left with little choice. He would have to just trust Cade and pray that it would work out for the best. He stepped out from behind the bushes and Cade turned toward him in a startle.

"Well . . . there you are. Giving me a right fit." Cade raised the lantern to light the path to their feet as Davin, Dusty, and Nelson emerged as well.

"This here is Ling." Cade pointed the torch toward a slender, ponytailed, and pockmarked man, and they could see the concern in his narrowed eyes.

"Light out," he said bluntly and with authority. Then he reached out and took the lantern from Cade, opened its wick door, and blew out the flame.

They didn't need his guidance to see far down the hill, and shrouded by the tree branches leading up the winding dirt path were two bouncing specks of light.

They were being followed.

Chapter 35

WANTED

 The idle prattle of infants and babies hummed in the background, but Ashlyn could barely hear any of this as she lovingly combed the horsehair brush through Gracie's light brown curls that were velvet to the touch.

Ashlyn sat in a chair with her daughter in her lap, both of them admiring her handiwork in the oak framed mirror.

"Mama." It wasn't a question, but rather a jubilant uttering from the little girl whose smooth cheeks drew to dimples. Her long black lashes and emerald eyes made her gaze distinctive, which in the mirror mostly was set upon her mother.

Gracie had grown up so much when compared to the tiny, frightened, and bruised newborn who was handed tenderly to Ashlyn by her father. At the time of the difficult birth, they were in the midst of heavy weather at sea aboard the *Stella* on their journey to San Francisco.

Ashlyn recalled peering up with exhaustion from her miserably uncomfortable cot in their cabin and seeing the happiness in her father's eyes. It was the first time through her ordeal where he looked upon her without traces of disappointment. It was devastating to Daddy when he learned she was pregnant out of wedlock. Having happened only months after her mother died, she feared it would amount to a final emotional blow.

But it was the baby in his arms that changed him and brought him out of his grief. The name came easy to Ashlyn, because from that point forward, her daughter always was the full embodiment of grace.

Yet it was her father's idea and at his insistence that they deny Gracie as their own flesh and blood. He said it was what would be best for the child, and it would provide them a clean start in a new world. It even would allow them to return home to Virginia someday without any tarnishing of their reputation.

She could only imagine what her mother would have thought of this careful ruse if she was still alive. Ashlyn loved her father, but it was undeniably Mama who was the core of character and faith for the Whittingtons.

Mama certainly would have frowned against Daddy's suggestion. Although she raised Ashlyn to be a proper Southern lady, she didn't worry much about the opinions of others. She said in the end it was only God's opinion that mattered.

Which for Ashlyn was the problem. With her moment of indiscretion, she had permanently spoiled the opinions of both God and man. She knew Mama would have forgiven her and told her everything would be all right, as she always did with such gentleness and eloquence.

But Ashlyn knew she would never be able to be like Mama: pure and upstanding, and this pained her more than anything. Perhaps her father was right. As cruel as it seemed, his path may well be the right choice for them and Gracie.

Ashlyn kissed her daughter on the cheek. "See how beautiful you are when you let me brush your hair?"

Gracie looked playfully into the mirror and turned her head from side to side before leaning forward and pressing her palm again the glass.

As she saw innocence reflected before her, Ashlyn shuddered. Had she put her daughter in harm's way? And all of the children, for that matter? If Seamus was as dangerous as Percy had intimated, then she had put them all at risk.

But how could this be? What danger could be in those blue eyes and that caring heart? Not one of his actions had betrayed his character. And what man of ill intent would risk his life in a fire for their sakes? None of this made sense to her.

Ashlyn wrestled Gracie back and spun the child and then hugged her tightly against her chest. Then she carried the child over and set her down with the two other toddler boys who were piling up some wood blocks. Ashlyn smiled when she thought how Gracie was the reason why the house was filled with three toddlers and four infants.

When word spread through the city that a young woman was serving as governess to the orphaned, what started as deception had resulted in blessing.

"And we know that all things work together for good to them that love God." It was all Ashlyn could remember of one of Mama's favorite lines of Scripture, but it was still dear to her heart. But how could it be true? She still loved God, but how could God love her after what she had done?

Ashlyn suffered a sudden jolt of terror as she was reminded that this was the very subject she was about to discuss with Percy. For the past couple of years, she had rehearsed the words, her facial expressions, the way she would respond to any of his reactions over and over again. But now that it was before her, she worried if she had the courage to say anything at all.

While drifting in these thoughts, she felt Priscilla tugging on her sleeve. The teenager had Isabella cradled in her arms.

"It's Annie. She's out front and there is a problem. I think it's Sarah Mae again."

Ashlyn left the children's room, then through the kitchen doors into the sitting area where she saw Annie halfway leaning out of the front door. Ashlyn opened it all of the way to see Sara Mae speaking in pleading tones.

Annie put her hands on her waist. "I's already told her, Miss Ashlyn. But we's got babies listens better than this one here."

"Sarah Mae," Ashlyn said firmly, "we have an arrangement. It is the same one we have with all of the children's mothers."

Sarah Mae bit her lip and put her head down. For a woman of her profession, it was clear she had made every attempt to dress as modestly as possible. But the dress she had chosen was worn and wrinkled and there were still smears of makeup on her face. "I know the rules, Miss Ashlyn, and I agreed to them fine. I'll be accountable if you say I must, but I was here in hope of some mercy."

"Now, we've discussed this many times. Having working girls around here would not be fair to the children, not to mention the outrage that would come from our neighbors."

"I know, Miss Ashlyn. That's why I was so careful to make sure no one saw me coming. I even hid behind that tree there for nearly an hour waiting for your next door lady to leave her porch. Please. I just want to hold my baby girl."

Ashlyn was baffled by Sarah Mae's persistence. There was always some level of regret with the women who left their children to La Cuna. Yet in all cases Ashlyn was able to eventually dissuade them until they became disinterested. But this woman was decidedly different.

"Your discretion is appreciated and I applaud you for this,

Sarah Mae. But it does not and cannot alter our arrangements in any way."

The woman pulled out a handkerchief and rubbed her eyes, causing it to smudge further. Then she pursed her lips. "Could I just see her? Could I just see my Isabella?"

Annie gave Ashlyn a look that was challenging her sanity for even contemplating giving in to this request, but she couldn't deny this. Who was she to judge harshly? Ashlyn backed out of the door. "Come in, Sarah Mae."

She stepped forward and grabbed Ashlyn's hand and kissed it fervently. "Oh thank you, Miss Ashlyn, thank you. I said a prayer that you would be merciful. Thank You, Lord!"

In the background Annie rolled her eyes to the highest point of heaven, and Ashlyn just gave her a guilty smile. "Go ahead, Sarah Mae. Before I suffer any more regret."

By this time, Priscilla had come out to the sitting room, still with Isabella in her arms. She glanced up to Ashlyn, and when she received a nod of approval, she gently handed the baby to her mother, whose full demeanor was brimming with rapture.

Once again, the sight of Sarah Mae holding Isabella brought Ashlyn back to her own festering anguish. How was she going to tell Percy? What would his reaction be?

Ashlyn didn't have the answers, and the uncertainty of it all was burrowing into innards and creating painful anxiety.

But she had made up her mind about one thing, and in this she was finally resolute.

Tonight. Tonight she would tell Percy everything.

The stars in the black sky were captivating. It would have provided the perfect backdrop for a symphony of romance, if not for the discordant pounding in Ashlyn's heart.

Returning from their short walk, Percy and Ashlyn saw that Annie had prepared molasses cookies and tea for them. She served them with a vase of fresh-cut daisies, all carefully laid out on a linen-covered table set up alongside the bench in the front of La Cuna. This would allow them privacy and the opportunity to enjoy the unseasonably warm night air.

This was all following the Southern dinner Annie had already fed them, which considering how low they were on supplies was both filling and tasty. Ashlyn well knew of Annie's ill-harbored feelings toward Percy, which made her friend's efforts even that much more magnanimous.

Then again, Annie knew how difficult this night would be for Ashlyn. Having accompanied Ryland and Ashlyn on their fateful sea journey to San Francisco, no secrets were kept from her.

Percy and Ashlyn shared awkwardness for several minutes, merely staring at the slowing activity of the street and listening to the dull trots of passing horses and carriages. Occasionally they would mumble a compliment about the cookies or tea.

Unfortunately, the truth was Ashlyn's nerves robbed her of all pleasures and she had hardly eaten any of Annie's masterful meal.

Having been so preoccupied with what she dreaded to broach, she finally determined her only possible relief was to finally take the risk. Just as she was about to speak, Percy leaned in and put his arm around her.

He cleared his throat. "Ashlyn, I have what I believe is . . . the most . . . glorious news to share."

Relief poured through Ashlyn for the reprieve and she rather enjoyed seeing her normally cavalier soldier squirming. She welcomed his rare display of vulnerability.

Percy removed her cup of tea and placed it on the table. He reached for her hand and clasped it with both of his. "I realize I have not been in anyway attentive to you since leaving Virginia."

This was an understatement, but she tried to affirm him anyway. "You have been necessarily attending to your career."

"Yes. Well. In visiting with you again, I have been painfully reminded of my affections toward you. Regardless of my pursuits, as noble as they may be, I should never have allowed such a precious flower to be left unwatered."

"Yes." She was confused as to where this was heading.

He squeezed her hand and locked his gaze with hers. "I want you to know I am aware of the burden you've been carrying. And it would be beneath all of my responsibilities to you to allow you to continue bearing it on your own."

"You know . . . about it?"

"I know everything."

The blood flushed through her entire body.

"In confidence, I enjoyed an intimate conversation with Mr. Parnell, and he offered with no lack of clarity the full difficulties of your father's affairs."

"He did?" Ashlyn's shoulders slumped. Oh, if he only knew the burdens she carried!

Percy straightened. "It is of Mr. Parnell's well-schooled opinion that even with the miracle of some gold discovery on Ryland's part, the entirety of what would be earned would be owed to him in full regardless."

"Mr. Parnell said that?"

"Which means there is only futility in going on some type of . . . gold hunt. Even if we find your father, we'll only be there to cover his debts."

Ashlyn felt numb.

Percy squeezed her hands. "This brings us to the more cheerful part of our conversation."

"Oh?" She heard the sound of a cart being wheeled down the dirt road and her eyes drifted for moment.

"I had my meeting with the general today, and I am pleased to say it was a much more profitable discussion. In fact, dare I say, it was exhilarating."

She turned back and saw his confidence had returned and she tried to tap into his enthusiasm.

"Are you ready?" He paused for effect. "I . . . we . . . have been granted a new commission in the Minnesota Territory."

"That is wonderful for you, Percy," Ashlyn said and then noted his odd expression. "It is what you wanted, right?"

"Ashlyn, dear." He picked up a cookie and snapped it between his teeth. "I said *we* have been granted a commission. And yes, it is challenging territory with much Indian activity, but this is a great opportunity. A great opportunity for us."

She shook her head. "I don't—"

"Oh, my dear, you are thick sometimes, aren't you? Don't you realize a fast-rising captain of the United States Army just asked for your hand in marriage?"

"He did? I mean, you did?"

He stared at her for a few moments, obviously dissatisfied with her reaction.

Ashlyn felt as if she was falling back into a confused abyss, and she struggled to paint an expression that wouldn't betray the bruising of her heart. Weren't these the words she had always dreamed Percy would ask her?

But it wasn't about Ashlyn anymore. It was about Gracie.

As Seamus had said, this was what was right. What would be best for her daughter was to be with her father. She would do anything for that child.

"Percy." His name came out as a faltering whisper. She put her hand to his smooth cheek. "Oh, Percy." Then she put her hand to her forehead. "But I can't just leave . . . all of this."

"I realize this is all so sudden, dear Ashlyn. Shame on me for expecting you to . . . just sweep into my arms. You've done commendable service here, one which both the city and the children will appreciate for years to come. But it's your time. Our time. We will most certainly want to start anew. Just the two of us to begin, but then our family." He smiled. "See. I am getting terribly ahead of myself."

"Then you do want children?"

"Of course. What would ever make you think otherwise?"

She wavered, even though she knew the door was now open. "Percy?"

"Yes, flower?" he said with expectation.

Ashlyn tried, but she couldn't get it into words. She started to cry instead.

In the street, a carriage slowed to a stop before them, and the brake cranked back and the horses neighed.

Percy looked at it with alarm and then pulled out his pocket watch. "Oh dear. That is for me." He lifted her up by the hands and stood before her. "Oh dear, dear Ashlyn. How cruel of me to thrust this all upon you." Percy kissed her on the cheek. "Although I do need an answer, as I am told they want us to leave with haste."

Ashlyn nodded, and tightened her lips as she looked down.

"You will give your Captain Percy an answer?"

"I will."

He started to leave but spun around and pulled a folded paper out of his coat pocket and handed it to her. "I almost neglected to give this to you. I am certain you will find it most disconcerting, as did I."

With this he stepped lively to the carriage, where the driver was waiting to open the door. In a few moments, the sounds of the hooves trailed away.

Ashlyn unfolded the document, and even in the limited light of the moon, it was clear what it was.

A wanted poster for a horse thief named Seamus Hanley.

Chapter 36
THE VOW

It wasn't as Ashlyn had imagined.

Ever since she was a child, Ashlyn dreamed of being one of those women who finds the perfect man, falls forever in love, and blissfully shares a lifetime of experiences and triumphs. And for most of her time growing up, this man had been the young, handsome Percy Barlow. He was only two years older than Ashlyn, but he always carried himself with a confidence and seriousness that made him seem so much more mature than the other boys.

As a teenager, Ashlyn would often comfort herself through the challenges of growing up by reminding herself that she would someday be Mrs. Percy Barlow.

Perhaps this all conspired against her on that last night with him before he departed for army enlistment. It was still hot and steamy toward the end of that summer day when she and Percy snuck away in laughter to the knoll overlooking her family farm. They unfolded the checkered blanket and lay down together.

She was twenty, and Ashlyn was certainly old enough to know she was putting herself in a compromising situation, one in which her father would never approve. But with her mother struggling with illness and Percy's imminent departure pressing down on her, she was in a place of emotional fragility.

This hill was a familiar one for the two of them. When they were much younger, the two would often retreat here to chase butterflies and frogs. But Ashlyn's mother had taught her new proprieties as she grew older and began to draw the eyes of many a young man in her small town.

So when Percy invited her to share in one last moment of reminiscing, she had a clear understanding of what his intentions were.

But as she lay there beside him, with the sounds of crickets and whippoorwills in the background, she had second thoughts. Suddenly, she was overwhelmed with guilt and became fearful of disappointing her parents, especially Mama who thought Ashlyn had gone to the market.

Percy must have sensed the fish loosening on the hook. He leaned in closely and gave her the wry smile that ruled her. "What if I was to take a bullet? We might not ever get another chance like this."

He pulled Ashlyn in close to him, and once she could smell him and feel his body pressing against hers, her resolve wavered.

"Don't talk like that, Percy." She held him and buried her head in his shoulder. Would she ever see him again? What if he did die while serving his country?

"You do love me, don't you?" He tucked her hair behind her ears and leaned in to kiss her and she turned away.

Percy guided her head gently with his hand and looked deep

into her eyes. "You'll always be the only one for me, Ashlyn Whittington." Then he leaned in again and pressed his lips against hers, but this time, she didn't pull back.

Ashlyn knew there was something missing in her life and always believed it was within Percy's ability to fill it.

So she closed her eyes. And surrendered.

"You be gone in the head all day." Annie's voice broke in and Ashlyn realized she had been daydreaming, staring out the front window of La Cuna.

"It's nothing." Ashlyn was embarrassed and tried to remember what she was supposed to be doing.

"You find that cow?"

"What?"

Annie reached her ebony hand out and snapped the empty milk bottle from Ashlyn's hand.

Ashlyn laughed at herself. "I am terribly sorry, Annie. You sent me to fill this up for you, didn't you?"

"No needs now. Babies done git tired waiting for you and walks themselves over to the neighbors."

"Did you really ask the Andersons again for milk?" Ashlyn sighed. "How was Mrs. Anderson about it?"

"Same as last. Milk comes with preaching."

Annie always made Ashlyn smile, even those times when such a feat didn't seem possible. But the woman stood before her, looked down, and fidgeted with her feet.

"I know what that means, Annie. What's on your mind?"

"I's afraid to tells you."

Ashlyn knew how the game was played. "Now, Annie. You know I am incapable of being angry with you. There are no secrets between us."

Annie's eyes widened.

"What . . . secret?" Ashlyn pivoted her head.

"I's done a wrong turn."

"What secret, Annie?" The kitchen door opened and one of the toddlers waddled up to Ashlyn and she lifted him into her arms. "How are you, Zachary?" She poked his nose. "What secret, Annie?

"I gives him the map."

"Who? What are you talking about?"

"The Irish boy."

"The horse thief?" Ashlyn's temper flared. She shifted Zachary to her hip.

"Ain't no horse stealer, that one." Annie parried with an expression of obstinacy.

Ashlyn glanced at the mantelpiece and saw the map resting on top of it. "It's right there." The boy started to pull himself up, and she brought him in close again and stroked the back of his head.

"I draw him a new one."

"Annie. Why?" She wanted to be angrier, but for some reason she couldn't.

"He's good people, dat one. He's gonna find your pappy. I knows it."

"You gave a wanted criminal the exact location of my father's gold claim?"

Annie put her hands on her hips. "I s'posin yous a fine judge of a man?"

A firm knock sounded from the front door, but both women continued to stare each other down.

Ashlyn pointed a finger at Annie. "We are not finished with this."

"Oh I's finished." Annie rolled her eyes but then seemed glad to escape to the front door and cracked it to peek outside. "Oh no. No. No. No. Done told you time again, you ain't welcome here none."

"Who is it, Annie?" They were comrades again. She set Zachary on the floor and he went back to the kitchen door.

Annie opened the wide with exasperation. "Sees for youself."

It was Sarah Mae, wearing a blue bonnet and faded yellow dress and carrying in one of her white-gloved hands a camel-colored piece of luggage.

"Sarah Mae?" Ashlyn nodded toward the bag in the woman's hand. "Are you leaving town?"

"Miss Ashlyn, may I come in?"

Ashlyn didn't bother to look at Annie's expression. She waved Sarah Mae in. "This isn't a good time. This isn't even a good day."

"I wanted you to know," Sarah Mae said, "that I have left my given profession. Forever. It was both Isabella and your kindness to me. And I've been praying about it and I heard the Lord plainly. I am going to straighten my ways."

"What wonderful news!" Ashlyn smiled at Annie. "Isn't that delightful?"

"Oh, I's delighted all righty."

Sarah Mae looked up at the ceiling, unable to make eye contact. "Which means . . . which means I do not have a job. So . . . I was hoping to work here."

Annie burst out in laughter and then covered her mouth with her hand and stopped suddenly. "Oh, sweet sunshine. She serious."

"Indeed I am." Sarah Mae set the luggage down and began pulling off the gloves from her hands, one finger at a time.

"Poor dear," Ashlyn said, "we can't even feed ourselves."

"Oh no, Miss Ashlyn." She reached into the top of her dress and pulled out a roll of dollar bills from between her ample cleavage and extended her hand.

Ashlyn closed Sarah Mae's hand around the bills. "That is very kind of you to offer, but we cannot accept what is ill earned."

Annie opened the women's hand and took the roll of bills herself, and then began to count what was there. "Thems babies never mind. It feeds them all same, ill earned or no."

Sarah Mae nodded. "Yes. Please take it. All of it. I want to stay and work at La Cuna as well. I'm still learning proper about babies, but Miss Priscilla, she's been teaching me just fine."

Annie lifted the luggage from the floor and put it in Sarah Mae's hand. "Money we take. But ain't room for no more birds in this nest."

The woman looked to Ashlyn for affirmation, but when there was none granted, her shoulders slumped. "I understand. I do. And you all been so kind and caring for Isabella. It was wrong for me to hope."

The kitchen door swung open behind them and Priscilla came in with Zachary on her hip. She seemed startled to see Sarah Mae standing there.

"Priscilla. Did you put Sarah Mae up to all of this?" Ashlyn's tone was more accusatory than she wanted.

Priscilla ran her fingers through the toddler's hair. "What do you mean?"

"About Sarah Mae. Living here. Working here."

"Oh that. Well, I suppose I might have said something about needing some help around here. But Sarah Mae has a heart for it. And she loves the babies, not just her Isabella. You always say, more hands moves the pile with smiles. Besides, she said she prayed and God told—"

"Yes," Ashlyn interrupted, "this I have already heard."

There was pounding on the door, with such firmness, it startled them all.

Annie peeked out the widow and turned back with her hands to her cheeks. "It's the captain."

Ashlyn started waving her arms. "All of you. Get in the back. Sarah Mae. You as well."

Sarah Mae's face glowed. "Does that mean—?"

"It only means I don't want you to be seen." Ashlyn sighed. "I am sorry. Yes. You can stay. How could we say no to God?"

The luggage hit the floor and Sarah Mae embraced her in tears. "Thank you, Miss Ashlyn."

Ashlyn remained stiff as the woman literally choked her. "There will be many rules and conditions."

Sarah Mae stepped back and was nodding in agreement.

"Absolutely no alcohol. No more paint on your face, and you'll dress as a lady. Lastly and more important, I do not want any of your friends around here. None. Allowing you here will already make La Cuna the source of all gossip. Do you understand?"

"Understood. And thank you, Miss Ashlyn."

Sarah Mae stepped forward to hug her again, but Ashlyn pointed. "Now all of you get gone."

As they scurried their way through the kitchen door, Ashlyn looked in the mirror and tried to pat down the uncooperative curls in her hair.

Pound. Pound. Pound.

"Coming. Coming." She flung open the door, and there stood, in full uniform, a winsome Captain Percy Barlow, except for his scowl of impatience.

"Why didn't Annie answer the door for me?" Percy took his hat off, wiped his hair down, and stepped in with boots polished to a brilliant shine. "I saw the ol' girl in the window gazing right at me as if I had flown in on a chariot drawn by horse ghosts."

"Oh, Percy, I am truly sorry about that. Had I anticipated you were coming we would have been prepared."

His forehead tightened. "You certainly did know I was coming. I told you I would be back today to gather your response as to last night's inquiry."

"Yes. I simply meant, I didn't know exactly when you would be here."

The door to the kitchen fanned open, and Annie walked in with a tray of lemonade. "I's thoughts you be a tad parched."

Ashlyn smiled and reached out for a glass, which was garnished with a slice of lemon, and Percy took one as well, without meeting the black woman's eyes.

"Thank you, Annie. Percy, let us sit ourselves on this couch." She went to move her feet but stumbled and, looking down, saw that Gracie had just wrapped herself around Ashlyn's ankles.

Annie's eyes widened.

"It will be all right, Annie." Ashlyn reached down and Gracie responded with her little hand. With her lemonade in one hand, Ashlyn bent down and helped the girl over to the couch where Percy was waiting. After setting the glass down, she lifted Gracie to her lap and noticed Annie still had the face of terror.

Percy gave a look of disapproval at Gracie. "Don't you want Annie to take the child?"

Ashlyn bounced Gracie. "It will be all right, Annie," she said firmly.

Apparently unconvinced, Annie moved slowly toward the door and even glanced back once before leaving the two of them alone.

Percy sipped loudly from his glass and then puckered his lips from the sourness. Then he put his arm around her. "I must ask you to forgive me, Ashlyn. This has been a day of challenges and not a few unpleasant ones. And on top of it all, I can spare only a few minutes."

Ashlyn held out a finger to Gracie, who clasped it in her tiny fist.

Percy tapped his hat on his leg. "Well. Before you formally give me the answer I am here for, there is another question I have for you."

"Yes?"

"That man. The horse thief."

Ashlyn took a sip of her lemonade and swatted away Gracie's hand as the girl reached for the lemon. She didn't care to hear Seamus referred to as a horse thief. Least of all from Percy, who did not know him as she did.

"Did you happen to know of him from back home? In Virginia?"

She shook her head. "Why do you ask?"

He watched her with traces of skepticism. "It's just that I saw him with Cade Gatwood, of all people."

"Cade?" Her grip tightened on Gracie.

"Oh yes. I was surprised to see Cade here as well. Something about him always made me wary."

"I don't understand." What could this be?

"Well, you see, I was doing some looking into this man. I was concerned about you, and certainly with his crime occurring so close to where I was stationed, it interested me somewhat. As I am sure you could imagine." He pulled out the wanted poster. "Yes, Seamus Hanley. Rather handsome fellow, don't you think?"

"You were saying you saw him accompanying Cade."

"Yes. Right. I learned he had purchased tickets for a riverboat ride. Several billets in fact. When I arrived at the pier, the ship was just leaving. I was too late. Then I saw this Seamus fellow on the deck. And sure enough, standing beside, in some heated discussion was our beloved Cade Gatwood. Most peculiar, wouldn't you say?" He raised an eyebrow.

Ashlyn was trying to process it all. She wrapped her arms around Gracie and pulled her in.

"Listen. Ashlyn. I don't know what kind of trouble you are in. With your father and his finances. This man and Cade. I'm not certain I even want to know. But I can take you away from all of this. You can leave all it behind and we'll start our new life together. The wife of a captain of the United States Army. Can't you see how perfect this is?"

So many conflicting emotions flowed through Ashlyn, but the ones that stung the most were about Seamus. Was he really a criminal? How could she have ever let the man into her house?

Then there was Percy's proposal. Most of her life was spent fantasying about being married to this man, and he was sitting beside her in the flesh, imploring her to say yes. Why shouldn't she? There was an appeal to this idea of leaving everything behind.

Gracie wriggled her way free and then sat again on Ashlyn's legs, this time in a way where she could sheepishly peek at Percy while still curled up in her mother's arms. Ashlyn kissed the child on her head, smelling her hair and skin. When Ashlyn looked up again, she saw a pained expression on the captain's face.

"What is it?" she said. "What do you see? You see yourself in her, don't you?"

"I realize . . ." his voice began to break, "probably what I'm asking you is too much. Perhaps, you should give it some time."

Ashlyn's resolve grew. "Don't you want to look at her?" She regretted saying this the moment she spoke. Now her sole intention was to shield Gracie from the pain of rejection.

"Why . . . didn't you tell . . . ?"

"You never answered my letters. And I didn't write of this for fear it would get in the hands of someone who could derail your precious career."

"That was indeed considerate of you." His gaze drifted away, and he stood and paced back and forth on the creaking wooden floorboards. Then he turned with rage poisoning his glare. "How would anyone know that . . . child . . . is mine? What proof would you have?"

"What proof? What proof?" Her emotions were so mixed up now it was hard to discern if it was anger, shame, or pure repulsion for the man who appeared pathetic and small before her. "My father. Annie."

"Hah! A madman and a worthless slave. What fine testimony that shall be!" Percy snorted, and when he looked at his daughter, there was a contempt that chilled Ashlyn's being.

"You can go now," Ashlyn whispered through gritted teeth.

"My intentions." Percy lifted his hat from the table, turned to the mirror on the wall and adjusted his hat, then straightened out his collar. Then he nodded, and rather than anger in his eyes, there was relief, a cowardice Ashlyn had never seen before but now realized was there all along.

He scampered out the door, and through the window he could be seen strutting away with steps that must have felt like freedom to him.

Numb, she offered no resistance when Gracie wormed from her grasp and climbed down to the floor. Then the child made her way to the coat rack, reached down behind one of the long hanging garments, and pulled something up.

With a smile on her face, she returned to Ashlyn who now recognized the object to be Gracie's favorite doll.

"Had a safe hiding place for her, didn't you?"

Ashlyn was grateful that Annie was leaving her alone to her thoughts. It was further evidence that her friend's ear most likely had been pressed against the other side of the kitchen door all along.

Surprising to Ashlyn was the lack of remorse she felt about Percy walking away from her life and her daughter as well. In some ways, she always knew what was finally plainly revealed. It was bittersweet, but there was peace in the resolution.

Her mind was a beehive, and tormenting her was the thought of Cade and Seamus in some type of collaborative, dark endeavor. And to think that Annie had given them the map!

It was time to act. She could no longer sit back and hope her father would someday return and make all of her problems go away. Percy's solution of running away was not an option. She needed answers to difficult questions.

Including one that had been buried for more than twenty years.

Chapter 37

FOWLER CREEK MINE

Ashlyn peered from behind a tree, across the street from the bank. She didn't need to wait long before hearing the bell of the door ring as two men exited the building, wrapping scarfs around their necks and buttoning tall coats.

"Tomorrow, Richard," Henry said to his employee.

"Yes sir, Mr. Parnell. Good night to you." The scrivener put his top hat on and with pomp in his step, he dipped his walking stick into the walkway and around the corner.

Henry watched him leave before putting the long iron key into the hole and twisting, causing the dead bolt of the bank's door to snap shut. Nervously, he glanced to his left and his right. He reached to slip the key back in his vest pocket, but it dropped and bounced on the ground. Henry cursed and bent down.

Ashlyn stepped out of her cover and crossed the dirt street, arriving just as he was picking up the key.

Mr. Parnell was startled by her arrival and his large body shuddered for a moment. He put his hand over his chest. "Goodness, Ashlyn. Did Ryland not teach you the dangers of sneaking up on old people?"

"We should go back inside," she said sternly.

"All right, Ashlyn. And then you can let me know what's on your mind as I am not used to seeing you so . . . agitated."

He opened the lock and entered into the room of darkness, and she waited at the door until she saw first the light of a match and then five wicks were aflame.

Henry held the candelabra in his hand, and he set it on his desk and motioned for her to sit. "Saving on oil. Everything adds up in difficult times. Come on, Ashlyn. Have a seat and let me know what it is that troubles you."

He dug the butt of a cigar out of his ashtray, put it in his mouth, and leaned into the candle, drawing in and sending smoke rising. "I am assuming there is a purpose to this?"

"You spoke to Percy?" Ashlyn fumbled nervously with her handbag in her lap.

Henry leaned back in his chair, and the red leather squeaked. He clasped his hands. "We spoke, yes. He mentioned something about a proposal. Is that what this is about?"

"You told him my father was bankrupt?"

"Regrettably. Everyone is bankrupt." The tip of his cigar glowed red and then he blew smoke from the side of his mouth. "You see, Ashlyn, I have discovered this core truth of the world. We are all broke. It's just some of us spend more than others."

"That's not why I am here."

"Then why are you here?" He filled his glass from a tin flask.

"It's about Fowler Creek." Ashlyn watched closely to see his reaction. "Fowler Creek Mine." She tried to remember if his hands always shook.

He took a slow sip. "Have you not spoken to your father about this?"

"My mother disallowed the subject to be discussed. She said discussing it would only bring Cade pain."

"And when your mother died?"

"I respected her wishes, even when she . . . left us. But now. Now it is time. What exactly happened at Fowler Creek?"

Henry leaned forward and pressed the stub of his cigar into the ashtray. "That was a long time ago, Ashlyn. Are you sure—?"

"What happened at Fowler Creek, Mr. Parnell?"

"Fine. But first tell me, why now? Why all of this interest?"

"Because Cade was here. In San Francisco."

Henry leaned back and crossed his arms. "Of course I know this. I know everything that goes on in this town. That boy is completely harmless."

"So you spoke to him? You talked to Cade?"

"I did not. He seemed to be avoiding me. But Percy did tell me Cade left to find your father."

Ashlyn was growing impatient. "Fowler Creek, Mr. Parnell."

"You know Cade's father, Urston, died at Fowler Creek? A mining accident." Henry narrowed his eyes and looked up as if he was reliving that day. "A terrible sight. One I'll never be able to clear from my mind. Digging him out and finding him . . . in that condition." He shook his head.

"Why has Cade never forgiven my father?"

"Yes. That question. I suppose it's helpful to know our arrangements. Urston was the one with the experience. He had mined plenty. Knew everything about it. How to test the soil, read the bends of the streams, find the veins. Your father and I—ha! We were green as could be. But when we heard there was gold in the Appalachians and the rush was on, we were arms and elbows in the crowd."

Henry filled up his glass again and the sound of the pour was loud. "Your mother?" He rolled his eyes. "Called it gambling. The pursuits of fools. The diversion of Satan. And worse. Me, I was unmarried. Still am, of course. But back then I was in no hurry.

"But your father. Ever since the moment we arrived and set up camp, he was pressing, pressing. Wanted to strike it rich before he had to slink back home. Urston kept pressing back, telling him to be patient. That a proper shaft couldn't be rushed and he, of course, knew.

"So. One evening, Ryland was pushing us once again. Driving us." He looked up to her. "Are you all right with hearing this, dear?"

Ashlyn shifted in her seat. "Go ahead."

"So one night, Ryland says he'll go to camp and start supper. He leaves Urston, myself, and another man—a hired man, not a partner like the three of us. And Urston was in the mine, trying to get more rocks dislodged, and boom. It all happened so suddenly. We tried digging him out." Henry stared down into his glass. "But it was too late."

Maybe she would have been better off not hearing it all. "This is why my father took in Cade, right?"

"Yes. Your father, for all of his shortcomings, remained a man of integrity. There was no way to repay the loss of a father, but Ryland made every effort. Cade was just a few years old, and you know better than any, he raised him up like one of his own. At least as much as Cade's mother would allow. She was bitter to Ryland as well. That's why when Cade got older, he turned so against your father."

Ashlyn sunk back into her chair and rubbed her aching temples. But there must be more to the story. Cade had so much bitterness. She remembered something he had mentioned. "This other man that you speak of? The fourth man?"

Henry nodded curtly.

"Was his name Cotton?"

He eyed her suspiciously. "Yes. Cotton Waller. He was just a laborer. A runaway slave actually. How did you know this? Did you father mention the man?"

The tone in which he was pressing made Ashlyn uncomfortable. "No. Cade told me about him."

The banker stood from the desk. "Cade? Are you sure?"

"Well, yes. Shortly after he arrived here. What is it, Mr. Parnell? What do you know?"

His voice rose to a shout. "Be perfectly sure, Ashlyn. It was Cade?"

"Yes. He . . . uh . . . said the man summoned him when he was on his deathbed. Cotton Waller. Yes, I am quite certain."

The banker pulled on the folds of skin under his chin. "This is quite serious, Ashlyn. Quite serious."

"What is it? Who is this Cotton? You are frightening me."

He ran his fingers through his hair. Then he reached down on his desk and picked up his bronze globe. Carrying it to the wall, he swung it into the glass display holding his pistol. He removed it as well as two bullets, and then loaded them into the pistol.

"Your father's life is in horrible danger. Fortunately, we are only one day behind them, but there is not a moment to waste. I wanted to spare you of all of this, Ashlyn. It was such a long time ago." He pulled his hat and coat from the rack and then tucked the gun into one of his inner pockets.

Ashlyn grabbed him by the arm. "Tell me the truth now. Is Cade going to rob my father?"

Henry looked down at her hand grasping his arm, and she released it. "Ryland's role in the death of Cade's father is much more . . . involved . . . than I portrayed. There is no way to say this other than to be indelicate. Cade is not interested in Ryland's gold. He's hunting your father down for revenge."

Chapter 38

THE SHADOWS WE FACE

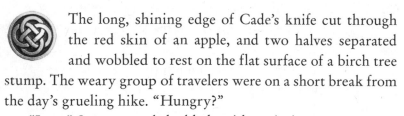 The long, shining edge of Cade's knife cut through the red skin of an apple, and two halves separated and wobbled to rest on the flat surface of a birch tree stump. The weary group of travelers were on a short break from the day's grueling hike. "Hungry?"

"I am." Seamus eyed the blade with curiosity.

Cade speared one of the apple halves with the point of the blade and extended it out to Seamus.

"Obliged." Seamus pulled off the piece of fruit and bit into it, finding it sweet and crisp. "Who do you think is following us?"

The Southerner lifted his boot on the stump and tied his leather shoelace, which appeared frayed and about to split. "Hard to know. But ain't surprised none, with you totin' a price."

"What about you?" Seamus put the rest of the apple in his mouth. "You aiming to get a piece of the reward? Five hundred dollars? That will spend long."

"That ain't the business I'm attending to." Cade grinned. "Not yet, at least."

"That business of yours? We will be having that conversation soon, you know."

"I told you, Seamus. Plain up. Thems just words between Ryland and me. You gonna need to let that dog lie."

"Help!"

The call of distress was from Davin, who was backed up against a large boulder, and the source of his terror was a coiled snake, diamond skinned and with its tongue lapping the air.

Seamus moved toward his little brother, but Ling grabbed him by the arm.

"No try," said the guide. "One bite, boy die."

Davin spoke in a wavering pitch. "I saw something. Shiny. But then . . . the snake came . . . please . . . just get it away."

Cade unsheathed his knife from the scabbard and shifted it from one hand to the other.

"No move." Ling crouched and tiptoed toward the serpent. But then it reared its head and the guide froze.

Seamus circled around every so slowly. "Stay still, Davin. We'll get you."

Davin's lips quivered and he closed his eyes. "Get it away, Seamus."

The snake rattled its tail, and its head gyrated keeping its black, beaded eyes fixed on Davin.

Then, calm as a windless day, they were dumbstruck as Nelson strolled over to the snake and kneeled beside it, and it pivoted its coil around to him. Rather than displaying a hint of fear, the teenager appeared fascinated with the deadly creature.

Dusty went to grab Nelson but Ling restrained him.

Inching his hand toward the viper, a becalming smile crossed Nelson's face. Suddenly, he snapped his hand around the rattler's neck, and then stood with the reptile's tail and body writhing in convulsions.

"Snake," Nelson proclaimed proudly, raised his trophy to them, and then backed up.

Seamus grabbed Davin's wrist and yanked him out of the way, causing him to fall, and then the boy scurried to his feet and hid behind them all.

Mesmerized, they watched without words as Nelson took his free hand and slid it down the length of the snake until he was able to hold it low enough so it could no longer flap around. Then he brought the viper's head closer to him, its mouth open and its fangs exposed. For the first time Seamus had ever heard him do so, Nelson laughed.

"Toss 'er, boy," Dusty said. "Toss 'er."

Cade stepped closer with the knife, but Nelson shook his head and turned his body to shield the animal. Then he carried the snake over to a patch of sagebrush, kneeled down, and released it on the sandy dirt. It scurried away out of sight, and the ruffling sounds soon faded as well.

Nelson stood and dusted his hands, then he turned, suddenly alarmed at the petrified expressions staring back at him. His nostrils flared and he started to shrink as if fearful he was in some sort of trouble.

Finally Davin, who had been clinging to the back of Seamus's legs, stood and approached Nelson with open arms, giving his friend such a sturdy hug it lifted Nelson off the ground and he reached up to secure his hat.

Dusty let out a hoot of relief and bent over and put his hands on his knees. "Think I near split my gut."

Cade patted Nelson on the arm. "This boy ain't got no yeller down his back."

Seamus squared up to Nelson and put his palms on the boy's shoulders. "You nearly put a fit in all of us. You can never do that again, Nelson. It is fine not to fear the snake, but it's unwise to put him to the test or he'll fill your blood with poison."

Nelson appeared confused.

"But I owe you well and good for stepping in for my brudder. You're a brave lad, and Davin's been right all along. You speak just fine."

"This is it!" Davin held up a small yellow rock. "I saw a glint of it on the trail, and when I reached down, that's when I saw the snake. Do you think it's gold, Dusty?"

Dusty reluctantly accepted the rock from the boy but looked with embarrassment at the faces staring at him. He held it between his fingers and up to the sunlight and squinted. "Well, it be well known the ship's life can strip a man's recall. Like bark off a tree." He handed it to Cade. "You're a son of a miner?"

"Yeah. 'Cept my ma wouldn't let me play with these rocks after what happened to Daddy."

"Give it to Ling," Seamus said.

Cade passed it off to their guide, who seemed displeased to be around such greenhorns. Ling examined it and then placed it between his molars and carefully bit down. "Good gold. Maybe twenty dollar."

"Whoooh!" Davin jumped up. "We did it." He poked at Dusty. "I told you we'd find you some gold. Why didn't we bring shovels? We should be digging here."

"No gold here." Ling handed the nugget back to Davin. "Must fall out."

"Fall out?" Davin scratched his head.

Seamus eyeballed the ground around them. "Little brudder, he's saying it must of fell from some prospector's pocket or saddlebag as they were making their way down the hill."

"Well, this is for Nelson then." Davin held it out to his friend.

Nelson accepted it, looked at Ling, and then put it in his mouth and began chewing.

"No . . . no . . . no, Nelson." Seamus held out his palm and Nelson spat it out. Reaching into his pack, Seamus pulled out a small leather pouch with a long drawstring. He put the nugget inside and then ceremoniously hung the leather cord around Nelson's neck. "You slay the dragon. You get the gold."

Apparently tiring of the diversion, Ling ended the pleasantries. "Need go now."

They all groaned, being reminded of the ardors of the trail ahead. Dragging to their feet, they gathered their belongings.

Cade flung his pack over his shoulder. "How far to go, Chinaman?"

Ling looked toward the sun, which was on its descent from its high point. "Not long. Half day. But dark comes soon, so we find place for sleep."

Without further delay, they began winding again up the sinuous trail of the Sierra foothills, through switchbacks and over slippery patches of gravel and loose boulders.

The footing was unsure and caused more than a few stumbles and knee-scraping falls. But easing the pain of the hike was Seamus's enjoyment of the surrounding scenery highlighted by the tapestries of the emerging wildflower bloom; bee hovering bursts of lupine, buttercups, lilies, and bluebells. Their efforts were buttressed as well by fragrant breezes of mint, sagebrush, manzanita, and pine.

Belying the grandeur of the setting were some ominous reminders of the ever-present carnal threat of the backcountry. Rising before them were jagged granite peaks, splattered with snow patches that when combined with the approaching herds of brooding clouds served notice to the trespassers: The guns of winter were still loaded.

The more the pace of the winds increased and the temperatures sunk, the more Seamus was haunted by flashbacks of the last time he breached the Sierra range. He struggled to push back against the recurring visions of Shila's cold, brittle, blue-lipped body lying still in the snow.

Most important was the question he asked himself with each step farther. Was he recklessly directing them into danger? They had left Sacramento City with such haste, they had failed to be properly provisioned if the weather turned sharply.

It was a couple of hours into this leg of their journey when exhausted from their efforts and with their gazes focused mostly on the uncertain terrain beneath their boots, they were late to notice a cloud of dust approaching from up ahead.

They scuttled to a small pocket of bushes and boulders off the trail that would allow them to see what was approaching while giving them adequate cover.

"What is it?" Seamus asked Ling.

"Pack train. Burros."

"I'll say, Chinaman." Cade pulled a mesquite branch down. "Seventeen. Eighteen, by my counting."

Seamus's voice lowered to a whisper as they came closer. "Where are they coming from?"

Ling started to rise, and Seamus grabbed him by the wrist. "Stay down."

"These men know Ling. Ling get answers."

He released his grip on the man but gave a questioning glance to Cade, who squatted closer to Seamus. They watched until Ling slipped out of sight, presumably heading back on the trail.

Soon, the sounds of the train grew louder: hooves crunching on the sandy trail, the rattling of harnesses, muted protests from the mules, and the chatter of men. Shortly, they could hear it all grinding to a standstill, and then they heard Ling's voice speaking to several others in a language they couldn't understand.

"What about the Chinaman?" Cade's expression didn't conceal his doubts.

"What is it about him you think we need to worry about?"

"Not us. It's Ryland. We ain't clear on what's he's sitting on, and it ain't proper to be spoilin' a claim."

Seamus tried to read the Southerner. "The way I'm seeing it is Ryland's got a bigger concern on his hands than Ling."

"That how you seein' it?" Cade pulled out his canteen and unscrewed the cap.

"That's right."

Cade took a drink and then held out the metal canister to Seamus who shook his head.

"We could do this the easy way," Seamus said, "easy for all of us, by just telling a little story."

Moving out of his crouching position, Cade sat in the dirt and wrapped his hands around a knee. "Whatta you wanna hear, Preacher Man? Preacher Man that's a wanted man."

Seamus listened for a moment, hearing Ling's conversation was still both lively and friendly, then continued with a quiet voice. "How about starting with Ryland and your pa?"

"Ain't the time for that story. That goes way back, and too thick. But I'll tell you this. You can go a long time thinking wrong 'bout somebody, never knowing who he really is. Me comin' here is about settling things up."

"And how am I to like the sounds of that, Cade?"

"Don't worry me none about you liking something, Preacher Man. Seems as I ain't alone comin' up the mountain with things needing settlin'."

A man's whistle arose, and the slow grind of the mule train could be heard making its way again. It seemed like a long time before Ling sifted through the bushes to join them, but Seamus figured he needed to wait until the strangers were out of sight.

"What did they say?" Seamus and the others rose to their feet and dusted themselves off.

"Friends of mine. Load up. Load down for hire. Say first time since winter."

"They catch eye of Ryland?" Cade asked, while in the process of removing his black bowler hat and pouring some water on his clustered hair.

"Ryland? No see for long time. But they say before winter. He hire train. Much heavy bags."

"Here's hopin' there's still bags to be filled." Dusty tightened the front strap on Nelson's pack.

"So they know where Ryland's camp is?"

"No. Ryland too smart. Say he meet with bags other place."

"Are you saying it's all gone?" Davin said with disappointment. "We're too late? They are out of gold?"

This brought a smile to Ling. "No gone. No gone soon." He then put his hand to his face and looked up and they all did as well. Drifting down from the darkness were flitters of snow crystals.

Nothing needed to be said at that point. In a few moments they were plodding forward again. Within an hour, Ling stopped and waited for them all to catch up. He pointed in the direction of an oddly shaped mountain, and with trepidation they started off of the main trail.

Seamus stopped to remove a pebble from his boot, and Cade waited with him.

"So, Preacher Man. Something I've been meanin' to ask."

"Since you have been such a flowing fountain of answers, go ahead and ask."

"Ash. What's your intentions?"

Seamus laughed. "Now there's some meddling."

"I told you. Ash's like kin."

Seamus turned his boot upside down and emptied it of dust and the offending pebble. "And you don't think kindly of having kinfolk getting mixed up with a horse thief?"

"There's some of that."

"Don't see as that would be a problem."

Cade raised his hands. "So what's with botherin' with all this?"

With his boot tied up, Seamus stood and tested it out. "You figure that one out, Cade, and be sure you let me know." He paused for a moment. "I suppose it's what they call faith."

"See we all have a little story, Preacher Man."

A swing of his pack and Seamus was set to go. He looked down to see how far they already traveled today. From their high point on the trail, they could see a fair distance down the mountainside.

"Spot them mules?" Cade asked.

"I am trying." Seamus squinted and stared for a while, straining to see any movement. It took a while, but when he finally spotted the train, they were actually fairly clear to see, like a centipede making its way downhill. He pointed the direction out to Cade. Then Seamus saw something else.

"You seeing what I see?" Cade asked.

"Uh . . . huh." There down below, having just passed by the pack of burros, were three solitary figures.

And they were heading up the trail.

Chapter 39

AROUND THE BEND

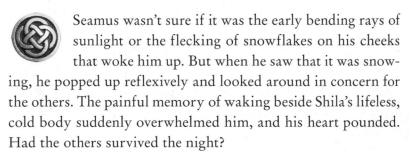 Seamus wasn't sure if it was the early bending rays of sunlight or the flecking of snowflakes on his cheeks that woke him up. But when he saw that it was snowing, he popped up reflexively and looked around in concern for the others. The painful memory of waking beside Shila's lifeless, cold body suddenly overwhelmed him, and his heart pounded. Had the others survived the night?

But instead of seeing deep powder and hearing whistling, freezing winds, there was only a soft white dusting of the high terrain. Above, the morning sun was piercing through the scattered clouds, which instead of being black and foreboding were sheep's wool with only touches of gray.

It wasn't even snowing. Looking up he could imagine the tree he had chosen for shelter was laughing at its prank as the overhanging tree branches still were misted with snow they had just released.

About ten feet away Ling sat on a boulder and crouched over a campfire, teasing at the lapping flames with his hands. They made the important decision late last night to keep the fire going. Having been confident they had been able to slip the three mysterious figures trailing behind them, it still was a considerable risk. But in the end they preferred being discovered over being consumed by the cold.

Seamus rubbed his eyes and yawned. He got up slowly, feeling every ache imposed by the cruel earth, wrapped his wool blanket around himself, grabbed his pack, and then found a seat at the pit.

"Morning, Ling."

The man gave him a curt nod and then began to work on braiding his long, black hair.

"How much farther?" Seamus reached into his pack, pulled out a tin can with dried dates, and began to chew on them, enjoying the sweetness of the wrinkled brown fruit.

"We close." Ling pulled out the map and unfolded it carefully. He tilted the map. Then he looked around, comparing it to their surroundings. Then again at the map. "Not far. Here now. Just need find creek."

Seamus shoveled a couple of dates in his mouth before realizing he didn't offer any to the guide. He held out the can. "Are you lost, friend? Before the others rise, this would be a good time to let me know. Do you really know where you're going?"

Instead of answering, Ling's gaze drifted to the right and then he slowly raised his hands over his head.

"What are you . . . ?" Seamus traced the direction of the guide's gaze and saw standing before them pointing a double-barrel shotgun was a brown-skinned man with a bushy mustache and a scraggly beard. He had overalls over a bare, muscular chest, and his worn pant legs were well short of reaching his tall boots.

Seamus lifted his hands as well. "Davin. Boys. Get up."

The armed man seemed alarmed to see the others rising from their slumber and shifted his aim back and forth and took a step back.

Ling stepped forward. "Put that down."

The man's eyes widened. "Don't move!" Then he lowered the weapon. "Ling?"

Ling clasped his hands together and bowed several times.

The man gave Ling a hearty slap on his shoulder. *"¡Que sorpresa!"*

Ling turned back and beamed. "This Ariel. Friend of Ryland. We here now."

"We're here?" The words were honey to Seamus. "C'mon, lads, let's gather your belongings and be on our way."

Ariel waved a finger at them and appealed to Ling with an accent that sounded like the local Mexicans. "Mr. Whittington. He no like much people."

"These friends," Ling said. "Ben say so."

Cade stepped forward. "Ryland is expecting me. Can you take me to him?"

The determination that steeled Cade's voice made Seamus leery. He eyed the shotgun in Ariel's hands and wondered if it might prove necessary. He started flooding himself with regrets about allowing Cade to come. But how could he have kept him from coming, short of tying him up or shooting him?

And why didn't he bring a weapon himself? What he wouldn't do now to have his ol' Brown Bess with him.

Ariel squinted at the Southerner. *"El Capitán, sí?* I send you letter."

Cade shook his head. "No. I ain't your captain. The name is Cade. Cade Gatwood."

White teeth flashed beneath Ariel's bushy mustache and he laughed. "Oh, you the *hijo.* Mr. Ryland's son, no?"

"That's about right." Cade nodded.

"*Sí*. Señor Ryland speak you all the time." Then Ariel's face changed to seriousness. "So. You know. You know about Señor Ryland."

"What about Ryland?"

"Oh. *Lo siento.* I sorry, Mr. Cade. Señor Ryland is sick. Very sick."

"Bring me to him." Cade strapped on his pack and the others scurried to gather their belongings as well.

Ling was kicking dirt on the fire, and when he caught Seamus's gaze, he beckoned him.

"What is it, Ling?"

"You here now."

"Oh. You're not coming with us?" Seamus reached in his pocket to pull out his billfold.

"Work done. Need go back."

"Understood." Seamus nodded to the others to start without him. "What do I owe you?"

"Ben pay Ling. He like Ryland. Say good man."

"Well." Seamus held his hand out to Ling and they shook. "I would say the same about you, friend." He went to leave but he paused, sensing the guide had something more to say.

"Yes?"

Ling's face was strained with concern. "Ariel. His brother. Good men. Very much trust. But . . ."

"But what?"

"This good find."

"Are you saying this is a good claim? The one Ryland has?"

"Yes. But good diggings. Much gold. Mean much trouble."

They followed Ariel around the bend and down a valley, and before long they could hear the trickling sounds of a lively creek, which was heavily covered by foliage.

The group pressed through branches and around low-lying bushes as their path thickened and then almost as suddenly it opened to a clearing and there at the bottom of a small hillside was a small waterfall leading into a tiny, pristine alpine lake. It was all nestled within a crucible formed of granite walls on all sides, which must have been what made it so remote and safe from transgressors.

Yet tearing at the beauty of the setting were the seemingly abandoned remnants of what once must have been vibrant mining efforts. Rusty shovels and pickaxes were scattered about, as were broken sluice boxes, empty bags, and rubbish drifting along the ground. Lining the water's edge were hastily constructed lean-tos and tents with torn canvas flapping in the breeze.

Ariel must have read their expressions of disappointment. "*Sí*. Much work to do. I just come back and find this. And Ryland."

"Show me," Cade said.

"*Sí*." He lowered his eyes. "This way. Just you."

Seamus stepped forward. "I'll be coming as well." He looked over to Cade, challenging him to protest. He was the one who led the Southerner here. It was his responsibility to protect Ryland. How devastated would Ashlyn be if he was to fail in this role?

Cade shot a glance of disgust at first but then acquiesced. "Yes. He's all right. A family friend."

"You all wait back here." Seamus saw that Davin and Nelson already had shovels in their hands and were starting to dig into a pile of dirt, while Dusty was bent over the lake and scooping up water to his mouth.

Ariel led Cade and Seamus to a shanty, which was the sturdiest structure in the camp but still appeared as if a large gust of wind would tip it over. There were gaps in the weathered, brackish boards and bent nails were hammered in rather than having been pulled out.

Before opening the door, Ariel seemed anxious to offer an explanation. "He very bad, I sorry. I leave camp for winter. Ryland stay. He no want to go. When I come back, this I find. Be ready."

"Be ready for what?" Seamus asked Cade, not expecting to get an answer and he didn't. Only a shrug.

As soon as the door squeaked open on its hinges, they knew. There was a putrid odor so rank, Seamus thought he would vomit. He pulled out his handkerchief from his pocket and covered his mouth.

Diffused light leaked in through the main cracks and seams in the walls and ceiling of the structure. A chamber pot was on the floor, but it was empty and not the source of the smell. There were a few items inside the cabin and all were crudely made on-site. A tree stump served as a stool besides a small table where there was a rusted iron scale. Another small table was on the other side of the room, and on it was a glass half filled with water, a melted, unlit candle and an old leather book.

Beside this was a bed, built with pine logs, still covered with bark. It appeared the mattress was nothing more than a stack of pine needles and lying on it, curled and feeble, was a man with long white and wild hair, covered with a cotton blanket. There was a gentle wheeze in his breathing, one Seamus recognized as that of a death pall.

The door opened behind them and a light and merciful fresh

breeze entered. Ariel propped a boulder in place to keep the door ajar.

Cade covered his hand over his mouth. "What is it? The stink?"

Ariel nodded. "Señor Ryland no talk much. But he say me he got lost in snow. Feet get, how you say, very, very cold."

"Frozen?" Seamus knew all about frostbite.

"*Sí*. They frozen."

"How long ago?" Cade asked.

Ariel moved over to the end of the bed and lifted the blanket. The stench rose causing Seamus to step back. Worse was the sight of Ryland's feet, which were green, swollen, and most of the toes were black.

The old man grunted and strained to twist and lift his head, revealing lips chapped and torn, his pale face beaded with sweat.

"*Perdoname.*" Ariel dipped a rag into the bowl of water and squeezed it out. "Head, very hot." Then he went to place it on Ryland's forehead, but Cade reached out a hand.

"May I?"

"*Sí.*" Ariel gave the towel one last snap and handed it to Cade, who rolled the stool beside the bed.

Cade took the towel and wiped Ryland's face, gently and slowly, and then dipped the cloth in the bowl and repeated this again. When he looked back at Seamus and Ariel, his eyes were red and moist. "His ears work?"

Ariel shrugged. "Sometimes, *sí*. Sometimes no."

"Pappy," Cade said, his voice soft and breathy. "Pappy, can you hear me? It's Cade. It's me, Pappy."

Ryland's eyelashes fluttered for a moment and a fevered smile came over his face. "Cade? Cade? Son?"

"Pappy. You just lie yourself still. I'll do the talkin'. Before you . . . 'fore you go." He started to choke with emotion. "I just here to say sorry, Pappy. I done treated you poorly." He started to sob.

Seamus nodded to Ariel and they both went outside to give Cade his peace. Whatever fears he had about the man turned out to be all wrong. At least they remained misunderstood. There surely was unresolved anger and bitterness in the Southerner, and of the worse kind. It just wasn't targeted toward Ryland. So what could it be?

Seamus was relieved to be outside of the cabin and in the fresh mountain air again. "Why didn't you take him to see a doctor?"

"Señor Ryland say no. Won't leave dig. I try. I try much."

Seamus looked around the camp. There was a rather large operation on this field. "How many were here? How many workers? Before the winter. Before they left."

"About ten, I think. Yes. *Diez.*"

"And they are all gone?"

"*Sí.* With much gold. *Mi hermano.* My brother Marcelo. He go home to Argentina. To wife. To children. Maybe back. Maybe no."

"What about you? Why didn't you go back to Argentina?" Seamus could see Davin had his shirt off and was working up a good sweat with his shovel.

"Me no wife. Nice here and more gold. I like Señor Ryland."

"If you like him so much, why did you leave him here alone?" He watched Ariel closely, trying to discern if he was telling the truth.

"Like Señor Ryland. No like snow."

Seamus laughed. "Yes. That is true enough for me as well."

Ariel eyed Seamus. It was clear he was sizing him up as well. "And you?"

"Yes." Seamus raised an eyebrow. "What about me?"

"You know Señor Ryland?"

"His daughter." He reached into his pocket, pulled out the photograph, and held it out to the man.

"Ashlyn? *Muy bonita, sí?*"

"Yes, she is." Seamus gave it a good glance himself before he returned it. "But she is broke."

"Broke? I no understand." Ariel opened the breech of the shotgun and laid it limply over his shoulder.

"Broke means no money."

"I know what broke mean." He sat back on the edge of the sluice. "But Marcelo bring Ashlyn the gold of Ryland. He send all."

"Your brudder?" Seamus tilted his head with cynicism.

For the first time, anger appeared on Ariel's face. "Marcelo bring gold to Ashlyn. Before he go home."

"Were you with him?"

The question tripped up Ariel for a moment. "No, señor. Marcelo go to San Francisco with gold. I last here with Ryland." He paused, and Seamus thought he detected guilt. "Before I go south for winter."

"Then how do you know your—?"

"Marcelo bring gold." There was vehemence in his voice. Then he put his head down. "Unless."

"Unless what?"

"Unless Marcelo die first."

Seamus could see the strength of integrity in the man's eyes. And if Marcelo was of the same ilk, Seamus believed every effort would have been made to deliver Ryland's portion to Ashlyn. But what could have happened? There was only one immediate way to get an answer.

"We'll have to talk to Ryland."

Just as the words came out his mouth, they heard the squeaking of the hinges of the shanty and they looked to see Cade coming out.

Seamus was about to inquire, but before he could, the Southerner looked up at him and shook his head.

Chapter 40

COTTON WALLER

In the full pain of heat, they started digging the grave. Seamus had walked the outskirts of the camp with Cade and together they found a ridge with a good view of the mine below. They both figured the old man would have wanted to keep watch on his stake. The two of them stripped off their shirts, lifted their shovels, and began their task.

It didn't take long for them to realize the ground they chose was less than ideal, and Seamus endured Cade's cursing as they spaded more stone than dirt. There was a time when these same words would have flowed freely from Seamus's lips, but now they seemed foreign and offensive.

But if both the coarse language and the difficulty of the dig took the edge off of Cade's grief, then he wouldn't complain.

It was many hours of labor before they had dug down deep enough to be considered close to finishing. The light had waned by now and Cade threw his shovel up from the hole, climbed up, and sat down and lit his pipe. Seamus was all too pleased to get a break as well and grabbed his canteen. The two of them looked down and admired their work.

Cade gazed up to the sun. "Ain't time to do the service."

"Not today at least." How could they have service without a priest? "We are having a service?"

The Southerner pulled his pipe out and spat down into the hole. "Of course we's gonna have a service. You're the preacher man."

Seamus pointed to his chest. "Me?"

"You got a Bible, no?"

He was about to say no but remembered that Reverend Sanders had placed it in his pack for him. "Well . . . yes, but—"

"Then we got a service, ain't we?"

"I suppose we do." Seamus had no idea what he was going to do, but Cade was right. Ryland deserved a proper burial with some words shared. It was least he could do for Ashlyn. Oh, Ashlyn! How would she ever take the news? And who would be the one to tell her? He was convinced she would never want to hear from him again. But for whatever reason, that didn't keep him from prying in her business.

"Cade?"

He put his pipe in the corner of his mouth and leaned back, placing his palms on the ground. It was as if something in Seamus's tone had him bracing himself.

"What is with all of the mystery?"

Cade shrugged off the question.

"If all you wanted to do was speak kind words to Ashlyn's father, why didn't you just tell her? I mean, why put everyone through all of that?"

"It didn't seem nobody's matter."

Seamus tried to seek the hidden truth in the man's face, but it was buried deep. "There's something more to this. You're not finished with what you came to do."

Cade grinned and turned to Seamus. "You impress me, Preacher Man."

"What is it? What happens next?"

"The matter ain't yet settled. That's all."

"Tell me, Cade. What about your father? What about Ryland?" He held out his canteen.

Cade accepted it and took a swig. "A man named Cotton." He handed the water back to Seamus.

"I don't understand."

"He was there. When my pappy, my blood pappy passed. Momma always told me somethin' was afoul. She never forgave Ryland. Said he was pushin' them. Working 'em too hard and that was the cause of the accident. I told her, no Momma. Ryland, he's a good man. But she said, no son. Someday you'll know.

"All the while, Ryland took me in. Just like his boy. Treated me right. No different than his Ash. But I got older. Dumber. I started believin' my momma. Turns out she was right all along."

The words were like daggers to Seamus's gut. "Ryland was to blame for the accident?"

"No. Not that part." Cade picked up a rock and threw it down the hole, and it rattled below. "There was blame. Blood on hands. Just those hands weren't Ryland's. That's what I came to say."

"It was this Cotton? He was the cause?"

"Nah." Cade grabbed his shovel and climbed back down and started digging.

Seamus wasn't ready to work again. He had to make sure Ashlyn was safe. He went down in the hole as well and grabbed Cade's shovel. "I need to know, Cade. Who is this Cotton? What did you learn?"

Cade tugged on the shovel, freeing it from Seamus's grip. Then he dug it into the dirt and leaned on the handle. "You want this? Your hands dirty? Is that right, Preacher Man?"

It was a good question and he thought for a moment. Seamus nodded. "Yes. You know I love that girl. I like you as well, Cade." He looked around the walls of dirt. "Can't you see? I'm in the hole with you, brudder."

The Southerner eyed Seamus for a while. Then he relaxed. "All right then, Seamus Hanley. You in the hole."

As these words came out of the man's mouth, Seamus gulped, but he meant it. He wanted to walk through this with Cade.

"Cotton Waller. He was at Fowler Creek Mine. A runaway slave. Black boy. All his life, he carries a secret. Of how my pappy died."

"Why didn't he tell anyone?"

"Who was going to believe a runaway? Get himself lynched either way."

"So he finally told you?"

"When he's near dying. Nothin' left to lose and only days to spare. He sent a son. All the way from Tennessee to fetch me, to see his old man before he died of 'sumption.

"Turned out, I knew the story some. Only I didn't know Ryland left the claim site that night to make supper. They sent Cotton to git some berries. This left my pappy and this other partner behind to shut things down.

"Cotton heard arguing. That boy came with a bucket of blackberries and he's lookin' through the bushes. Watching. That's when he saw it."

"He saw the mine collapse?"

"Nah . . . he saw my pappy arguing with this man and being told this and that about his fair share."

Cade pulled his shovel out of the dirt. "And one of these

here." He examined the edge of the blade. "It came down hard. My pappy went down. Cotton said he saw the blood. The body being dragged in the mine. Before it all came down. As this man's wiping his hands of the dust and his crime and before he started hollerin' for help, well that's when ol' Cotton found his feet."

Seamus moved the shovel away from his face with his arm. "He was murdered? Your father was murdered?"

"That he was. All for a bigger share. All for gold." Cade put both hands on the handle and then drove the edge into the ground. Then he tossed the shovel full of dirt out of the hole.

Seamus reached for his shovel as his mind whirred with all he had heard. "And this man?"

"Yes," Cade said. "I do believe you know of him."

"Henry. Henry Parnell."

Cade turned and smiled. "Now there you go, Seamus Hanley. You now official. You in the hole with me."

Chapter 41

THE BLESSING

 As the sun dipped over the granite peaks, Seamus felt a palpable drop in the temperature, and he rubbed his hands together to get some warmth.

He needed some time away from the others to process all he had heard and to do something he hadn't done since he left San Francisco: have some time alone with God.

Seamus sat on the cliff's edge and dangled his feet down. There must be a five-hundred-foot drop from where he was. But the fear he had was not from the heights, but from trying to figure out what he would say at tomorrow's mountaintop funeral service.

After all, this was Ashlyn's father.

From where he sat, the ground was sandy. A few pebbles cut loose and tumbled over the ledge and bounced and hopped their way toward the bottom. There was something eerily exhilarating about being perched on this precipice. He was firm and safe, but it gave him a sense of awe to be so high up and able to see for miles and miles around him.

He reached into the pack beside him and pulled out the leather-bound book Reverend Sanders had given him several months ago. At the time, Seamus was almost insulted by the gift. *What am I going to do with this? I don't even understand any of it.*

But as he had time to study it with the brothers, it slowly began to make sense. There was power in the words. Seamus rubbed his hands across the smooth leather with the words *The Holy Bible* imprinted upon it.

He laughed at himself as he thought of some of the first questions he had asked of the brothers. They were patient and kind with him, but even they couldn't hold back a smile at times.

When he opened the cover, a piece of paper folded inside was caught in the breeze and started to flutter. He grasped at it, rather recklessly, and had to grab on to a tree root to catch his balance.

Now the paper was crushed and he set the Bible down so he could straighten it out. It was a note from the reverend. It saddened Seamus to think of the disappointment he must have caused the man once he learned his prized protégé was actually a criminal.

> *Dearest Brother Seamus,*
>
> *When you read this, no doubt the enemy of all mankind continues to cause you to believe you are not worthy of God's love. I saw the deep remorse in your eyes and it pained me so. You are burdened by your past. Just as we all are.*
>
> *I regret to say that there is nothing you can do on your own to erase your past. No roads are long enough to lead you away. There are not enough good deeds you can ever do to cover up your shortfalls. Lastly, you*

cannot save others when you are incapable of even saving yourself.

All of these are great lies, and they only lead us to foolish pursuits. Emptiness. Despair.

What I have to say to you, dear son, is you were never meant to leave those behind. Those things you cannot change.

Instead, you are to embrace them because they are your gift. Neither is there anything for you to run from or for you yet to find. For He has found you.

God comes to us in golden splendor, and His radiance in our lives far outshines any other treasure, any other accomplishment, and our lives become richer the more we understand this.

Your friend, the Indian boy, knew this, and I promise you as he smiles down from heaven, he is proud of the man you have come to be.

You will never be alone again. God will use you in mighty ways, my son. Of that, I am well convinced.

Celebrate that you have been taken to so many dark, difficult places in your life. For now you know the way out and can well lead others to the light. You are free, Seamus. Rejoice! Your life is no longer about you. It is about the blessing you have received and all you will now share with others.

In His Love,
Reverend Charles Sanders

P.S. Will they miss you when you are gone? Yes. I already do.

Seamus read the letter through several times, and each time it drove deeper into the core of his spirit. As the wind began to whistle and sing praise to the Creator of all that abounded around him, he found strength in the knowledge of who he was. Who he was in God.

The words echoed through the cool air of the valley, and freely with élan through the chambers of his soul and Seamus began to weep. First slowly and then with joyful abandon.

Above, eagles flew, wide-spanned and angling with grace, and then added their voices to the chorus.

And it sounded like forgiveness.

Chapter 42

WHAT LIES AHEAD

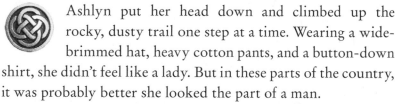 Ashlyn put her head down and climbed up the rocky, dusty trail one step at a time. Wearing a wide-brimmed hat, heavy cotton pants, and a button-down shirt, she didn't feel like a lady. But in these parts of the country, it was probably better she looked the part of a man.

It was early enough in the morning that the sun was just making its first appearance, but she could already tell it would be a hot day. She had never seen so much snow in her life, and under any other circumstances she would be enjoying the liveliness of streams, the burst of mountain flower blooms, and the emerging greenness of spring.

Up ahead waiting for them yet again was their guide, Mac, who was tall, thin, and bore a long drooping blond mustache that made him appear perpetually sad. He leaned with his arms crossed and his back against his burro, who was equally unimpressed by their pace.

When Ashlyn arrived, in between the guide's tobacco spits, she heard his protests, ones that were quite familiar to her now.

"I should have charged by the hour."

Ashlyn looked down the hill a good fifty yards behind them to see Henry Parnell waggling, weaving, and cursing. Although he dressed in his newly outfitted mining pants, shirt and boots, his girth and unsteady feet betrayed him as an imposter. Every twenty yards or so, whether to find his bearings or to sue for rest, he would pull out a map, wipe sweat off of his brow, and then look lost in all directions.

It would have been comical to Ashlyn if the repercussions weren't so severe. Her anger was mounting with every bad turn and off-track decision he had made. And they had come so close. Yesterday they had passed a train of burros, whose drivers described having seen two men fitting the descriptions of Seamus and Cade, just ahead of them in a party of six.

But then they lost the trail, and seeing Henry jabbing hopelessly at the map made her furious.

She turned to Mac. "Do you think you could get us there?"

The man looked her up and down and squinted an eye as if he was measuring his response and determining whether he was free to speak plainly. "Well, ma'am, that is usually why people hire themselves a guide."

Ashlyn grimaced. "Yes. I see."

She tapped her foot as Henry stumbled his way up to them, and when he finally arrived, he was pasty and spattered with sweat. He plopped down on a boulder and groaned as he put his hand on the small of his back.

"How much farther, Mr. Parnell?" There was a harsh edge in her voice of which she was not ashamed.

"Oh. Just a moment." He pulled out his canteen and lifted it at a full angle and only a few drops trickled out. He handed the canister to Mac. "Here, sir. Fill this up, will you?"

The sinewy guide spat out a chunk of tobacco and walked over, then exchanged Henry's with his own canteen. "Take this one."

"Good. Thank you. Oh my. This thin air. It's enough to whittle me to nothing."

"How much longer?" Ashlyn was draining of all patience.

"Oh yes." He pulled out the map again and untangled it and then he spun it around. "Hmmm." Henry pulled a monocle on a chain out of his shirt pocket. Then he looked toward a mountain range, and then back at the map. "Yes." Again he glanced up and then to the map. "That doesn't seem to make sense."

Ashlyn stormed over and snatched the map from the banker's hands and gave it to Mac.

"What are you doing, Ashlyn?"

"My father could be dead by now. We've been lost for a day."

"It's a difficult map to read. And with all due respect to our friend here with the donkey, I am the most experienced one of the bunch."

"This is not Appalachia and that was twenty years ago." She gave him a disparaging glance. "And I would assume you were of . . . a much different constitution."

His eyes rounded at the offense, and he puffed out his chin. "Nevertheless. There are some skills you never lose."

"Why, Mr. Parnell, based on what I have witnessed with this trip, I would say you are in no haste at all to get to my father."

He poked a plump finger at her. "That is enough, young lady."

Ashlyn ignored him and turned to Mac. "What do you see?"

"Here." Mac displayed the map before them and pointed with a fingernail that was long, yellowed, with dirt underneath. "This right here is Miller Creek. Follow that, and we should be there."

Ashlyn looked up to the imposing mountains that lay ahead. "And how far, sir, is it ahead?"

Mac spit out another wad of moist black fluid. "It's not ahead." He nodded down the hill they had just climbed. "It's about two hours back that way."

Ashlyn felt throbbing pain in her boots, on her heels and at the tips of her toes. She didn't want to think of the blisters she had formed over the past few days. Her body ached all over, from the ardor of the hike and having to sleep on the hard, wet ground.

But nothing compared to the pain of regret she had in allowing Henry to lead the trail. Certainly, they would be too late to halt the tragedy. Oh, how she had failed her father!

At least now she was confident they were heading in the right direction as Mac hardly referred to the map and had nary wavered a step. He had them tracking alongside the creek, and despite the unpleasantness of having to wave off ravenous mosquitoes, she could sense they were getting closer.

The greatest drag on their progress came from waiting for Henry, whose complaints about the conditions and the tyranny of their speed only grew.

Finally, Mac said the words they had been hoping to hear. "Just up ahead."

Ashlyn's heart leapt. What would they find? She looked over to Henry, who suddenly appeared pale and spooked. "What is it?"

"No. No, it's nothing." He reached into his pocket, pulled out a pistol, and popped open the chamber.

"Nothing said about any trouble." Mac eyed him with suspicion.

"Don't worry. You've done your service for us. If you're certain we're here."

"Sure as can be. Those are tailings there. That means there's a digging close by, if we aren't standing on it. And judging by that gun, I'm assuming we aren't all that welcome."

Henry reached into his pocket and pulled out a billfold. "Why don't I just pay you and you can head back down the trail?"

"What?" Ashlyn was beyond exasperated.

"You'll need to trust me," Henry said.

"As you wish, mister." Mac started to untie the packs from the side of the burro.

"That won't be necessary." Henry handed the guide several bills.

Mac counted the money. "Hey. I am not complaining, mister, but you overpaid me by a lot."

"That's because we'll be keeping the burro as well."

The mustached man took off his hat and scratched his head. "Then that will cost you another forty."

Henry stared at him for a moment. "Fine." He peeled off a few more bills and handed them to the man. "But it's time for you to leave."

"Gladly." He tipped the rim of his cap. "Ma'am."

Confused, Ashlyn stood beside Henry and they both watched as Mac reversed course and winded his way around the bends of the creek until he disappeared out of sight.

Henry tied the animal to a tree. Then he cupped some water to his mouth, took his hat off and poured some on his head.

"Now," he said with a wavering voice. "I think it's best you go ahead alone." He held up the pistol and sighted it with his eye. "I'll be nearby."

"What . . . what aren't you telling me?" Ashlyn's mind spun with fear and apprehension.

"I would be quite surprised if your father isn't already gone. You must prepare yourself for the worst, Ashlyn. I'm afraid you're in danger yourself. That boy. Cade. He is most unpredictable."

She glanced ahead in the direction of where the camp was to lie. "And you want me to just—"

"Go. And for goodness sake, take care of yourself. This will all be over soon enough."

Ashlyn's legs were stiff and unwilling to move, but she pressed ahead. What if her father needed her? What was she waiting for?

Something else was drawing her forward. Giving her strength. Yet who it was surprised her.

She wanted to see Seamus again. Horse thief or not, and as strange as all of these circumstances were, something told her deep within that he was someone she could trust.

Chapter 43

BENEDICTION

 He tossed the last few shovels of dirt on Ryland's grave, and then Cade stood back and removed his hat, and the others gathered around the dirt mound did likewise.

After a few uneasy minutes, Cade looked over to Seamus and nodded.

"Oh yes." Seamus cleared his throat. He didn't know if he was sweating from his turn at the shovel or from apprehension of this moment. "Cade has asked if I would be willing to offer a few words."

"Words? About what?" Davin squinted.

"From this." Seamus displayed the Bible and then thumbed in search of his verse as the thin pages fluttered in his hand. For a moment, Seamus thought of his friend Phineas Blake and his cargo load of French-language Bibles. What would he have thought of Seamus offering a benediction? Winn, no doubt, would have laughed.

That would be nothing as derisive as if the old Seamus could be observing this strange, new version of himself. What hilarity it would produce!

But then Seamus was reminded of Shila and became encouraged by the words he knew his Indian friend would utter: *"God man."* The thought made him smile and encouraged him as well.

And the reverend? Seamus could almost feel the large hands of his mentor resting on his shoulders. *"You are free, Seamus. Rejoice! Your life is no longer about you. It is about the blessing you have received and all you will now share with others."*

It didn't matter if Seamus was embarrassed. It wasn't about him anymore. He nodded and they lowered their heads.

"Dearly beloved. We are gathered here today . . ." Then he lost his place in his Bible and fumbled through pages for a few moments before glancing up with a touch of panic. "Dearly beloved . . ." Another long pause, and now the others were exchanging glances.

Dusty cupped a hand to his mouth and leaned into Seamus. "Something about ashes."

"Yes. Ashes to ashes. Dust to dust. That's right." Seamus swallowed and then only the whistling of the trees through the pines could be heard. He wiped the sweat off of his forehead and Davin offered a nod of affirmation.

"Right." Seamus closed the Bible and clasped it to his heart. Then the words came to him, as in a whisper to his soul, and they were startling. He had to keep himself from saying out loud, "Are You sure You want me to say that?"

But instead he let go and spoke without restraint. "I do not know much about this man's life. Other than to know where and how it ended. We do know Ryland Whittington was liked by many and loved by some. Including his daughter, Ashlyn.

His wife, may she rest in peace. And Cade here, who he knew as a son.

"However, these words are not for this man, who lay buried below. For he speaks now with his maker. And we cannot suppose how that conversation goes. But this man still teaches us while buried in the soil. For though he spent much of his life digging, searching, striving for gold and riches, we all stand as witness to the truth that he took none of it with him. Not an ounce. Not a single speck of gold dust."

He sensed the uneasiness of his audience and noticed Cade glaring at him.

"Spare a kind word or two, Preacher Man?"

Seamus held up his hand. "I am getting there."

"Hurry 'bout it, will ya?" Dusty looked warily at the dirt beneath him. "'Taint wise to be disturbin' the deceased."

Seamus raised his voice. "No. This man Ryland could not take any gold with him. But I can say without any hesitation that the last few breathing moments he spent with his son, Cade, were among the most precious of his entire life. For every father wills for his son a better hope, a better future, a better life than the one he lived. No doubt, in you, Cade, he saw the true treasure he had mined during his life. The question for all of us, those of us who continue to journey, is how will we respond? How will we honor our fathers and the dreams set before us?"

Seamus began to get his gumption. He almost wished now that the reverend were here to see him. "So are we not to seek treasure? Are we not to seek the prize? Yes. We are to seek, to strive, and to pursue with each and every one of our breaths. We are designed to pursue. To chase. To dig for this treasure. But—" The last word echoed and he held up a finger for effect. "The lesson, my friends and brudder, is that we are to choose our treasure most wisely. For that is all we have with our time here. It is all that matters."

He paused and wondered if he should say more, but he chose instead to let these words sink into his congregants.

"Are you . . . saying . . . we shouldn't dig for gold?" Davin knitted his brows.

"No, Davin. That's not exactly what I'm saying."

"What he say?" Ariel asked. "Gold *no bueno*?"

"No," Seamus said. "Gold is fine. It's for jewelry. And we need to have a means to support ourselves. There was gold in the temple and the High Holy. It's just . . ."

They looked at him blankly, but they had stopped protesting.

Seamus's heart was pounding. "That's all I wanted to say to you all. In fact, it wasn't my intention to do all of the speaking. How about if now we close our eyes and we can just think what we want? Whatever kind words we have. For Ryland Whittington."

They nodded, and Seamus watched as each of them closed their eyes, and then he did the same, relieved it was over. It was probably the worst sermon he ever heard, but he was exhilarated nonetheless. He reveled in the quietness of the moment. The songs of the breeze, the chipmunks, and the midday birds.

And then there was a piercing scream. "Noooo!"

They all looked up to see someone running toward them.

A young boy with long hair and anguish in his face reached down and picked up a small boulder and ran toward them with anger and rage.

No. It wasn't a boy. It was a woman.

"Ashlyn?" How did she—? What was she doing? First pure joy erupted at seeing her face, but then compassion flooded through him. What a terrible way to discover her father's death!

But she was not coming at them with the face of grief. It was with revenge and retaliation and she was heading toward Cade, who held up his hands and stumbled backward.

Seamus lurched forward, grabbed her by the waist, and lifted her off her feet.

"Let me go! Let me at him. Murderer! You killed him!"

He felt the full force of the rock she swung on the small of his back, and he toppled to the ground but took her down with him. Seamus rolled over atop her and pinned her arms.

She writhed and bucked like a wild bronco. "Murderer!"

"No . . . Ashlyn. There is no murderer." Seamus felt her pain and his face softened as she spilled tears.

"Cade! He loved you."

Cade went to kneel beside her, but Seamus nodded for him to move away.

"Ashlyn. It's not what you think." She began to relax and Seamus went to loosen his grip but she tried to burst free.

"Your father was sick. Ryland died of gangrene."

"What did you say?' She shook her head.

"Gangrene. He had frostbite."

The tension of her body let go and she cried now.

He rolled over to her side and let her sit up. He put his arms around her and she held him back. Deeper, harder as her body heaved with sobs.

"How?" she whispered.

"He got lost in the snow. By the time we got here, it was too late."

"When?"

"Just yesterday."

"Oh . . . I should have been here. I should have been here!"

Seamus moved the hair from her face behind her ears and wiped her tears away with his finger. He looked back and Dusty held out a handkerchief that didn't look too dirty. Using this, Seamus wiped the rest of her tears, then used the moisture to clear away the dirt smudges as well. He ran the back of his hand against her cheeks and wanted to draw all of her sadness out of her big, brown eyes.

Her temper flared. "But that doesn't mean Cade couldn't have killed him."

"Ain't true, Ash. I loved your father."

"All lies." She narrowed her eyes and appealed to Seamus. "Cade is lying. He was planning on killing my father. Maybe he didn't get the chance."

"Who told you this, Ash?" Cade kneeled beside her. "Did . . . Henry . . . tell you this?" The word *Henry* came out with a snarl.

She met his eyes. "Yes. Henry told me everything. No one knew of my father's business better than he."

Cade's lips thinned and his nostrils flared.

"Listen, Ash, and listen closely. Henry done killed my pappy. Ain't no accident."

"What?" Ashlyn started to shake her head, then climbed to her feet. Seamus and Cade did as well.

"That's right, Ash. Cotton, the ol' runaway slave, saw it all. Told me hisself."

She put her hands to her head. "But . . . how do you know this Cotton fellow was telling the truth?"

"'Cause he was dying. No reason not to. Henry took a shovel to the side of my pappy's head."

"And my father . . . ?"

"He never knew. Thought the same as all of us. And I treated him badly. That's what I came to say to him."

"But . . ." Ashlyn's expression turned pale.

Concern blazed in Seamus. "What is it, Ashlyn?"

"Here's here. Mr. Parnell. And he has a gun."

Chapter 44

IN THE WOODS

Seamus was frustrated with their indecision. They outnumbered him, and the double-barreled shotgun was more than a match for a pistol. But now it was dark and their advantage was lost.

Parnell was out there somewhere and they would have to sleep.

They sat around the fire as the flames towered above them. Their silhouettes would have made it an easy shot for a sniper with a rifle. But they decided if they were in the middle of the clearing, it would get them out of a pistol's range.

Still, this knowledge didn't make Seamus any less skittish. Every snapping of a twig. Every flight of a bat. Each movement in the shadows. Even just the wind bending the trees. They were all on edge.

Cade stood and glared into the darkness. "We just gonna sit here? Let him sneak up on us?"

"He mighta pulled anchor." Dusty whittled a pine branch.

Seamus turned toward Ashlyn, who was curled up against him. "Do you s'pose there is a chance he would just go back and leave us be?"

Ashlyn shook her head. "The bank is lost without the gold. He won't leave without it."

"What gold you say?" Ariel was polishing the barrel of the shotgun, something he had been doing for most of the day.

"My father's gold."

Ariel put the cloth down. "Gold in dirt."

"I do not . . . understand . . ." Ashlyn looked to Seamus.

He nodded. "Ariel says all of the gold left in December. Before the winter set in."

"But where did it go? Who did my father send it to?"

"So you never spoke to Annie about this, did you?"

She shook her head, her brown eyes glistening in the fire's flames.

"Mi hermano," Ariel said, "he is a good man."

"No one is questioning your brudder, friend." Seamus took Ashlyn's hand. "There was a box delivered to you before Christmas. Annie was saving it for—"

"The fire?" Ashlyn's voice sunk.

"Yes. She thought it well to wrap it as a gift for you and it burned I am afraid. But think now, Ashlyn. There was money in the box, but Annie was saying there was a wooden star in there as well. Maybe it was . . . a clue of some notion your father left for you. Perhaps your father knew already Henry couldn't be trusted."

"No. My father always was making shapes out of wood for me. Hearts, butterflies, tulips. I'm afraid it was mere sentiment."

There was a rustling in the trees.

"What was that?" Dusty stood.

Davin moved over beside Seamus and leaned in. Ashlyn

gripped his arm tightly, and Seamus felt the warmth and soft-
ness of her body as she clung to him.

"We oughta be the hunter." Cade reached for the shotgun,
but Ariel pulled it away.

"Sit down, Cade." Ashlyn frowned.

"He is right." Seamus stood as well. "We're just sitting here,
vulnerable and exposed. There is more of us. We should be taking the fight to him. It isn't as if Henry will be sneaking up on
us."

Again there was a rustling in front of them and they squatted to their knees. The noise was definitely from the grove of
aspen trees across the creek.

"Cade," Seamus whispered. "Why don't you circle yourself
around to the left, and I'll come from the other side. Ariel, you
keep them safe here, will you?"

The noise sounded again.

Something was coming. Seamus stepped forward and
squinted.

Four legs. It was an animal. A bear? No. It was a mule.
Seamus relaxed and turned back. That's when he saw Henry
with a gun pointed at Ariel's back.

"All right. Put the shotgun down. Easy. Easy. That's right."

The Argentine placed the shotgun on the ground and
stepped back.

"That long blade of yours, Cade. That's it. Toss that to the
ground."

Seamus held his breath. He felt Ashlyn sliding in beside him.

"Little man." He shook the barrel of his pistol toward
Davin. "Yes, you, son. Go ahead and bring me those weapons."

Davin looked to Seamus.

Seamus stepped forward. He recognized the pistol from the
day he was at the banker's office. "You only have two shots.
There are seven of us."

Henry laughed, his face looking sinister in the flicker of flames. "Was it two or three? And if it was two, then who should it be? Your dear Ashlyn? The boy?" He pointed his pistol at Davin. "Bring those to me now."

"Go ahead." Seamus nodded to his brother, who picked up the knife and shotgun and dropped them at Henry's feet.

Cade went to step forward, but Seamus grabbed his arm.

Henry kicked Davin, and the boy returned to the others. "Good. Now all of you take a seat. No one is going to get hurt. You're going to give me what I came for and me and the donkey will be gone."

Slowly, they returned to their places around the fire, but they nestled in close to one another.

"That's it. Everyone get in nice and tight so I can see you all."

Except for Cade, who remained standing.

"That's close enough." Henry cocked the trigger.

"C'mon, Henry. Why don't you and I settle this? This ain't nobody else's worries. No need others gettin' hurt."

"Hmmm. Too late for that, huh, Cade?"

"Why'd you do it?"

"What? You believe that old runaway slave Cotton Waller?"

"There's only one liar, as I sees it."

Ashlyn whispered in Seamus's ear, "Do something."

"Is that what you want to hear, Cade? That I took down the great Urston Gatwood?"

"Why, Henry? Didn't want to split three ways?"

Henry laughed. "That's what you think? No. Ashlyn's daddy, Ryland Whittington. He was the greedy one. But he wouldn't have had the courage to do what I did. Couldn't even had thought it up."

"Then why?" Cade's voice cracked. "Why you'd take my pappy's life?"

"Well, son. If it isn't greed, that leaves only one thing in the heart of men. What? You don't know what a pretty woman your mama was?"

Seamus knew that would take Cade over the edge. He pushed Ashlyn away and prepared to leap at Henry, but the gun rang out.

The explosion ripped through the darkness, and Cade fell back. They all stumbled in the shock.

Then the screams.

But they were not coming from Cade.

Henry fell to his knees and his hands covered his eyes, and even in the dim light, Seamus could see the blood flowing over his fingers.

"I can't see. I can't see!"

Ashlyn ran to Cade. "Are you all right?"

Seamus picked up the shotgun from the ground and handed it to Ariel. Then he saw the shattered pistol in pieces on the dirt. The old gun had exploded on itself when Henry shot.

"What happened?" Cade asked.

There was a gasp and the hulking body of the banker toppled to the ground.

Ashlyn kneeled beside Henry and pulled his hands away to see the wounds on his face. "There is so much blood."

Cade picked up his knife from the ground. "He won't steal me of the pleasure."

Seamus stood between Cade and Henry's still body. "He isn't worth it, Cade. Not to you. Not to anybody."

"This is justice. Ain't got no proof to try the man. Cotton's dead." Cade tried to push Seamus out of the way, but he held firm.

"Stabbing this man," Seamus said, "that won't bring your da back."

"I owe this to Pappy. Step back, Seamus."

He put his hand on Cade's shoulder. "Really? This is what your father would want? You to be a murderer?"

"How would I know what my pappy wanted? I was five years old when he was murdered."

"I was asking about Ryland." Seamus noticed something in Cade's eyes. "What is it? You told him, didn't you? You told Ryland about this before he died. There ain't no use denying it. I see it clear as day. What did he tell you?"

Cade started to cry. "He ain't tell me nothin'."

"What did he tell you, Cade?"

The Southerner looked at Seamus and the terror and violence was seeping out. He couldn't hold the anger.

Cade put his hand over his mouth. "Ryland told me. He says just like you said."

"What did I say, Cade?"

"That me . . . and Ashlyn. He said, he wasted his whole life. We's the only gold that mattered."

Chapter 45

REDEMPTION

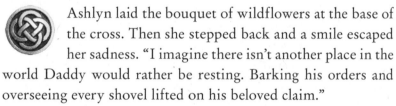 Ashlyn laid the bouquet of wildflowers at the base of the cross. Then she stepped back and a smile escaped her sadness. "I imagine there isn't another place in the world Daddy would rather be resting. Barking his orders and overseeing every shovel lifted on his beloved claim."

Seamus reached out for her slender hand and she grasped his and leaned her head into his shoulder. They stood together in a beautiful silence. He didn't want to interrupt her thoughts of grieving and quietly reveled that she needed him, soaking in the sweet stillness of their moment together.

Finally she turned and nodded and they walked away from the grave and to the overview. "Have you arrived at a decision?" she asked.

"About?"

"Your brother."

"Oh. That decision." He hadn't considered it much but knew he needed to do so now. "My older sister would throttle me if she knew I abandoned him up here in the wilderness."

"But . . ."

"But after enduring all he did to get out here to find me, I s'pose Davin deserves his poke at these mountains as much as any of these dredgers. Besides, having a wealthy brudder is something I could grow accustom to."

She laughed and they stopped at the ledge and looked down at the world that seemed so far away from them now. "And do you believe there is more gold to be found here in this claim?"

"Ariel seems to think so. Your father certainly did." He turned to her. "I've been wanting to ask you. What were you thinking when you heard your father is leaving all of this to Cade?"

She peered out across the canyon. "Daddy would have made that choice on only one condition."

"And what would that be?"

Ashlyn squinted in the sun's rays, her face soft and lovely even in the ruggedness of their surroundings. "If Daddy believed he already gave me all I needed."

He smiled at her. "Well, there is one way we can solve the mystery."

"Oh yes? And how precisely would that be, Seamus Hanley?"

"We only need to go to Argentina and find Ariel's brother Marcelo."

She grimaced. "Indeed. I am afraid as well we would discover not only Marcelo in Argentina, but the gold that was intended for us as well."

Seamus glanced behind them. "Make sure dear Ariel doesn't hear you speaking as such. He is thoroughly convinced his brother is above all reproach."

"Gold has a way of breaking the best of men. If you asked my father, he would tell you the same." She looked down below and seemed to be reminded of something. "I must return."

The idea of returning, of leaving this place, seemed unnecessary to Seamus. He had everything he needed standing beside him.

"Poor Annie." Ashlyn reached down, pulled up a flower, and tossed it into the wind and they watched it drift away. "I left her alone with Sarah Mae. We may end up with more violence on our hands."

"Oh, dear Sarah Mae." Ashlyn chuckled and lowered her head.

"What is it?"

Ashlyn wrinkled her nose. "Well, it's just that she tried to convince me that God spoke to her and said He had a new plan for her life and she was going to share it with all who had ears. Some kind of burning-bush experience, I suppose."

"And you aren't believing her?" Seamus couldn't help but touch her flowing auburn curls.

"It's hard not to doubt the woman, but it's just I wonder why God doesn't share those plans with us before we make such tragic mistakes." Her brown eyes locked on his and he thought he saw shame.

Seamus rubbed her cheek with the back of his hand, and he was embarrassed to see they were dirty, but she didn't seem to mind. "Without the storm, we would never treasure the rainbow."

She swatted him playfully on his arm. "See, Seamus Hanley? You have been spending too much time with Reverend Sanders. Why if you are not careful, he'll have you preaching in the streets."

"And this would be a bad thing?"

"I suppose I could get used to it. As long as you weren't spending *all* of your time tending to the congregation." Her face suddenly shifted to concern. "Gracie. The children. We need to get back. Oh, Seamus, what am I going to do?"

"What are *we* going to do?"

"It's all over. La Cuna. This was our last chance. We're ruined. There is no one left to beg for help."

Seamus hugged her. "There is always someone to beg." Then he looked deep in her eyes. "God will provide an answer."

They heard noise from behind, and there, standing with a shovel in his hand, was Davin. He looked at Seamus, appearing terribly apprehensive about getting a final answer, yet unable to survive the suspense any longer. "Well?"

"There is our answer right there." Seamus grinned. "My little brudder is going to find us some gold."

<hr/>

Henry Parnell was mounted on the burro, with a towel wrapped around his eyes, and clinging onto the neck of the animal.

Cade shook Seamus's hands. "You sure we ain't just leave him for the buzzards?"

Seamus scratched behind the ears of the donkey. "I am sure if we ask this fellow, he would agree with that." He patted Cade on the shoulder. "It's good your choosing not to ruin your life on account of this man. He's done all of the damage he will. Besides, you've got a fine claim to manage."

"Yeah. I guess we'll aim at seeing what the old gal has left in her."

Davin came up and gave his brother a hug.

Seamus kneeled down beside him. "Now remember the terms of our arrangement, little brudder. I'll be sending Clare a letter right away, letting her know you are safe except for a wee case of gold fever. And I'll be back myself in a month to make certain you're doing well."

Dusty put his arm around Davin. "Boy'll be well tended."

Seamus stood. "Wouldn't be leaving him here if I wasn't plain clear on that, Dusty." He gripped the man's hand. "You've been a good friend to my brudder, and a fine man as well." Out of the corner of his eye, he saw Nelson pacing.

"What's with the admiral? He's awful fidgety."

Davin shrugged.

"Hey, Nelson," Seamus said. "Aren't you going to give me a proper good-bye?"

The teenager nodded and Seamus put his arms around him, but he received it stiffly. Clearly something was disturbing him.

"What is it, Nelson? You can tell me."

He looked at Seamus and appeared conflicted. Then it seemed as if a decision of some sort had been made, and abruptly he took off his hat, looked at it sullenly, and then held it out to Seamus.

"What?" Seamus looked to Davin, but he was just as confused.

"For you," Nelson said. "My treasure." He held out the hat again. "For Seamus."

Seamus received the hat, although he could sense the loss and regret in the boy's eyes.

"That might just be the finest gift I ever did receive." Seamus's eyes watered. "And I can't think of a safer place for it to be than on your head." He put it back on Nelson's head and squared it away.

"But I'll be back to visit my hat soon. And all of you as well." Seamus fastened on his pack and Ashlyn did as well.

Then he gave a slap on the burro's hindquarters and they were on their way.

Seamus held Ashlyn's hand and he saw that it gave her comfort. And he tried his best to shield his concern and the growing unease in his stomach.

How *were* they going to save La Cuna?

What kind of provider would he ever be? His mission had failed. They were utterly, completely broke.

Chapter 46

JUSTICE

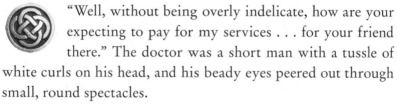"Well, without being overly indelicate, how are your expecting to pay for my services . . . for your friend there." The doctor was a short man with a tussle of white curls on his head, and his beady eyes peered out through small, round spectacles.

Seamus glanced at the adjoining room where Henry was slouched over in a large leather chair. "Firstly, the man is no friend of ours."

The doctor's demeanor sunk.

"But I think you'll find plenty in his wallet to cover your fees, and I would encourage you to compensate yourself most generously."

The man rubbed his hands together. "In that case, you can expect he will receive the very finest of medical care."

Ashlyn grimaced. "Your best? Oh no. Surely there are other patients more deserving of your best."

"Huh? What?"

"Good day, sir." Seamus tipped his hat and put his arm behind Ashlyn and led her out the front door. Once outside, with the afternoon coming to a close, it was clear they would be too late to catch a steamship home.

"Seamus. Are we intending on merely letting him go?"

"That's a hard one." Seamus glanced both ways down the road, which was bustling with carriages, wagons, mule trains, and mostly men of all nations. He nodded and then the two of them started down the side of the road. "As Cade said, there is one thing about being guilty and another about proving it. It's a banker's testimony against the rest of us. Out here, justice is done with a bullet.

"But if it's a consolation, ol' Henry will be blind for the remainder of his life. And . . . and . . . the best evidence of his chicanery will be in the papers at the bank."

"As if we don't have enough to concern ourselves with." She squared to Seamus. "Oh, I do miss Gracie and the children so. Is it really too late for us to go home?"

"'Fraid so. But we'll leave as soon as the sun winks at us in the morning. This I promise. In the meanwhile, what's your pleasure, young lady?"

Ashlyn didn't hesitate. She turned and pointed to a hand-painted sign that read, "Hot Showers."

Once inside the large barnlike building, Ashlyn insisted on paying for the shower herself with some of the few coins she had left. He sat on an empty oak barrel in the crude waiting area and watched as she turned and waved, giving him a reluctant smile.

He warmed with pride. Could this indeed be true? All of this was surreal to Seamus. He pulled out Ashlyn's ragged photograph and all of the memories of his difficult journey in finding her were suddenly recalled with vividness. But now, for the first time, he didn't experience the tinge of voyeuristic guilt he had in the past when she was some woman who didn't even know his name.

Now she was truly his Ashlyn, and he could adore her as long as he wanted.

He wanted to celebrate all of her qualities: her kindness, intelligence, and her Southern grace. He wanted to savor each of her traits. Her sweeping auburn curls draped over those delicate shoulders. The gentle curves of her face. Her smooth skin. Those inviting brown eyes, both vulnerable and alluring.

"She's quite beautiful."

Seamus glanced up to see Dorrie Hayes, dressed in black leather, standing above him, leaning over his shoulder. At first it startled him and he wanted to flee, but then he relaxed, assenting to his circumstances.

"Oh, she is all that and much more." Seamus admired the photograph again. "One could go his whole life never experiencing such joy. Such perfection."

Dorrie nodded. "It will give you something to think about, won't it?"

"You mean, when I'm hanging from the gallows?"

She shrugged. "That's not up to me. I'm just the delivery girl."

Then he noticed Wo Lin moving calmly toward him with a twisted smile, readying himself for a fight.

Seamus had an odd sense of compassion for Dorrie. How did the bounty hunter deal with hate and revulsion she must endure? He rose slowly and held out his hands. Wo Lin was on him, moving swiftly for such a large man. Seamus's wrists were bent behind his back, and soon ropes were being tied.

People started to surround them and stare.

"So why do you do this?" Seamus asked Dorrie.

"No one asks me that," she said wryly. "It's kind of you to ask."

Wo Lin tugged on his arms and Seamus was lifted abruptly to his feet.

Dorrie turned her attention forward. "Folks, can we clear a way out of here, please?"

"What did he do?" A small boy with a muddy face came up with a mischievous grin. "Did he kill someone?"

Wo Lin gave him a tug, and Seamus felt his shoulders being pressed painfully. Around him people started to gather and stare.

It was unexpected, but Seamus started to get emotional as a deep sense of loss overwhelmed him. What would this do to Ashlyn? Who would help her care for the children? He had tears on his face but couldn't wipe them away.

"That's it right there," she said, peering back at him with disgust. "Why do I do this?" Dorrie said. "It's all in the pleasure of seeing tough guys cry."

Chapter 47

WASHED AWAY

 Ashlyn felt as if the water was melting two years of dirt off of her body and down into the drain. The sign lied about it being a hot shower, but even a lukewarm one was most invigorating under the circumstances.

As she scrubbed her body with the long, wooden-handled brush and fragrant soapsuds, Ashlyn also felt the anxiety in her life washing away. She laughed and perhaps even shouted when she pulled on the chain and the restorative waters rushed down.

It brought her back to a day in her life as a little girl. What was she? Eight? Nine? Her mother was dressed in her finest Sunday clothes: violet taffeta, a flowered bonnet, and she smiled sweetly at her daughter.

And there was little Ashlyn, cold and shaking, but mirroring Mama's joy. Then the minister read some words from the Bible and asked her a question. She said yes and meant it. Then she was plunged into the chilly waters of the Gardner River and then up again into the sunlight to the chorus of cheers and shouts of adulation.

Yes. This shower reminded her of that special day.

Then just as suddenly, the voice came. The one that assailed her all of the time. The one that mocked her, tripped her, sapped her of her hope.

Who was she fooling? She would never again feel the thrill she experienced the day of her baptism. She was unworthy of the peace she always witnessed in her mama's eyes. She could never be the mother to Gracie that Mama was to her.

Of course not! How unfair for her to burden Gracie in such a manner. And poor dear. For the remainder of her life.

Ashlyn didn't want to descend further into the darkness. Not today. But she couldn't fight off another memory. The bleak one. Of that evening in her farm home in the Shenandoah mountains.

Having returned from her foray with Percy, her clothes ruffled, hair unkempt, and wallowing in shame, she opened the door to the house to encounter an eerie silence. Something was amiss. Terribly wrong.

"Mama? I'm home. Mama?"

It was several hours before Daddy returned home, and until he arrived Ashlyn had sat alone in the stillness, punishing herself with hate as the shadows of regret penetrated the core of her being.

It was the last night of Mama's illness, her pain, her suffering. But it was the first night when all of Ashlyn's began.

She tugged on the rusted chain of the shower and the water snapped off and Ashlyn lowered her head. For a moment. Then she battled against the hurt. No. She wasn't going to ruin this day. This moment.

Ashlyn didn't feel shame around Seamus. His blue eyes breathed confidence and affection into her, and his heart replenished her dignity and worth. He reminded her of what it was like to be a lady. He reminded her she was a lady. Just like Mama.

She loved this Irishman. She adored that he traveled from far to find her. That he saved the children of La Cuna from the flames. And that he would search for her father. But most of all, it wasn't what he had done for her, it was the man Seamus had become. Even in the few months she had known him, Ashlyn had witnessed the change.

Ashlyn couldn't wait to see him again. She had things to settle. He needed to know she was sorry. Sorry, that she ever questioned his character, that even for a moment she had believed the horrible things Percy had said about him. How could she, when Seamus only ever saw the good in her?

She would tell him all of this. And without delay.

Ashlyn dried herself with the towel, which wasn't all that clean but served its purpose. She had brought all of her clothes with her in the shower bin since there weren't any special privacies allowed to women.

Once dressed, and with her hair tucked under her hat, she stepped out and lowered her eyes to avoid the ogles of lustful miners.

Then she turned the corner and prepared a smile for Seamus in the lobby.

But he was gone.

"That was it?" Ashlyn couldn't contain herself. She looked back and the deputy sheriff glanced up from his newspaper and gave her a stern look. "Sorry," she said. Then she turned back to Seamus who sat on the other side of the bars in the cell. "Are you serious? That was the entirety of your great misdeed? Your horse thievery?"

Seamus put his head in his hands. "I know it was stupid."

"Stupid?" She glanced at the deputy, then whispered, "Stupid, yes. But they don't hang stupid people. Just horse thieves."

Seamus dragged his stool across the brick floor closer to her, and he offered his hand through the bars, which she reluctantly took.

"Ashlyn. But I'm afraid I did take the horse. And I had no intention of returning her until that corrupt lawman stopped me in the road. By then it was too late. The crime was committed. A man's got to face his due."

She softened her tone. "But you were alone and hungry and desperate. It was the mountains that culled the madness in you. That was then. Look at who you are now."

Seamus cupped his other hand on hers. "I know this is hard on you, Ashlyn. Difficult to understand." He looked around the interior of the cell, where another man was sleeping off a long night of drink. "But I have a peace about this. It makes little sense to me either."

How could he be so foolish! This was no time for his chivalrous thoughts. She would beg, plead for his innocence. "And I suppose it matters little that I most certainly am not at peace with all of this!"

"Shhh," he said with a nervous grin, looking to see if the deputy had stirred.

Then Seamus's face grew stern. "But you mustn't stay. Promise me you'll leave in the morning, at first light. You must not allow yourself to be known as associating with a convicted horse thief. You shouldn't even be here. It will ruin you. Please, Ashlyn. You must think of Gracie. Of the children. Please. Just go."

The floorboard squeaked and metal clanked. "It's time, miss." The deputy stood above her, sorting through a large ring of keys. "We're closing for the night."

"Can I have just a few more minutes? Please?"

"No, miss. I have a wife waiting for me."

"Would it be all right, sir, if I slept here for the night?"

"'Fraid not. We're locking up." The deputy took her arm and guided her toward the door.

"Good-bye, Seamus." She didn't want to take her eyes off of him for fear it would be the last time she would get the chance.

Then she was outside. The road before her was busy with traffic, pedestrians, revelers, and those with no place to go. She should have been hungry, but she couldn't even think of food.

There was a bench outside, in front of the window inscribed with gold letters spelling *Jail*. She sat and waited until the deputy backed out of the door and turned the long key into the lock. He tossed the keys in his hands, gave her a glance of pity, and then walked away in the other direction.

She waited until he was out of sight, and then Ashlyn lay down and rested her head on her satchel. It wasn't safe to be out on the street and it was already getting cold, but she wasn't going to leave his side. Never again.

Then Ashlyn closed her eyes and prayed. Just like Mama taught her.

Chapter 48

GUILT

This wasn't the first time Seamus had to walk while in shackles. He was guided by the deputy through the street crowded with many who were finger-pointing and gawking, and the hateful faces glaring at him reminded him of the horror he experienced in Mexico City.

There, as a captured member of the fabled San Patricios Army who fought for the Mexicans against the victorious Americans, he was spared the punishment of hanging. Instead he received fifty lashes. As terrible as that day was, as much as the searing pain remained embedded in the scars in his back, Seamus would choose the whipping again if it meant he could spend the rest of his life with Ashlyn.

But he tried to put these thoughts behind him. As valiant and composed as he had been in speaking to Ashlyn, the reality of his situation was closing in on him. His knees wavered and his anxiety and fear threatened to rip out whatever courage remained.

He had to keep it together. And thinking of Ashlyn wouldn't help this cause.

Had she listened to him? Was she already on her way to San Francisco and moving on with her life? It was the right thing for Ashlyn.

He waddled his way through the oak doors of the court-house, the clanking of chains drawing the attention of those who had come to spectate.

Seamus was lying to himself. He desperately wanted to see Ashlyn again. He was tired of being alone. Was that selfish? His gaze darted back and forth and he saw faces of anger and curiosity but no Ashlyn. His heart sank.

Then he saw her.

She had been crying, her face bludgeoned by grief, but seeing her brought him immediate joy. He smiled broadly and tried to wave before realizing his hands were bound by chains.

His eyes tracked her until he arrived at his place of dishonor, a large oaken chair facing the tall bench before him. He sat as the deputy adjusted the chains so he wouldn't have to sit on them.

At this point, a man stood straight as if at attention before the bench, and he was dressed with puffery and was gawky with a smallish nose. "Your honor, we now have the case of the United States Army vs. a . . ." The man fumbled through his papers. "A Seamus Hanley, of Roscommon, Ireland, dishonorably discharged from service in the military as a . . . defector." As these words came out, there was a gasp from the audience who had stifled their chatter and were now settling into attention.

"He is today being charged with horse thievery, and from the U.S. Army, no less."

Seamus couldn't keep from craning his neck to glance at Ashlyn, as if each look was a cool drink from a glass that would soon be empty. When he finally looked toward the front of the room, he saw perched high above the bench, presumably the judge, a man with a closely cropped beard and round-rimmed spectacles worn low on his nose.

"Very well, sir," the judge said without looking up from his papers. "And how does the accused plead?"

Seamus looked back at Ashlyn, and he expected her to be lobbying him with her eyes. But instead she gave him a nod of confidence and a reassuring smile. He turned to the judge. "Your Honor. Guilty as charged."

A few shouts of surprise came from the gallery.

The judge hammered his wooden gavel. "Quiet." He pulled his glasses from his nose. "Well, sir. It is most kind of you to be considerate of the court's schedule. However—" He stopped suddenly. Then he leaned forward. "Do I know you, sir?"

Seamus looked to his left and right. Then he pointed at himself. "Did you mean me, Your Honor?"

"Yes. You. Haven't I seen you somewhere?"

Seamus squinted and tried to see if there was something he recognized in the man. As he looked closer there indeed was something familiar about him.

The judge stood up from his desk. "Did you not . . . are you not the one who rescued my son?"

Seamus's memory returned to the day of the steamboat races. That's right. The judge was the father of the boy he rescued, and Seamus could even recall the unique intonation of the man's scream for help.

"Uhh . . . yes, Your Honor. That was me as you say."

The judge climbed down from around his desk, and his face was spilling with gratitude. "Unbind this man so I can shake his hand."

The deputy paused for a minute but then went about unfastening the handcuffs and the leg irons and then pulled free the chains, causing a great clatter. The judge reached out and swallowed Seamus in his arms. "Dear, kind sir. Thank you. Thank you. Oh, my wife and I do thank you."

There was a clearing of the throat. "Your Honor. May I beg the court's attention to this case?" The prosecutor's face was soured. "As grateful as we are about your son's good fortune, with all due respect, there is still justice to be measured here. While obviously having recorded an incident of heroism, this . . . man still remains a proven war defector and an accused horse thief."

The judge looked over to the prosecutor. "Yes, Mr. Griggs. You are most certainly correct. Very much so."

Seamus watched with disappointment as the judge circled back around to his seat at the desk and put his glasses back on.

The judge read a paper before him. "Now . . . Mr. Hanley, right?"

Seamus nodded.

"It says here that you responded at the scene of a stagecoach crash."

"Uh . . . yes, this is true, Your Honor."

"And it was there . . . you rescued one of the horses."

"Well, that wasn't exactly—"

"So am I to understand you are guilty of being a horse rescuer? That's quite a heinous crime, sir."

"Your Honor, please," the prosecutor said. "You're making a mockery out of this."

"Mr. Griggs." The judge leaned forward. "In all of my years serving at this bench, I have never had a more profound opportunity to issue justice. To have my son, my only son, at the cusp of death, only to be rescued by one who was so selflessly willing to make the ultimate sacrifice. And here, this man, this brave man is in the court before me." The judge took off his glasses. "Do you not see the perfect irony in all of this?"

There were a mix of grumbles and affirmations in the audience.

"Your Honor." The prosecutor raised his nose. "Once again, I must implore you. At stake is the very character of our laws."

"No, Mr. Griggs. At stake is the very character of this man before us. And I will no longer stand by as you, and those assembled here wishing to be entertained by a hanging, continue to harass such an upstanding citizen." He hammered his gavel and stood. "Not guilty and case dismissed." The judge unfastened his robe. "And with such a sweet chord of justice struck, I am concluding my day of service before there is the remotest chance of tainting this most glorious moment."

Seamus was stunned as he watched the judge descend from his lofty chair and head to his side chambers. But just before he left through the door, he spoke again.

"And Mr. Griggs. Please fashion a writ for Mr. Seamus Hanley exonerating him for all perpetuity of these fallacious charges." He looked at Seamus. "I think you'll need that, son. Your picture is in many places."

"Yes, sir. And thank you, sir, most kindly."

Ashlyn hurried up to him and Seamus swung her in his arms.

She leaned into his ear. "Let's get that piece of paper and leave this town before the judge changes his mind."

"But Ashlyn?"

"Yes, Seamus?"

"I was considering to ask the good judge to marry us."

They didn't feel completely free from the nightmare until the steamship pulled away from the banks of the Sacramento River.

It was only while standing along the guardrail, with the great paddle churning behind them, could they celebrate, and they did it in silence, a prolonged swaying embrace of relief and exultation.

The ship's captain was gracious and honored when they asked if he would marry them, and he performed a ceremony, simple and sincere, punctuated by the boat's roaring whistle as well as the applause and shared merriment of many of the ship's passengers.

After the full day was winding down and the steamship was approaching its destination, the two of them enjoyed the sunset as San Francisco drew nearer.

"Seamus?" Ashlyn's voice was almost a whisper and hinted of sadness.

"What's troubling you? I thought this all would bring you cheer." He smiled at her. "I am not even a horse thief anymore and I've got the papers to prove it."

Ashlyn shoved him playfully. "Oh no. It's not. Despite how the day started, it was the most glorious of endings. The happiest of all times."

Seamus put his hand on her shoulder and raised his brow. "Well then, my dear wife, what is it?"

Her face warmed at the sound of this briefly, then she glanced down. "It's just now as we're returning home, it's painfully clear to me that we have no choice but to close La Cuna. We simply cannot, in good conscience, carry on as we have. If we are unable to feed the children properly, if we cannot care for them as they certainly deserve . . . it is cruelty for us to keep them."

He gently lifted her chin. "Is this what is spoiling such a perfect face with sadness? After the miracle of today? Can you not see God's hand in this? We will work harder. I'll work harder. I'll get a job. A second job. Maybe even a third."

Seamus glanced up and saw the captain looking down at them, and he exchanged a wave. The captain of the ship? A peculiar thought came to Seamus. Yes. Of course.

"Ashlyn?" he said with excitement. "Remember when Nelson gave me his hat? Or tried to give me his hat?"

"Yes?"

"Do you recall what he said?"

"Yes, but I don't see—"

"What did he say?"

"Something about treasure. His treasure."

"Yes. It was his admiral's hat and he mentioned the word treasure. What if that was some kind of message for us? You know, God providing us an answer to the La Cuna problem?"

"I may not have married a horse thief, but clearly he is a madman. What are you saying, Seamus?"

"Didn't your father tell you he would take you home when he found gold?"

"Yes . . . he said he would buy the ship, hire a crew, and we would go home together. But that was just my father being my father. The dreamer. He never meant half of what he said."

"What was the ship's name? Your ship. One of the ghost ships in the harbor."

Ashlyn shook her head. "It was the *Stella*." Her eyes lit up. "It means star . . . in Italian. Seamus—"

"The wood star." He smiled as wide as his face would allow.

Chapter 49

HOMECOMING

Ashlyn and Seamus pranced down the streets of the Barbary Coast, in love and with the promise of treasure under their hats. They were both on the point of exhaustion for the day had been long and emotional. But their energy was boosted by their enthusiasm toward proving whether or not their newly discovered theory was correct.

Seamus reached for her hand. "Should we go straight to the harbor?"

"No. I want to see Gracie. I want to tell her about us. And Annie too, for that matter. And it would be no small luxury either to get out of these clothes."

"Should we just wait until tomorrow for the *Stella*?"

Ashlyn glared at him and everything in her expression declared a resounding "No."

"All right . . . then let us share our greetings and be hasty in getting to the harbor. It would be best for us to do this under the cover of darkness. If we do find the gold, we will not want the many eyes of this city upon us."

As they drew closer to the La Cuna, intense excitement and pride filled Seamus's spirit. It was all real now. He was married to the woman in his photograph, and the dream would grow larger as they were to discover their treasure. He got the girl and the gold. Could life be any better for him?

When they rounded the street corner leading up to the house, Ashlyn stopped suddenly. There, spilling out of the front door of La Cuna, were several women, laughing and frolicking.

"Are you seeing what I am seeing?" She gripped Seamus's arm.

"What exactly am I seeing?"

"Against my best judgment, I allowed Sarah Mae to stay and work in the house on the strict condition that none—and I did tell her none—of her friends would be allowed to visit. I leave the orphanage for a few days and I come back to find . . . to find it all . . . replaced with a brothel."

"Come now, Ashlyn. It would be a shame to taint this evening."

"Oh dear, what was I thinking. I am actually sad to say it, but Sarah Mae will have to go. Both she and her burning bush."

Seamus held her up, put his arms on her shoulders, and looked her in the eyes that were tinged with frustration. "Can we leave this be for tonight? Let us not spoil our great report, our wonderful news."

He watched as the words sunk in and her expression loosened and the anxiety was replaced with a nod and a smile.

As they passed the woman loitering outside and entered the door, they discovered Annie inside with one baby in her arm and a toddler wrapped around her leg, and she was drenched with exasperation. When she saw them, her response was surprise, but then it quickly changed to mortification.

"Ah, Miss Ashlyn!"

"What is it, Annie?" Ashlyn lifted the baby from her arms.

"Is all wrong. All of it. Miss Sarah Mae, she done break her promise."

"I know, I know. We'll settle all of this tomorrow." Ashlyn gave Annie a hug. "Everything will be fine."

"And . . . uh . . . Mr. Seamus, he's got kinfolk." Annie nodded over to the couch.

"Seamus, me boy." Into the light of the room emerged a man with gray hair and a beaming smile. He limped toward the two of them.

"Uncle . . . Tomas?" Seamus was looking into the very eyes of a ghost of his past.

"That I am." He gave Seamus a hearty hug, and the odor of liquor seeped through the pores of his face.

"How did you . . . ?" Seamus turned to Ashlyn who was begging for an explanation. "Ashlyn, this is my Uncle Tomas. From Manhattan."

"The very one!" He reached over and took her hand, kissed it, and bowed. "Pleasure to acquaint with you, miss."

"In fact, Uncle Tomas, you'll be one of the first to hear this from my lips, this enchanting woman here is my new bride."

"What?" Annie shouted out and put her hand over her mouth. "I knows it from the first day I see this boy. I just knows it in my soul." She held her arms out wide. "Ah, child, come to your Annie."

The two women hugged and cried, then they went in the back to prepare some celebratory refreshments, leaving Seamus alone with his uncle.

"Seamus, me boy." Uncle Tomas slapped him brusquely on the arm. "You've grown up well. But tell me." He leaned forward. "Where'd you hide the nip around here? I've got a throat that needs deparching."

"Oh. I regret to disappoint, but I don't partake anymore."

His uncle furled his brows. "Come now, lad. Really? Why, who would have guessed you be teetotaling?" He shook his head. "World's a changed place."

Seamus eyed the man he once idolized, and now the only emotion he could muster was pity. Tomas appeared tired and beaten. "Many things have changed for me since I was at the Five Points."

"That so?" Uncle Tomas raised a brow.

"'Tis." Seamus pointed them to a couple of chairs, and then both sat down.

"So tell me, Uncle, how are things back home? How is Clare? Is she faring well?"

Tomas eyed him suspiciously. "You . . . haven't spoken to Clare of recent?"

"Not for some time. Not since I left Manhattan. You know, to serve my country."

The man let loose a deep chortle. "Oh yes. Fighting with the Irish for the Mexicans. That's my boy. I heard all about it. Those Yanks didn't deserve you. They were just using our boys. I'm glad you went to the other side. So what was it, boy? Why'd you change up?"

"Wish I could claim it to be something noble." There was a time when impressing his uncle would have been so important. Did he truly once idolize this man? How long ago those days seemed! "I am ashamed to say it wasn't much more than a woman who persuaded me with affection and whiskey." Seamus was embarrassed to think of how shallow his pursuits used to be.

His uncle looked at him blankly but then laughed. "Have there ever been two finer reasons? You haven't changed one bit, boy."

Seamus wanted to correct the old man, but there didn't seem to be a point to it all. It was as if they were speaking two different languages. "So . . . Clare?"

"Oh yes. She's doing fine. We spent much time together, her and the family. You know how important family is. Don't you, Seamus? We've got to take care of each other. No matter what. Us against the world."

"Is Clare still mad?"

His uncle looked at him quizzically.

"You know. About Davin."

"Oh." His uncle's face unclenched. "Yes. Quite upset. And the boy at the pub, what's his name?"

"Billy?"

"Yeah, that's the lad. Does an honest pour, he does. He's the one tells me you were here. Billy says you have Davin too. Is that right? That will make your sister quite pleased. She's been worried awful about the boy."

There was something in his uncle's tone, and the flicker in his eye made Seamus leery. "No. He's at the mine."

"The mine? That's right. Your new wife. Her father, right? Hear he's done well for himself. You know, when I go ahead and fetch the boy, I suppose it would be good to put a shovel in some dirt, eh?"

Seamus stood and patted his uncle on the shoulder. "It's good to see you and all, but I'm afraid it's quite late. Ashlyn and me, we've had the longest of days. How about we share some supper tomorrow? We can talk about all of the old times."

"Tomorrow?" Frustration glinted in Tomas's eyes. "I suppose tomorrow is as good as any." He slapped his thighs and rose to his feet.

Annie came through the kitchen doors with a tray of sandwiches.

"Thank you, Annie," Seamus tried not to disclose his disappointment. "My uncle was just leaving. Could we paper up a few of those up for him?" She nodded and returned to the kitchen.

Uncle Tomas put his hand on Seamus's shoulder and squeezed it tightly, more so than was comfortable. "You know, son, do you recall where you stayed when you first came to the Five Points? I know all of those, uh, battles and time out here in California may have clouded your memory, but do you recall?" His eyes were bloodshot and he clenched his teeth.

"Ah yes, dear uncle. It was your hospitality when we arrived that kept us alive. I won't be forgetting that anytime soon."

His uncle loosened his grip and tapped him on the arm. Then a smile returned to his face, charm struggling to strain through the yellowing and decay of his teeth. "Tomorrow it is, lad." He put his hat on his head.

Seamus opened the door for him. "It's good to see you, Uncle."

Tomas nodded dully and then winked. "Tomorrow."

Chapter 50

THE *STELLA*

Seamus and Ashlyn held hands and ran, laughing in the full moonlit night.

When they had slipped out of the house, they felt like two teenagers escaping the scrutinizing eyes of their parents. It was the kind of exhilaration one would expect from two who were in freshly in love and on a mission to discover hidden treasure.

Though they were excited and running on unexplainable energies, they both knew the seriousness of their endeavor. Ashlyn was right. If they were unable to properly support the children of La Cuna, they would need to shut it down. But what would happen to the children?

When they arrived to the salt air and seagull calls of the harbor, the difficulty of their pursuit began to weigh heavy on Seamus. There before them were the many layers of hundreds of abandoned ships in various stages of decay: creaking, bending, and angling with the currents.

Having no boat of their own, what they were about to do amounted to no less than larceny. They walked the length of several piers before they found what they were seeking—a dinghy tied but not locked to the dock.

"Do you really believe this is proper for us to do?" Ashlyn glanced nervously around them.

"We must." Seamus held his hand out and assisted her into the wooden rowboat. "And if we find what we're hoping we find, the owner of this boat will be paid most handsomely."

"And if we do not find what we are seeking?"

Seamus didn't want to consider this option. Too much was depending on their success. "If it doesn't go our way, we will bake biscuits for the owner and beg for his mercy."

He untied the rope and settled into the boat and tried to find his bearings. Seamus gripped the oars, realizing he didn't know much about any of this. In a few minutes they were away from the dock, but he started to struggle, causing the boat to circle and Ashlyn to giggle.

"Would you prefer the lady did the rowing?"

"I would not." His voice held some agitation. "Perhaps you should just focus on your navigation chores."

Ashlyn craned her neck. "I believe I can find the *Stella*, although it was much easier to see from the shore. There are just creeping shadows out here."

"Don't put a flame to that lantern yet. It will give us away for certain."

She pointed ahead to the right. "It should be in this direction if my memory doesn't fail us. There. Yes. Follow that line of ships."

Seamus listened silently for a while to the dipping of the oars in the cool water, and he was grateful he had insisted Ashlyn dress in warm clothes. Though he worried about being spotted, they seemed to be alone except for the evening seabirds and the play and warbling of sea lions.

"What if this proves foolish?" Ashlyn posed with hesitation.

"You mean if there isn't any gold?"

"Yes."

Seamus continued to pull back on the oars. "If God wants La Cuna to stay open, there will be gold. That's what the reverend always says. God always provides."

The harbor fog drifted in as they weaved between the ghost ships, amidst the lofting smells of dead fish, rotting wood, and mildew. The waves splashing against the hulls and the moans of bending timber and strained ropes added to the eeriness of the evening. The farther they were from the shoreline, the more desolate and forbidden became this naval graveyard.

"Are we close?" Seamus's shoulders started to protest. "If not, the lady may indeed soon be required to row."

"It is one of the last ships." Ashlyn's voice was tinged with uncertainty.

They passed a few more great hulls, being careful not to be entangled by ropes and buoys, and then they came upon a large ship that seemed better preserved than many of the others.

They rowed up to the side of the bow, and Ashlyn said with delight, "I do believe this is the one."

"Go ahead and light it," Seamus said.

Ashlyn fumbled with a match and then lit the lantern and held it up. "There it is. See. The *Stella*. Oh, Seamus. This is it."

But now they had another problem. There was no way to get on board. Seamus looked inside the dingy and saw an anchor with a long rope. He stepped gingerly to the center of the boat and started at a crouch, rising slowly to a full standing position with the anchor and rope in his hand.

"Be careful, Seamus, or we'll be swimming in the bay."

He spun the anchor over his head very carefully, building up speed of the gyrations, and flung the anchor to the side of the boat. But it fell short of the target, bounced off the wooden planks of the ship, and crashed into the water, just narrowly missing landing back in the boat.

The movement of the anchor jolted Seamus and their boat rocked sharply left and right before he was able to regain his balance.

"Please, Seamus, do be careful. The water is freezing."

He got back on his knees and leaned over the side of the dingy and pulled up slowly on the rope until the anchor appeared again. Then he repeated his steps again, and the rowboat experienced a few more disconcerting rocks and wobbles before it steadied, and he hurled the anchor with full strength upward into the dark.

Clank!

It appeared to have cleared the ship's rail. He reeled in the rope gently until it tightened, and then he gave it a firm tug.

Ashlyn held the lantern up high. "Are you sure this is safe?"

Seamus yanked on the line again. "It looks sunk in well." Before she could protest, he pulled in on the rope, which drew the boat up tight against the ship. Then he planted a foot against the side of the *Stella*, gave Ashlyn a tip of his hat, and lifted himself up.

"You must be careful, Seamus."

Seamus shimmied his way up to the side of the ship, and as he got higher, he could hear a splintering from above. The anchor was giving way!

Now his concern was the anchor would fly over the edge and crash down on the boat. "Be on your eyes below!"

He continued to climb, moving his hands up the rope, and with each shifting of his weight, he could hear the cracking of the wood rail above.

Just a few feet farther.

Seamus let go of the rope and lunged to where he could grab the side rails, and he felt the splintered wood in his hands.

He worried that the slightest mismanagement of his weight would have him hurtling below with the wood in his hand.

Crack.

Then it all started to fall.

In desperation, Seamus released his hands on the rail and grasped for a cable on the edge of the ship, which fortunately was firmly attached to the deck.

He heard a yelp coming from below.

Now he was dangling over the edge. "I am fine, Ashlyn. I am fine. Did anything fall?"

"Just get yourself up!"

Prompted by the strength of her command, he kicked his feet up, and then still gripping the thick line tightly, he poked his head through the broken rail. He crawled to his feet, then examined his hands, which were chafed and bloodied.

But he was safe.

The fog was now so thick, he could barely see the light of Ashlyn's lantern, a dim glow through gauze.

"Are you still there below?" he asked.

There was a long pause. "No. I went fishing for whale."

"That's a fine thing. Because I am getting famished. Tarry a moment and soon we'll have you on board."

He was grateful for the fullness of the moon, which even filtered through the evening fog provided enough luminance to give life to the deck. He didn't have to walk long before he came upon a rope ladder. He flung it over the side of the ship and heard it plunge in the water.

"Did you hear the splash, Ashlyn? You need to row in that direction."

He didn't get a response, but soon he could hear the dipping of oars, and shortly he felt a firm tug on the ladder and then it was taut. In a few moments, he saw the glow of the lantern jostling in her grip and then Ashlyn's head pierced through the fog.

"Take it slowly, love."

She grimaced and grunted but climbed with determination, and before long he was taking the lantern from her hand and then lifting her from the rope and over the side of the ship, where she planted her feet awkwardly.

She exhaled and put her hands on her knees.

He lifted her arms and tried to dance with her, but she was stiff and unimpressed.

"We did it." He craned his neck and tried to coax a smile, which arrived with some reluctance. "We did it."

"We have accomplished nothing of value and nothing within the law. At least they won't need to discard your wanted posters. They will simply need to cross out the word *horse thief* and replace it with *pirate*."

"Arggh, Mrs. Hanley, shall we find yer treasure?"

"Now it is ever clear why you proposed in the first place. It was all about the Whittington dowry."

"So true. Although a wiser man would have seen the glint of gold before putting ink to the paper."

She frowned at him and probed the lantern into the murky air. "This way, kind sir."

Seamus held her arm gently and shifted to a more sobered tone. "You do know that the gold is in Argentina, don't you?" He hated to see Ashlyn's beautiful face blemished with disappointment, but he needed to settle her in on the reality of their limited hope for success. And if Ashlyn hadn't figured it out yet, she would learn soon enough she was married to a man who was more prone to hardships than easy breaks.

"Well, Mr. Hanley. I thought you were a man of faith."

"Faith is one thing. Expecting is another."

"Onward." She stumbled after tripping on a rope on the ground.

Seamus took the lantern and the lead. "Stay close to me."

She whispered in his ear, as if not to awake the ghosts aboard this abandoned ship. "It's down there. The hatch."

Seamus crouched down and lowered the lantern to the hatchway. It had once been locked, but part of the metal binding appeared to be lifted by a crowbar. "Appears someone has already made a visit below, and without a proper key."

"Could it be Ariel's brother, Marcelo?"

He raised a brow. "It is usually not the common practice for people to break in to leave a treasure."

Ashlyn waved her hand forward.

"I am under your orders, my dear." As he raised the hatch, the putrescence of decay and feces wafted upward and he reeled back.

When he recovered, he looked to Ashlyn. "You might want to cover your mouth with your sleeve."

They started to descend the wooden stairway and she was right behind him, clinging tightly. "What is that hideous smell?"

He finished the last step and then held the lantern out in front. "Rats. And many of them. And if we're quiet enough, we can hear them."

She made a noise that was half disgust and half fear, and her nails dug into him.

"Where's the cabin?" Seamus was beginning to wonder if any of this was such a good idea. He should have come on this expedition alone.

"Third to the left." She leaned in closer to him, and he could feel her anxious breathing on the back of his neck.

The wooden floor was slick and grimy, and he kicked his boots before him to clear their way of any scampering rodents.

He was relieved to get to the door, and when he turned the handle, it yielded easily with a squeak. "In here? Are you certain?"

"If you gave birth in a cabin, you would remember it as well."

They entered the tiny room, and seeing it didn't appear to be rat infested, Seamus shut the door behind them. "We're this close to knowing, aren't we?"

He shone the light up to where there were two cots. Nothing. Then he looked below the table. No sign of anything. They opened the slender closet.

"Now, don't get angry with me, but is there a chance we are in the wrong room?"

She just shook her head, and Seamus could see her disappointment, and for the first time Ashlyn appeared terribly exhausted. The day had finally caught up with her and he felt the dreariness as well. He sat on one of the cots and it sunk down strangely.

Seamus stood again and turned to Ashlyn.

"Yes," she said. "I saw that as well. Let me hold the light."

He reached down to lift the mattress, with some trepidation of what might be below. All they needed was to stumble on a nest of rats to end their search in the worst of ways.

And this might be their last chance to find gold.

Ashlyn leaned in. "Go ahead."

Seamus rubbed his two hands together and then took the corner of the mattress and lifted it slowly.

There before them, where there should have been a bed board, was a hollowed-out space packed with filled burlap sacks.

They exchanged expressions of glee, and Seamus instantly felt a replenishment of his strength and energy. "Bless your sweet, sweet, trustworthy heart, Marcelo, my favorite new Argentinean friend. Your brudder, Ariel, was as right as right could be about you, and I'd kiss you on the lips if you were smiling at me."

"Seamus!"

He tugged on one of the sacks, but it was too heavy to move with such nonchalance. He braced himself, grabbed it from either corner, and then lifted it out and, in one move, guided it to the floor.

He kneeled beside it and lifted it so the tied end was standing upright. Then he worked the knot on the rope and, once freed, dug his fingers in and pulled out a handful of dirt.

Ashlyn lowered the lantern to his hand, and both of them pressed their faces as close as they could in the dim light.

At first it appeared to be dirt, but as Seamus moved his finger around, the sparkling of gold flecks was undeniable.

"Is it dirt or gold?" Ashlyn asked.

"Both." Seamus plucked out a sizable nugget and held it up to her. "They had concerns about getting this out before the snow arrived for winter. So it's not very refined, but this is pay dirt all right."

He stood and lifted out another bag. Then another, And another. There were five bags in total. They both stared in silent awe at what was piled up before them.

"What do you imagine is the worth of all of this?" Ashlyn asked.

"More than La Cuna will ever need."

Ashlyn leaned over and hugged him and kissed him on the cheek. "Do you know what this means, Seamus? Not only can we feed the children, but we can expand the house and bring more in. We can add beds and more cradles. And our own bedroom. Then we can pay Annie a proper salary and give her a room to board as well. Even Sarah Mae. We'll make her job official."

"I thought dear Sarah Mae was getting a good shove to the street. Along with her burning bush."

Ashlyn laughed. "That dear woman. She knows more about faith and forgiveness than I ever will. Oh, Seamus. This is so . . . so marvelous. I will take that dance now."

"No dancing until we have all of this out of here and safely onto the shore. Much to do still, I am afraid."

Then they both looked down at the large, heavy sacks piled on the floor.

"How are we ever going to carry these—?" Ashlyn began.

"Not the faintest of notions."

Suddenly they heard a sound from above and their cheer suddenly drained. At first Seamus dismissed it as just the grumbling of the tired wooden planks, but shortly it was clear they were hearing footsteps, steady and with purpose.

They were not alone.

Chapter 51

WHAT SLIPS THROUGH FINGERS

"Who can that be?" Terror lit up Ashlyn's eyes.

"I have no . . ."

Then the hatchway creaked, followed by the sound of one coming down the steps. Seamus flashed the light around the room, looking for anything that would suffice as a weapon. Nothing.

"Put out the light," Ashlyn whispered.

But it was too late. The door before them opened slowly, and Ashlyn gasped and leaned in to Seamus, and he positioned himself between her and the door.

As the door opened, a much brighter light shone, so strong it obscured the face behind it. But what could easily be seen was the glistening silver steel of a pistol pointing at them.

"Ah . . . the true blessings of life. Sweat and blood and gristle we sacrifice. A dark journey through hopelessness, never getting a single break, when one day, alas, perseverance and a faithful heart finally reaps the prize. Sweet justice. Sweet, sweet justice."

Seamus recognized the voice even before Uncle Tomas's wrinkled face became visible, his ravenous smile emitting a sinister laugh.

"She's a real beauty that one, me boy Seamus. To think, for a wee moment, I thought you might be ruined for good. But the gold. That's what this is all about. I see you haven't lost the talent I saw in you from the start."

"Ah, my poor uncle. You'd be disappointed to learn just how little this dirt here means to me."

Uncle Tomas scratched his chin. "Is that so, eh?" He chortled again. "Well, in that case, you won't be minding to haul that dirt off for your ol' uncle. As it's the kind of dirt that matters to me."

"Where would you like it?" Seamus started to bend down for a bag.

"A few precautions first, son. Like your precious one there. She'll be with me." He held out a hand to Ashlyn. When she didn't come, his temper flared. "Or I could just shoot her, as she's not all that necessary to our little piece of business here."

Seamus stood. "I'll help you all you want, Uncle. But you won't touch the lady."

Uncle Tomas pulled back the trigger. "I am a gentle creature, laddie. Just want me gold, and you can squander your life with whatever love you choose. But meantimes, you'll just follow what I say. Now me and the girl will be up on the deck, swappin' family memories.

"I can tell her how your dear, dear sister Clare put her uncle in jail. Through lies. Lies. Can't even show my face in the Five Points no mores, the place I practically owned. Because of your dear, dear sister. You, Seamus. You'll be loading me boat, and as soon as you do, you'll see your uncle good-bye. Clear, are we?"

"It will be all right, Ashlyn." Seamus nodded to her. "Let me get to my work and this will all be over soon."

Uncle Tomas's face softened. "Now that's a fine boy, now. Sensible lad. Come, my sweet. Let us make good use of our time together."

Seamus took Ashlyn's hand, which was on his shoulder, and tapped it gently. "It's going to be fine, Ashlyn. My uncle is a reasonable man."

"Yes, he is that, very much so." Tomas held her hand. "Now, give us a moment to get on deck, and then we'll be cheerin' on your strength. And don't delay or get any strange ideas."

His uncle was a professional villain. Seamus would need to play things the old man's way.

As the two of them disappeared from the room, he surveyed the room again with the lantern. Nothing lying around that would stand up to Uncle Tomas's pistol. And if Seamus didn't move quickly, he might only stoke the man's wrath.

He would do as he was told.

But as he labored to fling the first bag over his shoulder, he couldn't keep the dark thoughts out of his mind. "Lord . . . how could You abandon us so? Why give riches to this wicked man and deprive La Cuna of a chance to survive? Why?"

Worse. He had failed Ashlyn miserably. Seamus couldn't trust his uncle. How could he have ever allowed them to be followed? How reckless! All of his life he had made these kinds of mistakes, and he was haunted by his own foolishness once again. Was there any change in him after all?

The bag was so heavy, he had to reposition it on his shoulder to keep from stumbling. He grunted and headed out the arched doorway and then up the wood stairs. Already his thighs burned. But he was anxious to see that Ashlyn was safe, so he bulled his way to the deck.

There sitting in the lantern light was his uncle with his arm around Ashlyn's shoulder. He was fumbling his fingers in her hair. "Such a pretty one, isn't she? Handsome like you, laddie.

A fine pairing. What a glorious evening." He waved his pistol in the air. "The full moon. The labor of youth. And love. Love is all around us."

Seamus recalculated his strategy. Maybe it would be worth the risk of charging the man. He tried to think of whether he could shift the weight of the bag and hurl it in his uncle's location.

"Careful . . . not too close, boy. This trigger. I'm not used to it. It's seems to be edgy as well. Hate for it to go off . . . on accident." He pointed the gun toward the rope ladder. "Keep on it, boy. You'll notice there's only one boat there and it's mine. Didn't think you'd need yours."

Seamus repositioned the sack on his shoulder and made his way to the rope ladder. It was difficult to discern with the fog, but he could see the shadowy edges of a boat below. How was he going to do this?

He pulled down on the broken rail, it severed, and he tossed it behind him. Then slowly he turned and his foot probed behind him until it hit the rope rung. With his first step, the weight shifted with the bag, and he started to fall back but lurched forward with all of his strength and managed to recover.

Then, step by step, he went until he got to the boat. There, very slowly, he placed one foot down, then another and crouched and lowered the bag as gracefully as he could, but even so, it nearly took him over.

He let out a large breath, looked up, and then headed back again.

Once up, he looked to his uncle. "They are not going to all fit, you know."

Uncle Tomas laughed. "A crafty one you are, Seamus. But not a handful of it will be left behind. And if a fleck of dust makes it in the water, your little princess will be following in after it."

Seamus put his hands up. "Don't get bothered, Uncle. It's just as I am telling you, they aren't going to all fit."

His uncle tapped the barrel of the pistol against his own head. "Use this, boy, will ya? Empty the bags in the boat, and it will all fit fine."

"As you say, Uncle." There was no use in objecting and there was no merit in helping the crazy old man any more than was needed. Seamus headed back down below.

When he arrived to the boat with the next haul, Seamus followed his uncle's instructions. He untied the ropes of the bags and spread their contents evenly across the wooden floor of the rowboat. He eyed the rope in his hands but looked up and saw his uncle was now peering down, so he tossed it in the water.

This continued for the remaining three sacks, and although he was wearying under the strain of the load, he was developing enough technique to continue without incident. With each bag, his uncle's spirits rose, and he sang songs of back home and even entertained himself with dance, with Ashlyn being his uncooperative partner.

It was all hard to bear, but Seamus just focused on getting it done. By the time he emptied the last sack into the boat, it was filled nearly to its rim with dirt, and the weight had lowered the boat to where it was just six inches above the water. Seamus rested the oars on top and shook his head. It would be his uncle's problem to solve.

As he climbed up the ladder for the last time, he prepared himself to be as pleasant as possible. "There you are. I did all as you said. You'll need to climb in carefully below as it's a bit wobbly."

"You did fine, lad." Tomas waved him over to where Ashlyn was sitting quietly, with her arms clinging tightly to warm herself from the cold. Seamus took off his jacket and put it around Ashlyn. He felt the moisture of his labors under his shirt.

Then Seamus held his hand out to his uncle. "Well. We wish you well with all of your newfound wealth."

Uncle Tomas stared at the hand offered to him and started to laugh, and his whole body shook with glee. Then he lifted the gun and pointed it in the direction of the front of the ship.

"Now," Tomas said, "there's one other little matter to settle."

Chapter 52

THE SACRIFICE

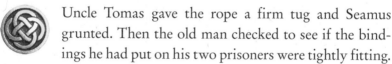 Uncle Tomas gave the rope a firm tug and Seamus grunted. Then the old man checked to see if the bindings he had put on his two prisoners were tightly fitting.

He stepped back and put his hand to his chin and admired his work. "A fine job. A fine one if I may say. A good touch, don't you think? Standing the two of you up front so you can watch me leave. Observe me rowing away with all of that dirt that doesn't matter a bit to you."

He leaned in toward the two of them and looked out in front of the ship. "It's a bit foggy, I'm afraid, but you'll see me well enough. And I'll be certain to wave."

Then his uncle sat himself down on a barrel. "But that's the thing. This whole plan about waving good-bye to you. See, as amusing as it would be, there's a problem with the plan.

"There's a good life for me, all right. This is true. While I have enough there in the boat to buy me all I want of it. Never be short of a fine shot of Irish rye. Best cigars. And girls? Ha! A man should fill his final days with pleasures, don't you think? Find myself a nice place in the city. Maybe not Manhattan. Too many eyes there. The country perhaps? Or even back home in Ireland.

"But then there's just one thing. Here I have two people who could take that from me. Steal it all away. The only two people who could do that. What would you do, Seamus?" He stood and ran the pistol alongside Seamus's cheek and brushed back his hair and then traced it against his scar.

"Leave him alone," Ashlyn said through gritted teeth.

"It is fine, Ashlyn. It will be all right." But Seamus didn't feel all right. His stomach was sickened with regret. *Please Lord. Please spare us. At least spare Ashlyn. For the children. Take me. I am fine with whatever You have in store.*

Uncle Tomas moved around to Ashlyn, leaned forward, and ran his fingers along her cheek. "So soft. So pretty. What a shame it would be?" He kissed her cheek. "Even a foul creature like myself has an appreciation for art."

He came back around to Seamus, who was panting with fear and anger.

"Have you an answer to my question, boy? What would you do?"

Seamus strained for the right words and he prayed fervently. All he could hear, over and over again, were two words: *Trust Me.*

"I have your answer, Uncle."

He laughed. "Now that's me laddie. What is it? What should I do?"

"You should put a bullet in my head. Then you should leave her be."

Uncle Tomas crossed his arms and sagged his head. "So, so

disappointing, my boy. Just when I thought there might be a future for you yet, you throw up false chivalry."

Seamus felt the strength rising. "But you haven't heard my reasoning."

His uncle waved his hand.

"I'm a war defector. A horse thief. No one would care a blink if I was to vanish. If you keep me alive and harm her, you'll know I'll track you down to all ends of the earth and I will never cease until I get my revenge."

Tomas scratched his pistol against his temple. "There's some logic in this. Maybe I've taken you too lightly is the problem. But why wouldn't I just off the lady as well?"

"It's not your worst option, I must confess," Seamus said. "Yet this is the better one. I won't be missed. But Ashlyn here is beloved and well respected for her mission of the orphanage. If she was to vanish or be found bloodied, there would be a mighty rage across the city. You've been seen at her home, the night of her disappearance, so your drawing with a rich price would be everywhere you went. I know well the danger in that. Always peering over your shoulder. Robbing you of your pleasures."

Uncle Tomas laughed and clapped his hands. "Well played, boy. Well played." Then he wagged his finger. "Still, still . . . I'm not convinced. Keeping her alive seems to be a greater risk."

"Ah . . . but that's where you're mistaken, dear uncle. Because you have all of the leverage."

"And how's that?"

"Because one word of what happened tonight from her lips, and you would take your vengeance out on the children."

"Seamus!" Ashlyn gasped.

"No." Uncle Tomas circled around and glared at Ashlyn. "The boy's right. He's counseled me well. You wouldn't be wanting to lose your husband *and* the little ones."

"No, Seamus!" Ashlyn blurted, staring down the gun. "Stop this talk."

"Trust me, Ashlyn." *Trust Me.* The words flowed clearer and stronger.

Uncle Tomas circled back around to Seamus and put the gun to his temple. "I'll fire it true for you, lad. You're at least deserving of that."

Seamus closed his eyes. *Trust Me.*

"No, I beg you!"

"Shut up, woman!" Uncle Tomas's response reduced her to sobs.

"I love you, Ashlyn."

"Such a sweet boy." Uncle Tomas's tone grew soft. "Such a sweet, sweet, boy." He pulled back the trigger.

In his head, Seamus flashed back to that wintry night when his friend Shila smiled at him for the last time. *Trust Me,* he heard the voice whisper again.

Then it came to him suddenly. The next words.

"But dear uncle, there is one other consideration."

"Ah, this isn't where you grovel, is it? You don't want to lose my respect as you'll be dying with or without it."

"You'll want to hear me out." Seamus turned and was staring into the black eye of the barrel.

Tomas lifted the pistol. "Make it good, and short." He looked out to the horizon. "It will be light soon."

Seamus could smell his uncle's putrid breath. "If you put me down, you'd be rich and free. But that's not what you really want."

"And what would that be?"

"Vengeance. Beautiful vengeance."

"I'm listening."

"Here is how this works, and I think you'll see to it warmly. You leave us tied up, where we can only watch helplessly as you oar away with our treasure. As far out as we are, it could be a day, maybe more, before we're spotted, and you'll be long away and enjoying your great prize. But here's the best part of it, Uncle. I'll write my sister a long letter and she'll get every detail, so Clare knows, she knows all too well that you triumphed. You won in the end. And if I know my sister, she'll carry that painfully for the rest of her life."

Uncle Tomas rubbed his face. "It is . . . it is perfect. But why aren't I just writing the letter meself, in me own pen?"

"Because you would be writing your own murder confession. And they would hunt you down with the proof in their hands. No. It's perfect this way."

His uncle squinted and then he paced back and forth, tapping the tip of the pistol against his own forehead. Then he let out a laugh. "It's brilliant!"

After walking over toward them, he lowered himself to their eye level. "Yes. The view from here will work. You'll see everything."

Chapter 53

The Harbor Rises

Uncle Tomas went out of his way to make sure they could see him in the distance as his oars dipped into shadowy scales of light from the full moon reflecting on the waters. With laughter in his voice, he broke into song.

"You know how much I love you?" Ashlyn whispered and her eyes glistened with relief and joy.

"Yes." Seamus smiled.

"I thought you were dead. And if I had been untied, I would have strangled you myself. How could you put me through that?"

"I may not be dead, but we are without a grain of gold." He felt defeated as he watched his Uncle Tomas row at a tauntingly slow pace.

"None of that matters to me. We'll begin again. We'll take Gracie. The others are now in God's hands."

Uncle Tomas started to move on the boat, first crouching and then standing up in the distance.

"What is he doing?" she asked.

"If I am not mistaken, the man is mocking us."

"What a great fool he is."

"Yes. But I, for one, am grateful to still be around to witness such mockery."

She chuckled. "Yes. We do have that, don't we?"

Now, with their view wavering in and out through the fog, they saw Uncle Tomas was at a full stand, his arms raised to the sky, shadowed against the moonlight. And he broke out in song.

> *Never a fairer lass than my sweet Adeline.*
> *Whose taste of the sweet life was equal to mine*
> *A tip of my glass, to one ever so sweet,*
> *And with all favor, until we again meet.*

"Farewell, dear Seamus," he shouted from afar. "Give me best to your sweet sister Clare."

With this he turned and sat in his seat, then grabbed an oar, but the boat tilted and he waved his other arm to compensate, and then it rocked side to side. But this time, he could not recover and the boat dipped into the water, and suddenly it flipped over and the burden of its weight took it down.

Seamus watched in shock as filtered by the mist, he saw a flash here and there of arms flailing with desperation and agony in the nebulous waters.

"Help me, Seamus. I . . . can't . . . swim."

There was no hesitation in Seamus's response. He began to war against the ropes that bound him, lurching his body violently to free himself.

"Please . . . help . . . me!"

Pain rifled through Seamus's body as he drew on all of his

inner rage and clenched every muscle. He started to scream in the horror of the moment.

"Hold on, Uncle. Hold on."

Yet despite his greatest efforts, the rope barely budged. His uncle's careful work in binding them proved to be his undoing. But Seamus refused to give up.

After a few minutes, Ashlyn's screams pierced through his misery. "Stop, Seamus! Stop! You'll kill yourself."

He collapsed, his body and emotions drained, now held up only by his restraints.

"He's gone," she said quietly. "He's gone."

Seamus looked up and as far in the distance as he could see, there was no boat. No sign of his uncle. It had all been swallowed up by the waters.

"There's nothing you could have done, my sweet."

"But I wanted . . . to save him. I wanted to save the old, tired, horrible man."

"He wasn't yours to save."

They both grieved silently and looked deep into the horizon, and the murmuring of the ghost ships grew in the chilling night air.

But above it all, Seamus heard the words: *Trust Me.*

Chapter 54

COMING HOME

An old Chinese fisherman discovered them.

The ropes hadn't loosened much in the twelve hours or so that they had been left to the elements, and after they survived the cold air of the night, the sun had beat them into near submission when it was at full strength.

But the ordeal was behind them, and they were more than relieved to have their feet back on the shore and heading on their way home.

It was hard to feel broken when they had escaped death and had all of their lives before them. But as they made their way back to La Cuna, Seamus sensed Ashlyn was experiencing a sense of loss. Her ministry would never be the same, and all she had built would be coming to a close. And then there was the children.

He reached out and held her hand. "I wish I could have done better."

She squeezed his hand. "It was an unrealistic dream to keep the doors open. Perhaps this is God's way of fixing something that started off with a lie."

"I don't believe that one bit." Seamus put his arm around her shoulder and pulled her close. "If not for you, who would have given those babies a chance at a better life? What would have been their fate?"

"Yes . . . but what now?" She sighed. "I didn't have an opportunity to discuss any of this with poor Annie. This will break her heart completely. She tried to talk to me about something, but our time was so scarce before you and I left . . . for our treasure, and I wanted to spend all of it with Gracie and the children. I imagine it was me knowing deep inside it would be the last night of La Cuna."

"I wish I had words for you worth saying." He leaned in and kissed her on the cheek.

"Well, if that's not the very expression of marital bliss." A deep voice bellowed from behind.

They turned to see Reverend Sanders coming toward them down a cross street carrying a large package in one hand and a leash in the other. There prancing alongside him on the street was Trip, clean and with a coiffure to the standards of French royalty. The reverend skipped a few steps and then embraced them both, engulfing them in his broad arms.

"What joy do I have on the feet of this great news?" He lifted the package. "So much so, I brought a gift in celebration. Although I suppose it's more for Seamus, truth be told."

"You did not need to bring that," Seamus said. "If anyone owes anybody a gift, it would be me." He kneeled down beside the dog, who still had his limp, but otherwise seemed rejuvenated.

"What have you done with this dog?" Seamus allowed the

dog to lick his face. "And I thought Brother Peter would be tending him?"

"Oh . . . well . . . that. You see rank does have some privileges." The reverend patted Seamus on the shoulder. "But as to the great news, the whole brotherhood is abuzz. What a most perfect ministry you have created at La Cuna, Ashlyn. Our Father loves redemption."

Seamus gave Ashlyn a questioning look, but she seemed confused as well.

"I don't know what . . ."

As they rounded the corner, they saw La Cuna ahead, and lounging around the front porch were several of Sarah Mae's friends, cradling babies in their hands.

"What is going on?" Ashlyn uttered, not hiding the dismay in her voice.

One of the ladies saw them approaching and hollered into the house. Shortly afterward Annie came storming out the front door, with Sarah Mae cowering behind her, bearing Isabella on her hip.

"What is the meaning of all this?" Ashlyn raised her hands in disbelief.

"Why, Mr. Seamus, you looks like a tomato, all burned. Here we is worrying and worrying and yous out in the sun. And Miss Ashlyn, don't you be angry with Annie. I tries to tell you about Miss Sarah. She ain't listen none, and you no time neither."

Ashlyn turned to Sarah Mae. "I hope you have quite an explanation."

"Yes, Miss Ashlyn, I've been meaning to tell you . . ." Sarah Mae's face flushed with worry and doubt.

The reverend put his hand on Sarah Mae's shoulder. "Go ahead, child."

Sarah Mae nodded and gathered herself. "It's quite wonderful, Miss Ashlyn."

Ashlyn's posture relaxed. "Tell me, Sarah Mae. I won't be mad."

"I's be mad enough for the two of us."

"Let her speak, Annie," the reverend said.

"Why . . . Miss Ashlyn. I know you said my friends weren't welcome. And we understand. But that was with our old ways. See? They are just like me now. When they heard I was with Isabella, well, they wanted the same. They've given up their ways. Now they just want to be around their babies."

"I tries chasin' 'em, Miss Ashlyn. I done tries hard."

"Miss Ashlyn." Sarah Mae touched Isabella's cheek. "Then when they saw their precious angels, why they were just asking for a second chance. The way I see it, everyone is deserving of a second chance."

One of the ladies, tall with a beauty mark, lifted her head. "We'll follow all of Sarah Mae's rules. And they are hard ones. No makeup. No cussing, drinking, or smoking. A Bible reading and prayers every day."

A blonde, husky woman stepped forward and held out some dollar bills. "And we're giving you all of our earnings."

The others nodded, and now Seamus and Ashlyn found themselves surrounded by these women, with tears of pleading in their eyes.

Seamus felt a tug at his pants. He looked down and saw Gracie staring up to him. He reached down and lifted her and then she held out a hand toward Ashlyn.

Ashlyn was flustered and then began to stutter, but then she reached out for Gracie and held her tight, rocking her.

Annie shook her head. "Whaz the neighbors gonna say? We surely gone now."

Looking at all of the faces peering back at her seemed overwhelming to Ashlyn, and Seamus put an arm around her. But then she lifted her head. "Miss Annie. I will deal with the neighbors personally. Now all you, stop standing around and staring at me. We've got quite a bit of work to do if we're going to make room for everyone."

She turned to the reverend. "Do you think we can trouble the brotherhood—?"

"It will be no trouble at all." The hulking man smiled sweetly. "We will have the brothers here with hammers and nails, and you'll have bunks set up by tomorrow."

The ladies broke into a wild celebration of hips swaying with the babies along for the cheer.

"And no dancing like that," Ashlyn said loudly. They stopped and covered their mouths and giggled.

"Trust me." Seamus turned to the reverend. "Those are the words I heard. The Lord will provide."

The reverend patted him on the shoulder, but then his eyes widened. "Oh yes. The gift."

He handed the package to Seamus, and they all gathered around with curiosity. "It's about time we corrected this serious issue about you being an imposter."

"Oh." Seamus lowered his eyes. "You saw the wanted posters."

The reverend waved his hand. "Not that. We're talking about a much more severe act of fraudulence."

Ashlyn put her head on Seamus's shoulder. "Go ahead. Don't keep us guessing."

He opened the box and pulled out a preacher's outfit: a black coat and trousers and a white collar.

"I had it tailored for you. I think it will fit you fine, but let me know if it needs adjustment."

Seamus recalled the first time he ever wore one of these, and the mere reminder of his friend Winn made him smile with melancholy.

"Put it on, Seamus." Ashlyn's eyes beamed with joy.

He took off his dirty shirt, and bare chested, he put on the jacket and buttoned it up slowly.

The reverend helped him fasten the collar. "Well, Ashlyn. What do you think about being a minister's wife?"

Ashlyn started to say something, but then she choked up and her eyes watered. "I think Mama would be proud."

Seamus put his arms around her, wrapping Ashlyn in all of his love, and they wept together as if they were the only two in the world.

After a while, he kissed her on the cheek, wiped away her tears with his fingers, and then looked down to view the new preacher's outfit the reverend had just bestowed upon him.

Was he prepared for such a task?

Yes. He was ready. At last, the words of Shila held true.

He was a God-man.

Still, it was overwhelming to imagine what might lie ahead. The uncertainty. The challenges. His need to be unwavering and steadfast. Seamus worried he might collapse under the weight of these expectations and prove to be a disappointment.

But as he looked into the assuring brown eyes of his bride and then to the pleased fatherly expression of the reverend, he heard the words again.

Trust Me.

EPILOGUE

 It was one of those days Clare thought she would never survive. The baby, now six months old, had usurped all powers of the household. Another strong-willed Hanley with the last name of a Royce.

On this day, Andrew's mother was in fine form as well, carving away at Clare's patience with the precision of a master.

However, when Andrew came home from the *New York Daily*, all was well again and her spirits were lifted. She had wrestled with him over his insistence she take time off from her position at the newspaper, but now she realized the wisdom in it all. The rest had been fruitful. She had more time to spend in her Bible, and she reveled in the discovery of the precious joys of motherhood.

Now with the little one to tend to and yet another on the way, the family had never been stronger.

Besides, she still got to write. Her editorials were now as scathing, powerful, and impacting to the community as any of her articles ever were. It's just that she could write them from home.

Clare handed the baby to Andrew. "Why are you home so early? What a pleasant surprise."

"I couldn't wait." Andrew reached into his pocket and withdrew a letter. "You're not going to believe this. Come let's have a seat."

They sat beside each other on the couch, as the remaining rays of the day's sun peered through the windows. She glanced at the front of the letter and gasped. "Do you suppose?"

"It came from the West. In one of the package ships. Must have been mailed a couple of months back. Well . . . come on, Clare. Open her up."

Her hands shook and she started to tear at it and then stopped. "We aren't barbarians, you know."

Andrew stepped up and returned shortly with an ivory letter opener.

Clare slid the letter opener under the envelope's seam, the paper tearing gently. Then she stared at it.

"Well?" Andrew put his arm around her.

"What if it's bad news?"

She reached in with slender fingers and pulled out the letter, closing her eyes as she unfolded it. Then Andrew leaned in and they read it together.

Dearest Clare,

I know the mere arrival of this letter will be the cause of anxiety. First to spare you of any further concern, I am most pleased to report that our dearest Davin is safe and doing well. However, I fear of his character being tarnished as it's been reported to me that he has done himself quite well in the California gold mines. I visit him often but have been unsuccessful in extracting the shovel from his stubborn hands.

As for me, I also am blessed with great riches. My new wife, Ashlyn, is the most amazing woman, and together we share the tremendous gift of a beautiful child. Her name is Gracie and she is most precious to me. There has never been a prouder father. We are working hard at our ministry and its reach has grown well throughout our city, for sadly there is a great need for our particular mission. It is a great joy for us to serve in this manner.

I look forward to hearing from you, and I am certain your letter will arrive back to me with many good reports as God has always placed His hand on your shoulder. So please respond quickly at the address below because there is so much more I wish to share. Wonderful, wondrous things.

> *Yours truly,*
> *Reverend Seamus Hanley*

Clare sunk into Andrew's arms and she wept without words for several minutes at the elation of these tidings. Her husband's hand lovingly stroked her hair.

Then, after a while, Clare sat up and read the letter again as tears blurred the ink on the pages.

"Seamus is well." The words barely lifted from her lips. "Davin is fine."

"This is most welcomed news." Andrew pulled out his handkerchief from his breast pocket and handed it to Clare, who laughed at her own emotions. She dabbed the moisture from her eyes.

"A minister? My brother Seamus?"

"This is good, right?" Andrew smiled sweetly, his eyes watered as well behind his round spectacles.

Clare stood and stepped to the window, where outside the flowers bloomed brilliantly of early summer. "You know, Andrew, I forgot about something. You remember when I told you how my littlest brother Kevan drowned in the creek back at our farm? And how Seamus was supposed to be tending him at the time?"

"Yes." Andrew nodded. "I do remember this. With sadness."

Clare heard the floorboard creaking and soon felt Andrew's presence behind her, then his hand reached around and rested on her dress, at her stomach, which was just beginning to show with new life.

She looked down and placed her hand on his. "Seamus, of course . . . well he was devastated. Inconsolable. He ran away. I thought he would never come back. But he did. Seamus did. Which took great courage because my father was so, so cruel to him. Especially after what had happened. Do you know what Seamus told me when he returned home? Why he returned home?"

Andrew began to sway gently with Clare, and they both watched hummingbirds at play in the garden. "I am listening."

"He told me he saw the white deer of Mallow."

"I don't understand." Andrew spoke softly, his mouth close to Clare's ear.

"Seamus said the castle of Mallow was in ruins. It looked dead. But then he saw the deer. The white deer of Mallow wandering through the grounds. Young. Alive. In some strange way, he told me, it gave him hope for his life. That someday he would get another chance."

"I like that story." Andrew kissed her cheek, and it tickled.

"I encouraged him, of course." Clare turned and faced Andrew. She wanted to look in his reassuring eyes. "Only I didn't believe it myself. I thought after what Seamus had done, I thought his life was ruined. That is. Until now. God has a sense of humor. Seamus? A minister?"

Andrew raised a blond eyebrow. "You did well, Clare. Despite the most horrible of circumstances, you kept your family alive. You gave them hope."

Clare recalled that fateful day several years ago when she and Seamus were coasting away from the green shores of Ireland, heading to the Promised Land of America, with laughter in their hearts, the seas opening before them, and the hopes of the family resting in their arms.

"Andrew?"

"Yes, love."

"Do you think we'll ever be together again? The whole family?" Clare tried to imagine how far and different California was from where she was standing. Gold mines? Granite mountain ranges and wide-open wilderness? Would she ever see Seamus and Davin again?

Andrew placed his long, slender hand on her cheek. "Somehow, my dear. I believe this letter is just the beginning of the Hanley story."

DISCUSSION QUESTIONS

1. What did you enjoy most about *In Golden Splendor*? Which were your favorite characters? Why?

2. Was there a character in particular you most closely identified with throughout the story? How so?

3. What did you see as the central themes in the novel?

4. Describe the relationship you have or had with your parents (or parental figures in your life)? What did you most appreciate? What would you have wished in your relationship to be different?

5. How has your relationship with your parents influenced your life for better or worse? Have you fully expressed your gratitude to them or, if needed, granted forgiveness?

6. Reverend Charles Sanders plays an important role in *In Golden Splendor*. How would you explain it?

7. Do you have someone like the reverend in your life? Who is it and how have they influenced your spiritual growth? Have you played this role in the lives of others? If so, share some examples.

8. What other characters in the book had a positive influence on Seamus? Which ones had a negative impact?

9. Why do you believe Seamus initially chose to live in the Rocky Mountains? Have there ever been times in your life when you've felt as if you've been forgotten by God? If so, are you still in that place today? Why?

10. Shila made the ultimate sacrifice for Seamus when they were in the snowstorm in the Sierra Mountains. Do you have people in your life who have made sacrifices for you? Who are they and what have they done?

11. At the moment when he discovers Shila has died, Seamus is reminded of a passage from John 15:13 that reads: "Greater love has no one than this: to lay down one's life for one's friends." What do you think is the significance of this verse at this time in the story?

12. Did you find thematic similarities in Shila's sacrifice and the one Jesus Christ made for us? How are they different?

13. Job 37:22 reads: "Out of the north he comes in golden splendor; God comes in awesome majesty." This verse speaks to the greatness of God. Take a moment to read the entire verse. Do you sometimes wonder how such an awesome God could be interested in having a personal relationship with each of us? Why do you believe He does?

14. Proverbs 3:5–6 reads: "Trust in the LORD with all your heart and lean not on your own understanding; in all of your ways submit to him, and he will make your paths straight." Are you someone who trusts God more than you do yourself when it comes to making decisions in your life? What are some of the areas in your life where you often stumble when it comes to trusting God?

15. How have things in your past held you back in your life? Have they impacted your spiritual life? In what ways?

16. Forgiveness plays a critical role in the novel. How are you at forgiving others? Seeking forgiveness from others?

17. Ashlyn was concerned that the mistakes of her youth would never be forgiven. Have there been times in your life when you felt as she did? Have you ever resolved these concerns?

18. Second Corinthians 5:17 reads: "Therefore, if anyone is new in Christ, the new creation has come: the old has gone, the new is here." What does this verse mean to you?

19. Have you ever asked for forgiveness from Jesus Christ? How did this change your life? If not, would you be interested in doing so now? If so, follow along with this prayer (or something similar in your own words):

Father, I believe You are an awesome God and that You always have the best in mind for me. But I also know that I have made mistakes in my life that keep me separated from You. I have tried to find my way out of the despair and darkness through my own strength and know now that this path only leads to the wilderness and loneliness. I know that Your Son, Jesus Christ, sacrificed His life so we may all be saved and that He is the only true eternal path to forgiveness. It is only through surrendering my life to Him that I can be forgiven and spend the rest of my days with You. So I ask now to receive Jesus Christ in my life, not only for the purpose of forgiveness, but also so He will guide and lead my steps for all eternity.

Amen.

Acknowledgments

The acknowledgements typically are the last words an author pens for a novel. However; they are also the most important. Because no book is ever entirely written by one individual, rather it is a compilation of a lifetime of experiences and relationships.

My most important relationship is with Jesus Christ, the Author and Perfecter of my faith, who brings all inspiration and purpose to my writing.

Then there is my beloved wife Debbie, who has sacrificed greatly in the writing of these novels, and has served as a constant encourager throughout the highs and lows of our publishing journey. My daughters Kaleigh, Mackenzie, and Adeline have been such a blessing as they've tolerated with grace and understanding my many long nights and weekends in the office as my deadlines approach. And they've been valued companions to me on our bookstore promotion trips.

For Sheila, my mother and editing assistant, who provided vital feedback and unwavering support. Also, for my father

Philip who cheered on his son as did my sisters Cathy and Jacqueline and my good friend Larry Smith.

I am blessed with the world's classiest and most capable literary agent in Janet Kobobel Grant of Books & Such Literary Agency, whose patience and mentoring has helped craft my career.

My hat goes off to all of my friends at the Books & Such Literary Agency, and my many author friends as well, who promoted my writing and lifted my spirits during challenging times. And to the folks at the Mount Hermon Christian Writers Conference, who have positively impacted the careers and souls of many authors.

For Julie Gwinn, who gave this writer his first publishing opportunity, and made the dreams of this trilogy come to fruition. And to the rest of the gifted team at B&H Publishing Group including my talented cover artist Diana Lawrence, book weaver Kim Stanford, marketing assistant Patrick Bonner, and public relations specialist Robin Patterson.

Special thanks to my editor, Julee Schwarzburg, who has such a unique talent at bringing out the best in a writer. Not only is she a genius at what she does, but she is a joy to work with as well.

And for my Author Insiders and friends on Facebook and Twitter who are so willing to share news about my novels around the world. What you do makes a huge difference.

Thanks as well go out to my staff at Global Studio, who put their heart and talents to work in publicizing the author and his books.

All historical fiction novels travel a road paved by the grueling work of scholars. There were so many excellent history books I depended on for the research of this book, chief among them being: *Americans and the California Dream* by Kevin Starr, *The Age of Gold: The California Gold Rush and the New American Dream* by H. W. Brands, *Rush for Riches* by J. S. Holliday, *Irish Californians* by Patrick J. Dowling, *San Francisco's Lost Landmarks* by James R. Smith, and *Historic San Francisco, A Concise History and Guide* by Rand Richards.

Finally . . . I have tremendous gratitude for my readers, who honor me with the gift of their time and imagination. And especially those who make the effort to thrill me with heartwarming reviews, kindly worded letters and who share me with their friends.

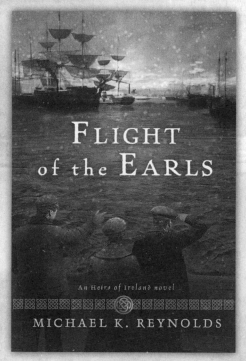

THE ADVENTURE CONTINUES

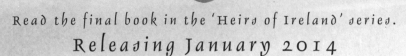

Read the final book in the 'Heirs of Ireland' series.
Releasing January 2014

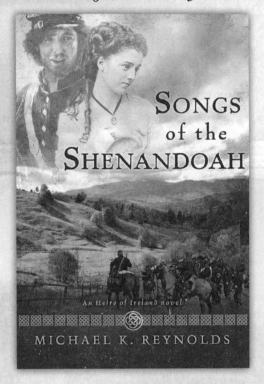

Siblings who immigrated from Ireland to the United States find themselves on opposite sides of the Civil War and struggling to understand God's purpose in the midst of unspeakable tragedy.